D0340662

ADVANCE PRAISE FOR *SHADOW FROST*

"A world of magic and intrigue is cannily laid out by a newcomer to the field of high fantasy. As expertly as she catapults a piano sonata into flights of tonal glory, Coco Ma lures a reader into the kingdom of Axaria."

GREGORY MAGUIRE,
New York Times bestselling author of *Wicked*

"*Shadow Frost* is a fresh, confident, and remarkably self-assured book...If Ma was this good at fifteen, the future of the genre is extremely bright."

TAMSYN MUIR,
author of *Gideon the Ninth*

"This is eighteen-year-old Ma's fantasy debut, but it already promises plenty of stunning storytelling and amazing adventures."

HYPABLE

SHADOW FROST

SHADOW FROST

COCO MA

Published in 2019 by Blackstone Publishing
Cover and book design by Kathryn Galloway English
Illustrated map by Jimmy Ma

Printed in the United States of America

First edition: 2019
Young Adult Fiction / Fantasy / General
ISBN 978-1-9825-2744-0

1 3 5 7 9 10 8 6 4 2

CIP data for this book is available
from the Library of Congress

Blackstone Publishing
31 Mistletoe Rd.
Ashland, OR 97520

www.BlackstonePublishing.com

To my favourite pianist and the first fan
of my book when it was only like, thirty pages long,
Manny Ax

NORD SEA
PRYDELL
ACADEMIA PRINCIPALIS
ERADORIS
ERADORE
ERMIR
GALANZIS
LETHOS
ICHAQAR
GALANZ
LETHIS
SYR SEA
IGNATIA
EYVINDR
WESTERWAY
VELCREST
VOLTERRA
XENITH
MOROVA
ZEMJA
MOROVIS
VOLTERIS

HOLLENFÉR
ARTICA
N
LORIC OCEAN
ASPEA
NYALKASTLE
IBRESEOS
OSTOK
HORN'S BAY
ORIELLE
AXARIS
LYRE RIVER
FIRE RIVER
IBRESIS
ASWIYRE FOREST
ALDVILLE
AXARIA
CORINTHE
CYEJI
GULF OF TEARS
FATALIAN PASSEN
BELMORA
OPREHVAR
OPREHVIS
CYEJIS
ORIS
ASVINDR OCEAN
THE MORTAL REALM

PROLOGUE

Eternity. It was as endless and gray as the bleak sky above, broken only by the craggy teeth of the mountain peaks. Gusts of snow lashed at barren rock, the bitter wind howling with the fury of a thousand souls forever damned.

An ancient mountain, taller than all the rest, pierced the blanket of ashen clouds in the distance, flurries of white spilling over its rugged crests.

One side of the rock face was peppered with a handful of tiny hollows. Each hollow led down through layers and layers of rock until they all opened into an immense cavern with an arched ceiling and vast walls, buried deep inside the earth.

Etched into the ceiling was a carving. A single word of wrath, in a language as ancient as the mountain itself, long ago abandoned and nearly forgotten by mortals. This was a gateway to a realm of merciless darkness, of beautiful horrors and bloodthirsty nightmares.

Hollenfér.

Hell's Way.

In the center of the cavern stood the Woman, her skin pink from the frigid bite of the cold despite the mask she wore to hide her face. She paid no heed to the iciness in her fingers as she chanted a feverish incantation under her breath. Lines of cobalt light raced from her palms, tearing through the rock floor and sending sprays of debris into the air.

Her breaths became gasps as she struggled to maintain her focus, muscles quivering from exertion.

A deep hum swelled from beneath the ground, rumbling the walls and felling dust from above in a whirlwind of soot-stained snow. The hum grew to a roar as the light surged forth from the ground, twisting and lacing together to create an egg-shaped cluster suspended high above her head. A mighty bellow shook the cavern as the cluster exploded, revealing a black mass writhing through the air in agony, shrieking and howling with rage. The Woman watched in awe, wrists twirling as she shaped its dark flesh, pulling and pushing, melding it as she pleased.

When at last she finished, the creature's howls had subsided. Gleaming red eyes drilled into the Woman's very soul as the creature lumbered onto its feet, its lithe, wiry body hunched before her, packed with muscle and covered in silken fur. It unfurled its wings like a pair of billowing sails, stretching them up toward the cavern arches. Somehow, its body seemed to draw light *inward*, consuming it.

Darkness incarnate.

The Woman took a step back, not out of fear, but in admiration. It was a lethal masterpiece—a weapon to grant her every desire and more.

"Bow to me," she commanded, still mesmerized. "I am your master, and you shall do as I say."

"I bow to no one," it rasped, claws clicking against the stone floor as it approached her.

"You shall do as I say," she repeated, drawing a small blade from her sleeve.

The creature hissed, lunging at her with incomprehensible speed. She laughed, clear and sweet, and slashed it across the face. It landed in a heap at her feet, blood dribbling from its muzzle. "I am your master," she whispered, lips curling in a cruel smile as she bent to stroke its ears. It remained silent as she sliced her forearm open with the same blade, mixing the beast's blood with her own. "You are bound to me now."

"I am bound to the earth," it growled.

"I need you to perform a task for me," she said, ignoring it.

"A task?" The creature's eyes glazed over in obedience even as the words left its mouth.

"A shadow. I need you to be a shadow … a shadow of death."

The trek back through the icy wasteland took three days, and the voyage south across the Loric Ocean to the continent of Aspea another week. They set sail in a small vessel, manned by a burly captain and a boorish crew who all seemed unfazed by the creature as the Woman guided it onboard. The temperature warmed as they crossed the great blue expanse, the captain navigating the treacherous waters with an expert hand and pockets weighed down with his reward.

Leaving the boat and its crew docked at a decaying pier on the westernmost shores of Axaria, they found a carriage awaiting them. The Woman locked the creature in the trunk and off they clattered into the night.

Under the cover of a moonless sky, the strange pair finally arrived on the outskirts of a small village that lay just on the fringes of a great forest. The Woman released the creature from the trunk and led it through the village. Shuttered windows and a peaceful, slumbering quiet greeted them. The cobbled streets were void of life—save for the Woman and the beast by her side.

The Woman paused by a brick-laid water well. The creature watched as she lowered the rope and drew up a wooden bucket. She raised the bucket to her lips with both hands and drank deeply. When she finished, the bottom of the pail still sloshed with water, and the creature saw that it had turned blacker than the sky above.

Unaware or uncaring, the Woman tossed the bucket back into the well, where it rattled off the brick and landed with an echoing *sploosh*.

Into the forest they delved, the creature merging with the gloom, invisible amongst the foliage. They forged deeper and deeper into the trees until they reached a branched archway leading to a clearing beyond. Tendrils of fog and mist crept through the stale air.

"Kill everything in your path," the Woman crooned as she turned to leave. "Carry out my bidding and satisfy your bloodlust." She faded into the fog, no more than a phantom wisp of smoke dissipating into the night itself. "Be my shadow." The creature felt a breeze caress its muzzle. A sudden, searing heat seeped into the flesh she had slashed open, though the wound could not be seen for the blood still encrusting it.

A reminder—and a warning.

The Woman vanished completely, her final command ringing through the clearing, yet no louder than a spine-chilling whisper.

"*Be Death.*"

CHAPTER ONE

Asterin Faelenhart ran a brush through her hair, violently untangling the stubbornest of locks with her fingers. She cast a fierce glower at her reflection in the vanity mirror. Emerald eyes stared back, glimmering with the flames of candlelight. Her scowl deepened as she glimpsed the ugly bruise blossoming across her cheek, stark purple against ivory.

Sighing in irritation, Asterin pressed two fingers to the blemish and murmured a healing spell. A tingling sensation enveloped the tender spot, the purple leeching away. Halfway through, she hesitated, debating whether her appearance or her pride were of more value.

Biting her lip, she imagined her mother's wrath at seeing her daughter as battered as a street brawler for the third day in a row. The bruise disappeared without a trace a moment later.

After dusting fine powder over her face, she twisted her ebony hair into a tight knot atop her head. She had to rummage through a drawer to find her tiara, its rubies twinkling as boldly as if they had managed to capture the candles' embers within. She found some pins to fasten the tiara onto her head. The last thing she needed was for it to fall off—again.

A knock echoed through her empty chambers. She rose from her seat, the fabric of her gown rustling as she left her bedchamber and crossed the antechamber into the sitting parlor, the fine-spun rugs softer than clouds beneath her bare feet.

When she looked up, the almighty Council of Immortals—the nine gods and goddesses of the Immortal Realm—stared down upon her from their thrones, painted in vivid, lifelike strokes along the parlor ceiling. Vicious Lady Fena with her circlet of fire and her foxes, elusive Lord Pavon half-hidden in hazy smears of gold with a peacock mask dangling from his slender fingers, and of course, the majestic Lord Conrye with his pack of snarling wolves and sword of unbreakable ice.

The knock came again, insistent. Asterin wrenched the door open and sighed. "What do you want?"

"Princess Asterin," said her Royal Guardian. He leaned against the doorframe, ankles crossed, his perfect mouth twisted in a smirk.

"Dinner isn't until half past six, Orion," she snapped. "Go away."

His ice-chip blue eyes glinted with mischief. "Such poor manners for a princess. Your mother wouldn't be pleased." She snorted at that. When *was* her mother ever pleased with her? He glanced from her cheek to his knuckles and then back again, all innocence. "Glad to see your bruise healed so quickly. Looked *quite* nasty."

She slammed the door in his stupid face.

"*Oi!*"

Asterin sucked in an exasperated breath. Although she loved Orion dearly, it was more an affection born from spending over a decade side by side. Only separated by six years of age, they squabbled on the daily, just like they had as children. A few members of the court pegged it as some sort of sibling rivalry, but Asterin could never think of Orion as a brother. He was her friend and mentor, but Guardian first and foremost. He put a sword in her hand and told her to try and beat him up, which didn't strike her as particularly brotherly.

Now she listened to the unimpressed *tap tap tap* of his foot outside. Oh, how she wished to bash his pretty nose in with a flick of her wrist or rip all his tailored finery to shreds with a wave of her hand—but she couldn't. The two of them had exactly one rule and one rule only—that they would never use magic against one another. Because history had proved magic could do terrible things when provoked, even accidentally—and great Immortals above, she was definitely provoked. She took another breath, forcing her pulse to slow and her mind to calm. "Please?"

The doorknob twisted into her side. She thrust her weight against the door as Orion shoved it open, his gleeful face poking at her from the crack.

"No can do, Your Highness," Orion said. "Your mother has requested your presence in her chambers." He shoved again, and her feet slid backward.

"I'm a little busy." She adjusted her stance to add pressure on the door. "Thanks to a certain someone."

"When I say requested, I'm being polite. So," he said, grunting as she gained on him, "I suggest that you go see her immediately." He suddenly withdrew, throwing her balance off and causing her to crash face-first into the wood with a *thunk.* She heard him stroll away, his laughter pealing through the corridor like an off-key bell.

Forehead throbbing and tiara knocked askew, Asterin hiked her silk skirts up to her knees, muttering vehement, very un-princess-like words beneath her breath as she stuffed her feet into some jeweled slippers and stormed out of her chambers.

Two guards waited outside her door, but she signaled for them to stay and bolted before they could protest. Peaked windows lined the white marble corridor, interrupted only by the occasional archway adorned with enchanted snow-laden ivy. The corridor opened into a large alcove and Asterin swerved right onto the spiraling grand stairway, just barely skirting past a cluster of tittering court ladies. Each glass step shone like ice beneath her slippers.

The sixth and topmost floor was reserved for the adjoined quarters of the king and queen, as well as their personal guards. Asterin passed the king's chambers. No one had occupied them for a decade.

At last, she arrived at her mother's door. Asterin drew in a deep lungful of air before rapping thrice upon the black obsidian, rubbing away the sting in her knuckles with a slight wince as the door opened. The round face of one of the maids peered out at her. Without a word, the girl curtsied and beckoned Asterin through the sitting parlor and into her mother's bedchamber.

Asterin toed off her slippers before entering, her feet sinking into the plush carpet. The teal curtains had been braided back, the last of the waning daylight bathing the walls in an amber glow. An enormous four-poster bed sprawled across the center of the room, a riot of peacock feathers fanning out over the massive headboard.

A slender woman stood silhouetted by the farthest window. Tendrils of blond hair so light they could have been mistaken for gossamer were piled in an exquisite coil atop her head. Shimmering blue silk—she only ever wore silk—cascaded from her shoulders, rippling on a phantom breeze. From the slant of her spine to the delicate tilt of her chin, her entire being seemed to exude an effortless elegance that Asterin had always struggled—and failed—to replicate.

And of course, it was impossible to miss the stunning diamond spires encircling her head like spears of ice, crowning her as Queen Priscilla Alessandra Montcroix-Faelenhart, ruler of Axaria.

Asterin performed her best curtsy, low to the ground, her skirts pooling like syrup around her. "Mother."

The queen turned, a single brow arched. Eyes of teal swept over Asterin. "Ah, there you are, Princess. You've kept us waiting … as usual."

Asterin flushed, averting her eyes. Only then did she spot the shadow in the corner, half-hidden by a candelabra. She plastered what could hopefully pass as a civil smile onto her face. "General Garringsford."

The general swept into an austere bow, the lines of her silver uniform sharp enough to cut flesh. "Your Highness." Her inflection sounded more command than greeting.

Carlotta Garringsford had first risen to her position as the General of Axaria when Asterin's father had been just a boy. And though illness had taken King Tristan nearly a decade ago, Garringsford still appeared not a day past forty, a few strands of silver amidst her perfect golden bun and several crinkle lines between her brows the only signs of aging. She trained right alongside the soldiers and personally kicked the recruits into shape without the slightest mercy. Rumor had it that someone once tried to stab her in the heart, but the sword had shattered instead.

Whereas Asterin had lost her father, Garringsford had once had two sons. They had both been killed while assisting a raid many years ago, not yet full-fledged soldiers—merely trainees that King Tristan had thought might benefit from the experience of tagging along with their superior officers to stamp out a very much underestimated threat.

Asterin swallowed the slightly acrid taste in her mouth and curtsied to her mother again. "What is it you need of me, Your Majesty?"

A smile, but that teal gaze was indecipherable, as always. "Why, is it such a surprise that I might desire my own daughter's company?"

"Of course not. But surely ...?"

Queen Priscilla gave a long-suffering sigh, as if Asterin had already disappointed her. "General Garringsford has brought you a gift." Her mother gestured, and the general strolled over to Asterin, producing a small chest from behind her back.

Asterin accepted it warily. A gift? From Garringsford? Now *that* was a surprise. She placed the chest upon the bed, the silken wood warm and rich beneath her fingertips, yearning for her touch. Even so, she hesitated, tracing the simple but beautiful metal embellishments.

The general tapped her foot, obviously trying to hide her impatience. "If you would kindly open the chest, Your Highness?" But only when her mother cleared her throat did Asterin finally flick the silver clasp and snap the lid open, ducking her head to hide her scowl.

Nine iridescent stones, nested upon a bed of viridian velvet, formed the outline of a triangle. They glimmered despite the deepening dusk, flat and round. Their surfaces were polished to a dark, oily sheen so glossy that she could glimpse her reflection, broken only by the different sigils carved into each of their centers.

Affinity stones.

The sigils represented the nine affinities—the nine elements, each hailing from a different kingdom and bloodline. The three core affinities making up the fundamental trinity—earth, water, and fire—cornered the triangle, the other six falling in between: ice, wind, sky, air, light, and illusion. Asterin had her own set of stones in her room, fashioned of ruby and silver, but these were unlike any that she'd ever seen. Affinity stones could be made from nearly anything so long as the sigils were carved properly, ranging from actual stones to metals, and even wood, but their effectiveness depended heavily on their quality and durability.

"They're beautiful." Asterin trailed her fingers along them, hovering over the empty center where a final stone representing the tenth element might have rested, had it not been long forbidden. *Shadow*—said to be the most powerful of all, equivalent to the power of the other nine elements combined. "Thank you."

Garringsford nodded, and then after shooting a quick glance at Queen Priscilla, ever her mother's obedient pet, she said, "I understand you've been trying to unlock a third fundamental, Your Highness."

Asterin's shoulders tensed. "What of it?"

"In order for our soldiers to reach their fullest potential, they must be trained in both physical and magical combat. I fear they are lacking in the latter, but I believe that watching you practice your magic might provide crucial insight on how to better train them."

Ah, Asterin thought, letting out a soft laugh. *The "gift" makes sense now.* "Is it truly a gift when one asks for something in return, General?"

"An exchange, then," Garringsford said bluntly. "Call it whatever you will, Your Highness, it matters not to me."

Asterin narrowed her eyes at the general, trying to gauge a second motive behind that impassive stare, tamping down the growing unease worming through her stomach. "I've never practiced under the watch of others."

Her mother glided away from the window, crossing beneath the glittering chandelier and approaching her. Asterin did her best not to shrink from that intimidating grace, suddenly reminded of a deadly snake disguised as a swan. "Come, my child," the queen coaxed. "Just pick up the stones."

Asterin didn't want to pick up the stones. *Garringsford* wanted her to, and Asterin would never trust anything the general said—not since her father's death. But her desire to please her mother overpowered her reluctance.

"The fundamental trinity," Asterin began, sweeping her hand over the triangle. She picked up the top stone. It illuminated as soon as she touched it. "Water." The two women came to her side, peering over either shoulder. "Earth." The earthstone came to rest in the cup of her palm beside the waterstone, their lights intertwining. With her other hand,

Asterin cradled the third core affinity stone. It stayed dark. "And fire. I've been practicing, but I can't seem to get it to cooperate."

"Two fundamentals," Garringsford said. "And an ice affinity, of course. Any others?"

Asterin nodded. "Light and wind, but those developed when I was older."

Although she didn't remember it—she had only been a month old—the tale of her Revealing Ceremony had been one of her father's favorites to recount. Revealing Ceremonies were momentous occasions, a tradition dating back thousands of years. In honor of the first—and only—child of the new royal family, noble and royal envoys from all nine kingdoms had been invited, and hundreds of Axarians had flocked to the capital to celebrate. The ceremony itself was simple—nine drops of blood pricked from each finger but the right pinky. One drop per stone. The sigils on the stones represented not only an affinity, but also a god or goddess—for the nine affinities originated from the blood of the Immortals. That blood ran through the veins of every mortal, no matter how small the quantity.

At her ceremony, three stones had glowed—those bearing the sigils of Lord Tidus, God of Water; Lady Siore, Goddess of Earth; and Lord Conrye, God of Ice and the House of the Wolf, whose stone had shone brightest of all.

Her kingdom had rejoiced. If any other stone had shone brighter, by tradition, she would have belonged to a different House, as her mother did. Queen Priscilla belonged to the House of the Peacock in Oprehvar—for it was Lord Pavon's power of illusion running through her veins.

Asterin returned the firestone to its place. "And you, General? What are your affinities?" She knew the answer, but it was worth asking just to see Garringsford grimace.

"I was born unifinitied," came the grudging answer. "Only ice."

Almost every person inherited at least one or more affinities when they were born, and most, like Queen Priscilla and the general, would only ever be able to wield their single element. Those who could wield two elements were bifinitied. Even rarer were the trifinitied, like Orion. Asterin was multifinitied—meaning she could wield more than three elements, though at the time of her Revealing Ceremony, the stones of Lady

Reyva, Goddess of Wind, and Lord Ulrik, God of Light, had remained inactive. Her wind affinity manifested when she was six, and her light affinity took three years to follow.

There were legends, too, of those who could wield all nine elements, known as the omnifinitied, their power equal to that of the tenth element—shadow, the affinity born from the powers of King Eoin, Ruler of Darkness. But the accounts of the omnifinitied that Asterin had come by were few and far between, and she certainly hadn't heard of any still living today.

Asterin prepared to call forth her water affinity, laying the earthstone back in the chest. "You might want to take a step back. This can get a bit messy."

"What incantations do you use?" Garringsford asked.

Asterin chewed her lip, wondering if she could get away with lying. She went with a half-truth. "A few here and there. My tutors forced me to use them as a child, but I've found that I prefer not to confine my magic to the boundaries of a spell."

Garringsford's brow raised. "That's practically unheard of."

Asterin opened her mouth to retort, but then her mother's hand fluttered onto her shoulder and squeezed.

"Perhaps you could give General Garringsford an example," the queen said.

How could she not oblige? "Fine." Asterin grimaced slightly, her tone far sharper than she had intended. Her mother's hand tightened on her shoulder, and Asterin couldn't help the small part of her that wished the queen would tell the general off for once. "I suppose you could use a simple summoning spell."

Garringsford's steel eyes glinted—a challenge. "Would Your Highness be kind enough to demonstrate?"

Asterin resisted the urge to grind her teeth and took a deep breath. When her mind cleared, she lifted the waterstone. "*Avslorah aveau*," she recited, the language of the Immortals heavy on her tongue.

A serpentine stream of water flooded into the air at her command, twisting and swirling around her fingers. She controlled it with ease, dividing it again and again until only individual droplets remained. Her palm rotated, and the drops surged upward, an army waiting for the charge order. At the snap of her fingers, they fell as one. Quick as lightning she grabbed the icestone from the chest, freezing the droplets into hail just before they shattered across the floor. Each fragment spread, silver frost racing up the bedposts and the walls—as well as Garringsford's boots, but the general failed to take notice.

Her mother's expression of absolute astonishment urged Asterin to the windstone. The temperature plummeted as she conjured thousands of snowflakes. She churned her fist, the snowflakes swirling faster and faster until snow became storm, howling through the room, tearing at the curtains and whipping General Garringsford's bun into a disheveled frenzy.

Asterin splayed her hand, and her storm echoed her movements, dispersing. Dropping the three stones she currently held back into place in the chest, she swiped up the earthstone and went to the windows. Pressing her face to the panes and squinting into the gardens below, she twisted her wrist upward. The wisteria trees shot up, their sinewy branches twining toward the sun with greedy fingers. As one, their buds erupted into full bloom, light purple blossoms cascading forth like dozens of waterfalls, hanging low. Asterin could almost smell their spring sweetness perfuming the air.

She was just about to reach for the lightstone when Garringsford's voice, edged with annoyance, stopped her. "Enough of your fancy party tricks, Princess. This isn't what I came here to see. How do you practice unlocking other affinities?"

Asterin's fist clenched around the earthstone, the wisteria blossoms outside withering along with her mood, but she forced herself to walk back to the chest, recalling the wonder in her mother's eyes. Swallowing hard, she took the firestone gently from its place. "*Avslorah fiere.*"

Nothing happened—not that she had been expecting otherwise.

Inhaling through her nose, Asterin let her eyes slip shut, focusing on the weight of the stone. *I was born with the power of the Immortals*, she thought to herself. *I was born with—*

"What are you doing?" Garringsford cut in.

She cracked one eye open. "Concentrating."

Not even a minute had gone by before the general interrupted again, her words dripping with scorn. "Well, we aren't here to watch you stand still, Your Highness. If you could actually do something, it would be most appreciated."

Deep breaths, Asterin told herself.

Another two minutes passed, and then a scoff from Garringsford. "Pray tell, what purpose is there in teaching soldiers to close their eyes?"

Queen Priscilla sighed and asked Asterin with a touch of derision, "Is there any way you can speed things up a little?"

Asterin's face heated, but she tried to ignore the sting of her mother's disdain. "I'm doing my best."

Garringsford shook her head and clucked. "I came hoping to learn from you, Princess Asterin, but as entertaining as your stunts are, I do have other matters to attend to."

The lingering patience Asterin had been desperately clinging onto evaporated. Her eyes snapped open. "Then you are more than welcome to leave."

"Perhaps I shall, since it appears that your 'practicing' is nothing more than a sham of sleeping," Garringsford said, and Asterin could have sworn she saw the woman smirk.

"I have stood like this for hours at a time, trying to unlock the third fundamental," she said, barely noticing as the firestone grew hot against her palm. "*This* is nothing."

"Hours wasted, then. You would be much better off practicing things you are actually capable of—"

"Shut up," Asterin snapped. A low rumbling sounded in her ears, but she paid it no attention.

"Asterin!" her mother exclaimed. "Apologize at once!"

Garringsford was definitely smirking. "It's fine, Your Majesty. It's always difficult admitting failure—"

Something in Asterin broke at the word. "I said, SHUT UP!" she snarled, the firestone scorching her skin.

As one, the other eight stones in the chest quivered and rose up into the air.

"Well done." The general sniffed, utterly unimpressed. "Floating rocks, very masterful. At least you can do *something* with them."

An ear-shattering *bang* tore through the room. The stones exploded in a flash of blinding light, dozens of white-hot shards shooting straight for Garringsford like a mouthful of jagged teeth. Blood misted into the air as cloth shredded.

"Asterin!" her mother shouted over Garringsford's shrill curses and the sizzling of flesh. "Stop this at once!"

"I don't know how!" she exclaimed, horrified.

"Drop the stone!"

She did so with a gasp, heart thundering in her chest. Immediately, as if she had severed her connection with her magic, the shards froze and rained upon the floor like an ominous chorus of bells.

Garringsford had gone terrifyingly silent. The color had drained from her face and the smirk was nowhere to be seen. Slowly, she reached across her own body and attempted to dig a particularly large shard out of her forearm.

Asterin stared at the firestone, lying innocently on the floor.

"Asterin, are you harmed?" Asterin had only begun to shake her head when Queen Priscilla thrust a finger toward the door, already turning her attention back to the general. "Fetch a healer immediately."

"Yes, Mother," she whispered, bile rising in her throat. Hastily, she scooped up the firestone and stuffed it into a hidden pocket of her skirts. Slivers of stone sliced her bare feet as she dashed out of the room, but she hardly felt them. She burst into the corridor, shoeless, gasps echoing through the nearly empty halls—luckily, most of the queen's court had already gone to dinner. Down the grand stairway she ran, only realizing how heavily her feet were bleeding when she nearly slipped, clutching the banister for dear life, a trail of crimson footprints spattered across the glass behind her.

Night had fallen, Asterin noticed, and it seemed as though the lamps could barely manage to ward off the ominous gloom. As soon as the thought struck her, the flames flared brighter. She averted her gaze, the firestone a dead weight in her pocket, and kept running. At last, she reached the passage leading to the medical turret and lurched up the stairs two at a time. Halfway up, she crashed into an apprentice, sending scrolls flying down the blood-streaked steps and scaring the poor man senseless.

Once assured that a healer would be sent to her mother's chambers right away, she found a deserted workroom on the second landing with its door ajar and scrambled inside.

Slamming the door behind her, she pressed her back against the wood, chest heaving. Forcing her breathing to slow, inhaling air infused with the calming scent of menthol and other bitter herbs, she uncurled her fists and took a tentative peek at the tender flesh. The firestone had burned its sigil right into her palm, and it throbbed something fierce. Twisting around, she discovered that the train of her dress was soaked with blood from the soles of her feet—a grotesque, weeping mess of gashes. Nothing she couldn't fix on her own, though.

"*Haelein*," she whispered, and her skin began to sew itself back together. Moments later, the cuts had closed completely, and the burn had faded without a trace. She couldn't find it in herself to care about the dress.

Fully healed, she slid to the floor, still breathing heavily. She grimaced when her hand smeared through a sticky puddle of blood. To the empty room, she asked, "What in hell was that?"

But of course, no one answered.

CHAPTER TWO

The bubbling chatter of the royal court rose above the clatter and tinkle of dishes and silverware as Orion sauntered through Mess Hall. He breathed in the mouth-watering aroma of roast. Three long tables swept across the length of the hall, draped in pristine white tablecloths and decorated with blue-flamed candles set amid bouquets of floribunda roses and blushing bellflowers. Even on an ordinary evening like tonight, plump candy goldfish with sugar-spun tailfins swam through the air in a kaleidoscope of colors over gravy tureens or darted between gigantic marzipan mushrooms.

Orion tore off a chunk of mushroom and popped it into his mouth on his way to his customary spot beside the Princess of Axaria. They always sat at the end of the farthest table, closest to the exit and secluded from the rest of the court—an overpopulation of fake smiles, acute ears, and loose mouths. The empty chairs surrounding them were reserved for Captain Eadric Covington and Asterin's Elite Royal Guard, but their absence probably meant they were running drills.

Princess Asterin herself was bent over her plate, cutting into a pork chop, her ebony hair veiling her face. Orion reached for a hunk of soft cheese as he sat down and took a bite. Then he swiveled to face her, an elbow propped on the table, and waited.

Without even looking up, Asterin asked, "What time are we training tomorrow?"

Orion raised an eyebrow. "I have to go to the residential district to visit my father, so it'll have to be before dawn."

"All right." She stayed focused on her pork chop, apparently unaware that she was sawing away at the bone.

He resisted the urge to pull her hair to get her attention like he used to when they were younger. "Not even a complaint? What's wrong?"

A hesitation. "I'm fine." She gave up on the chop entirely and shifted her attention to stirring peas in a puddle of gravy instead.

"Don't lie. You aren't still mad at me for clobbering your face, are you?" he asked, peering at her, still unable to see past the impenetrable curtain of black. "I can apologize, if it'll make you feel better."

She looked up sharply at that. *Finally*. He shot her a grin.

Rolling her eyes, she said, "I'll tell you later," and promptly shoved three forkfuls of mashed potato into her mouth to prevent further conversation.

"Whatever you say, Princess." Orion drummed his fingers on the table, eyes darting around the hall. His gaze inevitably landed back on her. "No, but seriously. What happened? Did someone *else* punch you?"

She huffed in exasperation and pushed her plate away. "No one punched me, but I almost killed my mother's pet. Accidentally, of course."

His face split into a grin. He and Garringsford shared a mutual dislike. "Nice."

"*No*, Orion, not nice."

He took a sip of wine from her glass. "Sure, whatever. How?"

"I don't really know. I held a firestone, and then the rest started floating, and then … they all just exploded."

He clasped his hands to his chest. "That's fantastic! I'm so proud of you!"

She swatted him. "Orion."

"Right, that's terrible." He reached for the bread basket. "Why did they explode?"

Asterin shrugged. "Beats me. All I know is that she seriously pissed me off."

His lips twitched into a smile. "Then it sounds like she probably had it coming."

A thoughtful nod. "She kind of did."

He frowned. "But why was she there in the first place? You never practice in front of other people." As Asterin explained the entire debacle, Orion found Garringsford at the head table in her usual spot flanking the queen among the other important guests of the night. The healers had done their job well; looking at her, no one would ever guess that she had nearly been impaled just a few hours prior.

Technically, he and Asterin should have been up there, too, except Asterin hated the prying inquisitions and badgering that Queen Priscilla never seemed to mind from the guests—so Orion had developed the dreadful habit of "accidentally" pouring hot tea on the lap of whomever happened to be fortunate enough to be sitting next to him when Priscilla insisted on their presence.

The general caught him staring, and he quickly looked elsewhere, unnerved by the intensity of her cool gray eyes.

"How close were you to actually killing her?" he asked out of the corner of his mouth.

At that, Asterin smirked. "Pretty damn close."

Sweat poured down his neck as Orion sparred with Asterin the next morning, her bedchamber dusted in the pink light of dawn and his ears ringing with the dissonant clash of steel on steel.

His shirt was completely soaked through. The fabric clung to his body, and he caught Asterin stealing glances at his muscles. *No distractions*, he thought, and attacked with twice the brutality to remind her of it. She retaliated with vehemence, nearly skewering him with her longsword, Amoux. Distantly, he marveled at her improvement over the last few years. Though Queen Priscilla had shown nothing but disapproval of Orion training her daughter from the very start, she'd allowed it, and Asterin had defied all of their expectations. Discipline, talent, and hard work fueled by the burning desire to impress her mother had honed her into a terrifying force to behold.

But even so, he was her mentor. Her Guardian. He had taught her how to throw a punch, how to hold a sword. When she fell, he was the one to lift her back on her feet and push her onward. Faster, harder, stronger. He knew her strengths better than the back of his hand and her weaknesses better still.

And he never hesitated to use them against her.

Asterin released a sharp cry as Orion lashed out with his leg, tripping her and sending her toppling. She caught herself on the cedar chest at the foot of her bed, scraping her arm, but her stumble gave him the perfect opportunity to lunge. Orondite, his own blade, shrieked through the air and met Amoux with an ear-shattering *clang*. The impact vibrated up to his shoulders. Asterin's teeth gritted, back still braced against the chest. She lunged beneath his arms and rolled across the floor, Amoux nicking a chip off the bedpost. Too slow—he was already upon her. She barely managed to throw Amoux up again in time to deflect Orondite's vicious arc. Orion's biceps strained, keeping her down, but she managed to drag herself up onto one knee, and then the other, and then finally to her feet. She shoved him off and they circled one another, weighing, assessing, two predators sniffing out the other's weakness.

Asterin dropped her guard slightly, leaving her right side wide open. He seized the opportunity, feinting left and swinging right.

That was his first mistake.

Triumph flashed across her features as he fell into her trap. He cut upward, expecting her to hook and withdraw, but instead she hooked and struck him thrice in succession, delivering each blow with blinding speed and merciless precision. His grip slackened in surprise, and she threw herself at him, a half-wild snarl erupting from her throat. Her sword sang toward him, and with the force of a dozen men, she swung.

His feet left the ground, his entire body flying backward, Orondite wrenched right out of his grip.

His head smacked into the vanity as he landed on his backside, and Orondite smashed into the wall, leaving a sizable hole in the plaster and taking down an oil painting along with it.

Asterin stepped forward, the ruby eyes of her double-headed wolf pommel glinting in the light of her victory. Wordlessly, she rested her blade beneath his chin, expression colder than the iciest of winters.

Orion shot her a feral smile, blinking the plaster from his eyes. "I yield."

She withdrew and sheathed Amoux at her side, one hand outstretched. He grabbed it, letting her pull him to his feet.

Warmth spread through her emerald eyes as he placed a hand upon his heart and bowed. His entire head throbbed, he was covered in plaster, and he had never been prouder in his life.

Her face split into a mile-wide grin. A bubble of laughter escaped her lips. "Finally!" she said, punching her fist into the air. The rising sun cast her joy in a silhouette of gold. "I finally bested you."

Orion shrugged. "About time. And only once, after nearly a decade." But he laughed along nonetheless when she broke into a victory dance.

Then, as one, they turned toward the hole in the wall.

"Luna's probably going to kill you," he said sympathetically.

Asterin cringed. "Probably."

CHAPTER THREE

Asterin was halfway through fixing the hole when Luna walked in and caught her red-handed with a bucket at her feet and wet glops of plaster dripping down the wall. "What have you *done*?"

Smiling her best smile while Luna stared in abject horror, Asterin edged toward the bathroom in case she needed to make a quick getaway. "I, uh, tripped."

"You, uh, tripped?" said Luna, eyes wide with false wonder. "Into the wall? Through several layers of plaster?"

The smile stayed perfectly in place. "I … may have been sparring in my rooms."

Her lady-in-waiting and best friend of ten years groaned. "Again? How many times must we go over this? What is it about *not in your rooms* that you don't understand? What's wrong with *literally* anywhere else?"

"It's private here," Asterin said, righting a stool that Orion had knocked over. "There's plenty of room, and—"

A loud gasp interrupted her. Luna yanked her fingers through her honey-blond hair, rushing over to the fallen oil painting. "Asterin! This is a Van *Ryker*, for the love of the Immortals!"

"Oh, stop. I've already fixed the hole, anyway." Smugly, Asterin threw the trowel back into the bucket, splattering more plaster onto the rug. "Oops." Her work was far from flawless, but admirable, in her opinion—although white rock of the mountain. The guards on the Wall controlled the magical wards, and their combined defenses shielded the palace from any attack.

Asterin counted herself extremely lucky that her chambers were just high enough to peek over the Wall. She loosened her braid and let her hair whisk into the flurry of the wind. While she already missed the sharp bite of winter, she couldn't help but love the way spring seemed to breathe life into Axaris. Her city spread out before her, every district a precious treasure trove, winking and twinkling vibrantly in the afternoon sunshine, teasing at the riches hidden within the sprawl of winding streets. Thick plumes of multicolored smoke puffed into the sky from terracotta chimneys and the white columns of the manufacturing district, tingeing the horizon with the purple of twilight. She held up the firestone against the sky, fitting it into the outline of the sun, and pondered in silence.

At last, she hopped off the sill and flopped onto the bed. She threw an arm over her eyes and moaned, "I'm sore all over. My arms, my legs, my neck. Everything hurts."

"I do really hope it's only from fighting," Luna said.

Her neck swiveled. "What's that supposed to mean?"

A nonchalant shrug. "I'm just concerned about your well-being. I mean, you haven't requested any contraceptive tonics. It wouldn't be fit to have a seventeen-year-old princess carrying an heir already—"

Asterin let out an indignant squawk, a furious blush rising to her cheeks. "Luna!"

"I'm only saying!" Luna exclaimed.

Asterin might have harbored a *minuscule* infatuation with her Guardian, and sure, sometimes she got sidetracked when they sparred, but she'd seen him shirtless before, and anyway, it wasn't like she had started frothing at the mouth or anything. She had self-control, thank you very much. She never thought about his perfectly sculpted body. Ever.

Well, maybe once.

Or twice.

She groaned, collapsing back onto the bed and burrowing beneath the duvet, face hot, poking her head out only when a knock sounded from the door.

Luna obviously didn't think so. The girl shot her a fearsome glower a snatched the trowel out of the bucket and began smoothing out the clum While she worked, Asterin nosed into the closet and dug through a pile clothes strewn on the floor. She emerged with Garringsford's firestone.

Luna squinted. "Is that new?" The trowel skidded against the wa "And is that *blood*?"

Asterin discreetly rubbed out the dried specks with her sleeve. "C course not. Our dearest Garringsford gave it to me. Supposedly, sh wanted to watch me practice magic for the betterment of our soldiers though only the Immortals know what her true intent was."

While Luna gawked at her, Asterin strode to the other end of her bedchamber and yanked the drapes out of the way before flinging the windows open. A great gust of wind blew into the room, cooling the beads of perspiration slicking her skin.

She stepped onto the windowsill and leaned out, inhaling the crisp early spring air and sighing in contentment. Once, she'd had a lovely little balustrade balcony—until her mother had ordered its demolition after the guards kept catching young Asterin practicing handstands on the railing. So, dangling over the empty void as far as she could and straining to catch a full view of her beloved city had become her alternative. Sure, the four-story drop to the courtyard guaranteed a few broken bones, if not death, but the palace itself had been built upon a mountain in the center of the kingdom, a stunning plummet of sheer white rock rising a thousand meters above sea level.

At the foot of the mountain lay the city of Axaris, the jewel and capital of Axaria. Quadrants unfolded around the mountain like petals, dividing the city into districts—trade, entertainment, manufacturing, and business. The residential sectors encircled the quadrants in a ring, flush with greenery. Eight main roads carved through the districts like veins, each leading to different parts of the kingdom. And here, in the center of it all, a heart connecting everything to everywhere—the royal palace. Her home.

Then there was the Wall—a towering slab of steel-reinforced stone surrounding the palace on all sides, patrolled by guards day and night. The only way to the palace was through the Wall, and the only way through the Wall was up the palace road, a wide marble path bordered by grass and th

Luna straightened, dusting plaster from her hands. "I'll get it." Moments later, she returned with a garment bag. "Your new dress."

That perked Asterin up enough to crawl out of her makeshift cave. Luna helped her first into her corset and petticoats and then into the gown, lacing up the back while Asterin ran a hand down the taffeta skirt. "It's gorgeous," she said. Thousands of tiny crystals had been sewn onto the bodice, sparkling like fresh morning dewdrops.

Luna made a *tsk* sound, pinching the back collar. "It's a little too big around the bust. We'll have to arrange an appointment with the seamstress."

"Or I could just eat a lot of cake," Asterin reasoned. Her lips pursed critically, and she motioned for Luna to unlace it. Somehow, though the dress itself was spectacular, it just didn't look quite right on her. "Or you could! Although you'd have to eat a lot more cake than me. I bet you would look much better in it, anyway." She shimmied out of the dress and handed it to Luna.

Luna laughed, disappearing into the closet to hang it up. "I think not." She returned with a bathrobe, tossing it at Asterin's head. "Imagine the fits the other court ladies would throw if they saw me wearing all those diamonds—me, a commoner! A nobody, without a single drop of noble blood in my body. They complain enough as it is that I'm your lady-in-waiting."

Asterin scoffed. "I haven't a care in the world for who you descend from, be it the King of Ibreseos or a troll."

Luna perched on the bedpost across from her and laughed again. Sweet laughter, so familiar that Asterin had to smile along. "A troll, really?" Her best friend reached forward to tuck a lock of hair behind Asterin's ear. Blue eyes the shade of cornflowers in late bloom searched her face. "Are you thinking about us again?"

"Maybe." Luna knew her all too well. More often than she cared to admit, Asterin wondered how things might have been. Luna was more of a princess than Asterin could ever be—charming, pretty, and courteous. She was the heiress Queen Priscilla had always dreamed of. Not the sword-wielding, quick-tempered daughter she had ended up with instead, prone to dredging up trouble whether she sought it or not.

Luna sighed, heading for the bathroom. The rush of running water carried into the bedchamber, the sweet scent of winterberry and evergreen oils wafting out on curls of steam. When Asterin drifted through the door, Luna was crouched over the claw-foot tub.

Her friend glanced up. "I might not be as docile as a mindless royal," she said, "but I'm no leader. And my magic is pathetically weak compared to yours. This kingdom needs a fighter to rule. A *powerful* fighter. Someone like you."

Asterin boosted herself up onto the porcelain countertop, shoulders slouched. "I can barely even control my powers, Luna, and they're all I have."

Luna snorted. "What happened to beating the pulp out of guards during training?"

"Yeah, well, I get an earful from my mother every time she sees me so much as carrying Amoux," said Asterin, turning her stare up to the ceiling. "You know … sometimes I almost feel like my mother would rather have me dead than on the throne."

Luna clucked, dipping her fingers in the water to test the temperature. "Don't say such things. She may be hard on you, but she's still your mother. She loves you in her own way. And besides," she added, shooting Asterin a sidelong look, the corner of her mouth twisted slyly upward. "She ought to die *eventually*."

Once the bath had filled, Luna departed to run some errands. Asterin slipped out of her robe and stood before the mirror. Her eyes slid down the curve of her neck and hips, arms and thighs toned and taut from years of training. Her fingers brushed across smooth, unmarked expanses of skin she knew had once been scattered with scars—at least, until she'd learned to heal them, though perhaps a little too well. So many years of sparring, and not a scratch to show for it.

She eased herself into the bath, her sore muscles sighing in relief at the hot water. She plonked the firestone into the tub's depths and watched it sink. Never had she displayed any potential in fire. It was well known that possessing two fundamentals usually allowed a wielder to unlock the two secondary elements connecting them—for example, water and earth were connected by ice and wind. So theoretically, if she did possess fire, the final affinity in the fundamental trinity, through practice and patience, she might be able to harness the power of all nine elements.

But how had she made those other stones explode? More than likely, her emotions had played a significant role—but she hadn't *wanted* to hurt Garringsford. At least, she didn't think so. Yet even then, there was no way all of the stones should have responded to her, unless …

Asterin sat up suddenly, sloshing water out of the tub in her haste. "Unless I *am* omnifinitied," she whispered to herself.

Luna interrupted her wallowing to ask if she still planned to attend dinner—Asterin declined, preferring to stew over her revelation in the warmth and comfort of the water over the cacophony of Mess Hall.

Finally, when the water bordered on ice cold and her skin was as wrinkled as a prune, she stepped out of the bath and wrapped herself in a fluffy towel. The sky outside had softened to a dusky orange. Luna returned, and they lounged on the bed in their dressing gowns.

Asterin nibbled on fruit and cheese, wincing while Luna struggled to comb out the seemingly infinite snarls in her hair. Asterin popped a grape into her friend's mouth. "So, how is everything going with Eadric?"

She could hear the smile in Luna's answer. "Lovely as always." A pause. "He's been so busy, though. We only manage to see each other once or twice a week."

Asterin gaped, dropping her melon slice on a pillow. "That is unacceptable. Come on." She hopped off the bed, dashing for the closet.

Luna blinked owlishly. "Wha—"

After throwing on a loose cotton blouse and trousers, Asterin tutted and picked out a sheer gold dress with a plunging neckline. She brandished it at her friend. "Put this on. That's an order." Cheerfully ignoring Luna's flustered protests, Asterin helped her into it and zipped up the back before diving back into the closet to find a pair of matching slippers. "These, too. Hurry up!"

A balmy breeze caressed her skin as Asterin nudged the windows open, icestone in hand. Frost crackled from the sill at her command, shooting to the courtyard far below. Notches carved themselves down the center, smoothing out into a narrow crystalline staircase. The sun had set, but the ice caught the glow of lamps, gilding the steps gold with flickering firelight.

Luna, long accustomed to her escapades, only sighed and stepped obediently onto the sill. To fill the silence as they descended, she chattered on about her latest work of art—a sculpture, one of the many displayed in the parlor-turned-workshop that Asterin had set aside for her. They were all true masterpieces, every single one of them.

"Can I commission one of Garringsford?" Asterin asked as they passed a second-floor balcony.

Luna frowned. "What for?"

"Could you give her bullhorns? And a duck's beak. And a pig's snout."

A snigger. "I can't give her both a snout and a beak at the same time."

They hopped off the staircase and into the flower bed undetected, or at least ignored. Like Luna, the patrol guards knew better than to question the notorious schemes of the Princess of Axaria. After picking their way around clusters of fresh buds cast gray in the shadows of the poplars standing sentinel overhead, they strolled arm in arm toward the training ring, tucked behind the stables and the guardhouse. The night was pleasant, the leaves rustling and the crickets chirruping in harmony with the soft whickering of horses.

Then came a *thud* and a chorus of victorious whoops.

Luna yanked Asterin to a standstill just before they rounded the stables, eyes wide and frantic. Finally, she had understood where they were heading. "Eadric can't see me in this!" she whispered furiously, flapping her hands at herself. "There's even a thigh slit! I look—"

"Gorgeous, as usual," Asterin said with an eye roll. Then she dragged her friend out into the open, forcing her over to the training ring's wooden fence.

Large blockades had been positioned inside the ring, encircling two vaguely human-shaped targets pockmarked with gashes and holes. Blue cotton spilled from the wounds of one and green from the other. Two figures guarded the targets, one apiece, each wearing either a blue or green band across their forehead. Asterin watched as a slight girl with fiery orange hair leapt from a blockade behind the much taller soldiers, roaring a terrific battle cry with her sword brandished.

Luna gasped as the blue-banded soldier whirled around and crossed two long knives over his head, barring the girl's attack on the stuffed target with a screech of steel. They fought like wildfire and tempest, blades slashing swift and precise, but then the girl dropped low enough to slide between his legs and deliver a killing blow straight through the blue target's back and out the other side. A yelp came from the green-banded guard as a spear flew out of nowhere and burst right through the second target's neck, showering clumps of cotton everywhere. The guard looked up in time to see a second girl drop from the top of the blockade and land nimbly on her feet with a smirk.

A tall man in full uniform appeared from the deep shadows of the two blockades, his broad chest and shoulders nearly filling the space completely. "Death by severed arteries. Nice work, ladies. Alicia, try withholding your battle cries. Even though you won, you gave away your position and lost the element of surprise. Casper, keep your guard lower next time. And Gino, always stay alert to your surroundings—projectiles have to fire from somewhere or another. Good aim, Hayley. Try to extend your follow-through for more power, like this." At his beckons, Hayley retrieved the spear from the green target's neck for him. He backed out of sight. Asterin felt the anticipation mount, and then a blur of silver hurtled from the darkness, the spear plunging straight through not one but both targets. It lodged into the blockade directly across the ring with a wooden *thwack*. Pandemonium erupted from behind the blockades, whoops of dazzled awe drowning out Luna's timid squeak.

"Captain Covington!" Asterin called out.

One foot braced against the blockade and muscles taut against his uniform, the captain yanked the spear free and glanced up. He caught sight of Luna immediately. Asterin watched in delight as his jaw dropped to his chest. "Fall in," he managed.

The shadows of the blockades shifted, and four more figures emerged. They jogged over to the four soldiers already lined up, some still with cheeks flushed from the excitement. As one, Asterin's Elite Royal Guard lowered to one knee in salute, right hands clasped to their shoulders across their chests.

"Your Highness." Eadric strode forward and bowed his head to Asterin before gently grasping Luna's hand and raising it to his lips. "And Miss Luna."

Captain Eadric Covington was the commander of her Elites, as well as Asterin's most trusted and capable soldier. The son of a Cyejin lord, he had first entered the royal ranks as an Elite himself when Asterin had only been a child. Cyejin heritage had given him hair streaked with tawny brown highlights that reminded Asterin of the cacao nibs her father used to have imported from Morova, straight brows, and dark eyes that shone like pine honey in the sunlight. Built like an ox, his mouth was set in a line so firm he appeared constantly unimpressed, although currently his gaze was nothing but adoring.

And roving—down the dress. One of the Elites cleared his throat and Eadric's eyes snapped back up, sheepish. A faint blush had worked its way up his neck, perfectly matching Luna's.

"Doesn't she just look stunning in gold?" Asterin asked, gleeful.

"But she always looks stunning," Eadric said, confusion crinkling his brow, so genuine and honest that Luna hid her face behind Asterin's shoulder in embarrassment. One of the Elites *aww*ed. Without so much as a glance, the captain said, "One hundred push-ups, Jack." The *aww* deflated into a quiet grumble. "Make that two hundred!"

Asterin surveyed her Elites, eyes lingering on the two empty spots at both ends of the row—five males and five females traditionally made up the guard, but she was currently missing two.

"All right, that's enough for tonight for the rest of you," Eadric said. "Clean everything away and patch yourselves up before bed. And if I hear about any buffoonery, I'll have you running ten laps around the palace every morning for the next week. Do I make myself clear?"

"He's such a mother hen," Luna murmured with a fond sigh, just loud enough for Asterin to hear.

Eadric nodded as the Elites drowned out Jack's grunts of "Thirty-three … thirty-four …" with their choruses of "Yes, sir!"

"Dismissed," he said. Then he extended an arm to Luna. "Shall we?"

As the three of them wound their way back to the palace, Asterin hung back, perfectly content to behold the couple from a distance. Eadric's chest puffed as Luna raised onto her tiptoes to kiss his cheek. The hardness in his face transformed to soft wonder every time she beamed at him.

Then Eadric halted in his tracks, staring upward. "Is that a staircase made of ice?"

"Yep." Asterin skirted past him and began climbing.

"What if it melted while you were on it?" the captain spluttered.

"Don't be silly, Eadric," Luna said, following suit. "Asterin's ice doesn't melt."

He rubbed his temples. "So this is how you've been duping your guards?"

Asterin paused her ascent to glare down at him. "My guards are oafs."

At that, the captain held his hands up in surrender. "It's not my fault your mother ordered General Garringsford to assign you palace guards until we can fill complete rank for the Elites."

Asterin just shook her head. "Are you coming or not?" She peered down to see Eadric eyeing the staircase dubiously.

"What?" Luna asked, confused.

"I'm taking the palace stairs, like a normal person," Eadric declared, and dashed off.

"Boring," Asterin said. Luna hummed in agreement.

Once they had safely arrived back in her chambers, Asterin commanded the staircase to liquefy. It streamed into the flower bed below.

Luna laughed. "No wonder those flowers look extra perky." A firm knock drew them toward the entrance to Asterin's chambers.

"—and both of you are incompetent," Eadric was berating the guards stationed outside when Luna opened the door. Both girls sighed, pulling him in by the arm and shutting the door. His expression turned serious as he turned to Asterin. "Your Highness, I just ran into a messenger. You've been summoned to Throne Hall."

Asterin made a face. "At this hour? By whom?"

"Your mother. Apparently, you've been sent a gift … from the Queen of Eradore."

Eradore. A starkly beautiful land on the opposite side of the globe, shrouded in mystery and magic. Other than the royal family, only special guests, residents, and students of the world-renowned Academia Principalis, the best school of magic, were permitted to cross into the inner city of the kingdom's capital, Eradoris.

Luna frowned. "I thought I heard that their queen passed away recently."

"It must be Queen Lillian's daughter, then," Asterin said thoughtfully. "What sort of gift?"

“I’d be guessing,” Eadric admitted.

Asterin stood, but fingers locked around her wrist and tugged her back. “You can’t go in that!” Luna cried, gesturing to her outfit.

Asterin raised an eyebrow. “What’s wrong with trousers?”

“Not the trousers, the *blouse.* The sleeve is still ripped from the time you fell out of that tree.”

Eadric took on a pained expression. “You fell out of a *tree*?”

Luna shooed him out the door and dragged Asterin back into the bedchamber. When she at last allowed the princess to depart, clad in a slim-fitting cobalt overcoat with pearlescent embroidery and sleek navy trousers, Eadric was nowhere in sight. Shrugging, Asterin sauntered down the staircase, hands slung in her pockets as she headed for Throne Hall.

His deep voice jumped out from behind her. “Your Highness.”

She almost hook-kicked him in the face. “Damn it, Eadric.” She had a vague sense it was his small retribution for the tree-climbing fiasco.

The ghost of a smile flickered on her captain’s face as he fell into step beside her. “My apologies.”

They had almost reached Throne Hall when General Garringsford rounded the corner, blocking the corridor. “Your Highness.”

“General,” Asterin said, eyes flicking to that perfect bun, every strand perfectly in place, as usual. “How are you faring?”

“Your concern is very touching, Your Highness,” she answered, voice too low for Asterin to discern the exact level of sarcasm. “The healers patched me up just fine. I do believe I owe you an apology.” She smiled, nearly as sharp as the glint in her flint-gray eyes. “I underestimated you.”

Asterin’s fists clenched in her pockets. “No hard feelings.”

“None at all. Anyway, your mother requested that I fetch you.”

“Her Majesty requested that *I* escort Her Highness,” Eadric said, voice flat; whatever had been left of his good mood vanishing. “Ma’am,” he added.

“Is that so?” Garringsford inquired. “Well—”

“How about you both escort me?” Asterin snapped. “We’re almost there, anyway.”

“Your posture is sloppy, Covington,” said the general. “Fix it at once.”

Eadric’s jaw twitched. “Yes, ma’am.”

They arrived at the entrance to Throne Hall, six of Queen Priscilla's guards snapping to attention outside the massive double doors. Asterin had spent hours as a child staring in awe at those doors while her father held court within. Hundreds of wolves had been carved into the dark oak, prowling down a mountain toward a lake. On the left, Lord Conrye rose above the peaks, wielding his legendary greatsword, Vürst—Frost, in the mortal tongue. Now Asterin's height matched that of the blade. Below, the ice god's wolf form rippled in the lake's reflection. Once, she thought that she had caught the piercing eyes of both human and wolf moving, though of course no one had believed her.

To this day, she still pretended that Lord Conrye was watching her from somewhere in the Immortal Realm, even though no one knew if the Council truly existed anymore, as they hadn't involved themselves with mortals since the time of legends.

Right before the guards opened the doors, splitting the two halves of the god apart, Asterin had to pinch herself—because as she walked by, she could have sworn those same emerald eyes followed her inside.

CHAPTER FOUR

"My daughter, Princess Asterin Faelenhart of Axaria," Queen Priscilla announced as Asterin glided down the crimson carpet stretching all the way from the hall's entrance to the throne. Eadric stationed himself at the doors while Garringsford sauntered over to the queen. Gold-flecked marble pilasters jutted from the walls, rising like colossal redwoods to meet the ceiling. Like the painting in Asterin's chambers, though here in sculpted magnificence, the Council of Immortals looked down from the ceiling around a massive ruby-encrusted chandelier, the gods and goddesses bearing witness to all official royal affairs. Lord Conrye faced the door to greet new visitors. The steel whip of Lady Reyva cracked over his right shoulder, and the trident of Lord Tidus crested a wave of marble at his left.

Two figures stood shoulder to shoulder before the throne, clad in identical green cloaks brocaded with swirls of silver. Their hoods obscured their faces in shadow. As one, they turned to Asterin and swept to the ground in deep bows.

The left figure spoke first—a female. "Your Royal Highness."

"Rise," Asterin commanded. They complied. When the girl lifted the hood off her head, bright auburn locks tumbled free, revealing a fair complexion, a pert nose peppered with freckles, and full lips twisted in a roguish smile. And her eyes. The girl's eyes smoldered beneath the high arches of her brows like a setting sun, molten gold and flecked with amber. She couldn't have been more than a year or two Asterin's senior, but the spark in those eyes held something else—something much older.

"Rose Fletcher," the girl began in introduction, her voice ringing out through the cavernous room. "And this is my cousin. We have been sent from the kingdom of Eradore by Her Royal Majesty, Queen Orozalia Saville of Eradore and the House of the Serpent. In honor of her recent accession, she has extended an offering of peace and allegiance to the nine kingdoms. We are two of her best soldiers."

Asterin stared when Rose bowed again. "*You* are the peace offering?"

"On her behalf, we are wholly at your service, Your Highness."

"*My* service?" Asterin turned to her mother for clarification.

Queen Priscilla waved airily, eyes almost turquoise in the light of the chandelier. "General Garringsford has her hands full looking after the newest batch of palace guard recruits, but I understand there happens to be two openings in your Elite Royal Guard, Princess Asterin."

For a moment, Asterin couldn't summon a response. It *was* true—Petyr and Tanya had been promoted to high-authority positions in Orielle, the seaport city on the west coast of the kingdom. Even so … surely her mother realized the risk of recruiting two foreign soldiers into her Elites. Asterin looked to Eadric helplessly. He shook his head. *Speak now or you'll have to hold your tongue.* Her fists curled and her mouth opened, but what could she say? Now that her mother had sanctioned it, there was no way to refuse, not now, not with Rose Fletcher's golden eyes locked upon her, lest she insult their queen by rejecting them.

Finally, Asterin bowed, first to her mother, and then the foreigners. "I am humbled by your queen's generosity. It is my honor to accept."

Queen Priscilla rose from her throne. "Wonderful. Now, I beg your pardons, but I must ask for your leave. I have some business to attend to." And with that she turned away to address Garringsford while simultaneously leafing through a pile of papers the general had produced out of nowhere.

Asterin spun on her heel, striding out of Throne Hall, Eadric and the two Eradorians following close behind. In the silence that followed, only her and Eadric's footsteps—the steady *click-tap* of hard leather soles—

could be heard. The Eradorians wore similar boots, laced to the knee—but their soft-soled steps were those of ghosts.

"Eadric, if you'd please escort these two to the barracks?" she prompted. "See to their uniforms as well."

The captain saluted. "Right away, Princess Asterin."

"Your Highness," Rose said, just as they were parting ways—Asterin to her chambers and her newest recruits down to the concourse, which separately housed both the palace guards and the Elites.

Asterin stopped but did not turn. "Yes?"

Rose spoke with a smile in her voice. "Forgive me any disrespect, but you seem rather apprehensive about this arrangement."

At that, Asterin huffed a laugh and faced her. "Forgive *me*, Rose," she said, not unkindly, "but I'm sure you can imagine my concerns. For one, your cousin has yet to even show their face," she pointed out, glancing at the shifting outline of hard muscle hidden beneath the cloak. Eadric's hand twitched to rest lightly upon the pommel of his sword.

"He's shy," Rose said, drawing a scoff from beneath her cousin's hood.

"For another," Asterin went on, "Eradoris has always been a city of great mystery to the rest of the world, what with the sequestering of your inner city and the royal family. Your kingdom reveals only the name of your ruler, and nothing more until the crown is passed on."

"For protection," said Rose.

"Yes, but from what?" Asterin asked. "Are guards not enough? The world hasn't seen war for over three centuries. The other kingdoms divulge all the knowledge that yours refuses to—and now your queen sends out two vessels of information to each kingdom? Perhaps you're spies—perhaps not. Either way, I can promise you one thing. I will not judge you differently from the other Elites unless you give me reason to, good or bad. Trust is earned, and once you have proven yourselves worthy, you will have mine."

Rose tilted her head, and Asterin got the sudden impression that she was being evaluated. Despite the girl's unremarkable height, something about her presence left Asterin feeling unsettled. She certainly had no desire to make enemies with this Rose Fletcher.

"And how might we achieve that, Your Highness?" asked the Eradorian.

Asterin resumed her way up the stairs. "That's up to you."

"Your Highness, one more thing," Rose called out. "We brought you a gift."

"Oh, enough with the damned gifts," Asterin muttered to herself, but pasted on a smile and plodded back down the steps to indulge her. "What is it?"

"An affinity stone," Rose said. Asterin nearly fled right then and there, Garringsford's shrieks echoing in her head. But then the girl added, "It holds the power of all nine elements."

"All nine?" Stones that bore two or three or even four sigils certainly existed, but nine … Asterin exchanged a quick glance with Eadric. He shrugged.

"Yes. Our queen struggled for years with her powers, but this stone allowed her to unlock the fullest potential of her magic—and I do mean the fullest."

Asterin stared openly at her. "Your queen is omnifinitied?"

Rose's lips quirked at her obvious interest. "Indeed. Behold the omnistone." She held out a small silk pouch, the same forest green as her cloak. "If it helps you like it did our queen, perhaps you could allow yourself to trust us a little more."

Eadric stepped forward, but Asterin held up a hand. She could handle this herself. She took the pouch, pulled its drawstrings open, and peered within. The stone rested at the bottom, a round teardrop the size of an eye and as clear as water. *So small and unassuming*, she thought, and slipped it out. She inhaled sharply as it rolled into her palm, the world dipping violently beneath her feet. Her eyes widened, her blood flowing with an electricity she had never before experienced. She could *feel* the stone's power, thrumming in her palms like the wings of a hummingbird. "What—"

Suddenly, Rose's cousin was at her shoulder, a featherlight hand on her waist to steady her. "If I told you the omnistone could unlock all your affinities," he murmured into her ear, voice as soft as velvet midnight, "would you let it?"

Her lips parted. She wouldn't have believed him, if not for the overwhelming magic radiating from the stone. She had tried for *years* to unlock another element. Garringsford's words taunted her constantly. *It's always difficult admitting failure.* She imagined how far the general's jaw would drop and how proud her mother would be if she proved Garringsford wrong. She wanted it so badly that she could taste it. Asterin clutched the stone harder and gave him a nod.

Rose's cousin placed his other hand over hers and entwined their fingers, trapping the stone between their palms. Asterin resisted a shiver, the firm planes of his chest grazing intimately against her back. "By the way," he said, "this might hurt a bit."

Eadric's eyes widened. "Wait, hold on—"

"A lot," Rose corrected. "Ready?"

"What?" Eadric squawked. "Now? Here? Your Highness, this isn't a good idea—"

Asterin ignored him. "What do I have to do?"

"Nothing. Just trust me," that midnight voice whispered again, his grip tightening on her waist. Before she could reply, his hands grew hot, like coals. "*Helt Avsloradovion.*"

The unfamiliar incantation sent a wave of shudders roiling through Asterin's whole body. Her vision flared white and her knees buckled. The scent of smoke and cold mountain air enveloped her as she sank into the warmth of his waiting arms, and then everything went black.

CHAPTER FIVE

When Asterin fainted in the hooded Eradorian's arms, Eadric panicked. He drew his sword in an instant, fully prepared to start slitting throats. "What have you done?"

Boots thudded up the staircase. Three guards had spotted them from the concourse and rushed over to investigate. Rose's cousin adjusted Asterin so that her face was hidden in his shoulder.

"Fletcher," Eadric hissed.

The damned girl only raised her brows pointedly at the guards.

"What's going on here?" a bald one demanded.

Eadric gritted his teeth, sheathing his sword. "Leave us," he told them, not recognizing any of their faces. He eyed the badges on their dark sleeves. Pups, fresh out of training. They continued staring dubiously at him, oblivious to his rank. Eadric concluded that they were either blind or stupid—he was wearing full uniform, for the love of the Immortals. He stepped closer, lips inches from the bald guard's ear. "That was not a request, soldier." The man frowned, opening his mouth to protest, when Eadric shut him up with a snarled, "That was an order."

The man flinched. "Yes, sir."

"Yes, Captain."

All three of the soldiers paled with realization. In unison, they squeaked, "Yes, Captain!"

"You will not speak of this to anyone, not even your superiors. Should you disobey, I *will* know."

They nearly tripped over themselves in their haste to flee to their stations.

He watched them go, perturbed. *So General Garringsford is enlisting soldiers without my approval.* While the general—and only the general—did rank higher than him, protocol dictated that new recruits had to receive approval from both of them prior to entering the palace division.

"*Captain*, hm?" Rose said, interrupting his thoughts. She leaned against the banister, looking for all the world as if she owned the place. She tilted her head approvingly, those gold eyes catching the light.

Eadric's fists clenched. But he knew how to play the game, so he coaxed them loose. "Captain Eadric Covington, commander of the Elite Royal Guard." He leaned forward, gaze cold and a lazy smile on his lips. "I would say I'm at your service, but you're at mine."

Rose blinked at him, taken aback. "Uh. I—" She broke off as Asterin, still in the other Eradorian's arms, suddenly twitched awake and let out a pigeon-like coo.

Eadric hurried over. "Your Highness! Are you all right?"

She raised a hand to pat his cheek. "Soft, but needs a shave."

He stared incredulously and whirled on Rose. *To hell with the game.* "What … what have you done?"

Rose cringed. "I'm told that the effects of the stone can be a little disorienting."

"Does toast count as a vegetable since it's made from grain and grain is a plant?" Asterin asked.

"Just a little?" Eadric deadpanned.

"I'll prepare a tonic for her," Rose said. "She needs to sleep." Without another word, she headed up the grand stairway.

"Where in hell do you think you're going?" Eadric spluttered.

Rose halted and turned, eyes wide. "Oh my, you're right. I almost forgot about Her Highness. Cousin dearest, if you'd please …"

'Cousin dearest' had already scooped Asterin into his arms as if she were no heavier than a child, but Eadric knew from firsthand experience that one needed more than a little muscle to carry the princess. Asterin herself had fallen into a doze, nuzzling into her transporter's chest.

The situation was wildly spinning out of control. "The princess is not meant to be handled like a sack of flour," he growled.

A grunt from beneath the hood. "Who holds a sack of flour like this? Would *you* prefer to carry her? Hold on, don't answer that, of course you would. Listen, Captain Covington—if you can't even trust me to carry the princess up the stairs, how can you trust me to protect her as an Elite?"

Eadric found he had nothing to say to that. By the time he regained his verbal capabilities, Rose and her cousin were already two flights up and continuing to ascend with frightening speed. Who in the name of the almighty Immortals were these people? All the same ... Taking the steps three at a time, he called out, "Stop!"

Rose peered over the banister, gold eyes burning with challenge. "What now?"

He caught up to them on the landing and pointed down the corridor. "Fourth floor. Her chambers are on this floor."

The two guards that Eadric had told off earlier were notably absent from their posts. Luna opened the door on the second knock, her eyes lighting up when they settled onto him. Since the first moment they had met—or at least, the first time she had passed him by, Asterin hanging off her arm and howling with laughter, his stomach always kicked into flutters—then and now. He still remembered that sweet smile, blossoming at the end of whatever joke she had told to cause the princess to dissolve into stitches, still remembered the way she had curled a tendril of honey-gold hair behind her ear and glanced toward him, blue eyes sparkling brighter than a Cyejin sky.

Now, that same forget-me-not gaze shifted, landing on the two Eradorians, and of course Asterin, mouth lolling open. After a long silence, Luna turned on him, wrath blazing across her features. "Did you let this happen?"

Rose grinned. "He sure did! Mind if we come in?" The girl shouldered her way through without waiting for an answer, tugging her cousin and Asterin along with her, and that was that.

"You, mister," Luna said, eyes narrowed, jabbing a finger into his chest, "are in big trouble." Without another word, she spun on her heel and stormed off into Asterin's chambers.

Eadric just threw his hands up into the air in defeat.

Asterin woke to a grogginess beyond comprehension. She flinched as light seeped through her eyelids and she cursed the pain that stabbed through her temple.

One glimpse at her surroundings told her that she was in her own chambers, tucked snug into bed. Craning her neck, she spotted the figure sprawled in the armchair beside her. "Luna?" she croaked.

The girl turned her head sleepily, before shooting out of the chair. "You're awake!" she cried. Asterin winced. "Oh, sorry." Much quieter, she asked, "How are you feeling?"

A soft groan escaped Asterin's lips. "Like I've been run over by a wagon."

Luna fluffed the pillows and stroked her hair. "Poor thing. Don't worry, I yelled at Eadric already."

"For what?" Asterin said. "Wait …" It all came rushing back. The Eradorians, the omnistone—

The door to her bathing chamber swung open before she could finish her thought. Rose strode through. "Oh, good, you're awake. Thought I heard voices." Already she wore the black, high-collared jacket of the Elite uniform, silver epaulettes decorating her shoulders and the Axarian crest embroidered above her heart. A red stripe ran down the right side of her simple black trousers. She only lacked the signature crimson cloak, but she wouldn't receive it until Asterin and Eadric deemed her worthy.

Asterin shot the golden-eyed girl a weak glare. How long had she been out? "You can't just barge in here like this. And what were you doing in my bathroom?"

A glowering young man trailed into the room after Rose, and when his dark eyes pinned sharply onto Asterin, her breath hitched.

Her first thought was that one of Luna's sculptures had come to life—

broad-shouldered, toned forearms revealed by sleeves rolled to the elbows. His features were chiseled into a face of ivory, contrasted by the locks of dark brown falling across his forehead, artfully tousled as if he had just returned from a windy autumn stroll. High cheekbones swept down to lips soft and pink as sin with an angular jaw and—*Immortals*, she could have stared at him all day.

Her face grew hot as he surveyed her in turn. When he stepped closer, she fell into the bottomless depths of his eyes, a fierce, intense indigo flecked with starlight.

She descended into a coughing fit.

One of his dark brows arched. After she gave a last, pitiful cough, he opened his mouth to speak. She leaned forward in anticipation, and for a moment, time seemed to slow.

And then—

"You're bloody heavy for a dainty little princess."

Asterin gaped in outrage, shocked beyond words. And then she realized she recognized that midnight voice. Rose's cousin. The one who had held her and—oh, Immortals, had he carried her up the stairs?

"And you're spectacularly rude," she finally stammered out. *And spectacularly handsome, but still a total ass.* It made sense why he had kept his hood up now. If any of the court ladies had laid eyes on him, they would have long torn him to carrion.

He smirked. "My apologies. I only thought to be honest with Your Highness."

Asterin narrowed her eyes. "How very considerate of you, erm …?"

Rose suddenly piped up. "Dear me, I've still yet to introduce him, haven't I?" She threw her arms in his direction in a grand flourish. "Princess Asterin, meet my most *beloved* cousin, Quinnie."

Despite herself, Asterin snickered. After all that suspense … "Your name is *Quinnie*? No wonder you didn't want to tell us."

Quinnie scowled deeply. Asterin found herself taking great satisfaction in his displeasure. "Quinlan," he corrected. "Quinlan Holloway."

"Is that really much of an improvement?" Luna said.

Asterin suppressed a giggle. Then some fragment of recognition flickered through her and her eyes narrowed. "Holloway … I've heard that name before."

Quinlan shrugged. "From my father, most likely."

"Your father?"

"Yes." He didn't elaborate further.

"Well, anyway," Rose said to Asterin. "I've arduously prepared a tonic for your pretty little head, if you'd like to have it."

"I'd like to have *your* pretty little head on a stake," Asterin grumbled under her breath.

But apparently she hadn't grumbled quietly enough, because Quinlan burst out laughing. "Oh, I like her."

Rose pouted. "Who's the rude one now?"

"You are aware that I could have you locked up at my wishes, no?" Asterin said, only half-joking.

"Ah," said Rose with a grin. "Diplomacy at its finest. Fine, I surrender." She handed over a small vial filled with a reddish-orange substance.

Asterin uncorked it, sniffing suspiciously. "It's not poisonous, is it?"

Rose gave her a playful wink. "I wouldn't dare."

"She really would, you know," Quinlan said. An uncomfortable silence ensued. Sheepishly, he added, "It's not, though. Obviously."

"That wasn't terribly reassuring," Asterin said, but nonetheless, she sent a short prayer to the Immortals and tipped the contents down her throat. Her mouth filled with the taste of fresh summer berries and sun-warmed grass. Her headache had already begun to fade as she drained the last droplets, leaving her tastebuds with a pleasant tingle.

Rose took the empty vial from her. "Luna, darling, please look after her. The tonic will make her sleep like a rock, but she'll be fine in the morning."

Asterin found that hilarious and began giggling. "I'm a rock."

Luna sighed and eased Asterin back onto the pillows. "Whatever you did better be worth all of this."

"No!" Asterin cried out. "I'm not tired."

Before Luna could reply, Quinlan sat himself on the edge of Asterin's bed and brushed aside the hair from her damp forehead with a sly grin.

"Just close your eyes, brat." She could do nothing but stare, transfixed by his dimples. Then, to her dazed astonishment, he took a breath and began to sing. Her eyelids fluttered shut, fatigue sweeping over her like a heavy blanket. She drifted on the verge of sleep for a minute, clinging to the gentle melody for as long as she could, until at last she succumbed to an endless indigo darkness.

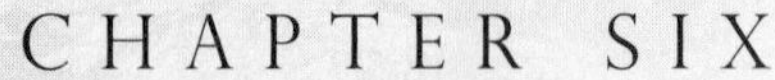

CHAPTER SIX

"Wakey, wakey!"

The whisper floated to Asterin through the darkness. She ignored it, savoring the blessed silence that followed. Then the heavy ripple of fabric cut the silence short and blazing white light pierced her slumber. "Close the damn curtains!" she howled.

When the curtains stayed open, she groaned and rolled onto her stomach, burrowing her face into the pillows. Those, along with the covers, were wrenched from her grip.

"Wake up, sleeping beauty," that voice taunted again. Asterin cursed it like a sailor, curling in on herself in a final attempt to fall back asleep. "Come on, you managed to beat me for the first time in your life and I return only to find that you've given up already?"

She shot up in bed with a little scream as Orion's grinning face swam into view. Heat radiated from her face as she yanked her satin dressing gown below her knees.

"Orion!" she shrieked. "I am not dressed!"

"Clearly," he said. "What a sight for sore eyes. That neckline is *sinfully* low."

"Well, I thought you were Luna," she snapped. "I saw no reason to cover myself."

"What? I don't sound anything like Luna!"

She shrugged and flung her finger toward the entrance. "Out!"

"I'll be back in two minutes." He winked and tugged playfully at her hem. "You should wear this more often."

Asterin whacked him in the head with the back of her hand. He just laughed and flounced out of her chambers.

After the door snicked shut, she flipped out of bed and prowled toward the bathroom, grumbling all the while—but before she made it halfway across her room, her window shattered and a man tumbled in.

Her magic reacted faster than she did, beyond her control yet again, spirals of jagged ice shooting straight for the intruder's heart.

Only as the man looked up and she met Quinlan's wide eyes did she realize her mistake.

"No!" she shouted, too late.

A wave of heat swelled over her as fire exploded from his palms, melting her ice into a deluge of water that splashed high enough to soak him from head to toe.

"What in hell was that for, brat?" he spluttered, drenched but unharmed. He clutched his hands protectively to his chest. "Is that how you say good morning? How rude."

"Immortals have mercy," Asterin said, clutching her chest. Her shock soon turned into fury. "Have you ever heard of using a *door*?" she yelled. "I could have killed you!"

"That would have been awfully ambitious of you," Quinlan replied nonchalantly, peering at his cupped palms.

Without a word, she strode over to him and slapped him hard across the face.

He blinked, cheek darkening with a hand-shaped print.

"What were you doing outside my window?" Her body trembled. "And don't call me brat, asshole."

His mouth snapped shut, and for the first time he seemed to focus. His eyes dipped down, snagging briefly on her neckline. He blushed. "Uh …"

She snapped her fingers. "Eyes up here, Holloway."

"Right," he said smartly. There was a pause. "Apologies. You look nice."

She glared at him. "You're dripping on my rug."

"Sorry."

"Are you really?"

He smiled sweetly, dimples and all. "Of course." He peeked into his hands again and then slowly unfurled his fingers. To Asterin's astonishment, a baby bird quivered in his palms, nothing more than a tiny ball of brown fuzz. It peeped up at her and chirruped bravely. "Nice defense spell on the window, by the way. If we hadn't made it inside a second sooner, you might have decapitated both me and this little guy."

This is an injustice, Asterin couldn't help but think, glancing between the baby bird and Quinlan's dimples. She pinched the bridge of her nose. "I can't believe I'm the one apologizing in this situation. And you still haven't explained why you even triggered my spell."

"I was just jogging through the gardens when I saw this little guy stuck on the railing of the balcony below your window." He paused. "And then I, uh, figured I'd might as well pop by to see if you were in. To say hello. To you. I mean, you to the bird."

Asterin's eyes narrowed. "And how exactly did you know that it was *my* window?"

Quinlan shifted his feet helplessly. "I don't know, I just counted all of the windows from outside. Your chambers are on the fourth floor, facing the gardens ..." He trailed off. "I am beginning to realize that I sound like a stalker." At Asterin's unimpressed eyebrow raise, he ducked his head. "I apologize. It was instinctual, not intentional, I swear."

"Stalking me, you mean?" she quipped.

"Of course not! I meant spatial awareness." He hid his face behind his wrists and peeked out one eye at her, the baby bird still hopping around in his cupped palms. "Please forgive me?"

Asterin sighed through her nose, trying desperately to maintain a stern expression. "You're still dripping on my rug."

"That, I can fix." Quinlan waved his hand and a warm wind wrapped itself around them in a hurricane of heat, whipping her hair into the air. The wind thrust her forward, causing her to stumble into his chest. He smirked at her and held her close, the scent of ash and smoke and northern air washing over her. One hand still cupping the baby bird and the other heavy on her waist, he leaned down, lips brushing her ear. "Feeling a little warm?" he whispered roughly, his tone sending involuntary shivers down her spine.

Asterin scowled and shoved him away, hating the smug quirk of his lips, the way her blood thrummed. The heat died down, leaving his clothes and her rug completely dry. She narrowed her eyes, face flushed, telling herself it was from the temperature. "You'd do well to remember your place."

"As?"

"As a *soldier*. Under my command. You aren't even allowed in my rooms."

"Who's not allowed in your rooms?" Orion asked, nudging his head into the bedchamber. His eyes landed on them, widening at Quinlan. "Who in hell are you?"

Quinlan raised an eyebrow. "Who in hell are *you*?"

Orion marched over, jostling Asterin behind him. "I'm Orion Galashiels, Princess Asterin's Royal Guardian."

Quinlan stepped closer with all the bravado in the world, chin high. "I'm Quinlan Holloway, Princess Asterin's …" He trailed off, glancing at her for help.

Asterin simply folded her arms across her chest. "Court jester."

"Wow." Quinlan backed down with a wince. "Ouch."

When Orion turned to her, she said, "While you were away, a present arrived from the Queen of Eradore. Two new Elites. I know Quinlan doesn't look like much, but his cousin Rose is fairly competent, trust me."

Orion didn't look too happy about the news, but then his boots crunched. He zeroed in on the glass still littering the carpet, and then the broken window. "Why …?"

"Don't ask." Quinlan passed the bird to Asterin without explanation and pulled an affinity stone out of his pocket. All at once, the shattered glass hovered into the air, glittering like frost, and then each piece ignited a fiery yellow. The glowing pieces whizzed high above their heads, amassing into a clump, fingers of blue flame licking at the ceiling but only melting the glass. Finally, Quinlan let the clump fall, catching it neatly in his hand and offering it to Asterin. "A paperweight for you, Your Highness. Careful, it's still hot." An understatement—when she held her hand over the glass, it rivaled the heat of a bonfire.

"You're a fire-wielder," Orion realized.

Quinlan bowed theatrically. "House of the Fox, at your service."

Fox. So fire is his most powerful affinity, Asterin thought. After seeing how masterfully he controlled his fire affinity, she couldn't help but admit her curiosity. Fire was the most difficult element to control, after all.

"At your service, my ass," Orion said, and Asterin noticed that the usual twinkle in his glacier-blue eyes had gone flat. "Get out of here."

Asterin gaped. "Orion."

"You said it yourself, Asterin. He's not even allowed in your rooms."

"Unless I give him permission," she retorted. *Why am I defending him?* She blamed it on Orion's uncharacteristic incivility. "Quinlan, my sword, please. By the dresser. I've got some ass to kick."

The Eradorian obliged. As he passed her Amoux, he gestured to her dressing gown and asked, "Aren't you going to change first?"

"Nope," Asterin said, scarcely noticing the strangled noise her reply choked out of him, already focusing on the task at hand. There was no way in hell she'd let Orion beat her—not now.

Her Guardian gave her a hard look. "Are you sure you want to do this?"

She pretended not to understand his double meaning, only crooking two fingers at him in invitation.

He scoffed, taking his time unsheathing Orondite, holding his blade loose in his grip. That was her first warning—that easy stance meant trouble. She stilled her breathing, Amoux steady and solid as she waited for the spring to recoil. For that single drop of rain to split the surface of the lake. For his telltale inhale—and there.

Orion shot forward, faster than a jungle cat, his sword cleaving through the air. She heard Quinlan suck in a breath. But Asterin was even faster than her mentor, Amoux nothing more than a blur. The cut that could have taken her hand off slashed through nothing. Orion drew back to right his blunder and she met him without hesitation. The collision of their swords nearly knocked her over—and before she could regain control, Orondite hooked around Amoux and wrenched upward. Tears pricked her eyes at the pain that shot through her wrist.

Focus.

Her Guardian drove his sword into hers again and again, pummeling her defenses as fast as she could set them up. She scrambled over the pile of pillows that Orion had abandoned on her floor earlier, struggling to recover from his attacks.

"What do you think happens when you put your trust into people you don't truly know?" Orion asked, hacking a pillow in half with an effortless slice and a shower of feathers. "Like your father did, all those years ago?"

Asterin swallowed. "That has nothing to do with this."

Slice. Two pillows sheared apart. "Of course it does."

With a snarl, she hurled herself forward and thrust. *Sloppy.* Orion parried her easily and bore down upon her blade with cruel, crushing strength. The strain on her wrist raked a groan from her throat. A chilling wind gusted through the broken window at her back. Her feet slid across the floor and an idea flitted through her mind.

"What do you think happens when you don't listen to the people you *should* trust?" Orion demanded. "The people who will stop at nothing to protect you when others betray you?"

She looked up, eyes blazing, inches from his face. "Door."

His ire flickered. "What?"

Asterin withdrew just as suddenly as Orion had at her door only a few days earlier. Except there was no door between them to crash into now—only air. As he staggered forward, he just managed to wrestle back his balance. But now she claimed the upper hand.

She met Orondite with fluid grace, moving like water, striking like fire, and fighting with all the ice she held within herself. She remembered the feeling of the omnistone's power singing through her body, now felt that power within herself as she delivered each blow with pristine accuracy and merciless strength. Sweat dripped down her neck, yet she did not waver. All she felt was the calm in her mind as she sought out his weak spot—one chink, that was all she needed.

When she found it, she was more than ready. Her Guardian swung high, and she dove *beneath* Orondite's rapid slash, coming up behind him. *Keep your guard lower next time*, she thought, and slammed the flat of her blade into the back of his legs. His knees buckled, and she darted around to his front, swift as an asp, springing into the air and delivering a final kick to his chest.

Orion toppled over and smashed into the floor on his side, skidding to a halt near the wall. He rolled limply onto his back, clinging Orondite, his chest heaving. When Asterin walked over and settled Amoux against his throat, his jaw had gone slack.

"I trusted you to teach me to fight, all those years ago," Asterin whispered. "How to protect myself. So that if I ever had to fight—"

"You would win," Orion finished, staring up at the ceiling. A slow grin crept onto his face. "I guess we both succeeded."

"I guess we did."

For the second time in her life, Asterin pulled her Guardian to his feet.

And then she grabbed Garringsford's firestone from her bedside table. Breathing in through her nose, she drew from the stone's power. When she exhaled, the tiniest spark skittered to life across her open palm.

Orion's eyes widened. "How . . . ?"

"It's all because of the omnistone," Asterin said softly. "I couldn't have done it without Rose and Quinlan's help." She turned to Quinlan, the baby bird still perched on his shoulder. "And for that, I'm thankful." She waved Amoux at the Eradorian. "Well? What did you think of our little battle, my Elite jester?"

Quinlan's indigo eyes glimmered with a new kind of respect, undimmed by her jibe. "Just remind me to never find myself on the wrong end of your sword."

CHAPTER SEVEN

Quinlan's first three weeks in Axaris flew by. Between training, guard duty, and tormenting the Princess of Axaria in his every spare moment, he hadn't touched his magic since the day he had burst through her window—and now it nagged at him, an incessant itch. Little spurts of magic weren't enough. He needed to let go, but even in the deepest corners of the palace gardens, he never knew who might be watching.

"Oi, Quinlan, coming to dinner?" Gino sang as he buttoned his jacket. Even in the dim light of the barracks, his spiked hair glistened with a copious amount of gel. Every morning, Gino woke before everyone else, just so he could hog the mirror. The other three male Elites already waited by the door—gangly Jack, with his easy, boisterous laugh; silver-tongued Casper, whose words were as sharp as the two ruby-hilted knives that always hung low at his hips; and grizzly bearded Old Silas, who Quinlan learned had only just turned thirty, but simply "Old" because he was the oldest Elite.

Quinlan shot them a grin from his bunk, hiding his jittering fingers in his lap. "You go ahead."

Jack blew him a kiss. "Bye, dear. Don't play with the stove, and remember, bedtime is at eight!"

Quinlan rolled his eyes. "So, light your bed on fire by eight. Got it."

Casper whistled. "Listen, Quinlan, there's no need for arson. If you want Jack in your bed so badly, just ask him."

Quinlan raised a certain finger, and Casper's uniform burst into flames. Old Silas just shook his head while the other boys fell over themselves in laughter as Casper yelped and dove to the floor, rolling and batting at himself to extinguish the flames before realizing they hadn't actually caused any harm.

"You sly fox," Casper said, grinning despite himself. He was the craftiest of the bunch and the only other male fire-wielder, and Quinlan had taken to him quickly. "The last time I tried that trick I nearly burned a man to a crisp. How did you do it?"

Quinlan winked. "Trade secret."

Gino's stomach interrupted with a deafening growl. "Food. Now."

The boys jostled each other to the door, still hooting, signature red cloaks billowing. Their guffaws faded and left Quinlan, finally, to the silence.

Three weeks had passed, and Quinlan still didn't have one of those damned cloaks—one side a deep crimson and the other sable black, marking him as an "official" Elite Royal Guard. Rose had been presented one a few days ago by Captain Covington after she had recited more poisons and their antidotes than all the other Elites combined, mended a shattered leg, and disarmed four patrol guards on the Wall from three hundred feet away with specialized arrows. His cousin had only rubbed it in his face about a dozen times so far.

For a moment, Quinlan simply closed his eyes and basked in the solitude, the crackle of the hearth his only companion. He loosed an exhausted sigh. His tailbone still ached from a week ago, when Princess Asterin had dropped by during a combat session and volunteered to be his sparring partner. Then, in front of everyone, she had knocked him, quite literally, onto his ass. Ever since, she'd "taken pity" on him—by forcing him to practice with her every morning. She'd gone after Rose, too, but even as children, Rose had always bested Quinlan in both hand-to-hand combat and swordplay. After a single duel, Asterin had grudgingly deemed his cousin's skills adequate.

Quinlan had never felt comfortable with any weapon save for his magic and the three priceless Ignatian daggers Rose's mother had gifted to him on his thirteenth birthday. Their iridescent blades were ribbed with countless folds from the deepest of the Ignatian forges, and he had yet to find something they couldn't slice through. Unfortunately, his new mentor expected him to demonstrate proficiency fighting with any weapon or object.

Even a carrot? he had asked, and the challenge had shone in her eyes before he'd even perceived it as one. *That* had been an interesting morning.

While he humiliated himself in carrotplay, Asterin had admitted to him that she still struggled to summon the other elements—but the omnistone had done its job, awakening her dormant powers. Now it was just a matter of training. Quinlan offered to help, but for whatever reason, Asterin was hell-bent on practicing in private.

Privacy. He definitely lacked that here. Looking around the male Elite barracks, complete with five neatly made bunks, a chest for possessions at the foot of each, a table in the center covered in a mess of playing cards and the odd bits and bobs the boys used for betting, and the adjoined communal bathing chambers, Quinlan couldn't help but wish for home. Home meant his own chambers. He hadn't shared sleeping quarters since studying at the Academia Principalis in Eradoris. And although he'd made easy friends with his fellow soldiers, they were just so bloody noisy. The girls' barracks were next door, and Rose constantly complained that they could hear the boys yelling through the wall, but Quinlan hadn't ever once heard even a peep from *their* side.

Ten soldiers in total made up the Axarian Princess's Elite Royal Guard. Only the Immortals knew what division he and Rose would have ended up in if those two spots hadn't been open—though, knowing Rose, she'd likely planned it right from the very start. While the boys had Old Silas, the girls had the youngest Elite—a fierce fifteen-year-old named Alicia, who Rose said could fight better unarmed in pitch darkness than most of the palace guards could in broad daylight. Aside from Rose and Alicia, there was the ever-silent Nicole, with her cool gray eyes and a sheaf of black hair that fell past her waist. She spoke twice a day if they were lucky, and Quinlan constantly forgot about her existence—at least, until she had her blade pinned against his throat. Laurel was Nicole's bright-eyed opposite—bubbly and chatty, distracting any one of them with her jokes and charm. Meanwhile, she was likely thieving away valuables or weapons from their person at every opportunity, that lovely smile never faltering. Finally, there was Hayley, the oldest of the females. According to Jack, she only had three facial expressions—impassive, irritated, and smug. From what Quinlan had seen so far, Jack hadn't been exaggerating in the slightest. She had also come *this* close to decapitating Quinlan once with—of all things—her shield.

From beneath his pillow, Quinlan pulled out the little silk pouch holding the omnistone, turning it over in his hands. Rose had planned for that, too, even though they'd both known it would be a gamble. And Rose hated gambling—but over the years, Quinlan had learned that when she did … she always walked away with the winning hand.

Either way, one thing was for certain—the Princess of Axaria was powerful. *I could have killed you*, she had yelled after he burst through her window. She'd come close, the brat, but he was used to people trying to kill him.

And what was more … she still had so much potential to fulfill.

Outside of training, Quinlan had started making increasingly ludicrous excuses to seek out her company. No matter how many times he riled her or pissed her off, she simply returned the favor. Most recently, she had invited him for a walk—just the two of them—in the palace gardens. While poking fun at one another, she had lured him unawares into a corner of the enormous hedge maze on the south side of the palace and then bolted off. It had taken him two curse-filled hours to find his way out, and he later found out from Luna that she had been watching him struggle for the entire time from an overhead window, weeping with laughter.

The truth was that Asterin had been the best distraction to turn up in his life for a long while. Something to focus on, to keep him from the memories he had tried for so long to keep buried, only to discover that the deeper he dug, the closer they rose to the surface. The sting of salt tears and blood dripping down his skin. That horrible, searing heat, scorching his back, his hands. The cold hopelessness of being alone. Now he forced himself to remember so that he could remind himself of how much stronger he had grown, but the pain never faded.

He rubbed the scars on his wrists, charmed into invisibility, his eyes flicking to the tattoo on his left wrist of a fox entwined with a serpent—marking his everlasting loyalty to the House of the Serpent. For a long time, his powers had posed more of a danger than protection. Only after years of training could he rein them in.

Quinlan tossed the omnistone aside and called upon a hail of fire arrows, his magic shuddering out of him with delicious relief. He watched as the arrows whizzed around the room, their smoky trails billowing up to the low ceiling. He didn't need a firestone, or any stone at all for that matter, but he kept one on him for appearances' sake. Relying on an affinity stone had only brought him a childhood of misery—but these arrows could deliver that misery tenfold. Could blaze through cities like a match lit to parchment, devouring all they touched to cinders, any building disintegrating to dust at the slightest wayward wind. They could burn through this very palace, taking everything and everyone he wished with it.

Including Asterin's handsome Guardian … Quinlan snorted at himself and rubbed his temple, his thoughts once more returning to the princess. His arrows dissipated with a soft hiss. A few glowing embers drifted down, singeing his tunic. The burn marks on the fabric faded away with a brush of his hand, the taste of ash and magic filling his mouth.

He cursed, suddenly remembering that he didn't live alone. Hopefully the fumes would fade by the time the others returned. They still had drills with Captain Covington to look forward to after dinner.

His stomach grumbled. As Gino so eloquently put it … *Food. Now.* Getting up from his bunk, Quinlan stretched and left the barracks, climbing the stairs and following the sound of Orion's unmistakable laugh to Mess Hall.

The other Elites saved his usual spot for him, between Rose and Casper. Quinlan's gaze lingered on Asterin, seated mere feet away—and yet, with the way her Guardian had her enrapt with some stupid story, it felt as though they were stuck in separate universes. Rose elbowed him, eyebrow arched. He cleared his throat and reached for a soup tureen, chancing a look over his shoulder to the flock of nobles in all their finery roosting at the head table, looking down on the rest of the court as they nestled closer around the finest of them all.

Quinlan had heard many tales regaling the beauty of the Queen of Axaria—and while few were actually true, he couldn't deny those about her eyes. They were the stunning teal of the Syr Sea, and, if the tales were to be believed, an extraordinary one-of-a-kind—not even inherited by her own daughter, who was currently biting down on a bread roll to stifle her laughter.

Asterin caught his stare and raised an eyebrow. *What, asshole?* she mouthed.

He shrugged, lifting his glass in toast. *To you*, he mouthed back. *Brat.*

Her smile could have lit the darkest of nights.

And though he'd never seen eyes quite like Queen Priscilla's before, he would trade them for a particular pair of emerald greens any day.

CHAPTER EIGHT

Eadric thundered up the stairs, only half-dressed. The message a servant had delivered to him was crumpled in his fist. Only four words had been scribbled upon it, in Asterin's hand, heavily underlined. *Urgent. Come at once.*

He flew down the corridor and burst around the corner to her chambers. He found Orion standing in the open doorway, unusually pale. Without a word, the Guardian beckoned Eadric into the sitting parlor, where Asterin waited beside a cart of untouched sandwiches.

"Your Highness! Are you all right?" Eadric demanded, heart pounding. He searched her blank expression. "Your Highness?"

Finally, she gestured for him to take the seat across from her. Her fingers were knotted in her lap, the knuckles bone-white. Quietly, she asked, "Did you know that thirty royal soldiers have disappeared?"

"Disappeared?" Eadric frowned. "General Garringsford informed me that the squads are just doing some rounds through the kingdom. They should be back tomorrow, actually."

"No. They won't be." She revealed a scrap of metal that she had been hiding in her lap, about the size of her palm and scorched black. Flecks of ash stained her trousers. "I was on my way to the stables when I intercepted a messenger by the gates."

Eadric peered closer at the crimson-painted metal. There was a flash of silver, the muzzle of a snarling wolf—

His eyes widened. "Is that ...?"

"The remains of an Axarian shield, brought by the messenger. There was a letter, too. He refused to part with either—at least, until I ordered him to." She turned the scrap over in her hands, before tossing it to him. "They're dead. Every single one of them."

In his shock, he nearly dropped it. The royal shields were the size of a carriage wheel, made of lightweight steel and strengthened with magic—resistant to fire, acid, various attack spells, and nearly indestructible by force. Eadric gripped the ridges even as they cut into his skin, struck dumb. Fellow soldiers that he'd known for years, all gone in one fell swoop. "But how?"

"I don't know," Asterin said. "I hoped you might have an idea."

He could only shake his head. "Who was the messenger supposed to deliver it to?"

Orion looked up from the ground. "Who else?"

"I think," said Asterin at last, expression grave, "that I need to have a conversation with my mother."

The three of them filed silently into Throne Hall. No sooner had the doors closed behind Eadric than they opened a second time. He leapt back, sinking to one knee, Asterin and Orion following suit as the Queen of Axaria stormed past, General Garringsford at her heels, as always.

"What is the meaning of this, Princess Asterin?" Queen Priscilla demanded. She shook her head at her kneeling daughter. "I do not appreciate being fetched at such short notice." Settling into her throne, she swept a hand. "Rise and speak."

Asterin strode forward, brandishing the chunk of shield. "What is this?"

The queen froze. "Where did you get that? Give that to me at once."

"Mother," Asterin hissed, shoulders shaking, though whether from grief or anger, Eadric couldn't tell.

"Your tone, Princess," the queen warned. "Hand it over." Asterin complied reluctantly. The queen examined the scrap of shield for a moment and then set it gently aside. They stared at one another, the tension mounting, before at last the queen exhaled. "Daughter—"

"I want answers," she said.

Asterin's mother raised an eyebrow. "Was that an order?"

Asterin averted her eyes. "It was a request."

The queen sighed. "I hoped you wouldn't find out. Not like this, anyway. How convenient for you that a guest arrived mere minutes ago … you may stay and hear him out. Carlotta, if you would please bring him in?"

The general nodded and disappeared through the doors.

The queen stood from the throne and descended the dais. "As of late, there have been an increasing number of reports describing some kind of monstrous beast terrorizing the outskirts of the kingdom. In particular, the Aswiyre Forest and its surrounding villages. It started by targeting wild animals, and then livestock, and now … humans. Regardless of day or night, man or woman, they are being slaughtered like cattle."

The doors opened, and they all turned to see Garringsford leading in an enormous, hulking stranger with a wiry black beard and caterpillar eyebrows that covered nearly all of his forehead.

Queen Priscilla waved to the man. "This gentleman goes by Crawson. He owns a farm near the southwest part of the forest and allegedly spotted the beast." She turned to Crawson. "Do you still remember what it looked like?"

Crawson stepped forward. In a gruff voice, he said, "No one who saw the damned thing would ever forget it fer the rest of his days, Your Majesty 'n' Highness. It had rubies fer eyes and fur blacker than coal, I tell ye. Claws fer cuttin' stone and fangs like rows of knives. And wings … wings stretchin' toward the sky, blockin' the clouds and the light of the moon, massive and webbed. It moved like a shadow, I tell ye, totally silent, slippin' in and out of wherever it pleased without the slightest sound, leavin' only carnage in its wake."

In the silence that followed, Eadric spoke first. *Tread lightly*, he reminded himself, chest tight. "Is there a reason I wasn't notified of this matter?"

Queen Priscilla fixed her cold gaze on him. "Simply put, yes. I knew you would have told Princess Asterin."

"And why shouldn't he have?" Asterin cut in. "You can't just bargain the lives of our soldiers—"

"Everything has a price," the queen snarled, so viciously that they all jumped. She took a deep breath. "I know the cost, daughter. I ordered ten soldiers to go and investigate. When they didn't return, I sent another twenty. And I am *well aware* that my decision means not a single one will ever return. As queen, I sometimes must make hard choices for the greater good. You would do well to remember that." She shook her head. "But of course I never intended to lose so many … I suspect that the demon can only be defeated with powerful magic, but we have no one qualified for such a task."

Asterin stepped forth. "I am." Her eyes blazed with determination. "I'm powerful enough. Let *me* go."

Asterin's mother stared at her. And then she burst into laughter. Hurt flashed across Asterin's face. Once the queen's laughter had subsided, she waved at Crawson. "Thank you, Mister Crawson, for your help. As promised, your bravery will be generously rewarded. Please wait outside. I will address you as soon as I am finished here." The grizzly man bowed and lumbered away. As soon as he left, Queen Priscilla stood from the throne. She strode toward Asterin and grabbed her by the shoulders. "Have you lost your mind?"

Asterin's jaw jutted out. "Why can't I go?"

The queen snorted delicately. "What makes you think that you can accomplish the task that dozens of my best soldiers cannot?"

"Because I'm omnifinitied."

Priscilla's mouth fell open. "You mean to say … but since when?"

"Since a few weeks ago."

Her mother's eyes softened. "Why didn't you tell me?"

Asterin averted her gaze, fists clenched. "Does it matter?"

"Asterin—"

"*Because I want you to be proud of me for who I am!*" Asterin hollered. The queen flinched, as if her daughter had struck her. "Not what

I can do. Nothing except for my magic has ever impressed you. Not my training progress or my combat abilities. And I know that you don't consider those to be 'ladylike,' but it's what Father would have wanted, and more importantly, what *I* want. And I'm proud of that."

Eadric felt a little breathless watching Asterin's back straighten while she confessed, as if each word was a physical weight unloading from her shoulders.

Asterin took a step closer, barreling onward. "Mother, this is the perfect opportunity to test my powers. Even without the control of the other elements, you *know* that I'm more powerful than any guard. This is my chance to see what I'm truly capable of. To see if I'm worthy of the throne."

"Even if you're more powerful than any one of the guards," Queen Priscilla argued, "their powers combined surely outmatch yours."

Orion cleared his throat, ice-blue eyes unwavering. "As her Royal Guardian, it is my duty to protect the princess. Wherever she goes, I will follow."

Eadric nodded. "As will I."

"There," Asterin said triumphantly. "Our powers easily match those of a dozen guards."

Priscilla observed the three of them. "You can't be serious."

"We're very serious, Your Majesty," Orion replied.

General Garringsford spoke up. "My queen … if I may. The princess has a point. How many more men—good, loyal men—can we stand to waste? When does the cost of attempting to kill the demon become too great? None of them stand a chance against it, but Princess Asterin has both the skill *and* the power." Garringsford turned to Asterin, who could scarcely hide her astonishment at the general's support. "I've seen her take on a half-dozen guards twice her size and come out unscathed. If there is anyone who can beat unbeatable odds, it will be her."

"Why, Carlotta," said the queen with a frown. "Where were your sweet words when Asterin was practicing magic?"

Garringsford's lips pursed, as if she were trying to summon a smile but could only manage a mild grimace. "Everyone needs a little push now and then. The point is that we simply cannot throw away the lives of our soldiers any longer. My queen, if Asterin has even the slightest chance of succeeding, then we *must* seize it."

"Please, Mother," Asterin begged. "What purpose does a ruler serve if they cannot protect their own people? If I'm your only hope, then *let me go*."

Queen Priscilla turned her back on them, seating herself on the throne. In a rare moment of vulnerability, she sagged against the armrests. "It seems I have no other choice."

Asterin exhaled. "Thank you, Mother. I won't fail—"

"I'm not finished," Priscilla interrupted. Asterin shrank. "Three is a sacred number, but it is not enough for the task at hand. If you can find three more brave souls willing to lay their lives at your feet, Princess, then I …" She rubbed her temple. "I will allow you to go. Keep in mind these are three lives *you* are willing to sacrifice, as well."

Asterin bit her lip, faltering, but Eadric knew that particular set of her chin all too well. "I will find another three," she said, voice perfectly even. "We'll slay the demon, no matter the cost."

"And if the cost is your own life?"

Asterin huffed a bitter laugh. "Doesn't everything have a price, Mother? You've sent me away to complete tasks before. For this one, I won't even have to leave the kingdom. And I will *not* fail."

The queen looked away. Finally, she said, "Immortals help me. You are fools, all of you. May the Council pity you and look down upon you in favor. Set out at first light. Head for the village of Corinthe, where the demon was last seen. Take whatever supplies you require. I don't want you in the village itself, however, in case the demon attacks it. Carlotta, your contact?"

Garringsford nodded. "He lives in the Aswiyre Forest, just north of Corinthe. I will send a message to him immediately and provide you with the maps. He goes by the name of Harry."

"The Aswiyre Forest is notorious for strange happenings," warned Priscilla. "Caves that come and go with the full moon, enchanted lakes. Proceed with the utmost caution. It appears that you may very well be Axaria's last hope, Princess Asterin." The queen flicked her wrist toward the doors. "Now get out of my sight, before I change my mind."

"We'll find the demon before it can kill anyone else," Asterin promised, eyes glinting with fearless conviction.

Queen Priscilla shook her head. "Just pray that it doesn't find you first."

Asterin didn't realize where her feet were taking her until she arrived at the door to Luna's workshop, tucked into a snug corner in the south wing. Still caught in a sort of trance, she knocked thrice. When there was no answer, she let herself in, taking a deep inhale of the musty smell of damp earth.

She had requested the old parlor be renovated into a workshop some years back as a gift for her best friend. Although Luna's duties kept her from working on her sculptures more than a few times a week, the room was filled with new wonders every time Asterin visited.

The girl herself stood in the center of the room, dancing around an enormous slab of white stone, chisel in hand. She hummed a little tune in time with her chips, the light of the single window glinting off her honey hair and a little wrinkle creasing her brow.

When Asterin tapped her shoulder, Luna jumped, the chisel clattering to the floor. "Immortals have mercy," she gasped. It took her less than a second to read Asterin's expression. "What's wrong?"

Asterin told her everything, from the shield and the deaths of the guards to the demon and the queen's requirement that she choose three more people to accompany her. Silence fell.

Luna reached out to grab her hands. "I'll go with you."

Asterin stared at her. "What?"

"I'm coming," her friend repeated, grip tightening.

"No."

"Asterin, all I have is you, Eadric, and Orion. I am sworn to serve you, just as they are. I may not be able to wield powerful magic, but … we've been together for so many years. I could never stand to lose you." Blue-flamed resolve burned in Luna's eyes. "I'll help you in whatever small way I can."

"Luna …" Asterin bit her lip, mulling her words over, still on the verge of saying no—but found that she couldn't. Finally, she asked, "You would trust me with your life?"

At that, Luna rolled her eyes. "As if I don't, every single time you dream up one of your harebrained schemes."

"Fine," said Asterin, chest tight, hating herself for bringing Luna—innocent, sweet Luna—into this mess. "Because that's exactly what you'll have to do."

CHAPTER NINE

The ten Elite Royal Guards were already lined up in the high-ceilinged concourse training hall when Eadric arrived. They snapped their heels and saluted, a synchronous *thump* of hands on shoulders. All were in full dress uniform, save Quinlan, who had yet to receive his cloak. Its absence from his shoulders left him looking strangely exposed—all the same, he stood just as tall as the rest.

"At ease," Eadric said and pulled the doors shut. The lamps flared brighter, the sole light source since there were no windows. "What I'm about to share with you is for your ears only: A beast of unknown origins has been terrorizing the people living near the Aswiyre Forest. The Queen of Axaria has allowed Princess Asterin the task of killing it, and as such, her Royal Guardian and I will be accompanying her. However, the queen has required that we choose three more of you to join us."

The Elites shuffled eagerly, but Alicia was the first to step forward.

"Sir!" Her ponytail swung as she saluted. *Ah*, Eadric thought distantly. *The boldness of youth*. "Captain, sir, I volunteer—"

"As do I," Gino cut in, and the floodgates opened.

Laurel and Hayley spoke at the same time, though neither backed down as their words overlapped, merely glancing apologetically at one another. The rest of them burst into clamor, even quiet Nicole, adding their voices to the chorus at double the volume in an effort to be heard. Only Rose and Quinlan did not make any move to speak.

"Silence," Eadric ordered, and immediately they stopped. "While I appreciate your enthusiasm, I ask that you wait until I have said all there is to say. Queen Priscilla has sent three dozen soldiers of Garringsford's choosing to slay this demon, and not one has returned." Even Hayley's impassive expression wavered at that. "We know almost nothing about the demon, other than its appearance and apparently unquenchable bloodthirst." He looked at each one of them in turn. "By volunteering, you are prepared to set down your life. You have until tonight to decide amongst yourselves which three will—"

"Two," Asterin interrupted, striding over.

Eadric hadn't even noticed her enter the hall. He frowned. "Who?"

She avoided his eyes. "Luna."

He blinked, certain he had misheard. "Pardon?"

"Luna. She wanted to come."

It took him several moments to recover. "And … you told her no, of course," he said. Asterin shifted uncomfortably. His breathing quickened, each inhale shallower than the last. "You have to tell her no," he said. His fingers had gone numb. "She'll die."

"There's a chance we'll *all* die," Asterin snapped, and then cringed. She exhaled, turning to the Elites. "And as such, I understand completely if none of you choose to volunteer."

"We all will," Quinlan spoke up quietly. "It's our duty." There were noises of agreement. "But the question is … how will you choose between us?"

Asterin seemed taken aback. "I …"

"Don't speak on the behalf of others, Holloway," Eadric interjected, and then added, "*even* if it's true," at the defiant expressions and protests. "Think this over, all of you. But know that if you feel obligated to volunteer simply because it is your duty, rethink everything. You must understand what is at stake, what the kingdom stands to lose if we fail."

"You're counting on power, aren't you?" Quinlan asked.

"Yes," he admitted. "But—"

A wall of scorching flame exploded from the ground, surging thirty feet into the air, separating Rose and Quinlan from the rest of the Elites.

Eadric staggered toward the flames, but the heat was unbearable. He could hear the others shouting behind it. "Holloway, what are you—"

"Hold on," Asterin said with her hand raised. "Let him."

"This is madness," Eadric exclaimed, sweat rolling down his forehead. The fire had no smoke, but each inhale burned his throat.

Asterin shook her head. "No. It's a test."

As if on cue, a cyclone of wind blasted through a section of flame, and Eadric caught sight of Laurel through the opening for less than a second before the inferno swallowed her back up. The flames at the far left of the wall hissed as Gino spewed a flood of water from his palms, but Quinlan merely narrowed his eyes and the flames roared hotter. The water gurgled and turned to steam. There came earth attacks and the rumble of a storm, but nothing could penetrate the wall. And Quinlan—*Quinlan hasn't even broken a sweat*, Eadric realized, stunned. What kind of power was this?

Just when Asterin raised her hand again to call Quinlan off, the middle section of the wall smothered out and Nicole came barging through. *She must have removed the oxygen with her air affinity*, Eadric thought to himself. Casper, too, had an air affinity, but nowhere near as powerful—and sure enough, Eadric caught sight of pockets of flame choking out, though never large or quickly enough for Casper to pass.

"Get back," Quinlan said, and before Eadric could argue, Asterin grabbed his arm and hauled him out of range.

Nicole let her makeshift door ignite behind her as quickly as she had extinguished it. *Every Elite for themselves.* Without wasting a precious second, she shoved her hand forward, the other clutching her affinity stone. Quinlan wheezed as she drew out the air from his lungs, but just as quickly, he recovered and mirrored the motion, drawing the air out of *her* lungs, the fire beside him still going strong.

"He's a bifinate," Eadric said. *But he's not the only one.*

Nicole strained, the veins in her neck bulging from asphyxiation. Teeth gritted, she threw herself forward. A crack split the floor and a hunk of marble rose into the air, with her crouched upon it, as she combined her earth and air affinities. She zoomed toward Quinlan at breakneck speed, but just as Eadric braced himself for the impact, the marble blasted apart to reveal the Eradorian safe and sound, his fingers splayed with casual grace. Nicole plummeted to the ground, barely managing to absorb the fall with a roll.

Eadric looked over to Rose, but she leaned against the wall, hands empty. "Quinlan is trifinitied, then?"

Quinlan stomped his foot into the ground and a slab of marble twice the size of Nicole's floated upward, taking her with it. The Eradorian flicked his wrist and the inferno parted to let her swoop through, tongues of crackling electricity lashing out at her legs when she tried to leap away.

By now, even Asterin's mouth had fallen agape.

Eadric swallowed. "So … he's multifinitied. Great."

Asterin nodded. "That's enough!"

Quinlan gave her a little finger salute and quenched his flames.

Rose still leaned against the wall, gaze calculating but otherwise unreadable.

The other Elites sprinted over to them as the last of the wall's smoldering embers drifted up to the ceiling, affinity stones at the ready even though most looked on the brink of passing out. A range of emotions played out across their faces—astonishment, shame, awe.

Eadric felt the sharp jab of Asterin's elbow in his side. "All of you, five laps around the garden," he commanded. "Take your time and walk it off. Quinlan, Nicole. You two stay behind. Fall out."

"Yes, Captain," they shouted back and dispersed—all but Nicole and the two Eradorians—before filing dutifully out of the hall.

Eadric raised an eyebrow at Rose. "What is it? I asked for five laps."

Rose exchanged a glance with Quinlan, mouth parting to speak, but her cousin shook his head and she merely saluted before jogging off.

Once they had cleared, Eadric whirled on Quinlan, seething. "What in hell were you thinking? What if you had lost control? You could have killed someone."

Quinlan met his glare without the slightest waver. "Control was beaten into me, Captain Covington," he said, voice soft. "Until the day I die, my magic will always obey."

"That's not the issue here—"

"The issue is who we're choosing," Asterin cut in.

Quinlan cleared his throat, eyes flicking to Nicole and then to the princess. "Listen, about that … could I have a word with you? In private?"

"There isn't time for that," Eadric snapped. "We have to leave before dawn."

"Actually," said Asterin, cocking her head. "I kind of want to hear what he has to say. Not to mention the reason why he never mentioned he's multifinitied."

Quinlan ran a hand down the back of his neck. "The truth is … I'm not multifinitied." He slipped a familiar silk pouch out of his pocket. "This omnistone is untouchable to those who aren't omnifinitied. For example," he said, sliding it out and bringing it near Eadric's body in demonstration. "Take Captain Covington." About an inch away from his chest, it wrenched out of Quinlan's fingers and flew backward, clattering to the floor.

Asterin frowned. "But … *you* just touched it."

Quinlan bent down to pick the omnistone up, before rising slowly and meeting her stare. "I know."

Before his words could properly sink in, Rose came jogging back around the corner, her expression conflicted.

Eadric rubbed his temple. "What now, Fletcher?"

She ignored him and spoke to Asterin instead. "I have something important to tell you. About the demon. And … myself." Eadric almost sent her back to the barracks, but the clear urgency of her tone made him hesitate.

The air grew tense. Rose refused to drop her unsettling stare, and finally, Asterin relented. "Fine. I'll give you ten minutes of my time." She cast an apologetic glance at Nicole. "Pack your things. I'll send for you later tonight."

The gray-eyed Elite gave the princess a dutiful nod and slipped away on silent feet.

Asterin sighed and turned away, her eyes lingering on the omnistone in Quinlan's hand. "Follow me."

Asterin brought Eadric and the Eradorians to her sitting parlor, where they found Luna and Orion already conferring in low voices. Luna threw herself at Eadric when he walked in, embracing him tightly—but while she smiled, his face had gone slack. Asterin swallowed her guilt, gesturing for Rose and Quinlan to seat themselves, and rang for tea.

Orion's eyes landed on Quinlan. "Oh, hell no."

Asterin glared at her Guardian. "Just shut up, Orion."

No one spoke—not even the maids as they poured out the cups.

Asterin's teacup rattled as she set it back onto its saucer, regretting the two spoonfuls of sugar she had dumped inside. Her eyes went to where Luna sat, curled up beneath Eadric's protective arm. "Luna, perhaps … I think it might be best if—"

"Don't even *think* about it," the girl growled.

"Fine." Asterin put her saucer down and turned to Rose. "Well? What do you have to tell me?"

"I was expecting less of an audience," the Eradorian replied.

Orion snorted. "And I was expecting to see Casper or Nicole or Laurel." He jabbed his thumb at Quinlan. "What is fireface doing here?"

Asterin chose her words carefully. "He proved himself worthy."

Her Guardian's glacial gaze narrowed. "Worthy … as in trustworthy? Like the eight other Elites we've known for years?" Asterin bit her lip. Orion sat back, arms crossed. "Yeah, that's what I thought."

"We *are* trustworthy," Quinlan said. "Both of us. We understand what is at stake. And we have far more to lose than your other Elites do."

"Quinlan," Rose barked, a clear warning in her voice.

"What do you mean?" Eadric demanded.

"Rose is—"

"Quinlan Holloway," Rose snarled, standing up. "That is *enough*."

Quinlan stood too. "Then tell them yourself. You said you would."

Orion sipped his tea, legs crossed. "Tell us what?"

"How can you ask them to trust us when you can't even trust them?" Quinlan hissed.

"Both of you. Sit down at once," Asterin commanded. They sat, still glaring at one another. "I haven't the patience nor the time for your bickering. Whatever it is you wish to say, speak it, or don't. It's entirely your decision. But if you don't, we'll take Nicole and Silas instead."

After a beat of silence, Rose grudgingly began to explain.

"The queen—of Eradore, I mean—didn't send soldiers to *every* kingdom," she admitted. "Only to one. She had a vision. Of a great and vast darkness, descending not only upon Axaria, but the entire world, destroying each and every kingdom, one by one. Ibreseos. Lethos. Eradore."

Orion scoffed. "That's it? A nightmare?"

Rose sent him a cold glare. "We wouldn't be here if we weren't absolutely certain."

"And how can you possibly be certain?" Eadric asked.

Those golden eyes turned away. "Because the queen also foresaw the attacks of the demon you learned of today. She saw *you*, Princess Asterin. That's why we came to Axaria, and not Oprehvar, or Galanz, or Morova, or any other kingdom. Whether you believe us or not, that's the truth."

Asterin eyes narrowed. "You've been here a whole month, and never have I heard a word from you about the demon."

"We didn't anticipate the attacks to happen so soon," said Rose, biting her lip. "We didn't even know that they *had* happened until Captain Covington told all of us."

Asterin mulled over her reasoning. "So what are you, then? Are you really the queen's soldiers? Or perhaps I was right from the very beginning and you *are* her spies?"

Rose straightened. "Not quite, Princess Asterin. Fletcher isn't actually my true surname. It was a moniker given to me when I displayed a particular aptitude in archery at the Academia Principalis."

"Your name doesn't matter to us," Eadric interjected. "Just explain why Princess Asterin shouldn't send your heads back to your queen on spikes."

Quinlan growled, but Rose only smiled, a crooked tilt of her lips. "I fear that would be most unwise, Captain Covington." Her expression grew grim. "You can trust us. All of you. Because other than our lives, I stand to lose my kingdom and the lives of my people if this darkness falls and the demon is not defeated—and I cannot let that happen, no matter the cost."

Asterin felt those words resound with something deep inside her. "You speak as though the fate of your kingdom and its people rests on your shoulders."

The smile returned. "Why, Your Highness, that's because it does. For you see … my real name is Orozalia Saville."

A chorus of gasps, Asterin's loudest of all.

Saville. The royal bloodline of the House of the Serpent.

"And I," Rose continued, "am the Queen of Eradore."

CHAPTER TEN

By dawn, six horses were saddled up and ready to leave. Darkness had not yet surrendered to the light when Asterin strolled to the stables, a sliver of orange-hued fire peeping over the horizon. The comforting scent of hay and manure hit her the moment she walked in. White stone arches bowed over a wide aisle, stalls with elegant wrought-iron fencing and maple gates lining either side. A trio of stable hands rushed about, saddling the horses and fitting them with special horseshoes charmed by earth-wielders for hard travel. Packs were fastened, their contents triple-checked to ensure each contained all the appropriate gear for the journey ahead.

Asterin let herself into the stall at the very end of the aisle, where a magnificent stallion awaited her, his ears perked and onyx coat gleaming like oil. Lux whickered softly, his long neck arching as she stroked his velvet nose and murmured sweet nothings.

Footsteps approached, and when she glanced up, Quinlan had his elbows crossed over the gate, somehow even more handsome than usual with his sleep-mussed hair. He shot her a lazy grin. "Morning, Princess. How did you sleep?"

"Splendidly," she lied.

"I can tell," he said. "How long do you think we'll be gone?"

Asterin shrugged. "I'm hoping around a week or two. Find the demon, kill it, go home, that sort of thing. But if worst comes to worst … who knows? Definitely before the Fairfest Ball, though."

His brow furrowed. "I've never been to that."

"Oh, it's only the most exclusive party on the continent." Fairfest was the week-long spring solstice holiday in celebration of life, culminating in a legendary ball held in the Axarian palace. Kings and queens attended from almost all the kingdoms. Its counterpart was Vürstivale, the winter holiday in honor of the Immortals. "Only nobility is invited, but if you're nice to me, I can try and get you an invitation."

"Ah, but you forget, dearest princess." His lips curled upward. "My beloved cousin is the Queen of Eradore."

"Are you and Orozalia actually cousins?" she asked. "I thought that was just part of the ruse."

"Nope. Also, never call her by that name to her face, she hates it. We're genuinely family … which means I'm genuinely the Prince of Eradore." He paused. "Or rather, *a* Prince of Eradore. I could never actually rule, though, since I belong to the House of the Fox. The late Queen Lillian—Rose's mother—was my father's sister." And then, with blunt coldness, Quinlan added, "But he's dead now."

Asterin decided not to pry. She was just grateful Rose preferred *Rose* instead of *Orozalia.* "Does Rose have any siblings?"

He nodded. "Younger twins, actually—Avris and Avon. And I have an older brother, so even if us Holloways were House of the Serpent, I'd still be fifth in line to rule."

Asterin lifted her eyebrows. "An older brother?"

He chuckled. "Unfortunately, yes."

She chewed her lip, letting that sink in. "Would you want to? Rule Eradore, I mean."

Quinlan shuddered. "Immortals help me, no. I'd rather drown in a vat of wine."

"Would you look at the two of you, chumming it up!" They both startled as Orion materialized out of nowhere. He threw a brotherly arm around Quinlan, giving him a slap on the back hard enough that the

Eradorian wheezed in pain. Asterin's Guardian grinned and let himself into the neighboring stall, pulling an apple out of his pocket and feeding it to his palomino mare. "Hope you're good on a horse, Quinnie. Heard a rumor that Eradorians only ride mules."

"Watch it," Quinlan said. "We ride dragons for fun. I could sweep the floor with your ass in no time."

"Oi, relax." Orion grinned. He gave his mare a fond pat. "If I were you, I'd be jealous of Buttercup, too."

"Either way," Asterin said, "Lux could beat *both* your sorry asses without breaking a sweat." She beamed at her Iphovien stallion, a gift from her distant cousin, Duchess Rowena of Galanz. He responded with a merry whinny. Although all the royal steeds were bred beyond the highest standards for both speed and endurance, far more superior than the average horse, Iphoviens were the fastest breed in the world. Said to have once pulled the legendary chariot of the Goddess of Wind, Lady Reyva, they could travel unimaginable distances with little rest, so long as their riders managed to stay upright in the saddle. Asterin just hoped the others could keep up.

Quinlan's brow crinkled. "Lux? As in light? What kind of name is that for a black horse?"

Asterin opened her mouth to answer when Rose trudged into the stables, her auburn hair pinned into a severe bun worthy of General Garringsford, a bow and quiver slung across her back. *Fletcher*, Asterin remembered. The Queen of Eradore gave them a little wave. "So, where are we off to first?"

"The town of Aldville." In addition to a map to Harry's house, Garringsford had given her directions to the inn where they would stay, but Asterin knew the way to the river town well. "We can make it by nightfall. We'll have to take it slow while we're still in the city, but once we're in the countryside, we'll ride fast and hard."

"We're ready when you are," Eadric called from the other end of the stables with his massive horse, Grey, at hand. Powerfully built, the dappled thoroughbred huffed and pawed at the ground with impatience. Luna and her snow-white mare waited behind him, the girl looking as lovely as the sunrise itself in her fur-lined cloak and riding gear.

The six of them led their horses out of the stables and onto the pathway before mounting. Asterin took a deep breath of the cool morning air and swung into the saddle with practiced ease, Amoux sheathed at her waist and her affinity stones clinking in her pack. She had switched out her old firestone for the one Garringsford had given her, but the others had shattered beyond repair. She rested her hand on Lux's silky neck. "Onward, then."

They set off at a quick trot. Even the gardeners had yet to awaken, leaving the palace grounds empty and quiet as they passed the guardhouse. Magnolias and wisterias lined the path, branches almost entwining. Just up ahead, great rhododendrons boasted their magenta clusters, leaves and petals drooping with sparkling morning dewdrops as the sun began its ascent.

The warbling lament of a lonesome bird and the hollow *clip-clop* of hooves against stone filled the silence as they continued on. At last, they arrived at the Wall, slowing as they approached the gates—a great mess of iron metalwork and interlocking steel gears and pistons that Asterin didn't even pretend to understand, designed to open from the interior only. Sentries, positioned every fifty feet along the Wall's interior, eyed their approach, though many more patrolled the ramparts from above. Six guarded the entrance. They saluted as Eadric shouted a command, and the enormous gates groaned open.

"Your Royal Highness," one of the guards said with a bow as Lux picked his way past. He was a very attractive young man, with smiling blue eyes and copper curls. "Safe travels."

Asterin tipped her chin in acknowledgment. "Carlsby."

As Orion rode by, he leaned down out of his saddle and whispered. "I'll see you when I return."

Luna stifled a high-pitched giggle, and Asterin wondered what was so funny.

"Y-yes, sir," said Carlsby. Asterin glanced back to see Orion throw him a wink. The poor boy blushed pink from the tips of his ears to his neck.

Then the gates clanged shut.

Luna wrapped the reins tighter in her grip as they wound down the well-worn mountain road, marveling at the view as the city spread out beneath them. The early pink-and-orange sun rays cast an almost liquefied glow over the gabled roofs of Axaris, the beginning sputters of smoke from ruddy terracotta chimney pots drifting toward the lightening sky in curls of white. When Luna looked back, only the pastel turrets of the royal palace were visible over the lip of the Wall.

A decade had flown by since she had arrived at the palace from the Oprehvean orphanage she had called home, alone and traumatized from a childhood she couldn't quite remember. For her own safety, she had never left—not even once.

"We're passing the wards now," Eadric warned from ahead.

Luna shuddered involuntarily as she felt the swell of magic rush through her body, something she'd always longed to feel, coating her veins in an electrifying heat powerful enough to incinerate all of them from the inside out. Elemental sigils illuminated in streaks of all colors pulsated overhead, arcing above them and spreading into a rippling tunnel of light. As they passed, the sigils flickered like torch flames, winking in and out of sight only to unfold again farther away, never allowing their party to escape out of their range.

Only when they crossed the last ward did Luna have the chance to catch her breath. *You're almost ready to pass out and you haven't even left the city yet*, she scolded herself, shooting furtive glances at the others, but they seemed unaffected by the wards. Was it because her magic was weaker than theirs?

"Are you all right?" Asterin asked quietly, loud enough for only Luna to hear.

"Yes, but that power . . ." Even her muscles quivered from fatigue.

"The guards opened a passage for us," said Asterin. "We only felt a tiny fraction of the wards' true power."

Luna shivered. "Almighty Immortals." How many ways could those wards kill a person?

"John works with the squad that maintains the wards sometimes," Orion said, overhearing them. "It's hard work."

Asterin frowned. "John?"

"Carlsby," Orion said.

"Since when have you known guards on a first-name basis?"

"Hm?" The Royal Guardian blinked, and then chuckled. "Oh, no, he and I go way back."

They continued down the mountain in silence. Luna watched as Asterin leaned forward and whispered into Lux's ears. The horse snorted and kicked into a gallop, easily overtaking the rest of the group. A startled Eadric shouted uselessly at her, spurring Grey and giving chase. Asterin let out a whoop as her Iphovien steed flew down the mountainside, girl and stallion blending into a single entity—hair, mane, cloak, and tail billowing behind them in a river of ebony.

Quinlan let out a low whistle.

"She's crazy," muttered Orion fondly.

Luna caught something inexplicable in the Eradorian's eyes as he stared after her and said, "A beautiful kind of crazy."

Quinlan inhaled the scent of deep-fried food as they passed through the main market square, stomach already grumbling. He'd missed breakfast. They moved in tight formation as quickly as they could, trying their best to avoid the stares of onlookers.

The only weapons Quinlan carried were his three Ignatian daggers—one sheathed at his hip, one strapped to his forearm underneath the sleeve of his tunic, and one at his thigh. The omnistone was tucked safely in his chest pocket.

After about two kilometers, the organized rows of market stalls began to thin, and the shouts of merchants and vendors flitted away into the wind like dust. Carriages clattered by, swerving aside to let their group pass when the road grew too narrow. They crossed beneath a beautiful marble archway marking the south residential sector, and Quinlan found himself admiring the architecture, the simple ornamentation of the sloping roofs and windows. In the distance, the mansions of the rich and noble rose above the grassy hillcrests of the west sector.

The houses, too, eventually began to thin, giving way to vast fields. They drove their horses faster, galloping past caravans and travelers on foot heading for Axaris. The capital sat comfortably in the middle of the kingdom, with the Ljre River and the sprawling Aswiyre Forest slashing across the land like battle scars. They would have to ride around the southern half of the forest to reach Corinthe—a two days' journey from Axaris, which was why they would have to spend the night in Aldville, halfway between Axaris and their destination.

A little after noon, a snaking expanse of green-blue water opened up before them, sparkling beneath the high sun. The Ljre River. They galloped alongside it, racing the white wisps of cloud above. Quinlan's eyes watered from the cold of the wind.

Only stopping every few hours to water the horses and to eat a quick meal, they managed to arrive in Aldville ahead of schedule, right as the sun began to set. Asterin guided all of them to a pleasant inn just on the edge of the town.

"The Rainbow Salmon," Rose read aloud, eyeing the leaping stone fish guarding the courtyard entrance.

"I know it's not a palace, Your Majesty," Asterin said, "but it'll have to do."

Rose grinned. "If the beds are any softer than the bunks in the barracks, it'll be heaven."

Asterin laughed at that and they rode into the modest courtyard, where the innkeeper and a handful of other staff greeted them with discrete bows, offering to carry their packs and handle the horses.

Quinlan dismounted and rubbed the soreness from his lower back with a groan. He felt something nudge his hand and looked over to find Rose tucking a small tin of salve into his hand with a wink.

He smiled, twisting the lid off and coating his fingers in salve. "Thanks," he called after her as she passed her reins to a stable hand and followed Eadric and Luna into the inn.

Asterin sauntered over, stretching her arms toward the sky and revealing a tantalizing sliver of midriff. "What's that?" Her face wrinkled as she peered into the tin. "Lard?"

Quinlan laughed at her expression and waved his fingers under her nose. "No. It's some leftover cooling salve Rose made for me after I started training with you. My tailbone has never been quite the same." He shed his jacket and pulled his shirt over his head to rub salve into his muscles, closing his eyes with a sigh as the refreshing evening breeze licked up against his exposed chest. He heard a squeak and cracked one eye open to cast a sidelong glance at Asterin. "What now?"

A furious blush had risen to her cheeks. "You … you can't just take off your shirt like that," she stammered.

"Why? Does it bother you?" he teased, nothing short of delighted.

"Yes! No! I don't care. I've seen shirtless men before anyway."

He quirked an eyebrow. "Oh?"

She scoffed at him and flipped her dark hair over her shoulder, still flustered. "Of course."

"She's seen *me* shirtless!" Orion yelled on his way into the inn, hands cupped around his mouth. A stable hand guiding Quinlan's horse toward the stables stifled a laugh, and it seemed that even the horse itself snorted quietly in amusement.

Momentarily taken aback, Quinlan's eyes flickered between Guardian and charge. He shifted his feet. "So, you two …uh … ever, you know?"

Asterin folded her arms across her chest. "Orion and me?" A nonchalant shrug. "Maybe. Who knows?"

"Tell me," Quinlan insisted.

"Why are you being so nosy all of a sudden, Quinnie?"

"Come on, tell me." He prodded her in the side. In a flash, her hand latched around his wrist and an arm locked around his waist. Her foot planted between his legs and before he knew what was happening, the world was spinning out of control, his bare chest braced against her back and his feet lifting clear off the ground—

His back slammed into the earth, knocking the air straight from his lungs.

Quinlan wheezed. "What in—what in hell was *that*?"

Astern crouched beside him, brushing a stray lock of hair from his face with a gentleness that sent shivers down his spine. "I thought you asked me to remind you to never get on the wrong end of my sword." Her head cocked. "Did you and your older brother never wrestle?"

"Taeron is more the bookish type," Quinlan managed, still struggling to inhale properly.

Asterin leaned back slightly. "I learned that move from Orion. Firsthand, of course." The light of the setting sun caught in her eyes like green embers. Her mouth curved into a dangerous smile. "That was a warning. Next time you poke me—" she bent forward again so he could hear her whisper. "*I break your wrists.*"

He disguised the hitch of his breath with a cough, blood singing. Try as he might, he couldn't tear his eyes away from that smile. She was so close—close enough that if he were to just tilt his face up the slightest fraction, he might be able to—

Asterin's eyes narrowed.

His face burned. "Right. So … you and Orion?"

She regarded him, and then pinched his cheek. Hard. "Why are you so determined to find out?"

"Just curious."

Asterin rolled her eyes, unimpressed, and then straightened, dusting herself off. She shot him a final smirk and sashayed away, providing him with a rather fetching—and very deliberate, he was sure—view of her backside as she disappeared into the inn.

Which left him to pick himself up from the dirt.

Later that evening, after a hot bath and a hearty dinner, they all headed upstairs to the second floor and said their goodnights before splitting off into pairs. Quinlan trudged after Rose into their shared room, complete with a well-loved chaise, wardrobe, and two beds indeed softer than their Elite bunks. While she busied herself with changing, he stared out the window overlooking the courtyard and the road beyond, enveloped by a clear, deep night, before drawing the curtains shut.

In his sleep, he dreamed of an endless cold, chasing him through the darkness. It wasn't one of those dreams where his legs felt too heavy to run or his feet were rooted to the spot. In this one, no matter how fast he ran, the thing behind him just ran *faster.* Slowly but surely, it caught up to him, looming overhead in a wave of shadow. When he looked up at it, his heart thundering in his throat, two yellow eyes and a wide mouth full of fangs gleamed back at him.

And right before that mouth yawned open to swallow him whole, he could have sworn the darkness grinned.

CHAPTER ELEVEN

Asterin woke with a start. Beside her, Luna slumbered on, her peaceful expression bathed in a soft, pulsing glow. With a frown, Asterin turned her head to the window, but it was still the dead of night—all was dark save for the stars.

Turning the other way, she realized that her bedside table was the source of the glow. Not the table itself—but the affinity stones she had laid out in a neat line before going to sleep. She reached for her icestone, only to recoil when it burned her fingers. Cautiously, she hovered her fingers over the other stones, frowning when all of them radiated the same heat. She sat up and swung her feet over the side of the bed. Her bare feet tingled against the chill of the floor and her arms prickled with gooseflesh as she eyed the stones warily.

The door burst open. In one fluid motion, Asterin grabbed Amoux from where it lay propped up against the bedpost. She had the blade raised and ready to strike in the half second it took Quinlan to barge in, his daggers flashing and indigo flames dancing at his shoulders.

He shoved her against the wall, muffling her scream of surprise with his hand. "Quiet."

She bit his thumb to force him to release her and hissed, "What is with you and breaking into my room?"

Ignoring her completely, his eyes went instead to the bedside table. It had begun to smoke beneath the stones. "This is bad," he said, flinging open the wardrobe and thrusting some clothes at her. "Get dressed." He pulled something out of his pocket and pressed it into her palm—the omnistone. "And use this, not your usual stones." His gaze met hers. "You might need it."

"Wait—"

Luna groaned from the bed and rubbed her eyes. They settled onto Quinlan and widened to full moons. "Qu-Quinlan?"

"Pack your things," he said. "Now."

Rose appeared at the doorway as Luna scrambled out of bed, her quiver slung over her shoulder and a ball of greenish light hovering above her head. She wore a strange bodysuit made from layers of blue scales that rippled turquoise in the ball's glow. "Any sign?"

Quinlan simply jerked his chin at Asterin's affinity stones. "Stay with them," he told his cousin. "I'll shield the window and seal the door. On *no* account do you let anyone—or anything—in. Understood?"

Asterin looked up halfway through lacing her boots. "Not even you?"

"Not even me." Quinlan raised his palms to the window and closed his eyes. "*Skjyolde*."

Light bled into the window in glittering rivulets, swarming thicker and thicker until the glass flared a blinding indigo. A wave of suffocating heat swept over the room, withering the frilled curtains. When Quinlan stepped back, the light had faded, the window seemingly untouched—but Asterin could sense a new energy, feel the trace of the powerful magic left behind like vibrations through the air.

Quinlan bolted to the entrance. "Be ready!" he warned before slamming the door behind him. Gold lines laced with red blazed between the door's crevices, crisscrossing over the surface until fiery light encased it entirely. Then that light, too, faded.

Something suddenly clicked in the back of Asterin's mind. "He … he didn't use an affinity stone."

"He doesn't need one," said Rose.

"How is that even possible?" Luna asked, pulling off her nightgown and digging through the wardrobe for trousers.

"Well, you would have to be pretty damn powerful to start with,"

said Rose. "But what no one really understands is that affinity stones aren't actually the source of our magic. Magic flows within our bodies just as blood does, though for weaker wielders, using magic without a stone is more like walking with one leg."

Asterin shivered. "Quinlan said that something was coming. Could it . . ." Her pulse quickened. "Could it be the demon?"

"Maybe." Rose slid her bow onto her back, the weapon's sleek limbs clinging to the rippling layers of scales on her suit. "We have to be ready for anything." She slipped a hand into her pocket and pulled out her sapphire tristone, the sigils of water, earth, and wind carved into its deep-blue surface. "You should try out the omnistone, Asterin."

The omnistone felt almost too warm between her clasped palms. When she inhaled, it grew heavier, as if drawing in her magic the same way some people used meditation to focus their powers. Expelling her breath, Asterin summoned a dagger of ice from one closed fist—or attempted to. Instead, a great blast of wind knocked Luna off her feet. Asterin gasped out an apology, stunned at the sensation—not only did the stone feel heavier, but her magic did too, somehow. She could feel the power of *all* the elements. Even when she summoned just one, the lines distinguishing them blurred together.

"Envision your intentions more clearly in your mind," Rose instructed.

Asterin closed her eyes and summoned her ice a second time, but the blade she conjured was made of water. Gritting her teeth, she focused on the image of the affinity triangle, zeroing in on the blurring elements and dragging them apart. Ice rose from water, but everything from its state to its utility was strikingly different, and using the omnistone forced her to recognize those differences. This time, when she exhaled and thrust her hand downward, the blade shattered into a thousand crystalline fragments against the floor.

Rose shook her head. "Not good enough, Princess. You can't close your eyes in battle."

So again Asterin summoned a dagger, and then another, and then another, growing more accustomed to that new, unfamiliar weight. Soon, she began combining her powers, until all the elements swirled around her in

a storm, wind whipping at her cloak, air blossoming into tongues of flame, sparks of electricity arcing along the spines of hoarfrost skimming the ceiling.

"Your energy isn't limitless," Rose warned. "The more magic you use, the faster you'll burn out—especially when using the omnistone."

Asterin nodded, letting her magic fade—only to have it flare violently at the earth-shattering roar that came from outside, so loud that it reverberated through her bones, its echoes rolling through the night.

The blood drained from Luna's face. "What was that?"

Shouts rose from the lower floor as a crash shook the building, throwing them all sideways.

"That came from downstairs," Asterin said, moving for the door. "We have to go and help them!"

Rose leapt toward her, barring her path. "We have to stay here."

"Your cousin's life could be in danger! How can you just stand here?"

"Quinlan likes flirting with death even more than he likes flirting with you," Rose shot back. "He doesn't need me to worry about him."

There was another deafening crash, accompanied by an outraged holler.

Luna turned even paler. "That was Eadric."

Rose's gaze softened, but she stood her ground. "He's the captain of the Elites. I'm sure he's—"

Her words were cut off by a sudden *pop* in Asterin's ears. The pressure in the room changed and she could taste the electricity in the air, crackling like embers on the brink of bursting into flame. *Eadric*, she thought just as a blinding fork of lightning hurtled down from the sky outside. The blast of thunder that followed rattled the window.

And then … silence. An unnatural silence, so heavy and dense that it seemed to envelop the entire room like pillowed fog. Asterin's ears had yet to unpop when the second explosion of lightning illuminated the night, but nothing followed.

"What happened?" Asterin whispered.

Rose swallowed. "I … don't know."

Asterin waited, counting her heartbeats in her head. *One, two …*

She had reached twenty when the unbroken silence overwhelmed her. She cursed. "We have to help them."

Rose shook her head. "Whatever is out there subdued Quinlan and the others in minutes. We don't stand a chance. *You* don't stand a chance."

"Do you expect me to just stand here and wait for whatever that thing is to come and kill us?" Asterin demanded. "We'll be trapped. I'm going."

"And I'm coming," Luna said, voice quavering. Asterin whipped around, halfway to the door. Luna straightened beneath her stare, fists clenched.

Rose stepped between them. "Neither of you are leaving. I'll knock you out first."

Asterin snarled. "I'd like to see you try."

"You asked for it." Rose flung out her arms. A current of wind swept Asterin right off her feet faster than she could comprehend and into the wall with a crash. She slid to the floor, groaning. While she struggled to stand up, Rose forced more wind upon her, shoving down every attempt.

"Rose!" Luna cried, gesturing frantically.

"I'm busy!"

"The window!"

They looked up just in time to see a churning mass of darkness swoop high into the moonless sky, blocking out the stars. It dove from above, a hawk with its prey locked in sight, smashing into the window headfirst. Quinlan's invisible shield launched it backward with a throb of light, the glass rattling. The dark mass shrieked and plummeted out of sight.

Without a word, Rose grappled for Asterin's arm and pulled her to her feet. They both hurried to the window, craning their necks to capture a glimpse of the courtyard below.

The mass looked like nothing more than a lump of blackness, jumbled on the pavement. And then it began to spasm. They watched as it took shape, lengthening into the muscular body of a predator, two wide ears popping out of its skull. It had two hind legs, but its forelimbs had been replaced with a pair of thorny, gnarled wings. A tail of barbs swept across the ground as it turned its head up and fixed its beady yellow eyes on Asterin.

She shuddered. "What in the name of the Immortals is that?"

"It's not the demon, is it?" asked Luna.

"No, it's a wyvern," Rose said. "They haven't been sighted in the Mortal Realm for centuries." Luna raised her airstone, only for Rose to smack it away. "You can't cast anything through Quinlan's shield. It'll backfire."

"It's preparing to attack again!" Asterin shouted. No sooner had the words come out of her mouth than the wyvern thrashed its wings, colliding into the window with enough force that they all leapt back. The creature shrilled in pain as patches of its leathery skin ignited in indigo flame and flaked away. It flailed midair for a moment before hurtling at them yet again. Asterin's heart seized as a single, hairline fracture raced down the glass with an ominous *crack*.

Rose pocketed her tristone and slid her bow off her back. "Shit."

"We have to get out of here," gasped Luna.

Asterin didn't dare take her eyes off the wyvern at the window as it hoisted itself higher in the air, wings pumping, preparing for another—and perhaps, final—assault.

"I'll hold it off," Rose said. "Luna, protect Asterin at all costs. When it breaks past the shield, you are both going to jump out the window. It's only two stories."

"Are you crazy?" Luna yelled. "Why can't we just use the door?"

"Touch it and you'll melt the skin right off your bones," Rose replied, reaching for an arrow. "Asterin, you cannot die here. You have no idea how much is at stake."

Asterin flexed her wrists. "If any of us are going to fight, we're going to fight together. None of us are going to jump out any windows, and none of us are going to die—"

She cut off as the wyvern barreled forward with a triumphant screech even while black sludge oozed from its blistering skin, as if it knew it had already won. The blow spread the single crack into a web.

All it would take was one more strike.

Asterin gripped the omnistone. "What do I do with this?"

Rose cursed again and nocked an arrow. "Shield. Make a shield. Keep it up until I say so."

Just as the wyvern poised itself to charge, Asterin thrust her arms out. "*Skjyolde*!" Magic erupted from her fingertips, weaving into a dome of translucent energy over their heads.

The wyvern lunged once more, and the window shattered, peppering the shield with glass. Even though Asterin braced herself, a groan still tore from her throat as the wyvern rammed into her shield, claws scraping mere inches from her face. She stared into its horrible yellow eyes through what now seemed like a too-thin barrier, her arms trembling the longer she resisted. "Rose," she gasped.

"Wait for it," Rose hissed from beside her, bow drawn.

Asterin snarled as the wyvern forced her back another foot, toward the scorching heat of the door. "Wait for what?"

"*Now*!"

Asterin relinquished her hold on the shield, the dome dissolving into nothing. Rose let her arrow fly, dead-on for the wyvern's heart.

The arrow found home, burying deep into its chest, but somehow, the wyvern did not fall.

Instead, it charged at Luna.

Time seemed to slow as Asterin watched it leap five feet into the air, razor-sharp talons extended. Her magic acted of its own accord, blasting straight from her core. Spears of ice shot from the floor and sent the wyvern tumbling sideways. Its talons punched into the floor, trapping it for a few precious seconds.

"Get behind me!" Asterin yelled, pelting more ice at it. But to her dismay, each blast was smaller, weaker. She yanked at the strings of her power. *More, more, why isn't there more?* she thought desperately.

The wyvern prowled closer, as if savoring every step. Its tail lashed out at her hand, but the pain was overshadowed by sheer horror when it knocked the omnistone right out of her grip. The stone sailed into the air and skittered behind the wyvern.

"Almighty Immortals," Asterin said. The three of them started backing away. "All right. While I distract it, you two get out of here."

"No," Rose said, eyes wide. "Asterin, listen. You don't need the stone. Your magic is a *part* of you. Your powers lie within your blood, closer within reach than you think. Harness it."

There was a thump at the door.

Asterin clenched her jaw and braced her palms outward, her heart pounding in her ears. The wyvern's tail scraped against the floor with an ear-splitting screech as it advanced. *Your magic is a part of you.* She tried to imagine it, envisioning her powers coursing through her veins, surging from deep within, flowing out of her fingertips.

"Come on, Asterin," Luna whispered. "You can do it."

A blade of ice the length of her arm surged from her open palm, slicing through the air like one of Rose's arrows. It pierced the wyvern's left eye and plowed clean through the back of its skull. The wyvern howled, lurching sideways, its good eye—blazing with yellow rage—darting until it found her.

With the last of her dwindling strength, Asterin threw up a final shield as the wyvern barreled forward, giving her no time to think, to doubt. Pain raced through her body as it collided into her shield, forcing her onto her knees.

She couldn't let go.

The corners of her shield crackled as the edges of her vision clouded black, blurring in and out of focus.

I can't let go.

But she couldn't hold on.

The pain became too much, her body driven far beyond its limits. She prepared to conjure a final blade of ice. When her shield dropped, she would go for the wyvern's other eye. She stared into its foaming maw, at the dripping fangs—

The door behind them ignited in an explosion of scorching heat.

A growl ripped through the room as a figure engulfed in indigo fire lunged through the last wisps of Asterin's shield just as it flickered out.

Quinlan leapt at the wyvern with an enraged snarl, knives flashing. The beast swerved in surprise as the Prince of Eradore leapt onto its back with acrobatic ease, dancing on his toes, maintaining his balance even as the wyvern bucked. Each strike, delivered with a calm, lethal grace, drew shrieks of pain from the wyvern, the iridescent blades Quinlan wielded somehow managing to slice clean through its hide. Black blood poured from its wounds and splattered onto the floor.

Asterin cried out as the wyvern whipped its tail in wild retaliation and sliced Quinlan across the forehead. Unfazed, he broke away, leaving the wyvern's neck wide open for the fatal blow. Quinlan's eyes met Asterin's for but a single heartbeat, his pupils blown wide and ringed with the deepest shade of blue she'd ever seen.

Before either of them could act, a howl erupted like a battle cry at her back. Asterin turned to see Quinlan's flames licking up the remains of the door. And poised beneath it … a magnificent silver wolf with luminous emerald eyes.

Asterin's heart stopped as those eyes met her own. She *knew* this wolf.

"Lord Conrye," she whispered, and she knew that she was right.

With a mighty pounce and a frigid blast of arctic air, the Protector of the North soared over their heads and sank his glistening fangs into the wyvern's throat.

CHAPTER TWELVE

Orion had fallen asleep before he could even bother burrowing beneath the covers, still in his riding clothes. Eadric had dozed off in the corner of their room, head lolling against the back of an armchair. After such a long day of travel, Orion couldn't help but nod off to the soft rumble of the captain's snores.

And then Quinlan had kicked down their door with a *bang*.

Eadric sprang from his armchair like a frazzled cat. "What's going on?"

When Orion stirred but refused to acknowledge Quinlan's presence, the Eradorian grabbed a pillow off the bed and smacked him in the face with it. "Get up."

Orion groaned and rolled onto his stomach. "Oi, out with you, you handsome bastard."

An embarrassingly high-pitched yelp escaped Orion when some sort of invisible hook latched onto his navel and flipped him over.

He cracked open one eye to find Quinlan's face looming a mere inch away.

"Unless you want to die," the Eradorian said, "you are going to get the hell up."

Orion scowled. "For Immortals' sake—" Suddenly, he sailed off the bed, cartwheeling through the air. The invisible hook tossed him out the open door in a heap. Orion clambered onto his feet and shook his fist. "That's *it*! You listen here, you little—"

"Yeah, yeah. Just shut up, okay?" Quinlan peered out their window and into the night, grip tightening on the curtains. "Something's coming. Something dangerous. And powerful." He grabbed Orondite and thrust the blade at Orion. "The others are safe. For now. But we have to warn the staff and evacuate the residents."

"Is it the demon?" Eadric asked in alarm.

"No idea. I just know that it's coming. I'd say we have less than five minutes."

The captain nodded grimly. "We'd better move, then."

Orion sputtered, clutching Orondite to his chest. "Hold on a second—"

Eadric glared at him. "There are people in danger. Save your sass for later."

They dashed for the second-floor landing and split up, running down the horseshoe-shaped hallway and banging on doors. Quinlan finished last, having just escorted the innkeeper and several other confused residents safely out of the building when the sound of beating wings approached.

"Downstairs!" Eadric exclaimed.

A roar boomed outside, shaking the steps as they descended and sending Orion tumbling ass over head to the main floor. Quinlan barely managed to shout a warning in time when the wall beside them exploded. They flew backward, crashing into the tables in the dining area behind them. Orion scrambled to his feet, coughing as chunks of brick and rubble rained down from the gaping hole the explosion had left in the wall.

A shadow fell over the destruction.

The first thing that struck Orion about their attacker was its wings—in lieu of arms and almost too large for the brutish, wrinkled body. Its filmy skin stretched over a sunken snout and skull, and when a pair of beady yellow eyes homed in on Orion, he found himself paralyzed. Its barbed tail whipped into the air to obliterate him off the face of the earth, yet he could only stand there, frozen to the spot.

"Move, idiot!" Quinlan yelled, diving out of nowhere and hurling up a fiery shield just as the creature's tail raked against it. The shield absorbed the impact with a blinding flare that burned tears into Orion's eyes. Arms encircled his waist, and Quinlan wrenched him into the temporary safety of the taproom.

"Immortals," Orion said as Quinlan deposited him against the back of a stool. "That's a wyvern. I've only seen them in paintings."

The wyvern screeched in the dining area, back arching. One flap of its wings demolished another section of wall, felling a chandelier. Oil spilled and flame raced along the carpets, but Quinlan extinguished it with a wave of his hand. The wyvern snorted, eyes narrowed to slits, and stampeded for them, tail swinging like an enormous bludgeon. Eadric shouted, and the three of them dove away just as it cleaved in half the stool Orion had been leaning against seconds ago. It smashed its tail through a row of glasses and a keg, showering beer foam onto their faces and accidentally trapping itself between a metal rail and the counter.

"Damn it, Orion! Where's your affinity stone?" Quinlan yelled.

Orion blinked, his whole body numb, gaze cemented to the wyvern as it struggled to escape. "Pocket."

Quinlan slapped him hard across the face. "Listen up, pretty boy," he hissed. "Asterin's life is on the line, and if you don't focus, she is going to die. Are you really her Guardian?"

Orion shot up, heat rushing to his face. "Of course I am."

"In that case, *get your shit together*."

Eadric sent a bolt of electricity at the wyvern's backside, affinity stone clutched in his fist. It shrieked, rearing in pain and subsequently wrenching its tail free. The captain charged at it with a fearless cry, sword swinging—but the metal simply bounced off, scarcely even chipping its hide. Undaunted, Eadric stomped a foot into the ground and held his affinity stone aloft. Orion's ears popped, the hairs on the back of his neck standing on end. The wyvern snarled, hesitating.

"*Náxos*!" shouted Eadric.

Orion threw a hand over his eyes as lightning erupted from the sky, snaking through the hole in the hallway and striking the wyvern right in its ugly snout. The walls shuddered with thunder, and the brickwork gave a wobble before caving inward. His gut lurched as he thought of Asterin and the others trapped above. Bracing one hand against the floor, he called out, "*Reyunir*!"

Lines of gray light shot from his other hand, encasing the crumbling foundations and splintering wooden beams. He forced his breathing to slow as he began binding the ruins back together. Then his eyes snagged on the humongous, gaping craters in the wall from the missing brick. *Almighty Immortals*, he thought to himself. *What am I doing?* How was he supposed to support an entire disintegrating two-story building all on his own?

As if sensing his doubt, Orion's magic wavered.

His heart missed a beat as a chunk of plaster fell from the ceiling, crashing into a stool not a foot shy of him.

Orion's cry for help died in his throat, however, when indigo filigree intertwined with his silver light like ivy and spread outward, reinforcing his spell and mending the damage enough to keep the structure intact.

From across the room, Quinlan gave him a firm nod and Orion breathed a sigh of relief.

Then, the wyvern opened its maw as if to breath fire. But instead of flames, a black smog spewed into the air, surging toward Quinlan and slithering across his body. The Eradorian let out a hiss of discomfort as the smog spread, encasing his entire body from the shoulders down before solidifying into jagged black rock.

"Run!" yelled Quinlan, but it was already too late. The wyvern breathed two more swirling clouds of smog and entrapped Orion in seconds.

Eadric raised his arms high above his head just as the third cloud swooped down over him. "*Lumináxos*!" he bellowed.

The second blast of lightning nearly fried Orion's vision. He heard a shrill of pain, the beating of wings, and then nothing.

It took Orion a minute to recover from blindness, and bright spots still danced across the room every time he blinked. The acrid scent of smoke swirled through the room. When the dust finally settled, only a charred spot remained where the wyvern had stood.

He hardly dared to breathe. "Did we kill it?"

"I guess," said Eadric, a thin wisp of smoke drifting up from the wild tufts of his hair. In the end, the smog had captured him, too, but at least the wyvern was dead.

Orion whooped. "That was brilliant! Hey, Quinlan! Did you see that? Boom, lightning blast!" He tried to clap his hands before remembering that he was immobilized. "Now, how do we escape this stuff?"

Quinlan squinted at the black mark on the floor where the creature had been, a crease forming between his brows. "Uh ..."

"What is it?" asked Eadric.

"This might not sound great, but I don't think ..." Quinlan trailed off. "I don't think we killed it."

They froze as a shadow peeled itself from the walls, gathering in a writhing mass of darkness. In its center glowed a pair of familiar yellow eyes.

Quinlan began to curse, rocking back and forth within his restraints but failing to break free.

The bodiless eyes regarded them with something like satisfaction before the entire mass glided away, disappearing through the hole in the hallway.

"I'm still holding my tristone," Orion declared victoriously, but when he tried to summon his powers, it felt like running into a brick wall. His rocky confines were somehow obstructing his magic.

"We need to get to Luna and Asterin and Rose before that monster regains its strength and takes a corporeal form again," said Eadric.

"How?" Quinlan asked. "Everyone else has fled. Nobody is coming back to save us."

Orion's breath hitched. They had failed, failed so miserably, and now the others were in danger. "Think of something, Holloway!" Desperation clawed its way into his chest, voice rising with each word. Asterin would die, and it was all their fault. *His* fault. "You're supposed to be smart!"

"Shut up! Can you keep your stupid mouth shut for ten seconds?"

Orion let out an incredulous scoff. "*My* stupid mouth?"

"It's always open, blabbering away! I can't believe you and Asterin—"

"Me and Asterin what?" Orion asked, voice suddenly quiet.

Quinlan bit down on his tongue, refusing to meet Orion's eyes. The Eradorian's ears flushed a bright pink. "Nothing," he snapped. "Never mind."

Slow realization dawned on Orion. "Oh. You're jealous."

"Shut up! *Shut up*, okay? We've got other problems right now!"

As if on cue, a tremendous crash sounded above them, followed by a scream and a thump from outside.

Eadric blanched. "That was Luna."

"I put a shield on the window, so it'll take a little more than a few blows from the wyvern," said Quinlan. "But I rushed it. The shield won't hold forever. We're running out of time."

"Do something," Orion said, voice cracking. "They're going to die. Do something. Please."

Quinlan shut his eyes, teeth gritted in focus. "I'm trying." The veins in his neck bulged with effort, and he cursed for the umpteenth time.

Panic shot through Orion's every cell. "That's it—this is the end."

In his head, he apologized to Rose and to Luna. He tried to remember the last thing he had said to Asterin. He prayed for her forgiveness for being the worst Guardian ever, a lump forming in his throat as he listed off everything else he wanted to apologize for.

It was a long list.

A second crash rattled the walls.

And then, just when he thought that all hope was well and truly lost, his ears picked up the muted sound of paws thudding against the ground. No, not his ears. He heard it in his *mind*. Eyes still closed, he held his breath, heartbeat quickening.

When he opened his eyes, daring to hope, there was nothing but darkness. Orion's stomach dropped like a stone. It had just been his imagination.

But then, as he blinked through tears, the impossible became reality. A shining silver wolf stood before them, casting a disdainful, green-eyed glare at him. Those eyes belonged to the Princess of Axaria—and the God of Ice himself, Lord Conrye.

Quinlan's eyes snapped open, his jaw dropping. "Is that—"

"Just shut up," Orion whispered, thanking all of the Immortals for this beastly savior.

Like a silver arrow, the wolf shot toward Quinlan, lunging for his confines with claws extended. The black rock blasted apart, releasing

Quinlan's suppressed indigo fire in an explosion of rubble. With a *hiss*, the debris dissipated back into smog … and then nothing.

Quinlan spared Orion a single glance. A question. *Orion* was her Guardian, after all. Not that it had made even a remote difference in the end.

"Go," Orion croaked. "Help them." With his blessing, Quinlan and the wolf flew out of the room, gone in the space of a heartbeat. At that moment, Orion almost felt sorry for the wyvern, almost wished it a quick death, for he had seen the promise in Quinlan's eyes.

A promise to destroy.

CHAPTER THIRTEEN

Jack and Hayley strode through Mess Hall, the clamor of the dinnertime rush rising around them. Jack rubbed his thumb and index finger together, a nervous tic he couldn't seem to drop. A servant had informed them that the Queen of Axaria requested their presence at the head table, and Jack didn't know whether to feel honored or petrified, so he settled for a mixture of both.

In perfect sync, they stepped up to a table set atop a raised platform and bowed to the queen. The rest of the court paid little attention to the two of them, although one man who gave Jack an extremely suggestive ogle received a glare from Hayley so vicious that he spilled wine upon himself. To the queen's right sat General Garringsford, her steel eyes trained intently enough on them as she sliced her steak that Jack had to will himself not to shrink. Immortals, he was *so* glad Covington oversaw them. The man was a total hard-ass most of the time, but all of the Elites knew he had a soft spot for them. Garringsford was intimidating as hell, inside *and* out.

"Your Royal Majesty," Jack said.

Queen Priscilla swirled a glass of wine in one hand, her fingernails painted in the same shade of blood red. "Elites. My apologies for stealing you away from your dinners, but I never had the chance to ask—which of the Guard did my daughter choose as companions?"

"The Eradorians, Your Majesty," Hayley said.

"Interesting choice." Priscilla tilted her head, waiting. When she saw that Hayley had nothing else to add, she frowned. "That only makes two."

Jack exchanged a glance with Hayley. "The third wasn't one of us, Your Majesty," he said, shifting. "I—I don't believe she was a soldier at all, actually."

The queen's glass halted midswirl, the liquid nearly sloshing out. "Do you remember what she looked like?"

Jack hesitated, bowing his head. "Her Highness mentioned a name … Luna."

"Speak up, soldier," Garringsford ordered, sharp as a whip.

"Luna," Hayley repeated for him, her gaze as flat and unflappable as ever.

Queen Priscilla set her glass down unsteadily, hands resting on the table. "*Luna*? But … why?" she murmured to herself, staring into the liquid as though it might give her an answer.

Jack and Hayley stood there in silence for a long, awkward minute before Jack finally gathered the courage to break the tension. Garringsford hadn't stopped staring at them, and it was seriously creeping him out. "Is there anything else we can help with, Your Majesty?"

The queen startled, resurfacing from her trance. "Oh my. I'm so sorry. Yes, of course. Thank you for your time."

They bowed again before making their way back to their table. As Jack slid into his seat, he turned to Hayley, both of them ignoring Casper and Gino's attempts to interrogate them about their little trip. He had to force himself to look away from Laurel's pleading expression, because *damn*, if those wide hazel eyes weren't irresistible. Silas flicked peas at Alicia, and one hit Hayley in the forehead. She sprang to her feet, wrestled the big man into a headlock and dumped a fistful of peas down his collar.

Jack stretched his legs beneath the table after Hayley sat back down. "So, what do you think that was about?"

Hayley glanced back up to the head table, where Queen Priscilla had stood to leave. Garringsford rose alongside her, but then the queen said something and the general lowered herself back into her seat, her eyes sullenly following the queen's retreat. "I'm not sure."

"Who's Luna, again?"

Hayley shrugged. "Isn't she Princess Asterin's lady-in-waiting? Anyway, it hardly matters. Judging by the queen's reaction … I doubt she'll make it out of that forest alive."

CHAPTER FOURTEEN

Orion nearly wept when the silver wolf trotted back down the stairs, maw dripping and fur stained black. Up until a few seconds before, when their confines had disintegrated to dust, they had been utterly, excruciatingly helpless. Quinlan trudged down the steps right behind the wolf. Blood trickled from a large gash on his forehead, but other than that and a small collection of claw-shaped slashes that would easily heal, he seemed mostly unharmed. Rose and Luna tottered down the stairs last, holding Asterin upright between them.

Orion wrapped all three of them in a bone-crushing hug, but eventually Rose and Luna untangled themselves from the hug to give him and Asterin some space.

"I'm so sorry," he croaked, blinking away the sudden onslaught of tears.

Asterin exhaled into his shoulder. "What for?"

"Everything."

She lifted her face, eyes blazing. "You have nothing to apologize for."

He closed his eyes, the reassurance of her physical presence washing over him. He stroked her hair. "I … I almost lost you. And it would have been all my fault."

She nestled closer. "Not true."

Orion felt Quinlan's scalding glare before he saw it. *Jealous?* he mouthed.

Quinlan gifted him an obscene hand gesture in response.

Orion smiled, and then said to Asterin, "Also, can we talk about the random wolf that showed up out of nowhere?"

She reeled back, eyes wide with disbelief. "Random wolf? Are you joking? You don't recognize him?"

Orion chuckled nervously. "No? I mean, yeah, I guess. He looks like Lord Conrye's wolf form, but all wolves—"

Asterin groaned. "That *is* Lord Conrye's wolf form, moron."

"What?"

At that moment, Lord Conrye padded up to them, and Orion suddenly realized how huge he was. Even sitting, his ears came level with Asterin's shoulders. And yes—there were those little half-crescent tufts marking the wolf's brow in ice white, and of course, the eerily luminescent green eyes that matched the paintings and sculptures around the palace, but … somehow, though Orion and every other child grew up learning about the legends of the Immortals and the origins of magic, it was hard to believe that they actually *existed* somewhere—even in an unreachable dimension, like the Immortal Realm.

Conrye dipped his massive head, brushing his muzzle against Asterin's curled fingers. She smiled and scratched him behind the ears.

Orion didn't know what to do, so he got down on one knee. "L-Lord Conrye. An honor, Your … Godship."

The god only yawned at him, revealing a flash of razor-sharp fangs. Suddenly, his ears perked and then flattened, lip curling back. He regarded Asterin for a moment before bowing his head, as if to say, *I must go.*

And then, just as quickly as he had come, he was gone, swifter than wind on silent paws, racing out of the hole that the wyvern had made in the wall.

Rose and Luna reappeared at Asterin's side, and Orion watched them help her out of the demolished building. Quinlan trailed on their heels, shooting Orion a final vehement glare on his way out.

Only now, when Asterin was safe, did the bitterness begin to seep in. Orion wanted to hate Quinlan for being stronger, for being Asterin's hero when it should have been *him*—but how could he, after the Eradorian Prince and Lord Conrye had just saved them all, when he had been trapped and useless?

"Orion," said Eadric from behind him.

"Isn't it hard to believe that after everything that just happened, meeting an Immortal wasn't even the craziest?" Orion said, trying to grin, but it felt like his face was cracking. Then he caught sight of Eadric's own downcast eyes and realized that he didn't need to fake his usual optimism.

"It's over," the captain murmured. "Asterin is alive, we're alive. That's all that matters. Let's go."

Luckily for them, Aldville was a large town, and they found alternative lodging without much difficulty. After resettling the horses, Eadric sent a messenger to the palace to request a clean-up crew, and they all gathered around the hearth in the commons—save for Asterin and Quinlan. Asterin retired to her room to rest, and Quinlan accompanied her so that he could monitor the toll that using so much magic had taken on her body.

And to guard her, Orion thought to himself. *That* little reminder stung like hell.

Orion shared a pot of tea with Rose, pouring and passing cups across the table in silence. Luna dozed on Eadric's chest on the couch facing the hearth, the snoring captain's arms wrapped around her. Orion tried to match their slow, unified breaths as he drank. Rose drained her cup and curled her knees up to her chest, giving a soft sigh before letting her eyes slip shut. Orion reached for the teapot, only to remember that he had emptied it on his last cup. The slumber he had found so easily in the evening eluded him now, leaving him restless and jittery. He drummed his fingers on his knees, gaze lingering on Eadric and Luna. A small coil of envy expanded in his chest. They looked perfect together, like two halves forming a whole, content in their own little world.

Orion sometimes wondered if he would ever be able to find that kind of happiness—not the fleeting moments in dark, hidden corners or behind locked doors tangled in silken sheets. He never kept track of those, not really. No, he wanted something more. *Someone* more. Someone who he loved and loved him back, more than anything in the world. *You love Asterin*, a voice in his head reminded him. But not in that way. He doubted he could ever be happy in a romantic relationship with her.

Eventually he did manage to drift asleep to the soothing crackle of the hearth, empty teacup still in hand—but after what felt like no more than a few minutes, he awoke to a shout, his cup shattering on the floor. His clothes were drenched in sweat, and his throat hoarse. He realized the shout had come from him. Heart thundering, he gradually came to his senses. Still panting, he licked his cracked lips, tasting salt. He must have had a nightmare, but for the life of him, he couldn't remember what it had been about—although even now he couldn't shake the sensation that he was falling down a bottomless hole.

A hand gripped his shoulder. His hazy vision sharpened to find Rose crouched at his side, face grim.

"Hey," she said gently, offering him a glass of water. "Hey, you're here. It's all right."

Orion clutched the glass like a lifeline, stomach roiling with nausea. His eyes darted around the room. Eadric and Luna had vanished from the couch. "What time is it?"

"The sun won't be up for another few hours," she said. "Everyone else has gone to bed."

He hauled himself out of the armchair, straightening a crick in his neck. "Except for you, Your Majesty?"

Her lips curved into a semblance of a smile. "I suppose so." She cocked her head, contemplating him. "You wouldn't happen to remember what your nightmare was about, would you?"

His palms turned clammy. "No."

"You were shouting, 'Don't go.' Over and over."

Orion looked away. "It was just a stupid dream."

"My dreams led me to Axaris," Rose said. "And when I dreamt that my father would die at the end of my uncle's sword, he was dead by morning."

"Uncle? You mean ..." His eyes widened. "Quinlan's father?"

Rose tipped her chin. "His violent, abusive father, yes. No one outside of the family ever learned of how my father actually died—just another one of Eradore's best-kept secrets."

Her sarcasm bit him. "Listen, Rose ..." He bowed his head. "About my suspicions when you and Quinlan first arrived in Axaris ... I never meant—"

Rose pinned him down with a flat stare. "Not everything is about you, Orion," she said. Those words hurt even more, nailing into something deep inside him.

"I just—I find it difficult to open myself up to people," Orion admitted. "And to trust them. A long time ago …" His throat closed up and he found himself unable to continue.

Rose sighed. "You know, I once had someone I would have died for ten times over. In the end, he broke my heart. It took me years to learn how to trust again, but when I did …" She shook her head. "All I'm saying is that you should learn to give people a chance, Orion."

He was struck by the pain reflected in her eyes, and he found himself unable to tear his gaze away from the hypnotizing flecks of charcoal amongst the gold. He had to remind himself that despite being the Queen of Eradore, she was still just a nineteen-year-old girl. "I'll—I'll try."

"I didn't want to trust the visions that led me to all of you at first," Rose told him quietly. "I had them every night. And every night, I saw a girl. Fighting. Every damn night, without fail, until I set foot in your city."

He swallowed his dread and dared ask, "Fighting who?"

"Darkness itself." Rose turned toward the window, fixated on a horizon Orion couldn't see. "She was the only shield against a tidal wave of shadows, but alone, she didn't stand a chance against them. They fell upon her like scavengers over a festering carcass." The hairs on the back of his neck stood on end. "And every time, as the shadows feasted upon her ravaged soul, a woman would emerge from the darkness." After the slightest of hesitations, Rose stepped toward the hearth and bent down to scoop up her satchel. From a side pocket, she removed a small object and passed it to him.

Orion frowned. It was a tiny iron figure of a butterfly, the patterns etched into its wings set with intricate swirls of black amethyst. He turned it gently in his hands and winced. The tip of a wing had nicked his palm. "What is this?"

"After my mother died a few weeks ago, I found this among her possessions. From the moment I touched it, I knew there was something wrong. It has an unnatural energy—a *dark* energy, just like the shadows in my visions. And that night, my visions changed. Instead of the shadows overcoming the girl, they were overcoming my kingdom. I could do nothing to stop them. But just when I thought all hope was lost, a silver wolf appeared and banished the shadows. And right before I woke up, it told me to come here. So I sent scouts to Axaria. None returned. I never planned such a prolonged absence from Eradore, but I'm not leaving until I know for certain that my people will be safe."

"Hold on." Orion frowned. "I've seen this figurine before. Asterin has one in her room."

Rose's expression darkened. "Do me a favor. When we get back to Axaris, burn it to ashes."

"What in the world for?" Orion spluttered.

"Each of the members of the Council of Immortals represents an animal. Lord Conrye and his wolf, Lady Ilma and her vipers, Lord Tidus and his serpent. Eoin, the God of Shadow, out of all the creatures in his kingdom, chose the black butterfly."

Orion rubbed his temple. "In my dream, I think I was falling." The confession dredged up a vague recollection. "Falling and falling. Endlessly. But it couldn't have been some kind of *literal* warning, right?" He chuckled half-heartedly. "That kind of thing would be impossible."

The silence dragged on and on, the cold in Orion's stomach only growing colder as the last of the smoldering embers faded upon lumps of blackened coal.

"In a world of magic," Rose said slowly, and he saw pity in her expression. "Nothing is impossible."

CHAPTER FIFTEEN

Asterin buried her fingers into the plush carpet and watched Quinlan pace back and forth in the light of a single candle perched on the corner of the bedside table, its flame dancing merrily. The room had a narrow bed for a sole occupant and not much else.

Quinlan halted in front of her, as if noticing her for the first time, and squinted in confusion. "Why are you still awake?"

"Can't sleep," she said, hugging her knees and looking up at him.

Quinlan glared at her and grumbled something underneath his breath. "Stop giving me doe eyes, brat. You know that there's a perfectly good bed right there, right?"

She scoffed. "Doe eyes?"

"Yes. You do that wide-eyed stare and bat your lashes like you're innocent or something, but you fool no one."

She blinked, bewildered. "Bat my eyelashes?"

He threw his hands in the air. "See? You're doing it again! The blinking thing!" He bent forward and did an exaggerated imitation for her.

"You have awfully long eyelashes for a boy."

Quinlan groaned, running his hands through his hair in frustration. "You are going to be the death of me."

Asterin sighed and stretched her arms above her head. "What a fine day that will be."

Quinlan scowled. She could hear him grinding his teeth. "You are ridiculous."

"I'm ridiculous? You're the one who climbed up four stories and smashed through my window just to show me a baby bird!"

"What was I supposed to do?" he grumbled.

"Oh, save it. That bird was unbelievably cute, though." Asterin smirked. "It made you look quite hideous in comparison."

Quinlan dove at her with a strangled roar. She let out a muffled *oomph* as they crashed to the floor. He straddled her waist, pinning her wrists above her head.

Lips parted, Asterin stared up at him, the carpet tickling the nape of her neck as she soaked in his wind-and-smoke scent. Her eyes traced the hard lines of his jaw, drinking in the creamy skin. The candlelight glinted like a halo along the silhouette of his rumpled hair.

Oh, this won't do, Asterin thought to herself and bucked upward, startling him enough that she managed to flip them over and lock his hands above his head instead.

Quinlan glared up at her. Then something over her shoulder caught his attention and he let out a gasp. "I think I just saw something move!"

She shouldn't have fallen for it, but she did, and the next thing she knew he had wrestled her back to the ground. "Not fair."

Quinlan leaned down and purred into her ear, "I never said I'd play fair."

As he drew back slightly, his eyes flicked to her lips.

Her throat dried.

It took all her self-control not to drag him down by the collar. *Don't let him make you his plaything.* She knew his type, and she refused to give him what he so obviously wanted. "Quinlan—"

"I was afraid you were going to die," he interrupted, eyes fixated on her mouth even as he spoke. His brow furrowed a moment later, as if he couldn't believe he had confessed such a thing.

"And I was afraid you were already dead," she said.

"You can't get rid of me that easily."

She bared her teeth. "Shall I try?"

At last, he blew out a long breath and cursed. "You are impossible," he snapped, rolling off her.

Asterin stayed on her back, curling her fingers into the carpet. Quinlan's ragged breaths filled the silence, and she glimpsed the flush creeping up his neck, tingeing his ears pink. "Why do you put up with me, then?" she asked.

"You're a good distraction."

Somehow, she was surprised by how much the offhand comment stung. Eventually, she managed to say, "You should get some sleep."

"Ah. Right." He got to his feet, scuffing the carpet with the toe of his boot. "Well, bye, then."

Despite her inner conflict, she blurted, "You could stay here, you know." Then she hastily added, "Since we're leaving so soon, anyway."

He coughed loudly. "Oh, I suppose." With a loud snort of indignation, he stomped over to her side and flopped onto his back. He threw an arm over his face, shoulder brushing hers.

Asterin almost laughed. "Has anyone ever told you that you can be incredibly melodramatic?"

"Thank you," he spat.

"That was definitely not a compliment," Asterin said. Quinlan swore colorfully under his breath, calling her a few choice names that she thought were entirely inappropriate for the situation. "How I pity the poor ladies pining for you back in Eradore."

He snorted at that. "And I the suitors in Axaria."

"You truly should. Nothing has ever worked out, and I've almost killed a few of them," she admitted in a hushed whisper. "I simply can't stand them, and accidents happen so easily." Her nose wrinkled as she recalled the most recent offender. "Though the last one was definitely asking for it. He kept gawking at Luna—well, everywhere but her face."

"And you let him keep his head?"

"He found all of his clothes swimming with the ducks in the pond." That drew a chuckle out of him, and she couldn't help but ask, "Are any ladies in Eradore desperately awaiting your return?"

"I wish," he responded with a dry smile. "Aunt Lillian was always trying to marry me off to the daughter of one of her closest friends. Her name was Pippa. She was a nice person and all. It's just that … well, I know it's terrible, but I could never say her name aloud in a romantic way without laughing. She always thought I was laughing at *her*."

"Poor Pippa. She probably deserved better than you, anyway."

"I courted her for about three months," he went on. "One day, we were walking in the gardens and she asked me to pick some white roses for her, which only grow on the east side of the palace. When I came back, I found her locking lips with the head gardener."

Asterin gasped, slapping a hand over her mouth to stifle her laughter. "Pippa!"

"Mind you, the head gardener wasn't a bad-looking man," Quinlan added. "If you overlook the oily goatee and the potbelly. Aunt Lillian laughed herself sick when she found out." He shifted a little closer.

"What about your mother?"

A pause. "She died giving birth to me. According to my brother, my father was never the same after that. He drank from morning until night, forgot that we needed to be fed, that sort of thing."

"That's terrible." Asterin swallowed. "I'm sorry."

A harsh chuckle. "That's not all. After my father realized how powerful I was, he took every opportunity to remind me that unless I trained until I bled, I didn't deserve my magic. He was jealous. He was only bifinitied, and weak at that. My very existence made him angry. He used to beat me, when I was too young to know that what he was doing was wrong or to fight back."

She couldn't believe her ears. *To hurt one's own child …* Priscilla had never raised a hand to her. Asterin's injuries had only come from fists she herself commanded to fly, fights she fought of her own free will. It was her mother's *words* that left the scars, a deep ache in her chest that chafed like a fresh wound every time she remembered all of her mother's scorn, the shame the queen caused her to feel whenever Asterin used her body to duel instead of dance.

Luna's voice echoed in her mind. *She loves you in her own way.*

"Do you think he loved you?" Asterin asked.

Quinlan's throat bobbed. "The only people he truly loved were my mother and Aunt Lillian, his sister," Quinlan said. "He didn't care much for my brother and me, but he hated King Bernard—Rose's father. Bernard was barely a lord, but Aunt Lillian still took him as her king. After my mother died, my father tried to convince Aunt Lillian to kill Bernard. Only the Immortals knew why. Maybe because he thought it was unfair that his sister's love still lived while my mother was dead. Of course, she refused, so he ended up killing the man himself."

"Immortals," Asterin breathed.

"After my father was executed, Aunt Lillian, despite still being in mourning, took me and my brother in. Raised us right alongside Rose and two newborns, Avris and Avon. The twins."

"Did you get along?" Asterin asked, trying to imagine a little Quinlan playing hide-and-seek with his cousins.

"The twins are devilspawn if you get on their bad side," he said, cracking a smile. "But otherwise, yes. My brother and I had a bit more of a … complicated relationship. Taeron … well, he's deadly smart. He spends all his time holed up in libraries or his room. Whichever has more books that he hasn't read. And he's handsome. Way more than I am." At her eye roll, he shook his head. "No, you don't understand. He's *perfect.* I'm not even exaggerating. My father used to say that Taeron was the only reason he bothered coming home. I could never compete with him, and he hardly even tries." Quinlan huffed out a miserable chuckle. "And he's so kind about everything that there's no way to properly hate him for it."

Asterin didn't know what to say to that. Orion was the closest thing she'd ever had to a brother, but he had never been her rival for attention, since *he* certainly didn't care about impressing Queen Priscilla.

"Taeron always tried to stop my father from hurting me. But Taeron did have a single flaw … he inherited almost no magical capabilities. No matter how hard he practiced, he could only ever summon enough flame to light kindling." Quinlan flicked his finger lazily, and a ball of fire engulfed the candle on the bedside table, consuming half of the wax in an instant. "All my father had to do was whisper a sleeping spell and Taeron was out. No bruises or broken bones, of course. Those were reserved for me."

Thinking of little Quinlan, hurting and alone … it was all Asterin could do not to wrap her arms around him and hold him close. She inched slightly closer to him. "Why?"

He shrugged. "It never occurred to me to ask. I just assumed it was meant to be. And physical abuse was one thing, but my father's favorite punishment was taking away my affinity stones."

Her head snapped toward him in shock. "He took them away from you?"

Quinlan stared up at the ceiling. "Yeah, when he beat me. So I had no way to fight back." He threw a few half-hearted punches into the air. "And then, one day, I learned how to wield magic without them." His lips curved into a wicked little grin. "Immortals, was he ever surprised by that."

"I wish I could've been there," said Asterin. "Oh." At the mention of affinity stones, she reached into her pocket and fished out the omnistone. "I almost forgot to give this back to you." It gave off a pearly, luminescent glow in her palm, soothing the darkness around it like moonlight.

"Keep it," said Quinlan softly.

"But—"

"I said keep it, brat," he repeated, reaching up and splaying his fingers beneath hers, gently curling them around the stone. "Only you and I can touch this stone, anyway, and I don't need it." His hand lingered a moment more against hers before dropping back to his side.

She gave in. "Thank you. Truly. For … everything." Her fingers felt blindly for his, and when she found them, she gave them a last quick squeeze. She hid a smile as he muttered something unintelligible, the tips of his ears tinged pink.

They lapsed into tranquil silence. She could tell he was struggling to stay awake, though she didn't know for whose sake.

Some time later, he murmured her name midway through a massive yawn.

"Yes?" she asked, rolling over to face him.

He rolled onto his side to face her too, though his eyes were closed. The tip of his nose brushed her forehead, and his breath warmed her skin. Asterin didn't dare move. A voice in her head warned her to turn away, but no matter how hard she urged herself to move, her body refused to listen.

"I'm glad you haven't tried to kill me yet," he mumbled, words slurring.

It took her a moment to understand his meaning. She blushed. "You aren't courting me, though." She watched the slow rise and fall of his chest, and then added half-jokingly, "Unless you are?"

But there was no response.

She tilted her face to look up at him, the candle burning low and the buttery golden light casting darkness over the planes of his face, only to find that he had already fallen fast asleep.

She sighed and closed her eyes. "Asshole."

CHAPTER SIXTEEN

The boy found the package in a dark passageway. Earlier explorations during his first four months working at the palace had revealed a sprawling network of such passageways in the underbelly of the palace—most allowed servants to scuttle about invisibly to do their work, but some seemed as though no one had disturbed their dust for decades. Lost in his thoughts, the young servant had taken a wrong turn or two, and now found himself dreadfully lost.

Most of the brown paper wrapping of the package had been torn to shreds. Even from afar, it smelled rancid, and at first he thought it might have contained some spoiled meat. But as he approached, he saw the remains of some greenish carcass within, entrails spilling out, glassy, yellow eyes oozing black pus. Scrawled on the side of the package was the sender's address, accompanied by a little note and a scribble that vaguely resembled the letter *N*:

The Rainbow Salmon.
Aldwille, Azaria.

Nice try.
—N

He bit down on his knuckle to keep from retching.

A trail of black pus led away from the package. Taking his lightstone out, the boy followed it, his heart thudding in his chest. He came to a dead end but traced his fingers along the wall and found a crack. *Just like in the stories*, he thought. A whispered, "*Ovrire*," and the panel opened with a rusty groan that echoed against stone.

A spiral stairwell descended into gloom, glistening with mildew and slime. With another charm, he summoned a ball of light that cast the walls in a sickly green glow. Water dripped from the ceiling, splashing onto his skin as he slipped into the opening.

When the boy reached the bottom, nose wrinkled and a damp chill settling into his bones, he let out a little gasp of awe.

Mere feet away, behind a pedestal with a little bowl atop it, a great stone archway rose out of the gloom. Beyond the archway stood the most magnificent fountain he had ever seen. Three massive butterflies hewn from black stone spiraled around a gold scepter plunging out of piles and piles of precious metals and jewels. The butterflies' glorious wings were encrusted with even more jewels—diamonds and emeralds and sapphires and still others he didn't have names for. Dark, glimmering liquid spewed from the crown of the scepter, cascading down the butterflies' slender little legs in dark rivulets.

The boy rubbed his hands together in delight. He would be rich! All he needed was a knife, perhaps, and then he could take all the gemstones he could carry in one go and sell them. He mapped out the calculations in his head. He had two pockets in his trousers and one on his tunic. He could stuff jewels into his shoes, too, and maybe even some in his mouth.

He sprang toward the archway, salivating at the fantasies flying through his mind. He would eat caviar until he stank of it. He would burn all of his itchy tunics, even the one with the silver embroidery that the servants wore for special occasions. And above of all, he would never wash another dish again. But just when he was inches away from crossing beneath the arch, footsteps echoed down the stairs. Heart pounding, he squeezed himself into a crevice in the wall, clutching his lightstone to his chest. *Should I attack them?* he wondered, scanning the chamber for some sort of weapon. He had his lightstone, but not much else. *What if they take the gems?*

Not moments later, a figure cloaked in black emerged out of the shadows, features hidden beneath a hood. From long sleeves crept ten bone-white fingers, thin and gnarled like spider legs.

Death, the boy thought, his desire for the gems evaporating faster than steam in a desert. He bit down on his tongue to keep from whimpering and tried to quell the quaking of his body. *That must be Death.*

Death proceeded to dip a finger into the bowl atop the pedestal, tracing three lines with a horizontal slash onto its white forehead. The mark flared briefly as Death crossed under the archway and into the chamber beyond.

Despite his fear, the boy craned his neck to watch.

A tarnished bronze chalice was mounted on another pedestal beside the fountain. Death tipped it into the fountain's stream. After the chalice filled, Death drew the rim to its lips and drank, long and deep.

Some invisible energy crawled over the boy's skin, electrifying his senses. Ghostly whispers breezed his ears, caressing him, chanting songs in languages so ancient they didn't even sound human. Death lurched onto its knees, bracing itself against the floor. A dribble of glistening saliva fell from its chin and spattered beside those hideous skeletal hands.

His lightstone slipped from his sweaty fingers and clattered onto the floor.

Death turned to him.

When Death stood, swaying almost drunkenly, the boy began to pray. Wet warmth spread down his trousers as Death approached. His legs gave out beneath him, leaving him to lie at Death's feet in a weeping pile. Eyes squeezed shut, he felt those horrid white fingers slither across his scalp like snakes and latch onto his hair, yanking him up into the air as if he weighed nothing.

Something forced his eyes open. Prayers still spewed from his lips when he saw Death's face. Death's beautiful, *womanly* face, her silky hair and cold eyes.

The boy finally began to scream.

The last thing he knew as Death smiled at him, sharp and silver, was a red-hot pain across his throat—and then darkness.

CHAPTER SEVENTEEN

The next morning, Orion awoke from a thankfully dreamless doze. Sunshine bled through the shutters of the room's single window, casting a ladder of pale white light through the slats and onto his bed. He rolled out from beneath the covers and got dressed, his thoughts still lingering on Rose's words while he packed up his things. Wondering what the inn might serve for breakfast, he stepped into the hallway just as the door across from him opened and out shuffled Quinlan, rubbing the sleep from his eyes with a little smile on his face.

Orion nearly dropped his pack onto the garish red-gold carpeting. "Were you in Asterin's room the whole night?"

Quinlan jumped so high that he smashed the top of his head into the lamp jutting out from the wall. He massaged the injury and shot Orion a pained glare. "Maybe."

Orion threw his pack down and rushed forward, shoving Quinlan against Asterin's door with a *thud*. "I swear to the Immortals, if you—"

"If I *what*?" he challenged, eyes blazing. "Took advantage of her?"

Orion's hand latched around the Eradorian's throat. "Did you?"

Quinlan's mouth thinned. "Of course not. Do you actually think I would do that?" At Orion's silence, something almost like hurt flashed across his face. "You … you still don't trust me. At all."

Orion's grip slackened. *Learn to give people a chance, Orion.* "Well, I mean, you kind of suggested it first—"

Quinlan smacked his hand away, expression closing off, and shouldered past. "We just talked about stuff," he said, voice cold. "Promise."

"What sort of stuff?"

Before Quinlan could retort, the door creaked open and Asterin nudged her head outside, stifling a yawn. "What's all the noise about?"

Orion jerked his chin at the Eradorian. "Beat it."

Quinlan just shook his head and stalked off toward Rose's room, shoulders hunched.

"Orion?" said Asterin. "What's wrong?"

There were so many things Orion wanted to say, but then he remembered the hurt in Quinlan's expression and his voice died in his throat. "Nothing," he finally managed. "Just get ready to leave."

He found Luna and Eadric outside, sitting on the steps to the inn and sharing a cup of hot chocolate from the kitchen. He tried to imagine Asterin and Quinlan in their place, and nearly stormed over to kick the mug out of Eadric's hand.

Before long, their horses were stirring up a cloud of dust, putting the town of Aldville behind them. They continued along the main road until it diverged southeast, toward Corinthe. They kicked into a gallop, the road soon giving way to worn dirt. It was a perfect day, warm and fresh, the early spring scenery passing in a vivid blur of lush green fields and sparkling aquamarine lakes as they flew across miles and miles of land. The sky stretched endlessly on, unblemished by even the slightest wisp of white, so bright and piercing that it hurt Orion's eyes to look at it. Wind whistled through his hair, and the drumming of hooves against the dirt road filled his head like thunder. They stopped only once to rest and water their horses, and so the sun hovered high overhead with afternoon heat when they at last arrived in the village of Corinthe.

Or at least, what remained of it.

Orion swung off Buttercup. "Immortals above."

The others followed suit, speechless.

Dust and debris hung around them in a veil, drifting aimlessly. Shapes emerged with each step along the road leading into the village—scraps of wood, skeletal carcasses of furniture, shattered glass littering the cracked cobblestones. Ruined houses loomed over them, ceilings caved in and doors missing from their hinges. The ground crunched underfoot, and it was all Orion could do not to check for bones.

It smelled like death.

They passed a water well that appeared untouched, save for the fraying rope dangling from the winch. The bucket lay upside down a few feet away, and when Luna nudged it over, she found a tattered doll trapped beneath. She bent down to pick it up. Stuffing weeped out of a rip across its face, one button-eye dangling from a lone thread.

"The demon did this," Asterin said, voice thick with rage and grief. "It must have."

Not a single being stirred the arid breeze as they led their horses farther into the village, all their senses on high alert. Orion kept a careful eye on Asterin's back, his stride quickening to match hers, one hand on Orondite's pommel. He wouldn't let Aldville happen again.

"There were at least three hundred people living here," Eadric said hoarsely. "But—"

"Where did they go?" Quinlan murmured. "There's blood, but … no bodies."

"Immortals," said Luna suddenly, looking sick. "You don't think the demon could have *eaten* them, do you?"

"Please stop," said Asterin quietly.

Soon they turned onto a lane of destroyed houses. At its end rose an enormous pile of earth, stretching twenty feet across and double that in height.

Asterin gave Lux a pat and started up the hill of dirt. "I'm going to get a better look at everything." The horse watched her go, swishing his tail back and forth and pawing at the ground.

Orion tugged Buttercup forward, but the mare planted her hooves in the ground and refused to budge. He handed her reins to Eadric and clambered up the slope after Asterin, stomach clenching with growing unease. Twice he nearly slipped, the loose dirt giving way beneath his boots.

Ahead, Asterin had already reached the peak.

"What do you see?" called Eadric.

Asterin failed to answer.

Orion finally managed to scrabble to the top of the hill. "What is …" His voice died in his throat as he looked down. Overwhelming denial washed over him, but there was no mistaking the horrid stench wafting upward.

"Orion?" hollered Eadric. "What's below the hill?"

"It's not a hill," he said. Everything seemed to slow as he turned and told the others. "It's … a grave."

Luna pressed a hand to her mouth, the doll hanging limp at her side. The Eradorians' eyes widened in shock. Eadric could only stare, expression utterly blank.

Quinlan was the first to spring into action, starting for the hill when Asterin thrust out an arm to halt him. "Don't," she commanded, her voice breaking on the end of the word. "These are not your people."

"Asterin," said Orion, reaching forward to grasp her wrist. She flinched, but he held firm and eventually she gave him a small nod.

Together, they looked back into the pit.

Heaps and heaps of corpses of all sizes were sprawled within the pit, some naked, others missing arms and legs. A strange black fluid oozed from their wounds, out of their mouths and ears. Nearly all of them were missing patches of skin from their faces, like the doll Luna still clutched to her chest, as if something had clawed their flesh right off.

Orion couldn't stand the sight for more than a few seconds, but Asterin kept on staring at the bodies for what seemed like an eternity, her expression unreadable.

"Asterin," he said to her softly, desperately, but she had gone mute. He grabbed her by the shoulders and shook gently. "Asterin. Say something. Please."

She clenched her fists so hard that they trembled. Then she opened her mouth, and at last, like a dam bursting open, the tears came, shaking her entire body with hysterical sobs.

Orion pulled her roughly into his arms, holding her close as if his life depended on it.

She buried her face into his chest, muffling her enraged howls.

"Don't cry," he breathed without thinking, but she drowned him out and he didn't repeat it.

A memory forced itself to the surface of his mind. The one memory that he couldn't bear to talk about, the one he had struggled to lock away all his life. But now …

Seven. He had only been seven at the time, growing up in a small town dotted with quaint little houses stacked one atop the other like books thrown together in a haphazard pile. There had been a central square with a large fountain, where the townsfolk gathered for holidays. Where *his* family had gathered, too. It was the only home he had ever known.

Orion remembered the weather. Rolling clouds of cinder flocked the horizon, bleak and dismal, the taste of a storm hanging over the town and the air sticky with humidity—perfect for fishing. On any other day, the streets would have cleared quickly—mothers calling their children inside from their games, vendors squinting upward as they packed away their goods and scurried for shelter.

But that day, the streets had already stood empty when the heavens opened up. The rain plummeted in cold, fat drops onto cobblestones slick with red.

Waiting alone in the central square, he had gazed up at the fountain, carved with the faces of the Council of Immortals. Lord Conrye stared down at him through the curtain of rain—a little boy, drenched from head to toe, golden hair plastered to his forehead and his face upturned to embrace the storm. But even with the storm and the scent it brought of something beginning anew, the stench of vomit and human waste still lingered. He wondered where the Immortals were, if they even existed. He wondered why they weren't here. Why they *hadn't* been here, when so many people had needed them so badly.

The rain cooled his burning cheeks, dripping past his lashes, but he ignored the sting in his eyes and the ache in his tired feet. He simply stood there, alive and whole, when he knew that he was supposed to be dead.

"I just wanted to go fishing," Orion had whispered up to Lord Conrye. A drop of rain trickled from the god's eye.

Though his gaze was fixed on the faces of the Immortals, they were not the faces he saw in his mind. No, he saw the faces of his friends from school. His neighbors. The man who sold roasted peanuts on the corner beneath the big oak tree with the branches perfect for climbing, the woman who sold jars of pitted peaches and apricots. The shoemaker. His son, who polished the shoes his father made from morning until evening. The bellmaker. The priest and his acolytes. The friendly baker who snuck him a fresh-baked cookie every time his mother sent him to buy bread.

Mother.

And Sophie, too.

Hirelings—those willing to commit any crime for the right price—had invaded their town to intercept a convoy containing a priceless nebula diamond heading for Axaris. The diamond, an affinity stone that could multiply one's powers a hundredfold, was a secret kept so close that only King Tristan and a few trusted advisors, including his Royal Guardian—Orion's father, Theodore Galashiels—knew of its existence.

But one of those advisors had betrayed him.

And when the hirelings came, they didn't just steal the diamond. They ransacked the entire town, taking everything they could possibly sell and cutting down anyone who tried to stop them. The best of King Tristan's soldiers had arrived to eliminate the hirelings, but by then, it had already been too late.

That day, Orion's street, bordering the edge of the town, had been the first to be attacked.

That day, his mother and baby sister had stayed home while he went to the lake to go fishing.

His fingers twitched, itching to lift the hem of his shirt so he could glimpse the smooth, unbroken skin that had been marred by a deep gouge just hours ago. His father had healed it with nothing more than a word and a touch.

Stupidly, he had dropped his fishing rod into the lake. When he climbed down the dock to retrieve it, he had slipped and impaled himself on a wooden spike sticking out of the shallows.

Managing to flounder onto a rotting, overturned boat beneath the dock's underbelly, he had curled up, trembling from shock and pain. Only minutes had passed when he heard the first screams shatter the air. And after that, the screams just hadn't stopped.

Maybe an hour later, the thud of hooves and boots. Shouting. The clang of swords.

When the fighting ceased, leaving behind a silence that almost felt worse, Orion had closed his eyes, too weak to cry for help, too scared that the wrong people would find him. A cruel, vicious wind bit at him. The blood loss and pain left him feeble, shaking like a leaf.

He had begun to drift off, wondering if he would bleed out before anyone would even find him.

And what if you do? a voice had asked. His eyes snapped open. He didn't want to die. *Hold on*, another voice whispered, far away and lovely, soothing his pain. *Just a little longer.*

"Orion?" yet another called, growing louder. "*Orion*!"

Only when he was being heaved out from underneath the dock by a pair of strong, warm arms did he realize the voice was not in his head. "Papa?"

"Orion," his father had rasped into his hair, hugging him so tightly that it became hard to breathe. "Yes, I've got you now. I'm here."

Another voice. "He's bleeding."

"Stay still," his father coaxed, placing a palm on Orion's torso. "It hurts, love, I know, but you have to stay still," he murmured as Orion hissed and squirmed. "Haelein." Orion's shivers died away as his wound closed up. He buried his face into his father's neck, too numb to do anything but breathe. "I saw your fishing rod floating in the lake. The Immortals were kind," his father whispered before tipping his head skyward. "Thank you. *Thank you.*"

"Theodore," a severe, female voice called out. "Did you find a survivor?"

His father clutched Orion tighter. "My son."

"Let's see him."

The slightest of hesitations from his father caused Orion to peek out from his little nook. He found himself face-to-face with an unfamiliar woman, her mouth pressed into a hard line. "Orion, this is Carlotta Garringsford, General of the Royal Axarian Army."

Garringsford's eyes narrowed. Then softened. "No tears."

"I don't cry," Orion declared tremulously.

A hint of a smile ghosted the woman's lips. "You must be very brave." She considered him, then looked at his father. "There's nothing and no one left for him here." Orion bristled, but his father remained expressionless. "We're regrouping in the square. Bring him along."

His father's jaw dropped. "Now?"

The general's nostrils flared. "Yes, now."

At that, his father's mask cracked. Since the last time he had visited, Orion now noticed the new lines wrinkling his brow. "But they're gathering the dead—you can't possibly mean to say that you … you want him to see … Carlotta, he's merely a child—"

"Papa?" Orion had interrupted in a whisper. "Where are Mama and Sophie?"

"Your mother protected Sophie with her life," his father growled. "She would have protected you with her life, too, because she loved you with everything she had. Do you understand, Orion?" His voice cracked. "She loved you with *everything* she had."

Orion bit his lip. "They're gone. Forever. Aren't they?"

His father nodded, eyes glistening. "But," he went on, placing a finger on Orion's heart and tapping it, "they will always be here."

General Garringsford put a hand on his head, surprisingly gentle. "What do you stand for, Orion Galashiels?" she asked him softly. He blinked up at her, uncomprehending, clinging tighter onto his father. "Do you want to protect the ones you love?"

He nodded slowly. "I'm going to be a Guardian one day. Just like Papa."

"Do you know what happens if you fail? If you make a mistake? If you trust the wrong people?" When he shook his head, she sighed. "Then you must be shown."

Orion hugged his father's neck as Garringsford led them into the square. He heard the wailing and the sobbing before he saw the crowds of hysterical survivors gathered around the bodies.

His father knelt beside two bodies draped in a single white sheet, laid out side by side. The outline of one was so tiny compared to the other. Orion wasn't naive. He knew that the bodies belonged to his mother and Sophie.

And then his father had lifted the sheet.

All thought flew out of Orion's head as he stared and stared. He realized in that moment that knowing and seeing were two very different things. He saw everything in flashes—Mother's crooked neck, Sophie's little necklace of blood, and above all, their stillness. Orion had heard that death could look like sleep, but he couldn't believe anyone would make that mistake.

He had still been staring when a horse thundered into the square, nearly trampling him. A distraught soldier leapt off its back and ran straight for Garringsford.

"General," the soldier panted, her eyes wide. The general raised her brow in question. "The four recruits, ma'am. They've disappeared. We've been looking for over an hour and we can't find them—"

The color drained from Garringsford's face. "What do you mean?" she snapped.

"We can't find them—"

"Simmons," Garringsford ordered, voice like the crack of a whip. A soldier standing by the fountain rushed to her side. "Take your squad and search the north quarter for the boys." Simmons whistled and signaled to her squad. They took off at a run. "Knoll, take east quarter—"

"General, ma'am," the soldier who had brought the message cried, "we already looked, we couldn't—"

"Then you didn't look hard enough!" Garringsford exploded, eyes blazing with rage. The soldier flinched and nodded. "Your squad has south quarter. Go, damn it!" she shouted. "Theodore, you're with me."

Orion's father stiffened. "But my son—"

"At least you know your son is alive!"

Her outburst echoed like a cannon shot in the abrupt silence of the square. Something passed over his father's face, and he placed Orion on the ground. "Orion," he said, crouching down eye-level to speak to him. "You stay here, okay? With Marc and Jan and the other soldiers. They'll look after you until I come back."

"Yes, Papa."

"Did both Alex and Micah come?" Orion heard his father ask as he and the general broke into a run.

"Yes, Immortals help me," came Garringsford's hoarse answer. "Along with those two others—Leila and Silas. Not one of them is older than fifteen. I *told* Tristan they weren't ready, damn it all to hell—"

They found them an hour later.

But only one still lived.

Two had been stabbed, and two had been drowned—though the soldiers managed to resuscitate Silas after dragging him out of the water.

When Garringsford knelt beside the corpses in the square, all the emotion had vanished from her face. Orion stood across from her, holding his father's hand. The light had gone out of the general's eyes, leaving them as lifeless as the bodies of her two sons.

Then something much darker manifested in her empty gaze.

"This is all Tristan's fault," the general whispered, fixated on the blossoms of red scattered across Micah's body, one hand gripping Alex's limp fingers.

"Watch your words," Theodore warned quietly. "The fault belongs to the hirelings, and the hirelings alone."

"No," Garringsford had said, tears streaming down her face. "This is on Tristan. He killed your wife. Your daughter. My sons. All of these people." She dropped Alex's hand and stood. "And he will pay the price."

Orion never did find out what price Garringsford had made Tristan pay, if she had followed through on her promise at all. And yes, the general would certainly make all of their lives back at the palace a little more hellish those next few years, but the two of them had shared their own hell that day, and neither would ever forget it.

"Orion. *Orion.* Let's go."

Orion blinked, surfacing from the memory to find Asterin looking up at him expectantly. She and the others were waiting below. He cast a final glance at the corpses and slid down the hill to join them.

"How did the bodies get here?" Rose asked in a hush. "Did the demon gather them in a grave for a reason? Maybe—"

"It's a killing pit," said Asterin brusquely. Rose fell silent. "The demon brought them here for execution." Her back was straight and her movements sure and steady when she took out the omnistone and held her palms up toward the dirt.

Nothing happened.

Orion's heart cracked. Asterin put up such a strong front, but something inside her had broken.

Then the earth started to move, mounds of dirt easing forward into the pit. Asterin turned, hands falling back to her sides as Quinlan took over the task of burying her people when she could not.

"Thank you," she whispered.

His only answer was a small nod.

Orion sent a prayer to the Immortals once the grave had filled, a small part of him wondering why he bothered, in the face of this slaughter—just as he had wondered all those years ago. Twice now, the Immortals had failed. Had chosen not to act.

"What now?" Rose asked.

Asterin stared into the shadowed thicket of trees rising on the other side of the grave. "We find Harry."

Luna shifted nervously. "Do you think he's even still alive?"

"We have to hope," Asterin said.

"Is it really safe?" Eadric asked.

"Well, given that those stains are still wet," Rose said grimly, pointing at a black smear along the ground, "the demon likely struck in broad daylight. I don't think we'll be safe until it's dead. We'd better find this Harry before dark."

"It's too dangerous," Quinlan said, shaking his head. "What if we run into the demon?"

Asterin swung Amoux savagely, the steel whistling through the air. "Isn't that the idea?"

"Asterin," Quinlan warned. "No."

She stared at him. And then she breezed past him toward the thickening gloom. "Fine. We'll just go without you then."

Quinlan's fists clenched. "Asterin! Get back here!"

Orion *felt* her anger spike, as tangible as fire.

The princess whirled around. "You do not have the right to tell me what I can and cannot do, Quinlan Holloway. This is my duty. I will *not* let anything or anyone stop me from defeating the demon that took the lives of hundreds of innocent people—my people. And if I fail to avenge them, I do not deserve the throne."

Quinlan faltered. "I didn't … I just meant that—"

"And furthermore, let me remind you that you're here officially as a soldier serving *my* kingdom, and therefore under my command, prince or no. You will obey my word or return to the palace. The choice is yours. But *you* do not, under any circumstance, rule *me*." With that, Asterin spun on her heel and strode away. The dense foliage of the forest swallowed her in darkness in less than a second.

Orion didn't hesitate for even a heartbeat before following her.

CHAPTER EIGHTEEN

Quinlan could only stare after Asterin as she vanished into the trees' embrace. The others departed in her wake, and even their horses spared him pitying looks. He longed to call her back, but his pride smothered his voice.

A hand squeezed his shoulder. "I'll let you sulk in peace," Rose said with a knowing look as she, too, turned her back on him. "Till 'morrow, cousin dearest."

"Till 'morrow," he echoed.

As their footsteps faded away, Quinlan slumped onto a chunk of broken limestone, bracing his elbows on his knees.

Pathetic, came the taunting laugh of Gavin Holloway. *You are pathetic.*

"Go away," Quinlan hissed at his father's voice, squeezing his eyes shut.

Look how easily she broke you. Pathetic!

"I'm not!" he roared to nobody. His horse skittered back, tail flicking, but all else remained still. "I'm not," he repeated raggedly.

A clump of bushes rustled a few feet away from the dirt path Asterin had followed into the forest. Quinlan's hand shot to the dagger at his thigh.

Lord Conrye emerged from the bushes, the soft thuds of his massive paws nearly soundless. The wolf came to a halt before him.

The first time Quinlan had seen the God of Ice was in the Eradorian palace's Throne Hall, the day after his father had killed King Bernard. However, unlike the sculpture that adorned the ceiling of the palace of Axaria's Throne Hall, it had been Lord Tidus's weathered face that greeted him at the forefront of the sculpture, as the powers of the House of the Serpent descended from the God of Water. Similar sculptures of the Council of Immortals could be found in the Throne Halls of all the nine kingdoms, with each House's god or goddess featured in the center. But no stone monument could ever come close to the actual weight of an Immortal's ancient presence, which Quinlan now found himself bearing.

They stared at one another for an uncomfortable minute—uncomfortable for Quinlan, at least. He tried not to squirm beneath the intensity of Lord Conrye's gaze.

Of course, he caved first and blurted out a nervous, "Nice to see you again."

Your sulking is childish.

Quinlan blinked. The god's words rang through his mind, clearer than if he had spoken them aloud. His father's voice was nothing but mist in comparison. He opened his mouth to defend himself, but the wolf cut him off.

There are no excuses, Lord Conrye growled in a tone so severe that Quinlan couldn't help but flinch. *Act like the fine warrior you have proven yourself to be.*

Quinlan scowled and ran a hand through his hair. "Did you seriously come here just to lecture me? You disappeared quickly enough back in Aldville."

Conrye snorted in displeasure. *The Council called me back to the Immortal Realm. And besides … we are not supposed to meddle with the lives of mortals.*

"Why return, then?" Quinlan asked.

Princess Asterin is a fine warrior as well. She helped train you back at the palace, yet you look down upon her.

Quinlan snorted. "I most certainly do not."

Your actions speak otherwise, Conrye insisted, tail twitching. *And the demon … you are right. Perhaps it just might be in the forest, lying in wait. What happens if it takes Asterin and the others by surprise? What use are your powers if not to protect, Quinlan Holloway?*

He froze, the question triggering a deluge of memories that flooded into his mind. His father, leaning over him with an expression twisted in disgust. His father, kicking him in the stomach, over and over, while Quinlan cupped a bird in hands smaller than the bird itself, refusing to kill it, protecting it even when he couldn't protect himself. *Especially* when he couldn't protect himself. His father had taught him that his powers were meant to manipulate, to hurt, to kill. Anything else was a waste. Quinlan swallowed. "I …"

You are not your father, Conrye snapped. *The powers you possess are not just a coincidence, or some accidental gift. They come with enormous responsibility—to protect those who need protecting, which you have done all your life—until now, of all times. Look at yourself. Are you a coward?*

"No," Quinlan growled with a ferocity that caused his horse to whicker beside him.

Then why are you running away when the others need you most? When he didn't reply, Conrye cocked his furry head to the side and asked, *How far would you go to help Princess Asterin? Could you teach her to wield magic without the use of the omnistone?*

He frowned, taken aback at the change of topic. "I—yes, I suppose so, if she lets me."

It will not be easy, the Immortal agreed, *and time is short. You must teach her.* The wolf looked to the sky. *With what lies ahead, I fear that her reliance on the stone may be her undoing.*

Quinlan's stomach twisted. "And what lies ahead, exactly?"

That, I cannot say for sure. But with the Immortal Realm in unrest, dark times are coming for both Asterin and the world as you know it. If the stone fails her and the demon attacks …

"Do you know where the demon is?" he asked.

I do not. Unlike that lesser wyvern, this demon is extremely powerful—powerful enough that it can mask its dark scent and aura, even from me. Conrye's eyes glinted. *It could be anywhere … it could be attacking the others at this very moment, and neither of us would even know.*

Quinlan's blood ran cold at the thought. He looked toward the thicket of trees in grim apprehension, the leaves rustling like phantom music. Then he grabbed his horse's reins.

Conrye dipped his head. *I must leave you here. Hurry. There is no time to waste.*

Quinlan gave Lord Conrye a final nod of thanks and guided his horse through the grass that separated Corinthe from the woods. When he reached the dirt path, marked by the ghostly prints of the others, he glanced back toward the God of Ice—but no trace of the wolf save for the mist in the clearing remained.

With a sigh, Quinlan plunged into the forest.

He had a princess to find.

CHAPTER NINETEEN

Asterin's blood boiled as she swung Amoux in a vicious arc, brutally hacking through the lower boughs of a pine tree. Lux snorted beside her, shaking a stray twig free from his mane.

"Northeast from here," Eadric said from the back of their procession, checking Garringsford's map.

"How much farther?" Luna asked over the hum of cicadas. She hopped over a rotting log. "The sun is already starting to set."

"I'd say another half hour, what with all of these blasted branches."

"I don't know," Rose remarked, ducking through the passage Asterin had created. "I feel like Her Royal Highness is doing a pretty decent job of clearing our way."

"I feel like we should be covering our tracks," Orion said.

Rose waved a hand. "No worries. Quinlan will take care of it once he finishes moping around."

Asterin halted so suddenly that Orion stepped on her heels. She whipped the omnistone out of her pocket and flung her arms up into the air with an enraged yell. The hundreds of branches, leaves, and chunks of wood littering the ground behind them rose as one, surging violently into the air like an army of wasps, and jabbed themselves back into place to make the trees behind them whole again.

She panted, expression fixed in a furious scowl, the outraged caws of crows and the *fwip fwip* of wings filling the air. Only when she turned around to see if her magic had worked did she notice her friends' stares—but they weren't directed at her.

"What?" she snarled. "What are you looking at?"

"Me," a voice called from above. Quinlan dropped down from the forked limbs of a maple tree ahead of them, hitting the ground in a low crouch.

Asterin swiveled back around to find his horse trailing behind Orion's mare. "How …"

Quinlan strode forward, stopping less than a foot away from where she stood. "I'm here to apologize." He squinted. "Also, there's a caterpillar in your hair."

She punched him in the jaw so hard that her knuckles split open. Quinlan recoiled, yowling, while Orion cheered her on and Luna yelled at the Guardian to shut up. Eadric and Rose just stood off to the side, heads shaking, with identical expressions of parental exasperation on their faces.

Asterin muttered "*Haelein*," and elbowed Quinlan aside, her raw and stinging skin already knitting itself back together as she stormed past.

"Hey, I said I was sorry!" he cried, cradling his face, nearly tripping over his own feet in his haste to follow her. She quickened her pace, but his hand latched onto her wrist and forced her to face him. His brow creased with genuine regret. "I mean it. Truly. You're right. It wasn't my place to tell you what to do. I'm sorry."

"All right."

His face lit up in a full-dimpled grin. "I'm forgiven?"

She shoved him into a bush—hard—and jogged away.

He was up on his feet in no time, spluttering indignantly. "Princess Asterin! Your Royal Highness!" he called, loping after her. "The most radiant of them all! The most dazzling! Coruscating!"

Orion smacked his forehead. "Describe *her*, damn it, not a *candle*!"

"Who uses *coruscating* to describe a candle?" Rose wondered.

"Scintillating!" Quinlan shouted.

"Shut up!" Against her better judgment, Asterin broke into a run, but thanks to Quinlan's stupid long legs, it only took him seconds to gain on her. Before she knew it, she was sprinting at full speed, struggling to fight down the hysterical giggles escaping her lips. Branches whipped outward as she tore through the trees, practically blind.

"Splendiferous!" Quinlan shrilled.

Asterin finally burst, howling with laughter—and still running as fast as her legs could carry her, her lungs burning and tears streaming down her face.

But then her stomach plummeted, her laughter turning into a scream as something seized her ankles and yanked her feet out from beneath her. Her vision reeled as she jerked into the air, pine needles stabbing at her from every direction. She heard Quinlan's startled shout, and after the world stopped spinning, she found him dangling upside down beside her from the next branch over. Her eyes landed on the thick ropes wrapped around both of their ankles.

Quinlan glanced to the ground, some thirty feet below. "Well, that was unexpected."

Asterin folded her arms over her chest. "You think?" A fall from this height would shatter their bones. "What now?"

He cocked his head and summoned flames to his fingertips. "We free ourselves."

Asterin realized his intention. "Quinlan, don't you *dare*—"

Quinlan ignited the ropes in an explosion of heat. Asterin screamed curses as the rope flashed white, spitting sparks back at them instead of burning. He made a noise of surprise and extinguished the flames.

"Are you out of your damned mind?" Asterin spluttered.

Quinlan frowned at the ropes and said, "They must have been cast with some sort of reflective spell."

"Your Highness?" a voice called from below before Asterin could snap at him again.

Eadric. "Wait!" she shouted. "Don't come any closer—"

A flurry of movement and several screams later, Eadric, Luna, and Rose had joined them in the trees, blinking and bewildered. Random limbs poked through the gaps of a thick net, their bodies tangled together and swaying back and forth in the slight breeze.

Eadric made the mistake of looking down. His face took on a greenish tinge. "Oh."

"Whose hand is that?" Rose demanded, the net rocking to the side as she jostled around. "Get it off my chest immediately."

Eadric flushed scarlet. "What? Oh, sorry." A boot connected with the back of his head and smushed his face into the net. "*Ow*!"

"Oops," Luna said sweetly. "My bad."

"Is Orion still down there?" Quinlan asked. "We have to warn him about the trap."

As if on cue, Orion came into view with their horses in tow. "Hello?"

"Orion!" Asterin yelled. "Don't move from where you're standing!"

He froze, slowly lifting his eyes to meet hers. His jaw unhinged. "What in hell? How—" He cut himself off, whirling to the left. "Someone's coming."

"Well, don't just stand there, then!" she exclaimed, head throbbing from staying upside down for so long.

Orion threw his hands into the air. "But you told me not to move!"

"Just go!"

After another second of hesitation, he bolted away and dove behind a tree trunk.

"The horses," said Eadric.

"Leave them be," Quinlan said. "We're stuck here, anyway."

They heard a rustle and the foliage dangerously close to Orion's hiding spot parted to reveal a figure sporting a long wool coat. Even from afar, it was clear that he was a hunter—not least from the quiver on his back and the monstrous crossbow in his hand, but from the way he moved. Each precisely placed step reminded Asterin of a panther, lean muscles coiled with powerful tension. He ambled beneath them, silently, as if he had all the time in the world, and tipped his head to the sky to meet Asterin's stare, that very intimidating crossbow in his hands cocked and aimed straight at her heart.

Asterin swallowed. "Please tell me that you're Harry."

A low chuckle, as warm as aged whiskey. "Indeed I am." The richness of his voice lingered in the air. "And you wouldn't happen to be Princess Asterin?"

She laughed. "Thank the Immortals, yes."

He looked them over, puzzled. "I was told that there would be six of you. Did something happen …?"

"Oh, no. Orion is … somewhere over there. Orion, you can come out now!" Asterin called. There was a prolonged silence. "Orion?"

"Sure, just … give me a minute," came Orion's muffled answer.

"What's the matter?" Asterin demanded.

"I'm—I'm stuck."

"*Stuck*?" she echoed. "How?"

"There's this … never mind. Just a moment—" Fabric ripped loudly, and Orion cursed.

"Would you like some help?" Harry asked politely.

"Actually, yeah, I think … yeah, that would be great, thanks."

Asterin strained to see, craning her neck as Harry walked behind the trunk of a nearby tree and out of view.

There was a crinkling noise and a surprised *oomph*, followed by a crack and more swearing.

Harry's voice floated up to them. "Move that knee a bit. May I—"

"Ow," Orion grunted. "Watch it."

"Immortals above," Harry said. More rustling. "Is that okay?"

"That's okay."

"I'm going to—"

Orion groaned. "Just do it."

"If you say so," Harry said. Another grunt. Asterin couldn't stand it anymore. She reached over, struggling to grab ahold of the nearest tree limb. Heaving herself up, she angled her body and whirled in a nauseating circle before finally managing to grab onto a limb of the next tree over. Now she could see farther. Her eyes zeroed into the murk behind the tree trunk.

The entire upper half of Orion's body was firmly lodged into a large hole at the base of the trunk, his posterior sticking high up into the air. Harry had his arms folded around the Guardian's waist, his chest pressing against Orion's back, trying desperately to haul him out.

"Immortals," Harry panted.

"Pull harder, you weak-armed pansy! Harder!"

"But your shirt—"

"Forget my shirt, just get me out of this stupid hole!"

"All right, all right!" Harry exclaimed. With a final tear of fabric,

Orion came tumbling out, profanities cascading freely from his mouth, mud clinging to his gracefully tousled hair. His chest was bare, exposing his sculpted torso.

"Well, hello there," Orion breathed, grinning coyly at Harry's stunned expression. "And thank you for your help."

"You're—you're welcome," Harry stammered while bending down to pick up his discarded crossbow, though his eyes seemed permanently glued to Orion's pectorals. Asterin could see Harry blush even from above.

"Nice to meet you," Orion said, holding out his hand. "Orion Galashiels, Royal Guardian of Princess Asterin."

Harry took the hand. "Harry." The two studied one another for a long moment, hands still joined, lost in their own universe.

"Hell-*o*-oo!" Rose interrupted at the top of her lungs. "Forgetting something?"

"Oh," Harry said, reddening even further. "Right, sorry."

Without warning, he lifted his crossbow in one swift motion and fired. The quarrel severed both ropes ensnaring Asterin and Quinlan, embedding itself in the tree trunk behind them with a *thwack*.

Asterin's scream caught in her throat as they fell together. Then Quinlan angled his body and shot toward her. He wrapped his arms around her waist and held her close, a mile-wide grin stretching across his face as his magic washed over them. She squeezed her eyes shut and clutched the front of his tunic for dear life. Her breath caught as a gust of wind caught them just before they crashed into the ground, their toes barely brushing the grass.

Quinlan searched her expression, his hands still clasped behind her. "Are you okay?"

She looked up from his chest. "You're the worst."

He winked. "Actually, I think I'm pretty amazing."

"Pretty, maybe. Amazing, not so much," she said, releasing his tunic. A surprised laugh escaped his lips. She raised an eyebrow. "Also, you can let go of me now."

He ducked his head and backed off just as a shriek followed by foul cursing pierced the air, scattering the birds in the trees. They looked up just in time to see three pairs of arms and legs flailing through the holes in the net now plummeting to the ground. Asterin summoned another blast of wind to cushion their fall. Eadric was still swearing as if his life depended on it when she and Quinlan hurried over to help haul the three of them out of the tangled mess of netting.

Eadric rolled onto his side with a groan and promptly vomited into the grass. Luna patted his back while making sympathetic noises. After his heaving ceased, he croaked, "Never again. Please."

Orion burst out from behind the tree trunk that he had gotten stuck in earlier and surveyed them. "Thank goodness!" he said, his blond curls damp with sweat, sticking to his forehead, and his pupils dilated to black moons. "Is everyone all right?"

Asterin frowned. "What were you doing back there?"

Before her Guardian could reply, however, Harry materialized from the other side of the trunk and cleared his throat. He straightened the lapels of his coat and bowed to her. "Your Royal Highness."

"Please," she said, "Asterin is just fine."

She took the opportunity to observe Harry from close up. He looked far younger than Asterin had guessed from his poise and the sound of his voice alone, with lovely dark-brown eyes and thick lashes crowned by wide brows, and an oval face framed by a soft sheaf of wavy hair the same shade as roasted chestnuts.

He brushed away a thin trickle of perspiration slipping down the coppery skin of his forehead and shot her a grin.

At first glance, especially with that warm smile, Harry appeared gentle, even harmless—but something about his presence made Asterin's every nerve tingle with caution, and her hand almost twitched toward Amoux.

"I apologize for the traps," Harry went on to say, "but with the demon rampaging about, I'm sure you understand my vigilance. I'm impressed that you managed to set off the net, though. It can only be triggered by a substantial amount of weight—say, a certain demon. Or … apparently three people simultaneously walking onto it."

That made her laugh. "We are indeed a talented bunch." Then she remembered Corinthe and her smile faded. "I don't suppose you knew Corinthe was attacked?"

Harry shifted uneasily. "How awful. Well, we'd better get moving before night falls," he said. "Shall we?"

Asterin nodded. "Lead the way."

As they guided their horses after Harry, Quinlan snuck up to her side. When she ignored him, he tried to play it off by stroking Lux's mane, but the Iphovien steed almost bit his hand off. He gave up his guise. "Listen, Asterin, I'm still sorry, by the way. I really am. I know that you're perfectly capable on your own, but … it's just that you're a lot more powerful than you think, and if you only had proper training—"

"Training?" Asterin cut in with a scowl. "I've had tutors all my life."

"And did those tutors know what being omnifinitied was like?"

Asterin mulled that over. "I suppose not." She paused. "Wait, are *you* offering to train me?"

His lips quirked. "What if I am? Would you accept?"

Her nose wrinkled. "I don't know."

"Come on, admit that you need me." He leaned in close to whisper, "Desperately."

She scoffed. But then she let herself think about it for a minute. It *would* be nice to train with someone who actually knew what it meant to be omnifinitied.

Asterin exhaled. "Fine. Thank you. For your *help*," she emphasized.

He smirked and then looked over to where Orion and Harry forged ahead at the front of the group. Harry was holding Buttercup's reins for Orion. "Hey, can I ask you something? Was he chosen?"

"What?"

"Orion. To be your Guardian."

Asterin nodded and explained. "His bloodline was, two centuries ago. With every new royal child born into the House of the Wolf, there is a Guardian. Orion's father was my father's Guardian. My mother married into our House, so she doesn't have one. Garringsford was assigned to protect her. Usually, there are fallback Guardians, siblings or cousins in case there are … complications. Orion had a baby sister, but they—his sister and mother, I mean—were killed in a raid. Nearly his whole town was annihilated. It was the worst Axarian massacre in over two hundred years." Her voice softened. "He never talks about it, but I think Corinthe reminded him of it."

Quinlan worried at his lip. "What about his father? Is he also …?"

"Oh, no. Theodore was given honorable discharge after Orion came of age." A leaf circled lazily above them and landed in Quinlan's hair. Asterin had to resist the urge to pluck it out and feel those dark locks between her fingers. She slapped herself mentally and went on. "Theodore lives in the west residential sector, now. Even though my father died a natural death, it was hard on him." She hesitated. "Well, as natural as an incurable illness could be."

"I heard about that," Quinlan said.

"It was some hopeless disease that no one seemed to be able to cure. Priscilla scoured the continent for healers, but nothing helped." Asterin sighed. "I think it was a mercy, really, when he finally passed. I remember … I was still young, but I remember. They wouldn't let me see him in the last few days, but, leading up to them, he'd always smile and laugh when I came to visit him. I could see the pain in his eyes, though. He tried to hide it from me … but for months, the illness had been rotting him from the inside out." She recalled the wracking coughs that had shaken his feeble, skeletal body, the sallowness of his skin. "My father was a big man, but that illness reduced him to nothing but bones." She turned her face up to the canopy of leaves, greens melting to gray as the last of the daylight dwindled to dusk. "I was glad when it was over for him. I didn't want him to be in pain."

Quinlan's shoulder brushed hers, his brow furrowed. "I'm sorry."

She huffed a laugh. "I've never heard you apologize as many times as you have today. I call that progress."

He let out a *harrumph*, yet she got the vague sense that he was secretly pleased by the comment.

"We're here," Harry called, putting an end to any further conversation.

They filed after the hunter down a narrow dirt trail, passing beneath the arch of two entwined pine boughs. Asterin paused, nearly causing Rose to crash into her. *What if this is a trap?* some small part of her wondered. But then Lux nudged her forward, puffing a cloud of hot breath into her hair, so she ducked beneath the trees and stepped into a large clearing basked in the golden glow of a dozen wicker torches.

Her eyes widened at the log cottage sitting in the middle of the clearing, lined with quaint little windows and a bright-red door. Bushy basswood trees and spindly hemlocks towered around the clearing in a near-perfect circle, crowded so densely together that they formed an impenetrable fence of needles and branches. The evening dewdrops clinging to their verdant leaves glittered in the torchlight as the six of them followed Harry up a cobbled pathway, bordered on both sides by grass dotted with white primroses. Tangles of wildflowers and ivy snaked along the eaves and the columns of the front porch in invitation, and a well-tended garden was fenced off to the side, a small barn resting behind it.

"Home sweet home," Harry announced with a grand flourish, bounding up the porch steps. "We used to keep cows and sheep in the barn, so there are pens for your horses. You can tie them out here for now while you get settled in." He reached down the collar of his shirt and pulled out an ornate iron key on a leather cord before unlocking the door and beckoning them in. They murmured their thanks as they passed into the snug foyer, sighing collectively at the rush of warmth.

The interior of the cottage was spacious, more so than it had appeared on the outside, and complete with a living room, a dining room, and a kitchen. Each room had a door that connected to the foyer. A staircase on their right led up to what Asterin supposed must have been bedrooms.

Orion bounded eagerly onto the large, worn sofa in the living room, moaning in contentment as he sank into the cushions. "Glorious."

Rose collapsed beside him and stretched her arms over her head with a sigh.

Harry turned to them with a pleased smile, his hands clasped behind his back. "Please make yourselves at home."

"This is an enormous cottage," Eadric said. "Fit for an entire family." A tiny note of suspicion edged its way into his voice as he asked, "No one else lives here with you?"

"Not anymore, no." Harry ambled over to the fireplace, feeding firewood into the lively blaze and giving it a few pokes.

"Not anymore?" Luna asked, flopping down onto the paneled wood floor and warming her fingers. Despite the arrival of spring, a chill hung in the air, a lingering promise that winter would return.

"The woodland lifestyle isn't for everyone," Harry said with a shrug, propping the iron poker off to the side. "You all rest here, and I'll go and bring the horses to the back."

"There's no need," said Asterin. "We'll handle it." When Eadric started toward the door, she waved him away. "And by *we* I meant *Quinlan*," she amended. "You keep Luna company."

Eadric grinned. "That, I can accept." He settled himself onto the floor beside Luna, slinging an arm around her shoulders. She rested her head on his chest and yawned.

Quinlan rolled his eyes but trailed after Asterin toward the front door without complaint.

Harry followed them into the foyer. "I'm going to grab some blankets from the closet," he said, one hand resting on the banister of the staircase. To the others, he called, "Let me know if you need anything else!"

Orion propped his legs onto the coffee table. "Thanks, Harry!"

"Yes," Eadric added. "Thank you." Asterin didn't miss her captain's eyes tracking Harry's retreat up the stairs, his expression darkening.

"Oh, actually, there's just one thing . . ." Harry paused in his ascent, ducking down to address them. Eadric's shoulders tensed as Harry caught sight of his expression, in place for just a second too long. Their host looked away, shifting and running an uncertain hand along the back of his neck. Eadric flushed. "There—there aren't quite enough beds for everyone. Forgive me, but someone will probably have to sleep on the sofa."

"No need to apologize," Asterin assured him. "We'll sort it out."

Her mind whirled with plans as she coaxed Lux into the barn. The pens were smaller than the palace stalls, but they could let the horses out in the morning to graze in the clearing. She brushed down Lux while Quinlan unsaddled Eadric's horse. They worked in comfortable silence, hanging up gear along the barn walls.

Asterin glanced up to find Quinlan smiling at her. "Stop that." His smile only widened. "Why is it so hard for you to follow orders?"

He crossed his right ankle behind his left and tilted his head. The sky had darkened, but it only made him look softer, smoothed out his edges. "I can follow orders." He smirked and lowered his voice to that lovely velvety whisper. "Just tell me what you want. Anything at all."

It was exactly what she hoped he would say. "Oh?" Her grin of triumph caused his smirk to falter slightly. "In that case, I order you to accept the fate of sleeping on the sofa."

Quinlan exhaled and trudged out of the barn. "Well played, Your Highness. *Well played.*"

CHAPTER TWENTY

The silence of the woods at night felt otherworldly to Eadric. Here, the sigh of pines and the whisper of wind along the eaves replaced the faraway shouts of patrol guards and the gurgle of pipes beneath the floors. The occasional wild howl rolled through the twilight, hungry and alone—so was it strange that a part of Eadric would rather surrender himself to the perils of the forest than confine himself within these walls?

Then Luna nestled closer to his chest and he told himself that everything would be all right so long as she was at his side. Almost everyone else had already gone to bed, but he was more than content to spend the rest of the night in front of the fire with her snug in his arms, although sitting on the hard oak floor had caused him to completely lose the feeling in his legs an hour or so ago.

He adjusted his position, wincing, and watched as Luna gazed into the fire. "This is nice, isn't it?" At the palace, their duties constantly got in the way of seeing one another. She hummed distantly. He brushed his thumb along her jaw. "What's on your mind, darling?"

She sighed and shot a glance at Quinlan, who had passed out cold on the sofa behind them. "I shouldn't be here."

He frowned. "What do you mean?"

"I'm not like the rest of you. I'm not powerful."

"So? That didn't stop you before."

"I know, I just ..." She laughed to herself. "Never mind, it's silly."

He tucked a lock of hair behind her ear. "No, tell me."

She looked away. He waited patiently, until at last she spoke. "Magic comes to all of you so easily, but I've always felt like something is *blocking* it from me." She bit her lip in frustration as she searched for the words. "Like a locked gate that I don't have the key to. I hoped that leaving the palace for the first time in my life might have changed that somehow."

Eadric frowned. "Like how?"

"Well, powerful parents usually make powerful children, don't they? And since I never figured out who my parents were ... I just—I just so badly wanted to be like all of you," she admitted softly. "And there's a part of me that keeps thinking that I could be, if only I had that key." She stopped and shook her head with a rueful smile. "Listen to me. I sound crazy."

"Not to me," Rose said. Luna and Eadric jumped, neither of them having heard her reenter. She had a towel wrapped around her head and smelled of lemon soap. Folding her legs beneath her with all the grace befitting a queen, she sat across from them on the other side of the coffee table. "Apologies. I didn't mean to startle you." She tilted her head at Luna. "But you should always trust your magic. Trust how you feel it should flow. If you think there's something more, something to unlock, maybe you're right. One of my professors at the Academia Principalis always said that magic is as much a part of you as any organ or bone. When something doesn't feel right, it probably isn't."

"If you don't mind me asking, what was the Academia like?" Eadric asked eagerly. The Eradorian school was the most prestigious magic academy in the world and internationally renowned for its contributions to the study of magic. Located within the inner city of Eradoris, admittance was nothing short of a miracle. It surprised him a little that Rose hadn't just studied with tutors as Asterin had, but he supposed that if the kingdom's future queen had wished to attend the academy, it probably hadn't been too much of a struggle to dredge up an acceptance letter.

"Brutal." And then, cheerfully, she added, "I got expelled."

"Expelled?" Luna blurted. "You?"

Rose nodded and began tracing shapes into the floorboards with her index finger. "I helped my classmate pass his end-of-year exam. Twice, actually. I should have been expelled the first time around, but my mother gave them hell over it. And I was one of their best students, so I was given a second chance … which I botched the following year. But I didn't care. Consequences be damned," she growled, startling them with her ferocity. "The examination system is merciless—the less powerful are at a severe disadvantage, no matter their other skills."

"Well, it *is* a school for magic …" Eadric couldn't help but point out.

"Magic is much more than just strength," Rose said. "It's about patience, focus, and keeping an open mind to all the possibilities." She snorted quietly. Fondly. "Not that he was great at any of that, either."

"Who?" Luna asked.

Rose's shoulders tensed. "My—my classmate." Her nails dug into the floor. "He was expelled, but I managed to get him a place to stay in the inner city anyway."

Luna's eyebrow arched. "You did all of that for a classmate?"

Rose ducked her head. "That's all I was to him, apparently, so … yes. In any case, I learned a lot from that experience, and to be honest, I think I ended up better off than I would have if I had stayed. Knowledge can be shared, but it is purest when sought."

"Why couldn't you just let him fail, though?" Eadric asked.

"Failure is unacceptable at the Academia," Rose replied, voice flat. "People who fail not only face automatic expulsion, but banishment from the city. That's why I had to help him." She flicked a bit of cinder off her boot. "And, unfortunately for me, I would do it all over again for him in a heartbeat."

A sudden chill brushed against Eadric's skin at the unforgiving ire in her expression.

Luna, Immortals bless her, yawned loudly, breaking the tension with her usual sweet smile. "Well, I'm beat. Shall we get ready for bed?"

Eadric smothered the fire with a few shovelfuls of ash, and the three of them trudged up the stairs, leaving Quinlan to his sleepy mutterings on the sofa—something about dueling with carrots. They kept the same sleeping arrangements as they had in Aldville, except Rose had the room at the end of the hall to herself. Eadric could hear Orion snoring softly from within their room. Luna tiptoed past him to the room she shared with Asterin, next to his—the door was ajar, but the lights were out. From Harry's room across the hall came only silence.

Just as Rose reached for her doorknob, the question that had been burning on Eadric's tongue since before they had even left the palace finally slipped out. "Why are you helping us, Your Majesty? You and Quinlan?"

Rose's hand stilled on the knob, her back to them. She didn't answer for a long while and Eadric wondered if he had overstepped.

At last, she released a heavy sigh. "As Queen of Eradore, it is my duty to protect my kingdom and its people at all costs. All I can tell you is that by being here, I am trying to fulfill that duty." She turned to face him and Luna. "Nothing is certain. All we know is, as the only heir to the Axarian throne, Asterin must survive. She is fair and kind, and her people *like* her. That alone could make all the difference. In times of great difficulty, Asterin Faelenhart will be a star in the darkness for not only the people of her own kingdom, but for people everywhere. They will look to her as a leader—as their ruler."

Eadric hadn't the slightest idea how to respond to that—but Luna only smiled. "With all due respect, Your Majesty, we already knew that."

CHAPTER TWENTY-ONE

"Two teams," Asterin declared the next morning, refreshed and ready to avenge her kingdom. "We'll split up into two teams to hunt down the demon. That way everyone on duty will be as well-rested and alert as possible."

Orion's eyes followed the princess as she paced back and forth along the length of the living room. Except for Eadric, the rest of them, including Harry, lounged about on the sofa and the floor. The captain had chosen to lean against the wall beside the fireplace, gaze flicking to Harry every time the hunter so much as moved a muscle.

"Even though it might have relocated after attacking Corinthe," Asterin went on, "chances are that it is still living somewhere nearby. So unless we receive reports indicating otherwise, we'll search every inch of this damned forest if we have to." She punctuated her statement by slamming her fist into her palm.

Orion picked at a loose thread on the hem of his shirt, gave up, and let his head fall back against the sofa. "So … what? Are we going to pick names out of a hat?"

Asterin shot him a withering glare. "I was thinking more by skill set. Quinlan will lead the first team, and you'll lead the second."

"What?" Orion blurted. "Me?"

Rose nodded her approval, tapping her fingernails on the coffee table. "And ideally, each team would have a strong healer, correct? As in, you and me?"

"Exactly," Asterin said.

Rose went silent for a few seconds. And then she smiled innocently. "I'll be on Orion's team."

Luna stood from her perch on the sofa arm at Orion's left. "Asterin, I want to be on your team," she said. "I mean, Quinlan's team. And you. Eadric can be on Orion's team."

"Hold on," said Eadric, pushing off the mantel. "That makes no sense."

Asterin's brow raised while Luna sat back down. "What do you mean?"

"Well ..." Eadric trailed off. "Orion and I are supposed to guard you."

"No, you're supposed to help me slay the demon," Asterin replied. "I'll be perfectly fine on my own."

With Quinlan, Orion couldn't help but think. He looked up to find the Eradorian staring at him expectantly, jaw taut with tension, as if he could read Orion's bitter thoughts.

You ... you still don't trust me. At all.

Since Aldville, Orion hadn't been able to shake off those words. And the truth was that he *still* didn't trust Quinlan completely—but he did know, without a doubt, that Quinlan would do anything to protect Asterin. And that between the two of them ... the Eradorian could protect Asterin better. Orion died a little on the inside at the self-admission, but Aldville had proved that. *Not everything is about you, Orion*, Rose's voice reminded him. And she was right—because in the end, it was always Asterin that mattered most, not his pride.

So when Eadric opened his mouth to argue, Orion cut him off while keeping his eyes firmly on Quinlan. "All right, then. I guess you're with me, Captain Covington."

Surprise flickered across Quinlan's features, along with a little bit of suspicion, but Orion couldn't blame him for that.

Eadric whipped toward him. "Orion, what are you—"

"It's like our princess said," Orion interrupted. "She'll be perfectly fine on her own." He exhaled and turned to Quinlan with the most threatening glare he could muster. "Hey, fireface. As team captains, it's our responsibility to protect our charges. If anything happens to either Asterin or Luna, I'll rip out your innards and string them up on Harry's porch for decoration."

The corner of Quinlan's mouth twitched. "I could say the same to you about my cousin."

Harry raised a tentative hand. Even the small movement caused his shirt to strain against that broad chest. "Excuse me, but I'd rather not have any bodily organs hanging from my porch."

"No offense, Harry, but it really isn't your decision," Orion said. "You *do* get to decide between my team and Quinlan's team, however."

"That is," Asterin cut in, "if Harry would like to be a part of this at all, which he may absolutely opt against."

"Nonsense," Harry said. Orion couldn't help but admire the confident puff of his chest. "I know these woods better than anyone."

Orion bit his lip, failing to restrain a grin. "Well, that's convenient. I have no sense of direction."

"I can be of use to you, then," Harry said a little too quickly. His face flushed a delectable shade of pink.

Orion's grin widened to a mile. "Oh, yes. I'm sure your knowledge of the woods will be *very* useful."

"Immortals have mercy," Eadric mumbled. Rose stifled a snort of laughter.

"Then we're done here," Asterin concluded, oblivious, and clapped her hands. "Our team goes out first. We'll rotate every day so the other team can rest as well as keep an eye on the immediate vicinity. Notify the other team if you find a lead, but ultimately assess the situation and make your own decisions. The moment one of us sets eyes on it, there is no chance in hell we let that demon escape." Orion shivered at the ice that crept into her tone. "We either slay it or die trying. Is that understood?"

Collective nods around the room.

Asterin smiled, but the light in her eyes had gone dark. "Excellent. Luna, Quinlan, come along. We've got a demon to hunt down."

Rain had fallen overnight, soaking the grass and setting the trees aglisten. Asterin tramped outside, Amoux strapped to her side, her eyes roving the trees hungrily. Luna came next, followed by Quinlan.

"Should we get saddled up?" Luna asked.

"We won't be taking the horses," Quinlan answered as he shut the front door behind him, a half-eaten scone in his hand. "The trees are too dense. They'll only slow us down." He popped the last of the scone into his mouth. "Let's get going. I'd like to be back before evening falls."

Asterin snorted. "You mean you'd like to be back in time for dinner." Still, he was right—it was too dangerous to search for the demon after dark. They hadn't the faintest idea as to the demon's whereabouts, how powerful it was, or even its size. All they knew was that it had managed to destroy Corinthe and all of its people in a matter of hours … so even now, in broad daylight, they would need to be constantly on their guard.

The three of them set off east, using Garringsford's map to mark their path. While Asterin knew that the chances of finding the demon were slim, especially on their first day, she still clung to the hope. She imagined it all in her mind—the hard-fought battle, the final strike. Bringing the body back to her mother with their heads held high. The queen would praise her for an excellent job, would be happy and proud—

She's never been proud of you, a voice in her head reminded her. *But perhaps, once you slay the demon … all of that will change.* Wouldn't it?

Asterin shook the thought from her head. They would kill the demon—not because she wanted to please her mother, but because her people deserved vengeance and a future ruler who was worth more than a smile and a pretty tiara.

Before she knew it, the sun was slipping inch by inch from its peak. Hours had passed, but they hadn't glimpsed so much as a hint of the demon's whereabouts—no abnormal prints, no territorial markings. Not even a rabbit carcass. They had found absolutely nothing. Still, she forged on until the sky wept streaks of crimson across the horizon.

Finally, when Luna kept clearing her throat and looking at the darkening sky, Asterin slumped against a tree in defeat.

Quinlan squeezed her shoulder. "We should head back," he said.

"Harry said he was baking a cake. If it'll cheer you up, I promise to give you my slice."

Despite herself, Asterin smiled. "Deal."

When they arrived back at the cottage, everyone was too busy with various chores to bother asking how the search had gone. Rose and Eadric were out back in the garden gathering fresh herbs. Harry and Orion stood side by side at the kitchen counter, chopping potatoes and carrots for a soup. It was obvious whose pile of vegetables belonged to whom.

"I'll go and check on Eadric," Luna said and hurried out the back entrance, leaving Asterin and Quinlan to loiter awkwardly in the kitchen. Neatly written recipes had been taped to the walls in a collage of yellowing parchment and cursive too far away for Asterin to make out clearly.

Orion shot them a grin by way of greeting and waved his knife in the air. "Look at me! I could be a chef!"

Harry rolled his eyes. "Sure you could. A bad one, *maybe*." Orion pouted. "Oh, Asterin, could you boil a pot of water?" Grateful to be helping with something, she hurried over. Harry jerked his chin at the row of cupboards lining the wall. "The pots are in there—no, the one to the left, yes, that one, second shelf."

She grabbed the gigantic stock pot Harry pointed out and filled it in the sink before lugging it onto the stove. She glanced at the empty oven, wondering if Quinlan had been joking about the cake.

Harry caught her looking and smacked his forehead with his knife-hand, much to Orion's terror. "Oh, the cake! I completely forgot. Orion, come with me to the cellar, I need to find the ingredients. Asterin, keep an eye on the stove, will you?" With that, their host snatched Orion by the wrist and dragged him into the foyer, whereupon he opened a door that Asterin had assumed was a closet but appeared to lead into the gloom of a basement. "Be back in a minute!"

The door slammed shut behind them.

Asterin shrugged and rolled up her sleeves to wash her hands. She sifted through the drawers for a long wooden spoon and then held the handle between her teeth so she could attempt to tie an apron around her waist.

Soft footfalls on the ceramic tiles approached from behind. Warmth washed over her as Quinlan's hands slid teasingly down her bare forearms and captured her fumbling fingers, halting her struggle. "Let me help you with that," he said into her ear, voice rough. His breath ghosted the nape of her neck, and it took every ounce of her utmost effort to repress a shudder.

With a deep, slow inhale, she forced her fingers to relax and closed her eyes, letting him take over. His lips crested the shell of her ear and her entire body stiffened, heat pooling low in her gut. A mortified blush rose to her cheeks at the involuntary sound that escaped her, jaws clenching on the spoon handle still clamped in her mouth. He chuckled softly, knuckles brushing the small of her back as he worked. She didn't know what to do with her hands, so she braced them on the edge of the counter and forced herself to exhale—albeit shakily.

After a moment, she felt the telltale tug of the finished knot, but then Quinlan made a vague noise of dissatisfaction. "It's not my best work. I'll try again."

He's playing with you, said that nasty little voice in her head. *You're just another Pippa. Another distraction.*

Asterin suddenly shoved herself away from him, shattering the moment, tearing free from the desire threatening to drag her under. She grabbed the spoon from her mouth and threw it onto the counter with a harsh clatter. "Water's boiling," she gritted out, even though only tiny bubbles lined the inside of the pot when she lifted the lid. She scooped up a handful of potatoes and flung them inside, hissing when water splashed across her skin. Not boiling yet, but still bloody hot.

Quinlan was silent. And then, quietly, he asked, "Am I doing something wrong?"

Before she could respond, Rose barged in through the back entrance clutching a bundle of herbs, Eadric and Luna on her tail. Eadric had a wicker basket swinging from his wrist. Rose took one glance into the kitchen and sighed. "Are you two flirting again?"

Quinlan spun around to face her. Asterin couldn't see his expression, but the image of his balled fists gnawed at her. "How about you stay out of this?" he snapped in a tone that had Eadric and Luna immediately retreating into the living room.

Rose tilted her chin, assessing. "Someone's being a little sensitive."

Quinlan scoffed. "You can't be serious. When you were with Kane, if I so much as said a word—"

Asterin felt the air crackle with tension as Rose froze, her knuckles bone-white around a sprig of rosemary.

Quinlan bit his lip. "I should not have said that."

"Get out," Rose said, voice clipped.

He held his hands up in surrender. "Sorry." With Rose's murderous gaze pinned on his back, he fled into the foyer and through the living room door.

The Queen of Eradore released a long-suffering sigh.

Luna popped her head back into the kitchen. Eadric was nowhere to be seen. "Can I come in?"

Rose pasted on a strained smile and began plucking herbs from the captain's basket. "Yes, of course."

Luna joined Asterin by the stove and the three of them lapsed into a companionable silence, maneuvering around one another in harmony through the kitchen, the calming scent of sage and robust oregano pervading the air.

"Can I throw these into the pot?" Rose asked, waving a handful of herbs at Asterin.

She shrugged. "Beats me. Harry and Orion haven't come out of the cellar yet."

Luna frowned. "Cellar? I thought it was a closet." She yelped when the pot hissed. "Immortals, I hate cooking."

Asterin laughed. "Come on, Luna, it's fun."

"Cooking is hardly *fun*." Luna sniffed. "All you do is chop little things into bits and pieces. And then you make them hot."

"Would you rather eat everything raw, then?" Rose asked.

"No, I'd rather have someone else do it for me."

"You'd rather have someone else eat raw food for you?"

Luna whacked Rose's arm with a wooden spoon.

Rose picked up a rolling pin from inside one of the drawers. "I don't want to fight you," the queen warned, more serious than Asterin had ever seen her. "But I have a rolling pin and I'm not afraid to use it."

"A rolling pin against a measly spoon? That's hardly fair!"

Rose grinned. "Never said I would play fair."

The cellar door opened and Orion came staggering out, a jar of dark cocoa powder in his hands and his face flushed, Harry at his heels with a sack of flour swinging from over his shoulder.

Asterin frowned. "Orion? Are you all right? You're awfully red." The last thing they needed was for him to come down with a fever.

Her Guardian fanned himself. "Never been better."

Harry cocked his head at Rose and Luna, who were circling each other and throwing taunts, right on the brink of a vicious battle. He opened his mouth as if to inquire but ultimately decided against it. Instead, he hefted the flour into Orion's arms, nearly knocking the jar of cocoa onto the ceramic floor. "Could you get started on the cake? I need to go and check the traps before it gets too dark. The recipe is taped to the wall."

"No problem." Orion bustled over to the wall, squinting up at the recipes and tracing his finger down the parchment. He hesitated. "Wait, when it says 'cup,' do I use an actual mug or what?"

Asterin sighed. "I'll help him."

Harry shot her a grateful smile and shrugged on his coat before hoisting his monstrous crossbow off a hook in the foyer. "Thank you."

Asterin waved as he maneuvered himself and the crossbow out the door. Orion had dipped his finger into the cocoa jar. She smacked his hand away. "Stop that!" She scanned the recipe. "Where are we supposed to find eggs? Did you see any in the cellar?"

Orion shook his head.

Asterin cursed and dashed for the bay windows in the living room that overlooked the clearing and the path leading into the forest beyond. Her eyes snagged on Harry halfway down the path, and she was just about to run out the door to call him back when something made her pause.

The light from the torches in the clearing gleamed off the pine boughs, astir with night wind, but she could have sworn that the swaying grass and primrose stalks stilled when Harry walked past. Her eyes narrowed at his retreating figure, a sudden unease settling into the pit of her stomach. The torches flickered, the flames bending away from the hunter as if to escape from their wicks. It was something about the way the shadows seemed to follow him, to cling to him like fog.

Then he ducked out of the clearing beneath the branched archway, and only when the hunter had vanished into the forest did Asterin realize that she had forgotten to ask about the eggs.

CHAPTER TWENTY-TWO

Her Royal Majesty

Queen Priscilla Alessandra Montcroix-Faelenhart,

Ruler of Axaria

requests the honor of the presence of

Her Royal Majesty

Queen Orozalia Saville, Ruler of Eradore

And the company of three escorts

At the annual Fairfest Ball

Six in the Eve of the Spring-Summer Solstice

The Palace of Axaria

Rose sighed and tucked the cream-white invitation back into its envelope, the crimson wax seal of the Axarian crest—two swords crossed behind a wolf head—brushing her fingertips as she slid the card into the inner pocket of her jacket. She left her room, Eadric's snores rumbling next door, and padded downstairs. Harry and Orion were puttering about the kitchen preparing breakfast. Quinlan's team had left before dawn. Orion was teaching Harry the words and the melody to the Axarian anthem in a voice that had both her and Harry cringing on the high notes. She slipped into the dining room and out the back door undetected, past the horses grazing in the clearing and behind the barn, where she had noticed a large flat rock the morning her team had first set out to search for the demon.

Tomorrow would mark the end of their first week demon hunting, and while Harry had been nothing but a wonderful host, Rose couldn't help but wish the beast would show up already—for Asterin's sake, if nothing else. With each passing day and the demon still nowhere to be found, the princess's mood grew increasingly volatile. And on top of that, she was giving poor, smitten Quinlan the cold shoulder, the Immortals knew why. Asterin was a bomb ticking down, and Rose did not want to be anywhere near her when she blew.

Settling onto the flat rock, Rose took out the Fairfest invitation again and wondered if she should accept. All she had to do was burn the seal, which would trigger a charm on the wax to confirm her attendance.

The invitation had arrived just days shy of her and Quinlan's departure for Axaria, but of course, newly crowned, she had expected it. The reigning monarchs of the kingdoms were always invited, along with scores of favored highborns from around the world. Invitation was exclusive—granted only by Queen Priscilla herself.

Rose remembered tiptoeing out of bed and eavesdropping on her parents' conversations—as all children do, though she doubted most children had to sneak through four parlors, two guardrooms, and a library to reach their bedchamber. The Eradorian palace didn't have hallways or corridors. Only rooms leading into more rooms, forcing guests to either learn the lay of the land or get lost—literally. Rose didn't have anywhere near the number of fingers needed to count how many ghosts supposedly roamed the palace, still searching for a way out.

On that particular night, after the arrival of the invitation, her father had urged Queen Lillian to make the long trip to Axaria. At the time, all Rose knew of the Fairfest Ball was that even the most lavish of parties paled in comparison. So naturally, she hadn't understood why her mother refused—and refused again and again, year after year.

If she were being honest with herself, she still didn't understand. Of course she could speculate—an issue of diplomacy or even something on a more personal level. But just like Rose had never found out why in hell her mother had named her Orozalia of all things, perhaps there simply wasn't a clear answer. Yet now, with her mother dead and that horrible vision of her kingdom falling to pieces so fresh in her mind, would it be wise to throw away the perfect opportunity to establish new alliances? To offer herself up to the other royals so that, in time, she could collect her dues?

Don't forget that it will be your first public appearance, she thought to herself. Attending would make a statement, but so would not attending. Either way, her choice would impact how the world saw her—and though she didn't want to care, she *had* to. She was the Queen of Eradore.

Lux trotted over to her, black eyes shining, and lay down beside the rock to sleep. Eyes closed and bathing in the sun, Rose couldn't help but absurdly wish that they could switch places. She slipped off the rock and lowered herself beside the stallion, stretching her limbs out. She breathed a lungful of the unmistakable scent of grass and soil and she sighed, a balmy breeze tickling her skin as it whispered across the clearing. Her eyes swept over what her mother used to call a seafoam sky—a muted screen of ocean blue peeping behind a churning, labyrinthine array of eggshell-white wisps, the gaps and seams constantly ebbing, shifting, devouring.

She hadn't slept well last night, only furthering the weariness of hunting through miles and miles of forest for the demon, and so it was with relief that her eyelids grew heavy.

Just a quick nap, she thought, letting the wind lap at her, tug her along the currents of slumber, and finally engulf her.

She must have napped for hours, because when she woke up, the light had dulled to an afternoon gloom beneath a thick blanket of dolorous clouds. Lux had abandoned her, opting to socialize with the other horses across the clearing instead. Their heads suddenly lifted, upper lips curled and tails clamping down.

Rose's nose twitched, catching an all-too-familiar scent from a childhood spent with Quinlan. Not seconds later, angry plumes of smoke billowed from the cottage, bright topaz flames crawling along the exterior. She scrambled up and sprinted for the cottage, nearly colliding into a rampaging Buttercup when the mare thundered past her toward the other horses, who were gathering as far away from the cottage as they could—except for Lux, who just whinnied for Rose to run faster.

She prepared to attack the flames from the outside, but then she heard the frantic shouts from within the cottage. *Orion isn't a water-wielder*, she realized.

Rose kicked down the back door and hurtled through the dining room. Smoke seeped from beneath the closed kitchen door, so she raced into the living room, which connected through the foyer to the kitchen. There was a curse from above and a half-awake Eadric toppled down the staircase wearing nothing but tight black boxer briefs. Rose burst into the kitchen with her affinity stone brandished and the captain at her heels, and shouted, "*Aveau explosa*!"

Geysers of water erupted from the floor, arcing across the counters and cupboards and surging right through the blazing remains of the oven, extinguishing the inferno in one strike. Rose thrust her hand up and the water glided along the walls and ceiling, penetrating every crevice, quenching every ember and flooding out the other side to douse whatever flames that had escaped her.

Panting, she turned to find Orion and Harry on the porch behind Eadric, gusts of wind blowing through the open front door. Harry looked shaken and Orion guilty, but they were both unharmed.

"What in hell happened?" Rose demanded, arm waving at the grotesque remains of the oven, the metal half-melted and twisted.

"We were baking bread," Orion said meekly.

Rose stared at him. She felt like she was scolding the twins back home—though, frankly, with all their mad experimenting, a fire would have been nothing. "Does baking bread involve burning down the house?"

Harry scratched the back of his head. "We got a little distracted."

A groan clawed its way out of her throat. "Can't you two make out *and* keep an eye on the oven at the same time?"

"What?" Orion spluttered. "W-we don't—we haven't ... we just—"

Eadric strode over to him and squeezed his shoulder, forcing the Guardian to look him in the eye. "All of us are here to support you, Orion, so please don't ever feel like you need to hide anything from us."

Orion flapped his hands frenetically, a scarlet flush creeping up his neck. "Thank you, but—"

"No buts," Eadric interrupted. "Unconditional love is all we have for you." Then the captain narrowed his eyes onto Harry. Rose couldn't help but take notice how intimidating he looked, even—no, especially in just his boxers, biceps rippling as he shook a finger in their host's bewildered face. "But *you.* If you hurt him in any way, shape, or form, know that I will hunt you to the ends of the earth and rip your organs to shreds. Understood?"

Harry gulped. "Very much so."

Rose sighed, eyeing the scorched walls, clutching her affinity stone. "I can make repairs to the house itself, but you're out of luck with the oven."

Orion winced. "Which means no cake for Asterin."

Eadric chuckled and clapped Orion on the back. "I'm not taking back what I said about unconditional love, but ..." His face suddenly went gravely serious. "That's on you, mate."

Orion looked to Rose in desperation, but she mirrored Eadric's expression, thinking again of the princess's inevitable explosion. "Sorry, Orion. Good luck."

As a last-ditch effort, Orion turned to Harry, but the hunter had already hightailed it out the back door.

Harry had a routine. Every evening, just after sunset, he would leave the cottage to go and hunt. And since the first day of their arrival, Rose noticed that Asterin had a routine, too. Every evening, the princess saw him to the door, but she had yet to return from her own demon hunt tonight with Luna and Quinlan, so Rose took it upon herself to substitute.

She leaned against the staircase banister in the foyer. As promised, she had restored the walls and ceiling with fresh lumber by melding it to the damaged wood. She'd even managed to replace the cupboards, but the plates—or rather, puddles—within were beyond saving.

"Six strangers stuffed under your roof," she mused. "We must be driving you crazy."

Harry's lips quirked. "I rather enjoy the company," he said, reaching for his coat. "It certainly gets lonely sometimes."

"Well, it's our honor," Rose said. "You cannot imagine how much we appreciate you letting us stay here with you. Our eternal appreciation wouldn't be able to express how grateful we are for your kindness and generosity. A million thanks."

Harry smiled. "Of course, Your Majesty. *I'm* just grateful that you fixed my kitchen."

"What?" Rose recoiled, heart hammering. "What did you say?"

"Fixed my kitchen? Oh." Realization struck Harry and he threw his hands up in defense, backtracking. "No, sorry, I didn't mean to alarm you—"

"I don't know what you're talking about," she said, mind working furiously. Had someone told him? Maybe Orion? But surely he wouldn't reveal her identity. Or would he?

"Immortals, I'm sorry, I shouldn't have said—I mean, right, you're right," Harry stammered, snatching his crossbow off its hook and fumbling for the doorknob.

Rose covered the space between them in two strides. She grabbed him by the collar before he could escape, dragging him away from the door. "How did you know?" she asked flatly. When he didn't respond, she shook him. "Who told you?"

He stared at her, brow furrowing. "No one."

"Then how did you know?"

Harry blinked innocently. "Know what?"

Rose didn't take the joke well. "I could snap you in half right now," she growled.

Harry didn't answer for a long moment. And then he said, "I went to feed the horses earlier while you were napping in the grass. I found Lux chewing up some fancy paper in the barn."

Rose's jaw unhinged. "My Fairfest invitation." She must have left it out on that rock. She remembered that impish glint in those black eyes and resisted the sudden urge to strangle Asterin's horse.

Harry nodded. "It was all torn up and … wet. It looked important, so I took a glance. I was going to give it to you, but … well, you seemed exhausted and I didn't want to wake you up. I brought it inside so the wind wouldn't blow it away."

"Where is it now?" Rose asked.

Harry took a moment to think. Then his eyes widened. "Oh. Immortals. Rose, I left it on the kitchen counter while Orion and I were making lunch."

She hadn't seen it during repairs. "So … you mean to say that …"

"It must have burned up in the fire," Harry finished, brow knitting. "I am so, so sorry."

His words sank in. And then she laughed quietly to herself. *I guess there won't be any unburning that, then.* "No, it's fine. Thank you for making that decision for me." He cocked his head in confusion, but then yelped when she yanked him closer, her voice stone cold. "No one, save the other five people living under this roof, knows of my identity. And those five already have my trust. If anyone else finds out, I will personally see to your suffering."

Harry blew out a long breath and muttered, "You Axarians are a scary bunch."

Rose smiled sharply at that. "That they are." She released him. "But I'm not from Axaria. I'm the Queen of Eradore, and believe me, by the time I'm finished with you, you wouldn't even remember the meaning of scary."

Harry hesitated a moment more before tipping his chin in accord. Then he darted out the door, ignoring the porch stairs in his haste, and melted into the night.

CHAPTER TWENTY-THREE

Harry snarled at himself as he bounded deeper and deeper into the forest. *You utter imbecile.* How many more of Orion's smiles would it take to render him a complete fool? *Of course, Your Majesty.* His words rang in his brain, an unintelligible loop. Almost no one except for Orion seemed to trust him, that much was clear. His mission grew harder and harder with every slip, every little lapse in judgment.

His mission.

He shook his head, refusing to think about it—not yet. He needed to clear his mind.

Finding a hollowed-out trunk, he shed his coat. The rest of his clothes followed. Next came the crossbow and quiver, and finally his boots, landing atop the pile with a careless *thunk.* He wedged a few leafy boughs on top. *Just in case.*

And then he closed his eyes and shifted.

The restrictions on his body lifted as he curled back onto his haunches. He dug his toes and fingers deep into the dirt, sighing in liberation as they morphed into paws. His nose elongated into a snout, his ears stretched, becoming flat and pert, and his legs lengthened into powerful hindquarters. No more did he have that fragile layer of human skin, but a dense coat of silky, obsidian fur.

His senses exploded—eyesight sharpening tenfold until he could see every single detail on each leaf and each clod of dirt, even in the dark. He couldn't believe the things these humans missed. Colors, smells, touch—he could feel the tiny pebbles beneath his paws, every bead of moisture clinging to his fur. With his hearing intensified, he caught the quivering of a rabbit in its hole from a mile away.

He couldn't help but release a moan as his wings broke past his shoulder blades. Relishing the caress of the night breeze along their ridges, he carefully tucked them at his sides. He couldn't fly tonight—Asterin and her team hadn't yet returned to the cottage. He could only hope they hadn't been lurking nearby when he had crashed through the trees.

Because of Asterin and Orion and the others, who would surely search for him if he disappeared for more than a half hour, he had been stuck in his human form for days—but he had never been able to stand being trapped in it for long. It was worth the risk. Now, when he became one with darkness, not even an Immortal would be able to tell them apart.

If he couldn't fly, he would run. Paws thudding against the ground, he hurtled through the forest, a black glimmer in an ever-darkening world. He could feel the shadows billowing behind him like a cloak, slithering across every inch of his body as he tore through the trees beneath the star-speckled sky.

His was the cursed gift of the god few mortals dared speak of. The ruler of darkness, the God of Shadow, the self-proclaimed King of the Immortals and all the other nasties crawling around the Immortal Realm. Harry's master had as many names as he had personalities—charming, cruel, generous—but Harry knew him simply as Eoin.

Eoin had been the first Immortal. With every god or goddess that came into being, Eoin's power only grew. Each Immortal, no matter how virtuous, brought darkness beneath the soles of their powerful feet and with the stains of the sins they had committed to rise above the rest. All together, ten strong, they formed the Council of Immortals to govern the growing Immortal Realm.

"We need a ruler," Lady Siore had said from her throne of earth and ivy. "Someone to ground us."

"No," Lady Audra had said, the sky beneath her throne an endless expanse of ever-shifting heavens flickering with lightning. "We are all equals."

Of course, this wasn't true, but Eoin said nothing. All were treated fairly, and he saw no reason to protest.

And then the other Immortals gave life to a new sort of beast—a fragile beast that Eoin's power would not allow him to produce. Mortalkind.

Eoin demanded that all mortals be destroyed. For how was it fair that the other Immortals could pass their powers through the bloodlines of other beings, a feat never before achieved, when he could not?

But the Council loved their little mortal descendants too much, and outvoted him.

"We have created them to exist on their own terms," Lord Ulrik, God of Light, had insisted, his lynx curled up at his feet. "That is their purpose—to choose their own paths, as we have. To further their own societies, their own humanities. We have forbidden ourselves from interfering with their lives, so there is ultimately no difference."

It was not enough.

Enraged, Eoin renounced the Council and built himself a new kingdom, far more magnificent than anything the other Immortals had ever seen. He built himself a new set of rules, created new nightmarish and beautiful creatures to roam his lands.

The wise and patient Lord Tidus had been the first to come and reason with him. Eoin snapped his fingers and the God of Water's body crumbled from the inside out. For a century, Lord Tidus lay broken at the foot of Eoin's throne. And when the other Immortals came seeking revenge, even their powers combined could not overcome Eoin. Only the nine of them united, including Lord Tidus at full strength, stood a chance against him.

"We are not equals," the God of Shadow announced. "I am no Lord. I am a King. And I do not care if you refuse to bow to me, because I can break you instead." And that he did.

Afterward, Eoin lost interest in destroying the mortals—he had already destroyed their creators, so what was the point? He wasn't a barbarian with a senseless thirst for death. In fact, he decided the Council was wrong to stay away from their creations.

The other Immortals could only watch as Eoin rose to the Mortal

Realm and meddled all he liked, restrained solely by the infrequency of total solar eclipses—the only time the two realms joined as one, allowing him to create a portal strong enough to withstand his power.

Eoin found that he adored mortals. They were as ever-shifting as he. Manipulative, loving, greedy. And over the centuries, he reaped the debts owed to him by the hungriest of mortals—hungry for power that only Eoin could loan them. Like he had loaned to the Woman.

The Woman. She had yet to tell Harry her name, so he'd taken to calling her that. She still thought she held dominance over him. But the blood oath, the obedience—that had all been a ruse. Just the way Eoin liked, because only Eoin could control him. Only Eoin *owned* him.

Harry was Eoin's pet. His property. He was an *anygné*, or a shadowling, in the mortal tongue. An immortal demon, enslaved by the contract he had signed centuries ago and couldn't seem to ever escape. If Eoin wanted Harry to do something, he did it. Somehow, the Woman had learned of the existence of shadowlings. Using her borrowed powers, she had summoned him through Hollenfér, one of the three gateways between the Mortal and the Immortal Realm, temporarily freeing him from his contract. That in itself was reason enough for Harry to carry out her bidding, as thanks. But after the Woman had dumped him in this forest, he had awoken one morning to find a message burned into his chest.

Obey the Woman. Her assets are of great importance to me.

The words—from Eoin, of course—healed as soon as he read them, but they were permanently seared into his mind.

Assets, Harry thought to himself as he raced the moonlight filtering through the trees and sailed over a river with one mighty leap. *What could that mean?* It couldn't be power. Eoin had more than enough of that. Some kind of army, then?

No human in their right mind dabbled with dark magic. The nine mortal kingdoms didn't share many international laws, but association with dark magic had long been forbidden. If discovered, the Woman would, at best, face permanent exile.

At worst, she would face execution.

And her reason for summoning Harry in the first place?

To kill Princess Asterin—and whoever else got in the way.

But why? Harry wondered desperately. Most likely, based on his past observations of mortals, the Woman wished to overthrow the crown. He didn't see how killing a village full of people had anything to do with that, though. And while he hoped that ultimately, their deaths had been a mercy, killing Asterin and the others was another matter entirely. He thought of Orion, with eyes as blue and dazzling as northern frost, as full of mischief as Eoin himself. The loyal captain, and the gentle lady-in-waiting who thought herself the best of Asterin's best friends. And the two Eradorians, one a queen—which the Woman couldn't possibly know, not that Harry had any intention of informing her. They were all good people.

No, it wouldn't be mercy—it would be murder.

You're no hero, he reminded himself. A hero protected the good people. A hero would save Asterin. *You're a hunter.* A hunter did anything he could to survive.

If he disobeyed the Woman, he would face Eoin's wrath. He had no choice.

The scent of hot, quivering flesh wafted beneath his nose. If he tuned his hearing just right—ah, there it was. Blood pumping through thick arteries, a hefty body.

He let his instincts take over, guiding him west. He became nothing more than the shadow of one tree, then the next. The young buck snuffled at a mulberry bush when Harry glided out of the darkness, jaw locking around its soft neck before it could so much as glance up.

By the time he at last returned to the hollow tree and shifted back into his human form, the moon was high and the constellations twinkled like shattered glass in the sky. Now, with all his senses uncomfortably muted and weakened, he stalked back to the cottage, the buck's body slung over his shoulder, bumping against his quiver with every other step.

He smelled the food cooking before he heard their voices. Warm, golden light flooded the clearing like sweet nectar as Harry reached the cottage. Asterin had returned. He could hear her yelling at someone. The others chattered, and Orion was singing the Axarian anthem again. Harry smiled despite himself. If he hadn't been so focused on listening to the sounds of the house, he might have noticed that he was humming along himself.

They were all good people.

As he pushed the door open, they rushed to help him, welcoming him home with laughter and light touches. Orion's hand lingered on his back, fingers tracing south. Even Rose gave him a little smile, though her gaze was wary. Only the captain's face showed not a hint of warmth, but that was nothing new.

The sooner Harry killed them, the better.

That night, after all the others had fallen fast asleep, Harry woke. A mirror framed in obsidian hung across from his bed, gleaming in the moonlight. At the top pulsed a symbol—three lines with a horizontal slash. The shadow sigil.

He got out of bed and approached the mirror on the wall. His bedraggled reflection blinked back at him, tufts of hair sticking up in every direction. But his sleepy haze vanished when he pressed his palm against the frigid surface of the mirror, the cold jolting him well and truly awake. The glass rippled, shifting from his reflection to a black void.

In a voice colder than the mirror's surface, the Woman spoke. "Shadow demon."

He resisted the urge to roll his eyes. While he could only discern a black void, he had no doubt that she could see him. "It's Harry."

"I shall address you in whatever way I desire," she snapped. *Stupid mortal bitch*, he thought. There was a pause. "Is it done?"

"No, milady."

"How convenient," she said. "Things have been postponed. I have other duties to attend to, and the last thing I need is to help arrange a royal funeral. Keep Princess Asterin alive and busy until I command otherwise."

To help arrange a royal funeral? So the Woman likely lived at the palace, then, working closely with the Queen of Axaria. "Yes, milady."

"And the blond one, too," the Woman added.

Harry tilted his head in confusion. "You mean the princess's Royal Guardian?"

"No, the girl. Luna. She is valuable to the queen. The others are expendable. Understood?"

Before he could reply, the mirror rippled again, signaling the end of the connection. Staring at his own reflection once more, Harry studied the defiant jut of his chin, the curl of his fists.

He forced himself to trudge back to the bed, where he plunked himself down and pondered the Woman's words, trying to dismantle the new information. He pulled the covers over his head like a shield and closed his eyes. If he wanted, he could shift, right now, and slaughter all of them in their beds. But now he had to wait, when with each passing day he grew more attached—not just to Orion, but to all of them. Fierce Asterin, sweet Luna, patient Rose. Protective Eadric, even though the captain still distrusted him. And Quinlan, who he sensed carried a great burden from a childhood of pain, but kept it buried deep inside. Just like Harry.

How can I kill these people? he thought, but for once, the shadows did not give him an answer.

CHAPTER TWENTY-FOUR

Despite Quinlan's optimism, they did not find the demon. Not the first week, nor even after the second. Asterin spent her off-days restless, fidgeting, waiting on edge for the hours to crawl by until dawn arrived. She had welts up and down her forearms from scratching at herself, trying to soothe an unappeasable itch for vengeance.

A little more than three weeks after they had arrived in the forest, the frustration became too much. They had covered miles and miles of ground, to the point where they had started mapping out repeat routes. Asterin felt pathetic. They didn't have a single lead. And her feet *ached.*

It's always difficult admitting failure.

She gritted her teeth and came to a stop in front of a towering spruce. She gave the gnarled roots a mighty kick. It felt so good that she did it again. "I am not a failure," she snarled, each word earning a kick.

"Calm down." Quinlan said, grabbing her wrist as she kicked the tree again. Luna observed them from a safe distance up ahead, hovering behind a bush.

"Why should I?" Asterin seethed.

"What did you expect?" He spread his arms skyward. "Look at this forest! It's huge."

"But we've been searching for three whole weeks and we haven't found *anything*!" She aimed another kick at the tree but Quinlan grabbed her outstretched leg and held fast.

"Don't get all pissy just because you haven't gotten a chance to slay the demon yet."

She scoffed loudly and shook herself free. "I'm not pissy."

"Right, and Rose isn't the Queen of Eradore," Quinlan quipped. "Look. You're pissy because you feel useless. We know, okay? All of us are frustrated. But starting tomorrow, on off-days, we're going to start your training. I don't know why you've been acting weird around me, but I don't care anymore. I told you I'd help you learn how to control your magic without the omnistone, and so that's exactly what I'll do."

It was irritating how easily he had seen through her. "I have control!" she exclaimed. A lie—she still couldn't summon more than an icicle without the omnistone. Remembering Quinlan's ease wielding not just fire, but all the elements, left her embarrassed and feeling utterly inadequate. "I don't need training. As long as I have the omnistone, I'll be perfectly fine."

"Is that so?" Quinlan asked, his expression cool. "Then let's blow off some steam, shall we?"

Before she could ask what he meant, he snapped his fingers.

There was a flurry in the air. A dozen arrows spilled into existence above Quinlan's head, spreading around him like a fleet of ships. He snapped again, and the tips of each arrow burst into flame, ruffling Asterin's hair with their heat, crackling and blazing as brightly as torches.

"Nock." Quinlan playfully mimed a bow. "Draw." The arrows pulled back on invisible strings at his gesture. "Loose."

Asterin reacted swiftly, the omnistone already in her hand as she leapt up, summoning a cushion of air to maximize her height. Four arrows whizzed beneath her. She twisted midair, cloak flapping and catching the tip of another. It singed the edge with a menacing hiss. Growling, she swiped at the silver clasp at her neck as she landed in a crouch. She let the heavy fabric fall away. It would only slow her down.

Quinlan, unimpressed, let loose the second wave.

Clenching the stone harder, she called on her magic, ready for his next attack. She hurled a blast of wind to deflect each arrow, even managing to extinguish some.

Despite the cool morning air, beads of sweat rolled down her jaw. She thrust her arms this way and that, trying to be everywhere at once, using her anger and frustration to fuel her already fraying concentration. But no matter how many arrows she diverted, or how many she sent back at her opponent, they just kept coming.

There was no way she could last much longer in a defensive position. There were too many arrows to keep track of, too many to dodge.

She spared a glance at Quinlan, expecting to see him at least a little winded, as he often was when they practiced swordplay, but not the slightest sheen of perspiration graced his forehead. He even had the audacity to examine his fingernails like a prim lady.

Finally deciding on a course of action, she lunged forward, arms spread wide. A whirlwind of snow howled around her as she surrounded her body in armor made of ice. The snow snuffed the arrows out before they could hit her, and though the impact of the arrow tips left cracks in her armor, she battled ahead, her palms crackling with the magic she kept trapped inside, waiting for the perfect moment to release it.

Quinlan's advantage was distance. He could reach her easily with his arrows, but she had a hard time getting anywhere near him. If she could close that distance, he would have less space to maneuver his arrows and she would have a better chance of making a hit.

With a grunt, she unleashed her magic, her blood singing as she let it wash over her in shuddering waves. Ice blasted from her fingertips, the sun glinting off the brilliant, blinding blue surface. She smiled to herself as she caught Quinlan's eyes widen just a fraction.

Her smile turned into a grimace as she felt an arrow clip her thigh.

Her ice vanished completely when a sudden explosion of fire swallowed her whole. Her armor melted off, water sweeping her off her feet, transforming the ground into a treacherous battlefield of slippery mud.

Asterin panted, her clothes soaked through and her tailbone stinging as she heaved herself to her feet.

"Tiring out already, Princess?" Quinlan drawled.

She caught a glimpse of Luna, inching forward into her peripheral vision, but when Quinlan sent the girl a warning ripple of heat, she hopped backward and sought cover behind a bush, receiving the message loud and clear.

Caked in mud, Asterin hissed, "*No*," and barreled forward once more.

This time, she created a pathway of ice, conjuring only patches at a time so that even when Quinlan melted through them as quickly as they appeared, she had already dashed left, then right, zigzagging over the mud.

Higher and higher into the air she forced herself, constructing a crystalline spiral staircase. The arrow wound drilled like a knife into her thigh, her breath coming in uneven gasps.

Asterin made her move.

She vaulted off the edge of the stairs, now over a hundred feet in the air, latching onto a tree branch and swinging like an acrobat, the bark biting into her palms and her gut clenching at the height. She swung up and pulled her torso over the branch, then swung her leg over and hoisted herself the rest of the way, tucking her feet onto the branch behind her for stability.

From her new vantage point, she had a perfect shot at Quinlan. Two spears of ice formed in her hands. He squinted up at her, lips parting in confusion and she hurled the spears with all her strength, commanding them to split and lengthen into a hailstorm of lethal blades.

Suddenly, the dozen arrows she had forgotten shrieked through the air toward her. They were everywhere, slicing through her clothes, descending like a flock of starving buzzards, burning and nipping at every inch of her. She struggled to keep her balance as she blasted ice at random to fight them off, panicking when she missed more arrows than she hit. Smoke filled her lungs and blood filled her mouth. She heard Quinlan curse in pain from her ice spears, but the arrows' barrage never faltered.

"Yield, Asterin!"

"No!" She yelled back, just as one of the arrows whizzed by her face. She jerked away from it, but her foot slipped. Her heart dropped to her toes as she plummeted out of the treetop, the ground racing up to meet her at an alarming rate. *I don't know how to land*, she realized in terror. Dirt erupted at her summons to soften her fall, but it was too little too late. She plowed through the teetering column, mud flying in every direction.

The force of her landing knocked the omnistone right out of her hand.

Quinlan stepped over her. He picked the stone up and threw it into the trees. "Yield." His torn clothing revealed three gashes, but he paid them no heed.

"No," Asterin gasped, head spinning from the pain.

His eyes bore into hers, cold and hard. "You lost. Even with the stone."

"Is this what you felt like?" she croaked, voice catching in her throat. "When your father took your stones away?"

"Yes." An arrow appeared at his shoulder. She flinched as it struck an inch from her knee. "Helpless." Another arrow fired between her fingers. "Weak." A third skimmed her cheek. "Like a damsel in distress with her knight dead between the dragon's teeth, knowing that she was next."

She bit the inside of her cheek so hard that it began to bleed. "I'm not a damsel—"

"I was talking about *me*," he snapped. "But then, I pushed and pushed at my boundaries until I finally broke free. Until I *became* the dragon." The arrows disintegrated to ash. His expression softened. "I just want to help you, Asterin."

Now that her mind had cleared of the anger, replaced by bone-deep exhaustion, she wished she had kicked herself instead of that tree trunk earlier. Quinlan had been kind enough to offer to train her, and all she had done was throw it back in his face. "I'm sorry," she mumbled.

"It's okay." He bent down to help her up, then raised a hand. The omnistone whizzed into his open palm. "Here."

She took it gingerly, staring at it for a long moment, and then at the blackened trees and waterlogged ground around her. Severed trees limbs dangled from above, jagged and dripping. Mud squelched beneath her. The earth dragged at her, as if wanting to bury her for the damage she had caused. She forgot her own cuts and gashes as she struggled to her feet and brushed a hand on a nearby branch. Chunks of bark crumbled at her touch, charred to ash from Quinlan's fire, and frost still clung like dust to the edges of the shriveled leaves.

Destruction. To her own trees, her own soil. Shame filled her. She had done this.

Curling her fingers against the dry, cracked trunk of another tree, she closed her eyes, forehead tipped against the bark in apology. She was no better than the shadow demon, laying waste to life.

For once, she tried to ignore the stone in her other hand, and remembered Rose's words from Aldville. *Your magic is a part of you. Your powers lie within your blood, closer within reach than you think.*

Slowly, slowly, the magic inside of her welled up, coiling and swirling through her skin and into the wood, winding its way through the trunk, wriggling higher and higher, until it twisted and turned into every single branch, every single leaf and bud. The blackened areas on the bark began to bleed away. The withered leaves slowly unfurled as they restored to their healthy green, and the spring blossoms swelled with life.

Keeping her hand on the tree, Asterin extended her magic even further, pushing until it connected with the next damaged tree, and the next, setting off a chain reaction. She exhaled, long and unwavering, and with her release of breath came the flourish of life. She gave the earth all the magic she had.

And the more she gave, the more the forest gave back. She inhaled, the air delicious and pure on her tongue. She spread her arms, drawing a flood of water out of the ground. Millions of glassy orbs sprang forth, sparkling and quivering. She clapped her hands above her head and the droplets evaporated into the sky.

Her exhaustion dragged her down, but her every pore tingled with magic as she bent down, scooping up a handful of rich soil and letting it trickle away through her spread fingers, cool and moist.

Quinlan stood with his hands on his hips, staring up at the sunlight filtering through the verdant leaves, dappling the moss and dirt in a dazzling array of gold.

Asterin toyed with the weight of the omnistone in her hands. *Closer within reach than you think.* She thought of the wyvern at the inn, that vicious yellow-eyed grin. She remembered that feeling of vulnerability, wanting to protect her friends but being powerless and utterly at its mercy. *I want to become the dragon, too*, she realized. "Quinlan?"

He turned to her, brows raised. "Hm?"

"I—I want to learn how to control my magic without the omnistone," she said. "I want to train with you, if … if you'll still have me."

Quinlan smiled. "Of course I will. But it won't be easy. I'll work you harder than anyone else ever has. You'll probably hate me by the end of it."

I could never hate you, she thought to herself. *Far from it.* But she couldn't find the courage to say it aloud. Instead, she held out the omnistone to him. "So, you'll keep this safe for me in the meantime?"

Quinlan clasped her hand tightly. She met his eyes, warm and strong and steady. "That, I can do."

CHAPTER TWENTY-FIVE

"By the Immortals, what happened to you two?" Orion snorted from the sofa as Asterin stalked into the living room, throwing her muddy cloak in a pile by the hearth.

"They had a little domestic," Luna piped in, kicking off her boots. She scanned the room for Eadric, but he must have been busy helping Harry in the kitchen, though the only sounds drifting through the open door were the occasional clang of pots and the tap running.

"About what?" Rose asked, not even bothering to glance up. She sat cross-legged on the living room rug surrounded by maps, her brow crinkled as she made markings with a quill.

"I threw a tantrum," Asterin answered, sagging against the sofa with a relieved moan. Quinlan gave her a nudge and she scooched over to make space.

Luna grinned and flopped onto her back on the rug beside Rose. "You really did," Luna said. Rose didn't seem to mind her there, though she manhandled Luna's legs to remove the maps pinned underneath to drape them over her stomach instead. That was when Luna caught sight of the rigidity of the Eradorian's shoulders, the tension in her jaw. "Rose? Is everything all right?"

Silence blanketed the room, broken only by the high whistle of a kettle through the door. Finally, Rose threw down her quill, her eyes flicking to Quinlan, then toward the kitchen. Her cousin nodded in understanding, hurrying through the dining room and into the kitchen. He shut the door behind him, muting the kettle.

"We need to talk," said Rose.

"About what?" asked Asterin.

"Harry." Rose hesitated. "There's something … off about him."

Orion waved her off. "Yeah, but he's *Harry.* He's been living all alone for who knows how long."

Rose shook her head. "It's more than that. Sometimes, when he comes back in the evenings, I swear that the light … shies away from him."

Orion rolled his eyes. "Right. That makes so much sense."

"Orion, I'm serious."

"Well, so am I! Come on, Rose. Don't be like Eadric."

Luna shot him a glare, causing the maps to shift under Rose's hands. "What's that supposed to mean?"

"Nothing." Orion exhaled. "Listen, you were the one who told me I should give people a chance when it comes to trust."

Rose lowered her head. "I know. And it's not that I'm saying we *shouldn't* trust Harry, but … I just think it's strange that the demon has never attacked him, while Corinthe—which is pretty damn close to here—was totally wiped out."

Orion stared at her. "So? Harry has a ton of traps set up around his house. Maybe the demon knows how to avoid them."

"Maybe …"

"And what do you mean that it's strange he hasn't been attacked? Do you *want* him to get attacked or something?"

"Of course not," said Rose. "But we still have to take everything into consideration—"

"No, no we don't!" Orion exclaimed, throwing his hands into the air. He sprang off the sofa, pointing an accusatory finger at Rose. "Why do you have to act like everyone has an ulterior motive? Not everyone is trying to stab you in the back! Even if Harry is keeping some sort of secret, what right do you have to call him out on it? You lied to all of us for an entire month about your identity!"

Rose's eyes narrowed. "Being a queen and a murderer are two entirely different things."

"I have to agree with Rose," Asterin admitted softly, glancing up at Orion. "I'm sorry."

The princess's Guardian reeled back as if she had slapped him, betrayal and hurt flashing across his face. With a disgruntled snort, he stomped off to the kitchen, letting himself in and slamming the door behind him with a *bang* that rattled the glass panes.

Luna watched him leave. "Should one of us go after him and make sure he doesn't say anything stupid?"

Rose sighed, folding her hands in her lap. "Quinlan is still in there, so I think it will be okay. Thanks for siding with me, by the way," she said to Asterin.

"Don't thank me." Asterin propped her elbows on her knees and lowered her voice. "The truth is, a few nights ago, when our team returned late, we saw Harry running away from the cottage, though he didn't see us. We tried to follow him, but he was too fast. Remember that deer he took down?" At Rose's nod, Asterin went on. "I didn't see a puncture wound from one of his crossbow bolts, but the deer did have teeth marks around its neck. Big teeth marks."

That was news to Luna. She hadn't noticed, and Asterin hadn't mentioned anything at the time. "Maybe a bear killed it or something and Harry just found it?"

Asterin shook her head. "I doubt it. But then again, it's not like Harry has bear teeth, so I didn't push it."

Rose sighed and made a mark with her quill. "If only he had more of an alibi."

"That tickles," Luna grumbled, shifting beneath the maps. She craned her neck. "What's all this, anyway?" The three continents—Aspea, Prydell, and Eyvindr—spread across the long scroll of parchment, the nine kingdoms neatly divided within. She rolled onto her stomach, tracing her finger along the marks Rose had made at seemingly random locations. "Artica." The uninhabitable, icy wasteland circling the north above Aspea and Prydell. She dragged her finger down a bold black line connecting Artica to a dot on the coast of Eyvindr. "Volteris." The capital of Volterra. Her finger continued, crossing into the Asvindr Ocean. Luna frowned. "And … the middle of the ocean."

"No," Rose said. "That's Qris. It's a tiny island that was colonized by Oprehvar, but very few people live there since it's basically a living volcano." She drew a final line, connecting the island back to Artica to form a perfect triangle. "This means something," she muttered to herself. "It has to."

Asterin sat up suddenly. "I have an idea."

Rose's eyes widened. "You do?"

Asterin waved a hand. "Not about the map." She rose from the sofa and began pacing.

Luna tilted her head. "Then about what?"

Asterin stopped. "The demon, of course. That thing Orion said earlier. About the demon knowing about the traps." Asterin resumed her pacing, faster than before. "We should set our own. Without telling Harry." She hesitated, mouth thinning. "Or Orion. As a precaution."

"It's a good idea," Rose allowed. "And we could set them up like Harry's net trap so that they can only be triggered by a substantial weight." She made a face. "But even if we cast invisibility charms to mask the traps, I doubt a net could hold the demon for longer than a few minutes."

"We don't need it to hold." Asterin looked at Luna. "Do you remember that time we played that prank on Eadric? With the dye bomb?"

Luna snickered. "Of course. His hands were blue for a month."

"What do we need to make the dye again?" Asterin asked.

"Not much," she replied, skimming through the list in her head. "Carbon black. Egg yolks. Honey. Some other stuff, depending on how long you want the dye to last."

"I can help with the chemistry," Rose said. "I don't think Harry has any eggs, but we can find an alternative. Vinegar with baking soda might work."

"We can rig the secret traps with the dye bombs," Asterin said. "Even if whatever or whoever we catch manages to escape, then …"

Luna's lips parted at the simple ingenuity of it all. "The dye will remain."

Asterin nodded. "So at least we'll know whether or not Harry is the demon."

Rose began gathering the maps. "Then let's get started. It'll probably take a few days to set it up, and we have to make sure Harry doesn't suspect anything."

"You know what?" Asterin said. Her eyes glinted conspiringly. "Just to be safe, what do you say we keep this a secret from the boys entirely?"

All three of them shared identical, wicked grins.

CHAPTER TWENTY-SIX

"All right, Princess," Quinlan said, standing in the clearing with the forest at his back. The horses were safe in the barn, and Luna was inside the cottage. He folded his arms, examining the princess before him from head to toe. The girl was already in a defensive stance, her expression wary, as if she half-expected to be ambushed by his arrows again. *Good.* "What are the two types of magic?"

"Spells and raw magic," Asterin answered without hesitation.

"Correct. Spells are commanded by incantations derived from the Immortal tongue. Raw magic is commanded by thought. Why do we need spells when we have raw magic?"

"Spells have specific purposes that raw magic cannot always achieve, like healing or shielding."

He nodded. "Exactly. No matter the affinity, no wielder can heal without the healing incantation. Energy shields cannot be produced by any element. Affinity stones are tools. They help us tap into the magic in our bodies, but that's it—they aren't the actual source of magic. *You* are. And you have enough power in your body to forgo the stone entirely. You just have to figure out how to release it."

Asterin made a face. "You make it sound easy."

"It will be, eventually. But you've been relying on affinity stones as crutches for your whole life. You'll need a lot of patience and practice to walk on your own." Quinlan pressed his palms together, twisted his wrists, then let his hands drift apart as a glowing orb of light slowly expanded at his fingertips. "Attention, control, and efficiency. Let those be your new rules. We'll begin with attention." He stepped off to the left while beckoning Asterin forward. "First, we hone your focus—you won't be able to summon anything without strength of mind." Taking a few more steps backward, Quinlan raised his right arm, and the orb burst into flame. "Try to dodge."

Asterin took up her defensive stance once more. With her knees bent and her fists loosely clenched, she coiled, ready to spring. Quinlan noted her eyes, riveted on his fire, her muscles drawn taut in anticipation.

Only to be hit with a scorching blast of flames from behind.

Asterin yowled, twisting around. "What in the Immortals—"

With a smirk, Quinlan extinguished it. "Pay more attention next time."

"You set my trousers on fire, you lunatic!" Asterin exclaimed, batting away the embers.

"Quit whining. In an actual fight, I would've set *you* on fire." Her mouth snapped shut. "When you beat my ass in swordplay, you told me that I had to be aware of more than just my opponent's weapon, right?"

"Yes." She grinned. "And then I cornered you up against an open window and you almost fell to your death."

He sneered. "Shut up. Anyway, this is the same thing. Since magic can take on infinite forms, limited only to the wielder's imagination, it is the most flexible weapon. So use that to your advantage." Quinlan reached into his pocket and tossed her the omnistone. "Here's your next lesson. Control."

Asterin caught it with surprise. "Why are you giving this back?"

"No offense, but you can barely summon magic without it. We're taking things slow." Quinlan splayed his hand outward, bright orange flame igniting in his palm. "Use your ice to smother the fire. However you choose to form your ice, keep it as close to the flames as possible. Remember, this is about precision, not power."

Doubt flashed across her features, but he gave her a nod of encouragement and dropped his hand, leaving the ball of fire to bob between them.

Slowly, a white shell of frost began to creep around the bottom of the ball of fire, but it hissed away to steam almost immediately. Asterin tried again.

Each attempt grew better and better, until her ice cupped half the flame—but by then, the bottom covering had melted and dripped onto the grass.

The back door opened and Luna drifted into the garden. Quinlan caught a whiff of something that smelled of fermentation. He frowned, but turned his attention back to Asterin when she let out a growl.

"This is ridiculous," she said, her shoulders hunching. Displeasure rolled off her in waves. The ground at their feet had begun to freeze over, bejeweling the grass with snowflakes wherever the melted droplets fell—but the flame still blazed strong. "I would never need to extinguish a fire like this in a fight."

"Don't be stupid." His breath clouded up in puffs of fog. "Of course you wouldn't. The purpose of this is to hone your control." He shifted, grass crunching underfoot, shivering. "So shut up and focus."

She clenched her jaw. "I am."

"Focus *harder*, then."

"I'm trying!" Asterin yelled. With a snarl, she stamped her foot on the grass. The temperature plunged. The frost beneath Asterin's feet exploded, racing outward and blanketing the entire clearing in ice. Her ice curved up from the base of the flame, up and over the top. The roof of Harry's cottage and the tree branches glistened white, icicles hanging from the eaves. Luna fled back into the house, her skin tinged blue. When Quinlan inhaled, it felt like he had swallowed a lungful of snow.

And yet, the flame still burned as brightly as before.

"Trying isn't good enough," Quinlan barked, throat raw and stinging from the frigid air. He met her livid gaze. "Just *do*."

With a puff of vapor and bitter cold that sent chills down Quinlan's arms, the flame sputtered out.

What remained was an egg-shaped hollow made of ice, lingering in the air for a split second before falling to the ground, the fragments splintering at their feet.

Asterin panted, grinning to herself in victory.

Quinlan bent down to pick up a sliver, holding it to the light. "That was terrible."

Her face fell. "Why?" she spluttered.

"Look around you," he chided. "Sure, you succeeded in extinguishing the flame, but look how much magic you wasted. What if the grass and the trees had been your soldiers? Or what if you'd been sitting atop your horse?" He flicked the scrap of ice over his shoulder. "You'd have frozen him half to death."

"What now?" she asked, defeated.

It was Quinlan's turn to grin. "Again."

To say that Orion was surprised to find snow decorating Harry's roof like a Vürstivale holiday greeting card after a weary day of demon-searching would have been a severe understatement. But with the passing of Asterin's every training session with Quinlan, the icicles dangling from the eaves receded slightly, and the temperature went from borderline glacial to an early spring chill.

Orion knew one thing for certain—Asterin had never been terribly aware of her own limits, for better or for worse. Sure enough, he came home with his team one day to find her passed out on the sofa, a cloth draped over her forehead.

Orion pressed the back of his hand to her cheek and recoiled at the heat. He glanced around the living room and growled. "Fireface."

Quinlan's head popped out of the kitchen. "I'm trying to make soup." He held his hands up when Orion opened his mouth. "I know. I overworked her. I'm sorry."

"Get her some tea," Rose said to Eadric as she hung her cloak on the banister in the foyer."

"I'll go grab some more blankets," Harry volunteered, and dashed up the staircase.

There was a yelp of pain and then metal clattering onto stone. "Quinlan, you idiot, you dented the kettle," Luna exclaimed from inside the kitchen.

Asterin shifted, eyes fluttering open and head turning as Orion crouched on the rug beside her. The cloth slipped from her forehead, but he caught it and cooled it with his magic before replacing it.

Asterin blinked up at him, focusing. "Morning."

Orion smiled, tucking a stray lock of ebony hair behind her ear. "*Evening*, warrior princess. How are you feeling?"

Asterin groaned, eyes closing. "Like shit."

Quinlan hobbled into the living room holding a bowl of broth and a mug of tea. "The others are going to start making dinner. Sorry about the noise, I dropped the kettle on my foot."

Orion snorted. "You deserve it. Look what you've done to Asterin."

The princess's eyes snapped open, glowering at Orion. "He didn't do anything. I did this to myself, and I regret nothing. Now let me sleep."

Orion fell silent. He glanced at Quinlan, expecting to see lips twisted in a smirk, but the Eradorian only seemed to have eyes for Asterin. Eyes full of concern, with a hint of tenderness.

Orion tried not to gag.

"She's been training with me every day," Quinlan said softly, placing the fruit and water aside on the coffee table and taking a seat on the table's edge. "Slowly but surely building up her endurance." He shook his head. "Anyone would be impressed by her determination."

"I … I wish I could help," Orion admitted, watching as Asterin's breathing evened out. "With her training, I mean." He had been her mentor for nearly a decade, after all. But his strength had never been in magic. In fact, Asterin had taught him most of what he knew. That trade was how she had convinced him to train her in combat in the first place. "But I would just spend the entire time stopping myself from wringing your neck anytime you pushed her too hard."

A wry smile. "You still hate me that much, huh?"

Orion blew out a long breath. "I never hated you. Well, maybe a little. But not anymore."

"Prove it."

"There hasn't ever been anything between Asterin and me. Romantically, I mean. She's like my little sister."

Quinlan gaped. "Seriously? So I've been freaking out over nothing?"

Orion blew out a second, much longer breath. "And I do trust you. More importantly, I trust you not to hurt Asterin. Even now, you're pushing her to make her stronger. So she can protect herself. Right?"

Quinlan nodded slowly at him, lips still parted like a fish out of water.

"As long as Asterin is safe," Orion said, "that's all that matters to me." With that, he maneuvered himself so he could lean against the sofa armrest and then closed his eyes.

Between his memories of the wyvern, his falling nightmare, and the images of the massacre at Corinthe, Orion had been struggling to find other thoughts to occupy his mind—but seeing Asterin throw herself into training until her body failed her sent a wave of nostalgia over him. That stubborn will to succeed had never bent—not when he first began training her, and not since.

After Orion's father had saved him from bleeding to death beneath that lake dock and he had said his goodbyes to the bodies of his mother and sister, General Garringsford had ordered Theodore Galashiels to return to Axaris with two squads and, of course, his son, while the rest of the soldiers stayed behind to bury the dead.

When Orion arrived at the Axarian palace, he had met King Tristan, a handsome man whose eyes radiated a reassuring warmth despite the pain from his kingdom's loss. There had been a royal funeral in honor of the victims, but Orion refused to leave his new chambers, eating nothing and drinking only when his throat was so parched that it hurt to swallow.

Perhaps a week later, he had finally ventured into the corridor and nearly crashed into a little girl. She hurtled past him, an affinity stone clutched in her chubby fist, shrieking with delight as not one but two nursemaids chased after her. A trail of ice followed in her wake, and the nursemaids toppled over the moment they set foot upon it.

Orion himself had burst out laughing, hysterical howls that folded his body in half. When the nursemaids attempted to rise, they slipped onto their backsides like overturned turtles, limbs flailing. Orion laughed until tears streamed down his face—tears of happiness. He never cried, but somehow, he knew that this didn't count.

He started eating again that day, and his smiles came easier and easier every day after that.

That was how he had first met little Princess Asterin, with her bright green eyes and her lovely round face, unbroken by trauma and full of joy.

He would think about her constantly in the coming weeks. He already loved her then, though he hadn't yet known it.

"You will protect her, one day," his father had told him when Orion shared the story of his encounter right before bedtime.

"When?"

"After you complete your training."

"Can we start? Now?"

A laugh. "No, now you must sleep. Tomorrow, if you'd like."

Asterin had just turned six when he had at last been allowed to formally meet her, with both of their fathers chaperoning the tea party the princess had courteously arranged. Over mini sandwiches, Orion vowed that he would spend every waking moment training to be her Guardian.

On his thirteenth birthday, his father deemed him qualified for his position. Until Orion turned sixteen, his father was technically both the king's and Asterin's official Guardian, but everyone had known that Orion was ready.

That was the year King Tristan had died. Orion couldn't remember how many hours he had spent sitting on Asterin's bed while the princess sobbed into his shoulder.

Only days later, the seven-year-old had kicked down his door, barging in with her chest puffed and her eyes alight with a determination that outshone her grief, dragging a sword that she must have stolen from the armory behind her.

"Wake up," she demanded.

Orion yawned and buried his face into his pillow. "Go away. The sun isn't even properly up yet."

The princess clambered onto his bed and began jumping, the springs squealing beneath her. "Teach me how to fight."

He lifted his head, nearly biting his tongue off as she launched into the air. "What?"

She brandished the sword—or attempted to. It was too heavy, and she slashed off the corner of his mattress instead. "Train me!"

"Put that sword down before you kill the both of us!"

She dropped it onto the carpet with a grumble, and then continued jumping. "Train me," she repeated.

"Why?"

"I want to be able to protect myself."

Orion sat up, positively affronted. "*I'm* supposed to protect you."

Asterin pouted, jaw set. "I'll let you use my affinity stones."

He snorted. "Father got me my own."

She faltered at the word *father*, then crossed her arms over her chest. "And how many can you actually use?"

He ducked his head, face coloring. "One," he mumbled.

"If you train me, I'll try and help you."

That perked him up. He hesitated only a moment. "Really?"

She nodded. "Sure! We can protect each other better that way. Deal?"

What's the harm, anyway? Orion wondered. King Tristan had known how to fight, so Orion didn't see any reason why his daughter shouldn't. "Deal."

He forced her through the same basic drills his own father had forced him through—running up and down the stairs, jumping over fences, sprinting through the gardens until she vomited into the flowerbeds. He taught her how to throw a punch without breaking her thumb and where the most delicate parts of the body were as well as how to target them. He taught her the way his father had taught him to wield a weapon, starting with wooden swords and hammers and pocket knives. Then he taught her how to manipulate any object—a candelabra, a belt—into a weapon. Only then did he put a sword in her hand. She took quickly to the steel, especially after claiming Amoux, her father's old weapon, even though she could barely lift it.

Orion was useless with a bow, so Asterin coerced another guard to teach her archery. She bribed the horse master to let her ride at twilight with only the moon for company, and the locksmith to teach her lock-picking. Whatever knowledge Orion couldn't provide her, she seized by other means. Her thirst to learn was insatiable.

And true to her word, Asterin did her best to help Orion hone his magical powers. Under her guidance, he mastered another two elements.

As the years progressed, he watched her grow stronger and stronger, until there came a day when she trounced three guards at once without using a single drop of magic.

With magic, a half-dozen wouldn't have stood a chance.

Of course, there were always blisters and cuts and broken bones, and once a punctured lung, but no injuries severe enough that they couldn't be fixed up with a few tonics and spells. Then, one day, Asterin had come to dinner with an untended bruise coloring her eye.

Queen Priscilla had all but dragged her by the ear into the corridor and exploded. "This is unacceptable and inappropriate. For the love of the Immortals, you are a lady!"

Orion stepped forward to take the blame, but Asterin had just crossed her arms. "So?"

Once Priscilla realized that Asterin would never conform to her expectations, she decided to put her daughter's abilities to good use by sending her and Orion on assignments around the kingdom. The queen frequently traveled to other cities and even continents for weeks at a time for important meetings, but there were other matters that required a more covert approach. For those, Priscilla would disguise Asterin and Orion with her illusion affinity, and then they would travel all over Axaria.

Asterin loved going on those assignments. In disguise, it gave her the chance to interact with her people, not as their future ruler, but as their equal. To hear what they *wanted* to say, rather than what they were supposed to say.

"Is this why you asked me to train you?" Orion had asked her once on their way back to Axaris. "So you could go out into the kingdom secretly? Without the Elites guarding you?"

Her eyebrows rose. "No. I would have found a way to do that, anyway."

"Then why?"

"I told you years ago."

"To be able to protect yourself?"

"Yes." When she spoke again, her voice was solemn. "My father died from an untouchable illness. But if it had been anything else, something he could have fought with steel, I know he would have. And …"

"And?"

She turned to him, eyes blazing. "If I ever have to fight, I will. And I will *always* win."

Orion awoke a few hours later, a blanket that smelled like Harry draped around his shoulders. Someone had left him a plate of stew with bread on the low table. Quinlan lay sprawled on the rug at his right, an arm draped over his eyes and a makeshift pillow that looked suspiciously like Asterin's cloak beneath his head.

He rolled the stiffness from his shoulders and turned in the darkness toward Asterin, slumbering peacefully on the sofa behind him.

"My life is yours," Orion whispered to the sleeping princess. "I know you don't need me, but I vowed to protect your life with mine, and I will never forsake that promise."

He turned back around, already drifting off when he felt a hand trail through his hair and come to rest gently against his cheek.

Orion smiled.

CHAPTER TWENTY-SEVEN

In the good dreams, it was always winter. Asterin loved winter. She loved the raw bite of bitter wind on her skin. The pale morning horizons, the slate-gray dawns bleeding into vermilion sunrises, setting the undisturbed snowdrifts ablaze with brilliant reds and oranges. The fresh, crisp air, kissed with the subtle fragrance of evergreens.

When it snowed back home, blanketing everything in sight in a thick carpet of white, she would sneak out of the palace before the sun came up and ride with Lux to the sacred grove of white birches bordering the southern residential district. It was where her father rested in the royal tomb, where all the other Faelenharts before him rested, and where she would rest one day, too. She never made it there unnoticed—Orion and a few Elite Royal Guards usually lurked nearby, but far enough away that she could imagine that she was alone.

Asterin would find a rock to sit on and simply wallow in a quiet that seemed to stretch on for eternity, serene and unbreakable. If she looked up she would see thousands of delicate flakes whirling in the breeze as they fell from the sky in flurries of virgin white.

But in this dream, when she sat upon the rock, the snow stilled and hung midair.

"Milady," a voice said from behind her in a tone so deep that it vibrated through her bones. Asterin turned to find herself staring at a massive man.

An ethereal glow pulsed around his figure. He was beautiful in a rugged, brutal way, from the severe cut of his nose and jaw to the windblown silver hair and familiar, piercing emerald eyes. A nonexistent wind carried the crimson cape flowing from his shoulders. Jagged steel embellished his pauldrons, mimicking icicles. He wore silver vambraces and a polished chest plate, the emblem of the House of the Wolf engraved into the center. A ruby-hilted sword with a double-headed wolf pommel identical to her own hung at his side.

What caught her attention, though, was his very presence—ancient and immense. Despite his middle-aged appearance, Asterin knew that he was no ordinary mortal. He was as old as time itself.

"Lord Conrye," she greeted without a doubt in her mind.

The God of Ice nodded. "Princess Asterin."

"Is this your … human form?" she asked.

"Indeed." His gaze fixed into the distance. "You have questions. Ask them."

She rose from the rock, still nowhere near eye-level with the Immortal. "Why did you have to leave? In Aldville?"

Conrye began to shrink to mortal height as he answered. "I was never supposed to be there in the first place, Princess. Immortals mustn't interact with their descendants—that was the promise all of us on the Council made when we shed our blood to create mortalkind. Lady Siore of the earth forged the nine kingdoms from her bosom, and each of us birthed a House to rule over those kingdoms, with magic—our magic—running through your veins. At the beginning, we guided you so that you might remember where you came from, and what you might become. But nothing more."

"But you broke that promise," Asterin pointed out. "You still came to save us at the inn."

"I came to save *you*," the God of Ice corrected. He huffed a laugh and shook his head. "I received the punishment I deserved from the Council, but I had sensed Eoin's hand, and intervened accordingly."

Asterin's eyes widened. "Eoin? The God of Shadow?"

"Yes. Not *himself*, not yet. He exempted himself from our rules long ago, and he fancies himself a puppeteer. How the Council continues to sit idly by while he interferes in the lives of mortals baffles me. I risk much by visiting you in this dream, but it must be done."

"What do you mean by Eoin's hand?" Asterin asked, her pulse quickening. "Did he send the demon to kill the people in Corinthe?"

Lord Conrye clasped her hands, his enormous palms dwarfing her fingers. "You must keep an open mind, Princess Asterin. The demon's actions in Corinthe may not be as straightforward as you imagine."

Asterin reeled back, snatching her hands away from Conrye. "What do you mean?"

"I can only advise you—" The Immortal suddenly cut off, his hand darting to his sword. The snow hanging in the air around him stirred, then hung still again.

"Lord Conrye," a voice like ocean thunder rumbled across the horizon. "Do not make me resort to threatening your seat on the Council."

"Lord Tidus," Conrye growled. "That old barnacled bastard." His eyes fixed back on Asterin. He spoke now with urgency. "Never let anger commandeer your decisions, Princess. Accept the truth for what it is, and your heart will show you the right path."

Asterin scowled. "Can you be a little more specific?"

Conrye began backing away. "No. I am not a fortune-teller, but you are of my blood, and that is the best advice I can offer you from personal experience. Now awaken, for the others need you."

With that, he shifted right before her eyes. His armor melded to his skin, transforming into a thick layer of fur. Seconds later, the wolf she had seen in Aldville bowed his head, sparing her one final glance, and then bolted away, nothing more than the glint of a knife's edge in a field of white. The snow suspended in the sky unfroze, their moment of stolen time dissipating like wisps of morning fog.

When Asterin opened her eyes, Luna and Rose hovered over her, their expressions alight with glee. Asterin smacked her lips, tasting summer berries.

"I made you a tonic," explained Rose. "Feeling better?"

Asterin sat up, her head clear and her body light. "Much."

Luna nodded. "Great. Because a flare just went up."

The demon! Asterin shot to her feet, vaulting over the back of the sofa and nearly crashing into the window. She spotted Quinlan loitering on the porch, staring into the distance. Asterin followed his line of sight up above the trees. And just as Luna had said, a bright red trail of smoke from a flare stained the evening horizon.

"It's close," said Asterin, feeling a little dazed. "Where's Harry?" She caught Rose and Luna exchanging a glance in the window reflection.

"Out," Luna said.

"We're bringing Quinlan along for backup," Rose said, "but we've instructed Eadric and Orion to stay here to keep an eye out for Harry and any … peculiarities."

Asterin grabbed her cloak off the sofa armrest and draped it across her shoulders, wondering for a fleeting moment why it smelled of smoke—of Quinlan. "All right, ladies." Rose and Luna followed her into the foyer. Asterin put her hand on the knob and smiled. "We've got ourselves a demon to catch."

Harry had sensed that the others were watching him more closely than ever before. Especially the girls. He wasn't sure what he'd done to pique their suspicion, but he felt the air go taut with tension whenever he entered the room. So he had managed to go a week without shifting, and every time he went to hunt he triple-checked for pursuers.

In the Immortal Realm, he sustained himself on nectar—but it turned to ash in the Mortal Realm. Human food didn't always provide him with the energy he needed, so he preyed upon livestock or game when the hunger became unbearable.

Tonight, his hunger had all but consumed him. He didn't have the time to go around checking his snares or searching for prey on foot. So he shifted into his demon form and barreled into the woods, promising himself he would stay close to the cottage and return soon.

Perhaps that had been his mistake. He felt the workings of the trap as soon as his front paws landed on the net—but by then, it was too late. He definitely hadn't set this one himself, and he hadn't even scented a trace of it, which meant that someone had charmed the trap into invisibility. The net yanked him up thirty feet into the air, and something wet and pungent exploded from a little tin canister attached to the very same pulley mechanism that Rose and Eadric and Luna had encountered a few weeks back.

Snarling, his tail and back legs getting increasingly tangled in the net, he gnawed on the rope, but it held fast. Also charmed. Whatever had sprayed from the canister now coated his fur. *Vinegar?* He thrashed around and smashed his right wing into a tree branch in a shower of leaves.

Be calm, he thought to himself. He forced himself to still, dizzy from swinging in circles so high above the ground. *You can escape before they find you.*

Sparks erupted from the branch above. Harry looked up to find that in his struggle to free himself, he had accidentally toggled some sort of switch. A flare shot straight up into the sky, marking a bullseye on his location.

Uselessly, he struggled again, thinking hard.

Shadow jump.

It was his only choice. He just prayed that he would have enough energy left over to make it back to the cottage.

Harry took a deep breath and started to rock back and forth. It only took a couple of pendulum swings before he felt the cool caress of the shadows of the tree boughs brush against him, and then he was gone.

Shadow travel was as simple as touching any shadow and jumping to another shadow elsewhere—anywhere, as long as there existed even the tiniest slice of darkness. But it required a tremendous amount of energy, and it could have devastating consequences on his body.

He transported himself to his hollowed-out tree and nearly fainted right there, wings hanging limply at his sides. A pair of terrified rabbits scampered past him for their burrow a few feet away, but two flicks of his barbed tail impaled them. Harry devoured both and then shifted back to his human form, spitting rabbit fur from his mouth. Staggering toward the stream nearby, he fell to his knees, naked, and dunked his face in the frigid water to wash the blood from his chin.

"Harry!"

He shot up at the voice, dangerously close, his blood thrumming. It was Asterin. He had no doubt that she had set the trap, perhaps with the help of Luna and Rose—he *knew* that they had been up to something. He guessed that they were heading for the flare and calling for him on their way.

A dark blue splatter reeking of vinegar stained his skin all the way from his chest down his right arm to the fingertips. He plunged himself into the stream and scrubbed vigorously, dread rising into his throat when it didn't so much as smudge. *To reveal me*, he realized. Only a huge mass could set off that trap. No mere mortal could have escaped it.

He was so stupid.

Kill them now. It's the only way out.

But he couldn't. If he did, he would be disobeying the Woman's orders to keep Asterin alive.

"Shit," he muttered to himself, and staggered back to the hollow tree, throwing his clothes on. Luckily, the smell was mostly gone, and his coat covered most of the stain. He convinced himself that as long as he kept his right hand in his pocket, everything would be fine.

He made it back to the cottage in record time, calming himself before he entered.

Eadric sat on the staircase, elbows propped on his knees, already tracking Harry's every movement with a flat black gaze. "Evening, Harry."

Harry swallowed. "Evening, Eadric."

"Catch anything?" the captain asked, jerking his chin at the crossbow Harry clutched in his left fist.

"Oh, is Harry home?" Orion called from the kitchen. Harry's knees nearly gave out in relief when the blond boy drifted into the foyer holding a frying pan.

"Yep." Harry forced a smile and hung up his crossbow. He strode over to the staircase, but Eadric blocked the steps from wall to banister. "Sorry, Captain. Do you mind?"

Eadric didn't budge. "Why are you still wearing your coat?"

Harry blinked, and then shrugged. "It's a little chilly." In one swift movement, he bent his arms behind him and let the sleeves slide off. With his right hand, he grasped the collar of the coat, concealing the stain from view. Then, trying to sound indignant, he said, "Could you excuse me, please?" It was *his* house, after all.

"Move, Eadric," said Orion with an eye roll.

The captain complied grudgingly, and Harry forced himself to take one leisurely step up the stairs at a time. He made it to his room and locked the door behind him, thanking Orion in his head.

Double-checking that his blinds were closed, he shucked off his clothes down to his boxers and stared at his reflection in the obsidian mirror. The stain was still there, like a half-shirt. He spat into his left hand and tried rubbing it off his chest again, unsurprisingly to no avail. With a furious growl, he clawed his nails down his chest, hard enough to draw five slashes of blood.

Panting, he weighed his options as he began to pace the room. When he came up empty, his eyes returned to the mirror, where his immortal body had already knitted the slashes together, leaving five pale lines of healed skin. Unstained skin.

He knew what he had to do.

Grabbing a pair of socks from the wardrobe and the largest blade from the assortment of knives in the bottom drawer, he walked back over to the mirror and balled the socks before stuffing them into his mouth.

And then he began to carve.

He sheared off the skin on his palm first, then each individual finger, then the back of his hand, gripping the knife handle as hard as he could to keep from shaking. Silver blood poured onto the floor, pooling around the scraps of blue flesh—which, parted from his body, had already withered like dead leaves. With every slice, he closed his eyes and did his best to wait through the pain. His body was still weak from shadow jumping and near starvation, but within a few minutes the skin on his hand had regenerated.

Another deep inhale and he dragged the knife down from his shoulder to his wrist, tears burning into his eyes. He pared his arm like a vegetable, biting down on the socks to muffle his scream. The blade caught on the back of his elbow and he had to pause, slumping against the mirror, the strip of skin hanging from his arm like a ribbon. Black spots blotted his vision. He blinked them away and finished the cut. Finally—finally, came his chest. His hand quaked so hard he nearly stabbed himself.

King Eoin has broken you a thousand times worse. This is nothing, he chanted in his head. *This is nothing*.

He closed his eyes and drank in the agony, letting his instincts guide the blade, sharp and true, running across his collarbone and stripping himself down to muscle and bone.

When it was done, Harry threw the knife onto the bed and collapsed beside it, curling up and burying his face into the pillow, chest jerking with empty breaths.

Downstairs, the front door opened with Asterin's return. He could hear all of them talking. The smell of stew wafted to his nose, teasing at his hunger, and he whimpered quietly.

He caught the shuffle of footsteps on the stairs. They reached the landing and grew closer, stopping in front of his door. He knew it was Asterin from the sound of her steps alone, but he humored her tentative knock. "Harry," she said. "Dinner's ready. Are you coming?"

Harry hauled himself out of bed and lifted the rug, moving it to cover the pool of blood and pile of shriveled flesh. He unlocked the door and cracked it open with a smile on his face. "Hey."

Asterin smiled back, but he could tell it was forced. "Eadric said you didn't look well."

"Sorry. I'm feeling a little under the weather." He ran a hand through his hair and joked, "Maybe you passed your cold on to me."

Asterin's brows shot upward. "Oh, Immortals, I hope not!" She paused. "You should come downstairs and have something to eat, you know."

"I guess." Slowly, he opened the door all the way, savoring the relief that washed over her features when her eyes ran down his body.

"Maybe put some clothes on, though?" she said.

Harry let his mouth fall open, cheeks heating. "Oh. I'm so sorry." He pushed out a laugh. "Just give me a minute."

He turned his back on her, feeling the telltale tingle down his spine that revealed she was examining him again. By the time he had pulled on a new shirt and trousers, her smile was genuine.

Once downstairs, he followed her into the dining room. Quinlan was in the middle of a story about some girl abandoning him in a hedge maze.

Asterin stifled a laugh. Rose and Luna looked up when Harry and Asterin joined them at the table, and Asterin tipped her chin almost imperceptibly. The girls' shoulders relaxed.

Orion came out of the kitchen balancing the huge pot of stew Harry had smelled earlier. The Guardian served Harry first with a wink, spooning stew onto the bed of rice on his plate until it nearly flowed off the edges.

After everyone had been served, Harry let himself dig in. Quinlan finished his story and Luna launched into a loving account of how Eadric had begun courting her. Between bites, Harry tried to imagine their blood on his hands. Tried to imagine their bodies slumped across the dining table among shattered plates and cups, their eyes glazed over and forever unseeing. No one could see Harry's legs tremble beneath the table as he took a sip of water.

Orion's knee brushed Harry's. He glanced up to find the Guardian with his head tilted in concern. "Everything okay?"

Self-hatred washed over Harry. He hated being forced to hide and lie to these people. Whatever torment he put himself through for them wasn't their fault, and he could never—*would* never resent them for that.

"I'm fine," Harry whispered, staring into Orion's ice-chip eyes. And he *was* fine. Orion's hand brushed the new skin of Harry's palm, and he shivered, remembering the pain. Yet at that moment, he knew with certainty that he would do it all over again to keep these good people safe. Surrounded by their smiles, and with Orion's hand in his, he could believe that everything would turn out all right.

That night, the Woman summoned him once more.

"Demon," the Woman said from the dark depths of the mirror.

He bowed his head. As usual, he could hear Eadric snoring in the other room. "Milady."

"Get it done by the end of the week."

Harry's breath caught in his chest. "End of *this* week?"

"Yes. And I want you to bring some sort of evidence to me."

Harry's entire body went cold. "Evidence?"

"Perhaps her heart in a velvet case," she said with a chuckle, amused by her own ingenuity.

"Yes, milady," he managed, even as the desire to rip her throat out—whoever she was—threatened to overpower every other rational thought in his mind.

"Fairfest Eve is soon. Bring it to me then, when everyone will be distracted by all the festivities. When you arrive in the capital, do try to be ... discreet. If you're caught," the Woman warned, "you'll be as good as dead."

How dead can an immortal demon get? he wondered.

"Do not fail me," she warned just before the black void rippled and faded.

Harry exhaled and sank onto the bed, picking at a speck of dried blood on the sheets. The Woman's words rang in his head as he eased himself back onto the pillows and stared at the patterns in the ceiling, his fingers steepled beneath his chin.

Once, a long, long time ago, Harry had been mortal. Then, there came a day when the moon had swallowed the sun, casting the land in a darkness as black as night, and the God of Shadow had come for him. Had claimed him.

With the powers Eoin had given Harry as an anygné—including shifting, healing, and shadow jumping—he could also identify others with shadow magic running through their veins. Dark magic left a unique signature, and when wielded, that signature could linger behind on a person for years. Then there were those who Eoin lovingly called *shadow-kissed.* The shadow-kissed had the god's sigil hovering above their heads, which meant that one day Eoin would come to claim them as his own.

Harry had been the debt his parents owed to Eoin in exchange for the power of the tenth element. And once Eoin claimed him, the God of Shadow had presented him with the contract. Harry learned that he had two options—sign or die. By signing, he would not only be granted immortality, but also the power of the tenth element to use as he pleased, so long as he followed the king's orders.

Not yet twenty years old, he thought the choice had seemed easy at the time. And so he had signed away an eternity, not caring much for the consequences. Not caring for time. Time didn't matter when you could have as much of it as you wanted.

But now, it did.

It mattered for Asterin, whose forehead burned with faded dark spells she knew not of. Spells that had set her down a path that could lead to her undoing. It mattered for Luna, whose veins coursed with suppressed power—and whose head was crowned with the shadow sigil, marking her as the debt someone owed to King Eoin. Marking her as shadow-kissed, just like Harry had once been.

Dark secrets and an unknown past were hidden within the blood and bones of the Princess of Axaria and her loyal friend. Harry just needed to figure out what those secrets *were*. But how could he reveal their truths without revealing himself?

Obey the Woman. Her assets are of great importance to me.

He could do that. In fact, the Woman's vague command to "get it done" worked perfectly to his advantage.

An idea finally formed in the back of his mind. He had always wondered why the Woman wanted to kill the princess, and maybe now, by helping Asterin, he could find an answer for himself, too.

As the early morning light crept past his curtains, the idea grew, pushing its way past the other thoughts crowding his head.

Harry's eyes flew open.

I need the lake.

CHAPTER TWENTY-EIGHT

The dappled sunlight warmed her face as Rose took a much-needed swig from her waterskin and wiped her mouth on her sleeve. It was always hottest during the afternoon in the Aswiyre Forest, when the air sweltered from the midday sun—but luckily the tangles of branches high above provided ample shade. Still, it seemed that spring had no place in Axaria. Summer was already well on its way.

A muffled, eerie quiet filled her head. Usually, birds searching for mates flitted above, their keening chirps accompanied by the soft rustle of leaves and the distant flap of wings. But not today. Rose tried to enjoy the silence, but she should have known it was more of a menacing omen than anything comforting.

Their little hunting party shuddered to a halt before the trunk of a towering fir tree.

"Are those ..." Eadric trailed off.

"Claw marks," said Harry. "Though never in my life have I seen markings from an animal so big."

"Might not have been an animal, then," Rose murmured.

"Big marks mean big claws," said Orion, brushing two fingers across the shredded bark.

Rose's heart skipped a beat. She pointed past the fir. "Look over there."

Not more than fifty paces ahead, the ground dipped deep into a wide ravine. She could just make out the entrance to a yawning cave hidden in the gloom of three uprooted trees propped atop it like matchsticks. The waterlogged loam leading up to the cave mouth was scattered with a trail of white twigs. Rose squinted. With a sickening lurch, she realized they weren't twigs at all, but bones, picked clean.

They all froze as a guttural growl ripped from the inside of the cave.

"Demon," Eadric breathed. "Let's go."

"Wait, we should go back and get the others," Orion whispered. "That thing is probably massive."

"We outnumber it four to one," Eadric argued, even while staring at the trail of bones. "What if it moves somewhere else? We'll have lost our only lead."

"It's clearly been camped here for at least a little while. I think it's worth—"

Harry held up a hand, silencing them. His nostrils twitched as he sniffed the air, eyebrows furrowed. Then the blood drained from his face. "We have to get out of here. Now." Despite his hushed voice, the command was sharp and unyielding. "Orion's right. We're not facing this thing with just the four of us."

"But—" Eadric protested.

"I get that you want its head," Harry hissed. "But if you wish to keep yours, we need the others."

Rose tightened her grip on her bow, an arrow nocked on the drawstring. The fletching was coarse and comforting between her fingers, ready to fly into the inky black depths of the cave the moment she drew the bow taut. "The faster we can round them up, the faster we can come back here and put an end to all of this."

"*But—*"

The creature in the cave growled again.

"Asterin put *me* in charge of this team, Eadric," Orion snapped. "And I am not going to disappoint her." Quieter, he added, "Not again."

A tense beat passed before the captain gave in at last. "Homeward bound, then."

When Orion burst into the clearing with the others right on his heels, it only took Asterin a single look at their faces for her ice, weaving intricate patterns between Quinlan's flames, to disintegrate.

Training was over.

"You found the demon," said Asterin. Her stomach leaped at the glimmer in Orion's eyes as he nodded, a sharp exhale tearing through her. She sprinted for the front door and pounded on it with both fists.

Luna opened it, a book in hand and one eyebrow arched. "It's unlocked, you know."

"Demon," said Asterin.

The book slipped from Luna's hand. "They found it?"

"Hurry." Asterin strode toward the trees, hearing Luna scrabble with the door behind her. Blood buzzing, she nodded at Orion. "Lead us there."

Quinlan's fingers snagged her wrist. "Asterin, let's not be hasty." He turned to his cousin. "What did the demon look like?"

"Well, we found these huge claw marks, larger than those of any predator," said Rose. "And a trail of bones leading to their owner's cave."

"So you didn't actually see the demon itself?" asked Quinlan.

Rose shook her head. "But demon or not, we need to investigate."

Harry led the way westward, more familiar with the forest's sprawl. Asterin's palms itched with the craving for long-anticipated vengeance. She could almost feel Amoux's thirst, waiting for blood. She kept herself occupied by running through the list of ways she had dreamt of since Corinthe to make the demon suffer, ignoring Quinlan's warnings that it might not even be the demon, but rather just some lesser creature, like the wyvern.

"All I'm saying is, don't get your hopes up," he said.

"I heard you the first dozen times," she bit out, her pace quickening.

Quinlan easily caught up to her. "Just don't do anything rash, brat."

She scowled, struggling to fight down the animosity she knew he didn't deserve. "Quinlan, how would you feel if some beast invaded your kingdom, massacring everything in sight?" Her voice wavered. "Corinthe has been wiped off the map."

"I would be desperate for revenge," Quinlan said, raising an eyebrow. "And rightly so. But please, if only for my sake, remember that your mother sent legions of trained guards to take down this thing ... and they all failed."

At last arriving at the fir tree, Asterin struggled to keep her jaw from dropping. The bark on the trunk had been mauled to ribbons—each claw mark at least the length of her torso and two fingers thick.

Quinlan let out a low whistle. "I'm still not convinced it's the demon, but I admit that whatever made these could do some serious damage."

Rose pointed up ahead into the dip of a ravine. "That's it. That's the cave." And just as the Eradorian had described, a trail of bones, leading to the entrance.

"We can't go down there," said Quinlan, scrutinizing the steep walls of the ravine. "If it corners us while we're trying to scramble back up out of the sides ..."

"Then we'll draw it out from here," Asterin replied, the omnistone warm in her hand. She kept Amoux sheathed. To get close enough to land a hit on the demon would likely be suicide. She glanced at the others, flanking her on both sides with their affinity stones and their weapons brandished. "Ready?"

Quinlan, at her right, gave her a firm nod.

Asterin took a deep breath, determination heating her blood. She thought of the endless hours she had spent training with him and released a ragged exhale.

She summoned her magic and sent a torrent of razor-sharp fragments of ice into the darkness of the cave.

A second passed, and then—

A mighty, enraged bellow exploded forth, scattering the birds from the treetops above. Dull *booms* rocked the ground, as loud as cannon blasts. Asterin's heart kicked into a gallop when she realized that they were footsteps.

She counted to five in her head as a dark shadow loomed within the cave, growing closer and closer to the light. Fluorescent eyes glared at her from the darkness.

The breath rushed out of her lungs in one long *whoosh* as the creature finally emerged.

In all honesty, Luna felt a little disappointed.

She had imagined that the demon would be a lot … bigger.

It was certainly ugly, though. Matted gray fur covered the top half of its sinewy, four-legged body. Silver scales ran down its torso, ending in a thick, reptilian tail. Its paws were monstrous things, with claws matching the size of the markings they had discovered on the fir tree. Among a row of needlelike teeth were two elongated fangs, dripping a bright fuchsia. Its eyes fixated on each of them in turn, brimming with purple hatred.

"Hold … hold on," Asterin stammered as the creature lumbered out of the cave. "That man, that witness—Crawson. Crawson said … *red* eyes." The creature's steps grew louder, and Luna had to fight the urge to cover her ears. "And black fur. And wings."

It took the others a long moment to process Asterin's words.

Luna's voice squeaked. "So … that's not the demon."

Harry clapped a hand to his mouth. "No, that's a *dybrulé*."

"Impossible," Orion said. "Dybrulés went extinct centuries ago."

Luna gulped as they all began backing away. "Apparently not so extinct."

The creature roared at them, clawing up the sides of the ravine. Quinlan held up a hand and the dirt walls loosened, causing the creature to slip back to the bottom.

"Somebody kill it," said Orion.

"We can't kill a supposedly extinct creature!" Asterin exclaimed.

"Then it's going to kill *us*!" Quinlan yelled.

Asterin shook her head. "We are not killing it."

"Then we run?" Luna asked anxiously. "Can we run now?"

"Running sounds quite good to me," Eadric agreed.

"We cannot outrun a dybrulé," Harry told them.

Quinlan nodded. "We stay and fight it, then."

Asterin glared at him. "No. We came to defeat the demon, not kill innocent beasts living peacefully in the forest."

"An innocent beast that's about to eat us alive!"

"Wait!" Harry cried. "I read somewhere ... a long time ago. Dybrulés are fire spirits."

"So we could douse it in water?" Orion asked. They all turned to Rose—except for Harry.

"No," he said, "we would need a much larger body of water." His eyes lit up just as the dybrulé let out another roar, the tip of its gigantic, ridged head just appearing over the crest of the ravine. Luna caught sight of its frothing maw, pulled back in a snarl, and gulped. "A lake. There's a lake nearby. Follow me, and run as if your life depends on it."

"Won't be too difficult," Quinlan said, thrusting out an arm. Chunks of earth tumbled down the lip of the ravine, burying the dybrulé up to its neck.

Together, they broke into a wild sprint, trusting Harry to lead them through the unfamiliar terrain of the forest. Not a minute later, an earth-shattering bellow exploded behind them. Luna stumbled and nearly lost her balance, only just recovering as heavy thumps shook the ground.

"Do dybrulés eat humans?" Quinlan yelled.

"I'm not sure, and I'd rather not find out," Harry gasped. He surged forward in a burst of speed, leaving the rest of them no choice but to press on faster.

They thundered through the forest, whipping past a blur of branches and leaves. Luna's blood pounded in her ears, louder than a drum. She didn't dare look back, petrified of what she might find behind her.

Despite its size, the dybrulé was definitely fast. It trumpeted another roar at their backs. Definitely fast, and definitely gaining on them.

"Almost there," Harry shouted. "When I say jump, jump!"

"Why are we jumping?" Rose shrilled.

They suddenly broke through the trees, the soil beneath Luna's feet giving way to loose shale and wet pebbles. A sparkling expanse of water stretched out before her.

"*Jump!*"

She only noticed the strange, greenish tinge to the water after her feet had left the ground, her heart plummeting to her stomach as she plunged into the icy lake. The water closed over her head, bubbles swarming to the surface. In a frenzy, she paddled so deep that her ears popped, terrified that the dybrulé might leap in after them. Spots of light flashed across her vision as her hands hit the bottom of the lake, stirring up clouds of sediment. Panic seized her. Was she running out of air already?

Trying to right herself only dredged up more muck, until she was totally blind and disoriented. Had the dybrulé retreated yet? Were the banks in front of her? Which way was the surface?

Finally, the sediment settled. But as her legs scissored through the water, her movements grew sluggish. Eyes wide, she craned her neck, heart jolting as she took in just how far the surface was. In her panic, she realized too late that she had forgotten to conserve air and watched helplessly as a stream of precious air bubbles escaped her lips.

Her skin began to tingle, intensifying into a needling sensation that spread all over her body. She writhed, pressing her palms into her temples as a hot stab of pain raced up her spine and into her skull.

Luna choked in a mouthful of water, lungs seizing and muscles convulsing. Her heart thudded in her ears. *Swim, damn it.* Fuzziness crept into the corners of her vision. Dark cocoons of shadows arced toward her from the lake bottom like ink spilling across parchment, and she felt their cold wetness slithering up her legs in ribbons of silk. From the cocoons emerged black butterflies, their wings slicing through the water.

Her friends were nowhere in sight.

No one would save her.

Come to us, the shadows whispered. The butterflies forced her arms open in embrace. *We are yours, and you are ours.*

When they attacked, her mouth opened in an agonized scream no one would hear. Her skin stretched, her bones compressed and shifted. Pain was all she knew.

Then in her mind, she saw Asterin on her knees, fighting the yellow-eyed demon with everything she had, willing to die to protect her and Rose.

For Asterin, she would try and hold on.

But it hurt, hurt so badly that Luna wondered if it was wrong for her to surrender. The darkness beckoned to her again. *Come to us. We will be one and the same. Succumb, and we will make you remember.*

Remember what? Luna thought.

And as though the words were an invitation, the shadows tightened their hold on her and dragged her into the oblivion below.

CHAPTER TWENTY-NINE

Eadric dove straight to the bottom of the lake. Somewhere above him, he heard the muffled *plooshes* of the others entering the water. He kicked toward a cluster of green plants, thinking they would provide him cover in case Harry had been wrong and the dybrulé could swim. Only as something slimy latched onto his ankle and tugged did he realize his mistake. In the shadows, the plants looked like ordinary pondweed, but as they yanked him closer, he recognized them as mordrillia, a poisonous plant notorious for its hunting methods—drowning its prey by injecting paralyzing toxins through its minuscule needles. Cursing inwardly, he reached for his sword and slashed himself free, but he was far too slow. He grunted as the mordrillia's teeth stung his calf, kicking away from the plant just as his limbs grew leaden and paralysis set in.

He wasn't too concerned about the poison itself—mordrillia hunted small fish, not humans. The toxins would wear off in five or six minutes, though he hoped someone noticed his absence a little sooner.

He was holding both his skystone and his windstone, but he could only use the latter—his sky affinity was meant for controlling the weather and storms, and the last thing he wanted to do was accidentally electrocute everyone. Without an air affinity, the best he could manage was summoning wind from above the surface to breathe. He channeled a tube through the deep water and sucked in the air, struggling to inhale as the toxins froze his body. *Stay calm*, he ordered himself even as his lungs demanded more oxygen.

This was the second time he had used this trick—the first was when he had jumped off a cliff on the coast of Cyejis to escape a pack of city guards. His father, a rigid, straitlaced lord of Cyeji who considered disobedience a crime, had enlisted an eight-year-old Eadric in boot camp to break his troublesome habits—stealing, mostly. Lord Covington had expected a disciplined son to return ready to shoulder the Covington inheritance, but instead Eadric had pickpocketed his commander's affinity stone out of boredom. And if it hadn't been for that pesky tracking charm cast upon the stone beforehand, he would totally have gotten away with it, too.

The city guards had dogged Eadric through the streets and cornered him on the cliff. So he did what any eight-year-old would have done to evade punishment—he plunged into the ocean. With the help of his breathing tube trick, he managed to stay there for hours. Unfortunately, when he finally resurfaced, the guards were waiting for him.

And it wasn't just them.

He still remembered the gilded carriage parked on the side of the road. There had been a woman inside, clad from head-to-toe in the richest blue, an enormous feathered hat with a veil tipped low over her face.

After his commander shouted himself hoarse at Eadric—the usual *you're an utter disgrace to your family's name*, blah, blah—the guards shoved him inside the woman's carriage, sopping wet.

"Who are you?" he had demanded, wiping the commander's spittle off his face.

"I'll ask the questions, Eadric," she said in a voice of smoke and satin, unconcerned that he was ruining her silk cushions. A whip cracked, and they began rattling off to the Immortals knew where. "Why did you steal your commander's affinity stone?" There was nothing accusatory in her tone, just simple curiosity.

He answered honestly. "I was bored."

She had taken off her veil then, revealing coppery curls and shocking him with eyes as bright and intensely blue as sapphires. "Would you like to do something exciting?"

I just did, Eadric thought to himself, remembering the commander's face, purple with rage. The man hadn't even noticed when Eadric had stolen his expensive-looking pocket watch. Now in the carriage, he reached inside his jacket, frowning when his fingers grasped nothing but air. After digging around unsuccessfully, he looked up to see the blue woman tossing the pocket watch up and down in her hand.

"My, my. Looking for this?" Her mauve lips curved into a wicked smile at his surprise. With a flick of her wrist, the watch vanished before his eyes.

He would never forget the awe he felt in that moment. "Who are you?"

"Eadric, I'll ask you one more time. Would you like to do something exciting?" When he finally nodded, she held out a cobalt-gloved hand. When he shook it, she said, "Then you may address me as Miss M."

One whistle from Miss M and the carriage suddenly swerved left. An hour later, they had arrived at the little white manor he would call home for the next eight years of his life—the longest boot camp in existence, he would one day joke to his glowering father.

Miss M ran an establishment for children as young as six and as old as sixteen, funded entirely by private sponsors. To outsiders, it was a reformation school. But what happened within the walls of Miss M's manor was a different story. In the mornings, Eadric studied history and math and literature. In the afternoons, he learned the art of deceit, behaviorism, sleight of hand, infiltration, and so much more.

For Eadric, it was a dream come true.

Students were allowed to visit family twice a year during Fairfest and Vürstivale, but Eadric preferred to stay at the manor. In fact, he only returned home once, after his mother had fallen ill. When his father attempted to weasel information out of him, Eadric stole the family heirloom—a signet ring his father had worn on his pinky finger since before Eadric had been born—and moved all the furniture in his father's office two inches to the left just for the lark of watching him bumble around, banging into table corners and knocking things off the bookshelves.

Before Eadric had become Captain Covington, he'd been a spy.

After Miss M had deemed him ready, he infiltrated dozens of cities, played countless roles from servant to son in noble houses across the continent, and obtained enough secrets to fill a palace vault. His mission success rate was flawless, no matter how treacherous the task. He was top of the class. But once he turned sixteen, Miss M had to let him go. So he packed his bags and took the first job Miss M found for him—an Elite Royal Guard at the Axarian palace. He left almost all the money he had earned over the years to his mother, but other than that, he didn't so much as write a letter home. Lady Covington had borne a new heir to her husband, and that was fine with Eadric.

When Eadric wasn't drilling or guarding the young princess, he trained on his own, missing the thrill of his old missions, the danger that had kept him constantly on his toes, trying to keep the ever-dreaded boredom at bay. His "dedication" and skill earned him the rank of captain at the ripe old age of twenty-two. That had been four years ago.

The instincts he had developed working for Miss M had saved his life dozens of times. Maybe it was stupid of him, but when his gut didn't trust something, he didn't either. And his gut sure as hell didn't trust Harry. But weeks had passed and Harry proved to be nothing but kind and dependable. For the first time ever, perhaps Eadric's instincts had failed him.

The light that trickled down through the water shifted, and he felt something cold and slick brush against him. *More mordrillia?* he thought. But nothing tugged at him, and the sensation only continued, the current of water around him rushing faster and faster until a violent surge sent him tumbling onto his back.

The sight above him made his heart stutter to a halt.

At first, he couldn't believe his eyes, for the things that had flipped him over looked like nothing more than shadows. Shadows, that had somehow taken a physical form, gliding through the water like immense birds of prey toward a figure bathed in ethereal light, her skin as white as snow in contrast to the gloom of the lake, her hair glistening like mercury, and her lips as red as fresh blood.

Luna.

He cried out to her, but he lost his voice to the watery depths. The darkness swirled and swarmed around her, and then pierced through her body in jagged shards.

He could hear her screaming. Teeth gritted, he willed his muscles to move, but they refused, no matter how hard he tried, and when the darkness finally cleared, she began to sink—fast.

Then, like a goddess descending from the heavens, Rose swept into the water, her hair billowing around her in a flaming cascade of scarlet. Pulsing green light throbbed from her palms, flickering briefly as one hand closed around Luna's limp wrist. She seemed to sense Eadric, lying pathetically at the lake bottom, and spared him a single glance, her gold eyes glinting like burnished stars. She gave him a sharp nod, and without another moment's hesitation, she bent the water to her will and rocketed to the surface with Luna in her arms.

Eadric cursed the mordrillia and forced himself to keep breathing through his wind tube. In the end, it wasn't Rose who returned, but a bare-chested Quinlan. He folded his elbows underneath Eadric's arms and pushed off the lake bottom. With several mighty kicks, the Prince of Eradore carried him back up to the light.

They broke the surface with a splash, both of them gasping for breath. The feeling slowly returned to Eadric's body as Quinlan dragged him to the shoreline, the prince's dark hair matted to his forehead and lake water dripping from his lashes.

With a breath of relief, Eadric found that he could wiggle his fingers and bend his legs, though he didn't protest when Quinlan continued to drag him across the pebbled shore to the fringes of the forest. He didn't want to be anywhere near that strange lake, with its glass-like expanse of green, not a single ripple or wave disturbing its unnatural stillness.

"Stay here," Quinlan said, propping him against a tree that overlooked the pebbly shore. "I need to find Harry."

"And the others?" Eadric panted.

"Safe."

Before Quinlan could elaborate, a head burst through the surface of the lake. Harry struggled toward them, coughing out water with each paddle. The water became shallow enough for the hunter to wade the rest of the way ashore. He coughed some more and took a moment to catch his breath. Then he shook himself like a wet dog, showering water everywhere. Eadric wiped his face, and Harry exclaimed his apologies.

Eadric waved him off. "We're soaked through, anyway."

"I can help with that," said Quinlan. Instantly, stifling heat licked along Eadric's body. His clothes, along with Harry's, dried within seconds. Quinlan dried his own trousers but kept his shirt off.

"Asterin," Eadric prompted. "And everyone else. Where are they?"

"Nearby. Rose is watching over them."

Eadric stared. "Watching over them? What happened?"

Quinlan pulled out a glass vial from his trousers pocket and turned toward the lake. "I ... I have a theory."

"Well, enlighten us, damn it—" Eadric's voice died in his throat as he caught sight of the bare skin on the prince's back. He heard Harry's breath hitch.

As if feeling the weight of their eyes on him, Quinlan froze at the lake's edge.

Jagged scars crisscrossed the prince's shoulder blades to his waist, pink and puckered, some winding onto his arms and even up his neck.

And then Eadric noticed the patterns, the shapes. They were like tattoos—no.

Brands, seared into his skin.

"Immortals above," Harry breathed.

Eadric swallowed. "Quinlan—"

Quinlan peered over his shoulder, leveling both Harry and Eadric with a sharp look. "Leave it. They're old."

"I've never noticed those before," Eadric managed, unable to tear his eyes away from them. Surely he would have noticed the ones burned onto his neck. They were beautiful—in a terrible, evil way.

"I had charms cast over them," Quinlan said flatly. "To conceal them. But I think the lake washed them away."

Eadric scoffed. "Water can't wash magic off like some sort of stain."

Quinlan crouched down and dipped the glass vial into the lake. Once filled, he capped it with a cork and held it up to the light, brows furrowed.

He gave it a little shake and the contents clouded over before turning crystalline once more. "No, it can't." He tucked the vial back into his pocket and pulled out two more to repeat the process. "But contralusio can. Upon contact, any charms and spells altering appearance—like the charms on my scars—are lifted. All that remains is the truth. You, Rose, and Harry weren't affected. But Luna and Asterin were."

"And Orion?" Harry asked.

"I don't know. I think Rose got him out of the water while I was looking for Eadric," Quinlan said.

Harry shifted uneasily. "If you say that contralusio lifts altering spells ... why were Luna and Asterin affected?"

Quinlan pulled his clothes back on and fastened his cloak around his shoulders. Then he beckoned for them to follow him into the trees, mouth pressing into a grim line. "I guess we'll find out when they awaken."

Eadric nearly tripped. "Awaken? Are they unconscious?"

"Not exactly," said Quinlan.

"What does Luna have to do with this, anyway?" Eadric demanded, remembering the horrible shadows in the lake. His voice rose with each word. "What exactly happened to them?"

Quinlan stopped in front of a curtain of foliage and faced him, hands raised in a calming gesture. "Eadric, you need to remember that what you see will be fact, and only fact," he said. "Nothing else. All that remains is the truth."

Eadric shook his head, trying to wrap his mind around Quinlan's words. He shouldered past the prince. Beyond the tangle of leaves lay a little grove—and in the center, Rose, kneeling between two bodies, unmoving save for the slow rise and fall of their chests.

Eadric continued forward in a trance until a twig snapped beneath his foot and Rose spun around, affinity stone raised.

She exhaled, shoulders slumping. "Immortals, you scared me half to death."

A strangled noise came from Harry. "Where's Orion?"

Rose stared at him. "What?" Her eyes went to Quinlan. "I thought you had him."

Confusion and then horror flashed across Quinlan's face. "Almighty Immortals."

But Harry was already running in the direction they had emerged from, crashing through the underbrush without hesitation. "Stay there!" he shouted, his tone brooking no argument.

"Will you be all right on your own?" Quinlan hollered after him, but the hunter was already gone.

If it had been any other moment, Eadric would have been running right after—no, alongside Harry. But he couldn't think of anything else as his eyes trailed over Luna's face, his insides turning to lead. At first, nothing made sense. He knew it was her, but it *wasn't* her.

Her skin had bleached alabaster white, almost translucent. Lying there, she looked more fragile than the most breakable porcelain, except for the new sharpness to her features—a pointed chin, a narrower mouth. Her face had shed soft cheeks for keen cheekbones that shadowed the lean hollows beneath. Her hair remained unchanged but for the color; once the gold of honey, it now gleamed like silver gossamer.

Then she began coughing, and Eadric fell to her side as her eyes fluttered open to reveal a lustrous teal that sent all of them—including the Eradorians—stumbling backward in shock.

Eadric would have recognized those eyes anywhere.

They were one of a kind.

And then, suddenly, everything clicked into place: why Luna knew so little about her childhood in that Oprehvean orphanage; why she had never known her mother or father, couldn't even claim a family name of her own; why Axarian guards had brought her, without explanation, to the royal palace to work the most enviable position of all—the lady-in-waiting to a princess—despite being a nobody.

All of them knew those teal eyes, like the shimmering tail feathers of a peacock …

For those eyes belonged to none other than Queen Priscilla Alessandra Montcroix-Faelenhart.

CHAPTER THIRTY

When Asterin had jumped into the lake, the dybrulé snapping at their heels, she sank straight down—and when her feet touched the muddy bottom, in her mind, she kept sinking. The dybrulé faded from her thoughts as her heartbeat stalled. Oblivion spread around her in endless waves on all sides. Perhaps this was the end of the universe, or perhaps she was stuck in some limbo, tethered to life only by a thread. But then the waves began to roil softly, and a line of golden spheres emerged from the darkness, glowing like torches along a riverbank, stretching out into the void.

The waves tugged at her. She drifted with them, a boat without oars, losing herself to the current.

She let out a little gasp when she peered into the first glowing sphere. A blurry image shone from within—a handsome man with a crown atop his head, gazing down at a tiny baby with a smile full of pride.

Her father.

She understood, then, that this was a memory. Her earliest, she supposed.

The waves continued to tug her along, and she stared into each little ball of light, each memory growing sharper as she drifted down the line. Her first winter, her first footsteps in the snow. Her first time riding a horse.

And then one particular light made her pause, a wondrous smile creeping onto her face. When she lingered on the memory, the sphere began to swell and expand until it had stretched into the size of a doorway. Her eyes widened as a gravity from within pulled her closer, the golden light swallowing her body entirely as she drifted through.

When she blinked, she stood in the middle of the palace ballroom, the air filled with laughter and sweet music. Two servants carrying a roast pig bustled toward her. She braced herself, only for her body to pass right through them. She tried picking up a glass of champagne, but she might as well have been grabbing mist.

In a daze, she wandered through the crowds of nobles feasting and dancing, their faces so vivid that she recognized almost every one—Lady Peonia with her usual condescending smile, Lord Valdric squinting through his monocle. Both had been from her father's old inner court. She hadn't seen them in years.

Asterin turned in a slow circle to take in the scene playing out around her—the long table running down the center of the ballroom, piled with flamboyant gifts and a birthday cake as tall as her, decorated with tiny silver flowers and light-pink frosting.

The sight of the cake sparked her memory. *My third birthday*, she realized. She searched the crowds for more faces she knew, for Orion and Luna, but then she remembered that she hadn't met them yet.

And then Asterin saw *herself*, her three-year-old self, tiny and giggling, running beneath the table and giving the cloth atop it a good yank. Plates shattered in her wake. A hysterical nursemaid dove beneath the table to grab her, but little Asterin darted away and ran for the cake, chubby fingers outstretched.

A man scooped her up just in time. "You little rascal," he laughed. Theodore Galashiels grinned as the little princess fussed and squirmed in his arms, finally mollifying herself by tugging at his thinning ducktail beard with a pudgy hand. The king's Royal Guardian stooped to look underneath the table. "Look what you've done to poor Madge."

"I'm so, so sorry," Madge gasped as she scrambled to her feet, on the verge of tears. "I—"

"No apologies needed," Theodore assured the nursemaid. He pinched little Asterin's cheek, unaware that she had frozen his whiskers. Cooing, she pointed down, and when he tipped his chin to look, his entire beard snapped off against his chest and shattered like the plates on the floor.

Asterin—present-day Asterin—slapped a hand to her mouth to stifle a burst of laughter before remembering that no one could hear her anyway.

"Just how many more beards will you have to grow to stop falling for that trick?"

Asterin's head jerked up at the voice, her throat suddenly tight. A path had cleared through the crowd to allow two figures to approach, the nobles around them smiling and bowing respectfully. Behind the couple trailed General Garringsford, her face unchanged by fourteen years' time, but Asterin barely noticed her. She had eyes only for the man approaching her younger self.

"It's not my fault your daughter is so clever," Theodore grumbled, tickling little Asterin's chin.

King Tristan smiled, coming to a halt at their side. Asterin had forgotten how her father looked then, healthy and well, his skin golden with life. His presence, from his strong voice to his posture, flooded the hall. "The cleverest. Asterin, my love, I have a gift for you."

Hot tears welled in Asterin's eyes as she watched the king present little Asterin with a tiara, the one that sat on her bedchamber vanity today.

"My mother wore this when she was young," her father explained, placing it on little Asterin's head. It was much too large, slipping past her brow and covering her wide eyes. With a laugh, her father adjusted it as best he could. "You'll grow into it," he promised, and then wrapped an arm around the waist of her mother.

Asterin turned to look at the Queen of Axaria, but her heart stopped. The woman her father looked at with adoring eyes was not Priscilla.

Priscilla had been replaced by another woman, with hair as black as polished onyx and emerald-green eyes identical to Asterin's.

No, Asterin thought.

Her heartbeat thundered, each breath shallower than the last. She stumbled backward, and the memory evaporated around her, returning her to the oblivion.

It wasn't possible. It simply wasn't possible. Asterin still remembered that moment, remembered how Priscilla had smiled her beautiful, prim smile and had summoned water droplets from thin air to dance around little Asterin—

But Priscilla couldn't wield water. How could Asterin have forgotten that?

She looked around at the rest of the floating orbs, wondering what other altered memories might await her discovery. As if sensing her thoughts, the orbs expanded, growing into a hall of doorways. Hastily, she flung herself toward the first doorway and plunged through it.

She arrived in her palace bedchamber, lit by the soft glow of a single candle. In the bed lay little Asterin, perhaps five years old. A woman cast in darkness tucked her in, singing a lullaby. The melody sent a pang through Asterin, excruciatingly familiar.

Priscilla, it was Priscilla tucking her in, surely … but Priscilla never sang.

In a trance, Asterin drifted closer to the bed. The candlelight flared brighter and caught those same emerald eyes from the last memory, as bright as the stars themselves, filled with a love and warmth that Asterin couldn't remember ever seeing in Priscilla's teal eyes.

But she knew what came next. Priscilla would blow out the candle on her way out the door, and whisper *Good night, child,* as she had done every night when Asterin was young—

"Sweetest dreams, my love."

The words she heard now, spoken so tenderly, and the ones she remembered with such clarity … Asterin knew for certain the words "my love" had never passed Priscilla's lips, and yet, just like that lullaby, they were so familiar that they warmed her from the inside out.

She entered the rest of her memories one by one: her mother holding her close, braiding her hair, eating with her, telling her stories, watching her grow up—except instead of Priscilla, this unknown woman had taken her place.

Or was it the other way around?

Then two more years passed, and the woman was gone, little Asterin was now six, and the memories continued with Priscilla's face, Priscilla's voice, and Priscilla at her father's side.

And then came King Tristan's illness. Asterin looked around her father's chambers at the ornate carvings upon the ceiling, at the nine suits of armor lining the wall, guarding the sickbed. The king's quarters had been closed since his death, and she had almost forgotten what they looked like.

Her father's illness had crept upon him like an autumn chill, beginning with dizzy spells that intensified to headaches and explosive migraines that forced him to retire from the throne to his bed. Doctors from all corners of the world were summoned, but none could make a diagnosis. Meanwhile, in his absence, the obligation to rule fell to Queen Priscilla.

By Vürstivale, Asterin's father could no longer move on his own. That winter would be his last.

Now, in the memory, she stared at his sunken eyes and the ever-darkening purplish bags. She reached out to lay her hand on his but clenched her fingers into a fist when they only passed through.

Just then, two legs dangled into sight outside the window overlooking the balcony. Young Asterin, now eight, dropped down onto the marble platform and hurried to the doors, tracking prints into the heaps of snow. She picked the lock and snuck inside the bedchamber, shedding her wet boots. Her ruddy cheeks paled as her eyes fell upon her sleeping father.

As if sensing young Asterin's presence, or perhaps simply stirred by the gust of cold that had followed her through the door, the king awoke and turned his head. "You shouldn't be here. I'm unwell."

"I know, Papa. General Garringsford told me that I wasn't allowed to see you, but it's been nearly a month and I miss you." Young Asterin scuffed the carpet with her toe. "Are you mad at me?"

Her father's face softened with a smile, though it wasn't like his usual smile from the older memories. Strained, the light not reaching his eyes—fallen and burnt and dull. "Of course not, my love. How could I ever be mad at you for wanting to visit me?"

Seeing the pain etched so vividly in every line of his tired face, hearing each breath rattle through his chest … a grief Asterin hadn't felt so strongly in years threatened to overwhelm her.

Young Asterin ran to his side. "You can't go. Just till the spring, Papa," she begged, silver lining her eyes. "The warm weather will make you better."

"I'll try, my love," her father rasped.

It was then that Asterin noticed something strange about her father's face. The veins up his neck ran black. She couldn't recall ever seeing that before. Yet suddenly, Asterin knew something she had never even suspected—it was poison, not sickness, eating away at her father's life with each passing day.

Young Asterin buried her face into her father's shoulder. "Promise, Papa."

"I promise."

Not a week later, the frost still thick on the balcony doors, her father closed his eyes, never to open them again.

The next day, dressed in her finest mourning black, Priscilla Alessandra Montcroix-Faelenhart claimed the throne as ruler of Axaria. Asterin remembered the cloud of sorrow at her lost love hanging over the queen—that memory had to be real, didn't it? General Garringsford was there, too, standing at Priscilla's elbow during the funeral. Asterin would never forget the moment her father had been lowered into his grave, but now she watched, feeling sick, as the tiniest smile flitted across Garringsford's lips.

Asterin emerged from the memories, her mind empty and her heart raw.

The golden light of the memories sputtered out like candle flames. The waves ceased, leaving her to hang in the empty oblivion.

She didn't know how or why her memories had changed, but she knew one thing for certain. That green-eyed woman—unknown and yet *so* familiar—was her mother.

Her real mother.

Which begged the question … *What had happened to her?* Asterin couldn't remember anything about her disappearance—or even her name, for that matter.

Even more alarming was the mystery behind how her memories had been altered. No magic or spell had the power to change memory, except for shadow magic.

But who would dare use the forbidden element? And who had poisoned King Tristan? Could it have been Priscilla? But Asterin knew Priscilla missed him desperately, knew she even kept a chest of old love letters somewhere. Priscilla had definitely married her father. Asterin had seen the official documents—although, she had to admit that they could have been forged. The *dates* had certainly been forged, if Priscilla had replaced

Asterin's real mother *after* Asterin had been born. All these years, Priscilla's coldness, Asterin's inability to please her … was it the result of having to raise another woman's child?

Frustration coursed through Asterin. Nothing made sense, and too many questions had been left unanswered. Not the least of which being who could have wanted her father dead, if not Priscilla? Someone seeking revenge? Power? Perhaps a soldier? A hireling?

The revelation jolted through Asterin.

General Garringsford.

General Garringsford, who had always harbored such barely restrained hostility toward Asterin, who never forgave King Tristan for sending her sons to their deaths in Orion's hometown. Asterin didn't know much about the circumstances of Alex and Micah Garringsford's deaths, but she knew that it had partially been her father's fault. They had only been trainees at the time, and when General Garringsford had protested against them accompanying the soldiers to intercept the hirelings, King Tristan had accused her of coddling her sons.

So that could explain the general's motivation for killing the king, but why replace Asterin's memories?

Garringsford, always walking two steps behind the queen, Priscilla's pet—but maybe not her pet after all. For as long as Asterin could remember, the queen had allowed Garringsford almost total control over the military. The general was more powerful than any other servant of the crown.

Control and power, without responsibility.

Armed with dark magic, Garringsford could even be controlling Priscilla from the comfort of the queen's shadow.

Could even have summoned a demon.

In fact, Garringsford could have orchestrated everything from the start. Garringsford, who had so generously convinced Priscilla to allow Asterin to hunt the demon. Garringsford, who had been around the palace longer than anyone, even King Tristan. For someone who had watched Asterin grow up, who had familiarized herself with her short temper and need to impress Priscilla, it couldn't have been difficult to predict that she would want to hunt down the demon herself.

Asterin wondered if she had blindly walked herself to her own execution—and taken everyone else with her.

Asterin's real mother and father were gone, and she would not look back and wish for what could have been—but their killer was still alive, and Asterin made a vow right then and there that she would make Garringsford pay for taking her parents away from her … that she would fight to protect her kingdom until Carlotta Garringsford breathed her last breath.

And so, when Asterin emerged from the darkness of her memories on that muddy shore and opened her eyes to see Rose's distressed face hovering inches above her own, she looked beyond her fellow ruler and saw not a bleak, dismal sky, but a silver dawn, full of vengeful promise.

CHAPTER THIRTY-ONE

Rose knelt in the mud over Asterin, on the verge of giving up hope that the girl would awaken anytime soon—or possibly at all—when her lids finally fluttered open. She exhaled. "Finally. Thank the Immortals."

Eadric had carried Luna into the shade on the other side of the grove, half-hidden by bushes as he stayed by her side and monitored her vitals. Both Harry and Orion had yet to return. Quinlan had almost decided to go looking for them, but when he saw Asterin struggling to sit up, he rushed over.

Her cousin dropped to the ground, helping Asterin upright. "Are you hurt?"

A moment of silence passed. Rose frowned, worried that perhaps Asterin had gone brain-dead or something, when the princess finally spoke, no louder than a dry rasp.

"I know we haven't killed the demon yet, but we have to go home."

Rose exchanged a glance with her cousin. He put a hand on Asterin's shoulder. "Did something happen after you jumped into the lake?"

Asterin stared into the distance beyond the treetops. "I—I remembered something. Many things. All these … forgotten memories. I saw my mother, but it wasn't Priscilla. It was another woman, with my hair and eyes and face. I can't even remember her name, but I *know* it was my mother."

Her words left them momentarily speechless.

"What do you mean?" asked Rose.

Quinlan's eyes widened. "Wait," he blurted out. "So Priscilla isn't your mother?"

Asterin shook her head. "Nor is she the rightful Queen of Axaria. With the help of shadow magic, someone used Priscilla as a puppet to replace my *real* mother." She stared at her lap, fists clenched. "And I think that someone is General Garringsford."

She went on to explain everything from the deaths of Alex and Micah Garringsford to her certainty that her father had been assassinated.

Rose pondered the information. Quinlan's face had gone blank at the news of Tristan's assassination. He now paced to keep the emotions she could sense stirring within him at bay. So little was known about the tenth element. Mind control didn't exist within the power of the nine elemental affinities, but shadow magic … the possibilities were endless.

"If Garringsford harnessed enough power to alter your memories," Rose said, "she might very well be using its power to control Priscilla, even now."

"I don't understand," Asterin said. "Why doesn't anyone remember my real mother? She was a queen. Surely other royals around the world must have met her, or at least knew of her."

Quinlan kneaded the heels of his hands into his closed eyes, his brow furrowed in thought. "Garringsford probably used a memory-erasing spell, but to affect so many people, so far apart …"

Rose's pulse quickened. *Could it be?* "The butterfly figurines. My mother had one, and Orion said that Asterin had one in her room as well. That dark aura … it must have been traces of shadow magic. With the right amplifying charm, Garringsford could have used the butterflies to spread the memory-erasing spell through the kingdoms like a plague, infecting thousands at a time."

Eadric jogged over, missing his jacket and cloak. "Quinlan, could I borrow your cloak?" He noticed Asterin, relief cascading over his features. "Your Highness, are you all right?"

Asterin swiveled around. Her head spun. Everything seemed to be happening at once. "Where are the others?"

Rose chose her words carefully. "Luna is … sleeping."

"And shivering, which is why I need your cloak," Eadric added, and Quinlan ripped off his cloak, then his jacket for good measure.

Asterin's brow creased. "And Orion and Harry?"

Rose couldn't help but feel grateful when Eadric answered. "Orion went missing after we jumped into the lake. Harry is looking for him right now, so—"

Asterin shot to her feet, rage cresting her features. "What do you mean, *missing*? Why in hell didn't any of you say anything?"

Eadric's fists clenched. "Because the first thing you would have done is run after him. He's supposed to protect *you.* As am I. Your safety comes first."

"Stop acting like your lives are worth less than mine!" Asterin exploded. "You are my friends! Friends always protect one another—"

Asterin cut herself off just as they heard the snap of twigs and leaves rustling. Quinlan's hands already smoldered with heat, battle-ready. Harry burst into the grove, shoulders heaving and Orion in his arms. The hunter fell to his knees, clothes and hair still dripping, and set the Guardian down. Rose's fingers already grasped his limp wrist for a pulse. Faint, but there. "He swallowed a lot of water," Harry said. "I got him to vomit most of it out and start breathing again, but—"

Asterin lunged forward and threw her arms around Harry, stunning him into silence. "Thank you," she whispered as Eadric and Quinlan helped spread Orion out on the grass.

Rose prepared her affinity stone. "All of you either have to leave or shut up so I can concentrate. I have to get the rest of the water out of his lungs."

Harry chose to stay, and Eadric returned to Luna, but Quinlan stormed off, posture strung like a bow drawn taut. Rose remembered that particularly hard set of his shoulders from when they were children, from before their fathers had been killed. It came with bruises and burns hidden beneath his clothes. It came when Quinlan visited the palace and Rose asked if he wanted to practice magic, and her cousin's smile would freeze and he would tell her with trembling courage that he had forgotten his affinity stones at home.

Rose had known he was lying. Her mother had told her that Gavin Holloway kept them locked in a case he carried around in his pocket.

"Asterin," Rose said quietly, tracing her thumbs across Orion's chest. "I know you want to help, but I can handle this on my own. Could you keep an eye on Quinlan for me? I'm afraid he might do something stupid if left alone."

"Why me?" Asterin asked.

Unbelievable, Rose thought, shaking her head. *You still haven't realized?* "Because, somehow, it's always you who knows how to set him right."

Quinlan wondered what General Garringsford's screams would sound like when he set her alight. Alive.

He leaned against a tree, bark scraping the back of his neck. He inhaled sharply through his nose, struck by a sudden flash of anger. Sparks popped from his palms, hissing onto the dewy grass. There was nothing more despicable than stealing a part of someone—an identity, memories, magic. It had been horrible enough when his father had taken away his affinity stones as a child, but that was exactly it. Just the stones. The embers of his magic had always flickered within him—he needed only to set them ablaze.

But Asterin's parents … she would never get her parents back.

He exhaled a plume of black smoke, lungs filled with ash, and forced himself to cool down. He remembered the first time he had used his powers without the stones. How good it had felt to be free. How good it had felt to hear his father's screams of outrage—and pain.

Heatless flames licked up the trunk of the tree he leaned on, leaping across branches and spreading until his entire world glowed red, smoke rising from the ground like fog. One thought was all he needed to make it burn.

Then something cold kissed his forehead. He turned his face up to watch as a second snowflake drifted down from the sky, its delicate needles catching the light before melting on his lips.

When his gaze lifted, Asterin stood before him, an apparition half-obscured in the thick gray haze. "Rose told me that I might find you like this," she said as she picked her way through the smoke and stopped a few feet away.

His voice was a sooty rasp. "How are you feeling?"

She stared up at the inferno devouring the treetops, yet never singeing so much as a leaf. "What's the point of fire that doesn't burn?"

"Potential," Quinlan said. "It is a sword to the throat that simply waits to deliver the killing blow."

Her emerald eyes had gone dull. "But why hesitate? Why give that mercy?"

"It is never a mercy to be at another's mercy," he said. "It only means you will suffer longer." He covered the space between them in three quick strides and grabbed her hands, enclosing them in his own. She looked up at him, her eyes reflecting the firelight. "Asterin, I promise you. I will make Garringsford suffer an eternity for you."

She let out a hiss, and he realized that his hands were smoldering like coals. Maybe he hadn't cooled down as much as he'd thought. But rather than release him, she only gripped tighter, jaw clenching as she embraced the pain.

"Asterin—"

She let go of his hands and wrapped her arms around his neck, her face nestled into his shoulder. His heart leapt into his throat, and hesitantly, he wound his arms around her waist, holding her close. The flames high in the trees wavered and then snuffed out, the smoke fading to a forgotten wind.

His chest ached with a daunting, new weight he had never felt before. His father would've called this a fatal weakness. *Never let your heart rule your head.* But this didn't feel like weakness. It felt like strength.

He swallowed and said, "When we kill Garringsford, Priscilla might be unfit to rule after being under her control. If worst comes to worst, you must claim the throne." He felt her shoulders stiffen. "Even if you have to fight for it. You *belong* on that throne, Asterin."

She withdrew from his arms and scoffed. "Quinlan, look at me. My Guardian almost drowned, I almost got all of us eaten by the dybrulé, and if it wasn't for you and Conrye, we would have been killed by the wyvern in Aldville. I can hardly protect my friends, let alone hundreds of thousands of people. I'm not wise like Rose, or even kind like Luna. I can't be queen."

He reached forward to cup her jaw ever so gently, tilting her face upward and wondering if she could hear his heart hammering. "You can be whatever the hell you want," he whispered. "And I promise you … I promise you that—that if you so desire, I will stay by your side through all of it." His face burned with embarrassment at his own words, but he barreled on, terrified that if they didn't get out now, they would remain buried deep inside him forever. "I will stay by your side, always. I won't leave you."

She stared at him. "Why?"

He found himself at a loss for words, his expression desperate as he willed her to understand.

"*Why*?" she demanded again, striking her fists against his chest. "I'm nothing to you. I'm just a distraction. I'm—"

Quinlan grabbed her fingers and held them against his heart. He heard her breath hitch as her fingers splayed open and the traitorous thundering of his pulse told her everything she needed to know.

"You? *Just* a distraction?" Quinlan almost burst out laughing. "Asterin, you idiot, I didn't mean it like that." All of a sudden, he couldn't get the words out fast enough. "When you're on my mind, I can't think straight. I forget about everything else. You *steal* my attention, all of it, every time I look at you. I—I never intended to … feel anything for you. But I just can't help it." His hands, still gripping hers, shook from nerves like they never had before.

Asterin's eyes widened to moons. "Me?"

Quinlan groaned aloud. "Yes, you, damn it. Most of the time you are unbelievably annoying and stubborn. But you are also the most brilliant, brave, and beautiful person I have ever met."

The hint of a growing smile. "Could you repeat that?"

"What, stubborn and irritating?"

She raised an eyebrow. "After that."

Her smile gave him courage. "Brilliant. Brave. Beautiful."

The light had rekindled in her eyes. "Sorry, I missed it again. One more time?"

Quinlan threw his hands into the air. "You're such an infuriating little …" He shook his head, soft laughter rolling through him. "Brat."

"Asshole," she retorted.

He sighed in exasperation, and then took her face in his hands and surged forward to kiss her, so swiftly and unexpectedly that she actually kissed him back.

The kiss lasted no more than a few seconds because he couldn't resist breaking away to let loose a giddy whoop, fist pumping the air. "Finally!"

"You're so obnoxious," she complained.

He only grinned and then kissed her again. When they parted, the color was high in her cheeks and her eyes shone as bright as jewels.

And then, from afar, a scream ripped through the air.

The blood drained from Asterin's face. "Luna."

Quinlan grabbed her hand, and then they ran.

CHAPTER THIRTY-TWO

If hell existed, this was it.

Knives shredded Luna's skin, cutting her apart. Then a needle sewed her back together. Then came the knives again, and then the needle, and then the knives, again and again. There was no end to the pain and suffering, and Luna's only thought was, *What did I do to deserve this?*

But now, something—someone dragged her back to the surface, back toward the light.

And it burned.

She hissed, clawing blindly in a futile attempt to slow her ascent, dreading the moment she would break into the real world.

"Luna," came the muted echo of a voice. The sound of her name tore through some boundary in the back of her mind, dredging up a recent memory, bright and fresh. She gasped, thrashing, only to choke down a lungful of water. She needed air, she needed the darkness—

"Asterin, wait!"

Luna jerked awake to find that she hadn't been underwater at all—it was just some horrible nightmare. It took her a moment to reorient herself. Two cloaks and a jacket she recognized as Eadric's covered her quivering body.

Rose and Eadric's blurred faces swam into view above her, but Luna could only see Asterin, storming closer and then stuttering to a halt, disbelief taking over her features. "What in hell?" The princess whirled on Rose, emerald eyes round. "You *knew*, damn it!"

"What is it?" Luna croaked.

Asterin's eyes shone with concern as she sank to Luna's side, her expression softening. "Immortals above. What did that bitch do to you?"

"What do you mean? What were those *things* in the water?"

"Luna, there's something you need to see."

Asterin conjured a stream of water between them and shaped it into a flat surface so that Luna could gaze into its reflection.

But the face staring back at her was not a face she recognized. The bones jutted out, the hair glowed platinum, and the eyes … swirling with hues of turquoise and teal. They certainly didn't belong to her. Yet when Luna blinked, the reflection blinked back. Dread coiled low in her gut when she realized that the reflection *did* belong to her.

Those eyes … she knew who those eyes belonged to, too.

"What—what happened to me?" Luna breathed, raising her hands to her face, fingers grazing the foreign contours. "Am I dreaming?"

Asterin watched her warily, gauging her reaction. "No, Luna. The lake we jumped into contained contralusio, a substance that reveals hidden truths. This … this is your true appearance."

"That's not possible—"

"What happened to your parents, Luna?"

Luna shook her head fiercely, tears rising to her eyes. "They died. I grew up in an orphanage, I swear it."

"Luna, please," Asterin begged. "Just try and remember what happened before you went to the orphanage. Anything."

"You know I don't like remembering it, I—"

A cold night.

"But why?"

"Because I can't really …" Luna stopped, covering her face in her hands. *A cold night. A bright blue ribbon. Moonflower.* "I could never really remember it clearly. It was always sort of a blur, and my head hurt every time I tried. So I stopped trying."

Her hands fell away as Asterin wrapped her arms around her, warm and solid. "I'm so sorry," her friend murmured. "We'll get our revenge on Garringsford. Together."

"Garringsford?" Luna echoed in confusion.

There was a series of curses from behind them, and they turned to see Orion struggling up, finally awake, hacking out watery coughs.

Asterin released her and rushed back to the edge of the clearing for her Guardian, leaving Luna feeling strangely abandoned. Eadric strode toward her, but Luna was already on her feet, following in Asterin's wake as she always did.

All of them surrounded Orion, his golden hair still damp from the lake. Rose reached for his wrist to check his heart rate, and both Asterin and Harry looked like they were about to keel over in relief.

But then Orion's eyes cleared and fixated on Harry, who knelt in front of him. A growl tore from Orion's throat.

"You liar."

Everyone froze at the wrath in the Guardian's sandpaper-rough voice.

Harry flinched, shoulders curling in. "What?"

"Don't play innocent." Orion lurched forward, grabbing Harry's collar with unsteady hands, and Luna had never seen such fury twisting his handsome features. "You lied to us," he said, "right from the very beginning. I should have listened to Eadric and Rose. They were right all along."

A torrent of emotions played out on Harry's face. "Orion—"

"What are you saying?" Asterin asked her Guardian, but from Quinlan's stance and the way that Rose slowly slipped out her affinity stone, Luna had a feeling that all of them already knew what lay ahead.

A dark chuckle escaped Orion. "I'm saying that Harry isn't just some hunter."

Luna inhaled, praying to the Immortals that his next words wouldn't be what she feared.

But they were.

"Everyone," Orion spat, "meet our demon."

CHAPTER THIRTY-THREE

Even after he had brought Orion safely back from the lake to where the others huddled in the grove, Harry couldn't break free from the images looping through his mind—plunging into the cold water, searching the depths, dragging Orion's lifeless body out, hollering incomprehensibly and pumping at his unmoving chest on the bank, leaning down to press their lips together, filling Orion's lungs with air, mouths wet from the lake water—

It certainly wasn't how Harry had expected their first kiss to go.

And when Orion had finally awoken, Harry had been so relieved to see those ice-chip blue eyes open that he didn't even notice their blazing wrath at first. When he did, he knew it was already over. His time was up.

Still, after everything that had happened, he could still try, he could still—

Orion laughed again, a hard, mean bark that grated against Harry's ears. "Stop staring at me like you think you can fool me. I saw you in the lake, Harry. I *saw* you."

Harry's heart plummeted. There was no way out of this. A part of him had sensed Orion wasn't totally blacked out when Harry, in his demon form, had found him and dragged him back up to the surface. He had shifted after jumping into the lake, though not because the contralusio had forced him to. The only truth the lake had revealed to him was just how shitty of a swimmer he was in his human form, and Harry refused to risk Orion's life for the errors his human form might make.

Now two hands locked onto Harry's shoulders, one from Quinlan and one from Eadric. Harry wanted to tell them that he wasn't planning an escape, but judging from their vice grips, he doubted they would care.

Orion released Harry's collar and stepped back in disgust. "You're a monster."

Harry closed his eyes. "I'm not a monster. I'm an anygné, an immortal being summoned from the Shadow Kingdom—"

"I don't give a damn about what you are," said Orion, an empty smile fixed on his face. "You're a monster for what you've done."

"Orion—"

"I don't want to hear your excuses, or your apologies. I *trusted* you."

In the silence, Harry could only hear his own blood rushing in his ears. Asterin had her face buried in her hands. Luna kept looking back and forth between him and Orion like she desperately wanted one of them to yell, *Just kidding!* And Rose … Rose just seemed resigned. Of course, Harry couldn't see Eadric's or Quinlan's expressions, but he could only imagine the captain's rage.

"Plotting away in some cozy little shithole with Garringsford, figuring out the most amusing ways to torment us—"

"Wait," Harry interrupted with a frown. "Who is Garringsford?"

"The General of Axaria, obviously. Your contact. The one who sent us to you."

Harry inhaled sharply. "The Woman."

Asterin glanced up. "The Woman?"

"Yes … she never gave away any hint of her identity, although I was fairly certain she worked at the royal palace. But I had no idea that she was the general … I'm sorry," he said, throat dry, unable to come up with anything else.

"That day I came upstairs to your room and you said that you didn't feel well …" Asterin trailed off. "It *was* you who set off our trap, right?"

Harry bit his lip. "Yes."

Rose tilted her head. "How did you get the dye off?"

Harry looked away, the weight of Orion's stare still pinning him to hell. "Does it matter?"

At that, Luna descended upon him like a furious wasp. "Of course it matters! Do you know how relieved we were when that trap confirmed you *weren't* the demon? So tell us how you got the dye off, Harry, or so help me, I'm going to—"

"I cut it off," Harry said quietly.

Asterin swallowed visibly. "What?"

"I heal very quickly. So I cut all of the dyed skin off."

Asterin stared at Harry. "Why would you do that?"

That drew a wry smile to Harry's lips. "Because my other option was killing you."

The princess huffed. "Why didn't you?"

"Because—"

"So you did kill all the people in Corinthe," Rose said softly.

Harry's voice died in his throat. They all waited for him to respond, but he found that he couldn't.

Horror dawned on Orion's features. "Oh, Immortals. You—you killed all those people in the village," he breathed. "It was *you*."

Asterin circled around him, out of sight. "Harry," she whispered into his ear, something broken in the way she said his name. "Did you?"

Harry closed his eyes and swallowed. *I don't want to hear your excuses, or your apologies.* "Yes."

Silence.

Followed by the high whine of steel unsheathing.

"Asterin," Quinlan barked, voice filled with alarm. "What are you—*Asterin*!"

And then Asterin plunged her sword into Harry's back.

CHAPTER THIRTY-FOUR

Orion stared at the end of Amoux, protruding through Harry's middle. He could hear himself yelling. Harry had bowed over, soundless. Still, the demon struggled to hold in a groan as Asterin slowly withdrew Amoux, only to plunge it back in a second time, silver blood soaking his clothes and pooling around his knees. After the fourth time, Orion could tell that Harry was fighting to stay conscious.

"Asterin, stop!" Rose tried to wrest Asterin back. "You'll kill him!"

"I won't," Asterin said calmly, shaking her off. "Look, he's already healing."

Indeed, the moment Asterin pulled Amoux out of Harry's back, the blood from the wound seemed to clot. Still, it didn't make it any easier for Orion to watch Amoux cleave through flesh and bone, again and again. Even though the wounds healed easily enough, from Harry's expression, no blow hurt any less.

Bile rose in Orion's throat.

This was Harry, after all.

No, he thought. *This is the demon.*

"How could you?" Asterin asked, voice shaking. "How? They were innocent. Tell me why you couldn't just end their lives, instead of torturing them like you did, and I'll stop, I promise."

"Torture?" Harry managed to gasp out. "I didn't torture anyone."

"Then why were they mutilated? Oozing black blood, missing the skin on their faces—"

"I didn't do that."

"Then who in hell did?" Asterin yelled, ramming Amoux into him with such force that the hilt slammed against his back and rocked him onto his hands.

"It doesn't matter. I deserve this either way," he wheezed, spitting blood into the grass.

Asterin pulled Amoux out of him in one smooth stroke and walked around to his front. Her fingers jerked his chin up. "Tell me." When he still didn't respond, she struck him across the face. "*Tell me*!"

Orion closed his eyes, unable to watch any longer. *He deserves it*, he thought. But in his mind, he could only see that warm smile, hear the peaceful, steady background *chop chop chop* during their conversations while Harry diced vegetables with his silly floral apron tied around his waist, could only remember going down into the cellar to talk about the things he didn't know how to talk about with the others—

"They were already dying," Harry said at last. Orion's eyes snapped open. "She poisoned them. The Woman. Garringsford. When she brought me to Corinthe, she poisoned the well."

A choked noise came from Asterin's throat. "What do you mean?"

"There was a well in Corinthe," Harry said, and Orion remembered it—remembered how strangely undamaged it had been in the face of all the other destruction. "She drank from it. Something dark leaked from her and into the water. I had no idea what it would do. When I passed Corinthe a few days later, the villagers had gone into a rabid fever, blindly slaughtering their own neighbors. The water rotted them from inside out. I thought … I thought it would be a mercy to end their suffering."

Asterin released her vice-hold on the demon and drove Amoux into the ground, rubbing her face with silver-flecked hands. Orion watched the fight drain out of her.

"And the thirty Axarian guards?" Eadric asked. "Were they in misery as well?"

"What guards?" Harry asked, blinking in confusion.

Eadric's hand twitched toward his sword, as if he wanted to take a turn at a stab or two. "The queen's men. The guards sent to kill you. Who never came back because you killed them instead."

Harry shook his head. "I never saw a single human even step inside this forest before all of you came. I swear it on my life."

"But the Axarian shield," the captain insisted. He looked to Asterin and Orion for support. "The one that the messenger brought in, remember? It was almost completely destroyed, melted through. Scorched to a crisp—"

"Forgive me, Eadric," Harry cut in. "But I think I'd remember if I could breathe fire."

Quinlan turned to Asterin. "Another one of Garringsford's lies?"

Asterin's hands dropped back to her sides. "Most likely."

"But where did the soldiers go?" Eadric demanded incredulously. "They couldn't have just vanished!"

"Garringsford has control over the military's comings and goings," said Asterin. "For all we know, they might be back at the palace."

Orion sat down heavily, ignoring the wetness of Harry's blood seeping into his trousers. He forced himself to face Harry. "So let me get this straight … Garringsford summoned you from the Immortal Realm and ordered you to kill us."

"No," Harry said. The demon met Asterin's gaze. "She ordered me to kill *you*. And whoever got in my way … except for Luna."

Luna's eyes widened. "Me? Why?"

"She said you were important to the queen."

Eadric snarled suddenly. "So why haven't you killed us yet?"

"Because I don't *want* to kill you, damn it!" Harry yelled. Eadric started forward, but Rose grabbed him by the wrist, holding him back. "I don't want to kill you," he whispered hoarsely, and Orion's heart cracked. Harry looked up at him, then Eadric, then Asterin. "Any of you." He exhaled. "When I first met you, I thought I could. But the more time I spent in your company, the more I realized that I couldn't do it. That I *wouldn't* do it, no matter what it meant for me."

"What power does Garringsford have over you?" Quinlan asked.

Harry shook his head. "Not Garringsford. King Eoin, the God of

Shadow." His lip curled back. "He is my … owner. I must follow his orders, and he wanted me to follow Garringsford's orders because of her 'assets'—as in control over the Axarian army."

"Eoin," Rose breathed. "What could he want with an army?"

"I have no idea," said Harry. "I'm sorry."

"There's something I can't understand," said Luna. "How in the name of the Immortals did Garringsford manage to get away with using shadow magic for so many years without anyone noticing?"

Rose made a noise. "At the Academia Principalis," she began, "I took a class on forbidden spells so that should I ever encounter one, I could recognize it. Centuries ago, a sorcerer created a spell using shadow magic called a suspicion dampener."

"I've heard about that," said Harry.

Rose nodded at him and went on. "Its purpose is to misdirect anyone who looks too closely at the caster's nefarious activities. And the only way to break it is to recognize that the caster is using the spell."

Orion glanced at Asterin's dark expression. "So Garringsford cast this suspicion-dampening spell …" He looked at the Eradorian Queen. "And we just broke it."

"I think so," said Rose.

"I always wondered if Garringsford was up to something more sinister," said Asterin, gripping Amoux's pommel with one hand until her knuckles turned white.

"But nothing like this," Eadric said quietly.

Rose pointed at him. "Exactly. The spell is just that powerful."

They lapsed into a tense silence, letting the realization set in.

Luna eyed Harry. "So … what exactly are you?"

Harry wobbled onto his feet. "Let me show you."

And then his body began to transform, tearing through his clothes.

It was a body that Orion had seen once before, in the water, just before he blacked out. But seeing it in daylight … His fingers inched forward to run along the ribbed, translucent membrane of the wings folded at Harry's sides. "You can fly with these?" said Orion. In response, Harry unfurled them slowly, as far as he could, until they extended twenty feet across from tip to tip.

"Shift back, Harry," said Asterin.

He dipped his head in compliance, and returned to his human form—but his clothes had been ripped to shreds when he had shifted. Now a dark, armor-like second skin covered him all the way up to his neck, glimmering as if hewn from rough-cut obsidian.

"I want to help you, Asterin," said Harry.

Asterin considered him for a long moment. "How exactly do you plan on doing that?"

Eadric whipped around to her. "You can't be serious. After everything he did—" The captain's mouth snapped shut when he saw the fire in Asterin's eyes.

"There are two kinds of liars," she said. "The ones that lie to protect themselves, and the ones that lie to protect others. Garringsford is one, and I believe that Harry is the other." The princess pulled Amoux free from the earth, gazing at the double-headed wolf pommel. "Someone told me to accept the truth for what it is, and that my heart would show me the right path." She looked up at Harry. "My heart hasn't forgiven you for lying, but we might need your help to get to Garringsford. And so … I accept your truth."

Eadric shook his head rapidly. "Your Highness—"

Rose stepped forward. "I accept your truth, too, Harry. You had so many chances to kill us, to hurt us. But you never did."

"Th-thank you," Harry whispered, his eyes wide with something akin to disbelief.

Orion swallowed the knot in his throat. Part of him wanted to echo Rose's words, but something deep inside him still bled, and it hurt. He had finally begun to learn how to trust, and Harry had shattered that. Out of everyone, even Asterin, Orion had felt like he shared something special with Harry. Something different. But had that been a lie, too?

Quinlan tilted his head. "What can you tell us about shadow magic?"

"Anything you want to know," said Harry.

"Are there any ways to kill an anygné?"

That caught him off guard. "Do you plan to kill me?"

Quinlan smiled. "If you betray us, then yes, without hesitation. Do you plan to betray us?"

"No," Harry replied firmly. "Cutting off my wings is the only way to kill me. But it's impossible to accomplish with mortal steel. Only King Eoin's sword, Nöctklavan, is sharp enough." He exhaled and squared his shoulders. "For centuries, I have slaved beneath Eoin's hand. I have never found the courage to disobey him, but then I met all of you and witnessed your strength, day after day. You taught me what bravery was. You taught me how to care." His eyes lingered on Orion. "Your kindness gives me hope that even though I am a demon, I can still be more." He bowed deeply. "And I will never forget that."

Asterin regarded the hunter for a moment longer before speaking. "It's settled then. Especially since we have no idea what more Garringsford might have up her sleeve. You're coming with us back to Axaris."

Eadric opened his mouth again, but Luna kicked him in the shin.

"We have no time to lose," the princess went on, sheathing Amoux. "We must return to the palace as soon as possible."

The others began following her out of the grove, even Eadric, albeit reluctantly.

Orion stayed on the ground, staring up at Harry.

"Do you hate me?" the hunter asked quietly.

Orion ignored his question. "Was anything real?"

Confusion flickered across Harry's face. "What do you mean?"

"I mean us. Were we real?"

Harry's gaze dropped to the ground, his face hidden in shadow. His shoulders began trembling. When he finally lifted his chin, to Orion's everlasting shock, those warm brown eyes brimmed with tears.

Orion shot to his feet, every misgiving flying out of his head. He wrapped Harry in his arms. How could he not, when Harry looked like his heart had been stripped raw?

"Almighty Immortals," said Orion as Harry muffled a sob into his neck. He cradled him closer, finding himself at a loss for any other words.

"Did you really think that?" Harry mumbled. "That I faked everything?"

Orion huffed. "Well, you can't really blame me for checking."

Harry buried his tear-streaked face into Orion's shoulder. "I could never do that to you."

"Hey." Orion grasped Harry's chin and tilted it up, their eyes searching one another's. "Listen, Harry. I might, in Asterin's words, 'accept your truth,' but I swear to the Immortals … if you leave us, I will never, ever forgive you. Promise me that you won't."

Harry tipped his face forward, resting their foreheads together. "Promise."

CHAPTER THIRTY-FIVE

Luna led her snow-white mare out of the barn and into the clearing, the reins gripped in her fist. The sky was an overcast slate, the air thick and humid. Ahead of her, Rose swatted at a cloud of black flies. It dispersed, only to re-collect around Luna's face.

She waved her hand irately—but then froze, feet dragging to a halt.

The low, incessant drone of buzzing black flies. Three children, sprawled in the late summer sunshine, sweating and eating fresh berries, the juices dribbling down their wrists and staining their skin pink and purple.

"Luna, are you all right?" Asterin asked from behind her. Lux nickered impatiently.

Luna blinked away the image. "Oh, sorry." She hurried to catch up to Rose, shaking her head to herself. Where had that memory come from? *One of those children was you*, her mind told her. But she didn't remember the other two children. Who were they?

"With her guard down, it'll be that much easier to finish Garringsford," Asterin said to the others. Quinlan trailed beside her and Harry waited for them down the cobbled path beneath the branched archway. Orion came out of the barn last, latching the door shut behind Buttercup. "Harry is supposed to bring my heart to Garringsford. She told him to meet her at the palace at eight in the evening on Fairfest Eve, three days from now."

"You know we can't just kill the General of Axaria," Eadric said. His brow hadn't smoothed since Asterin had overruled him about Harry. Luna knew he would never disobey the princess, but it didn't mean he was happy about the decision.

Asterin nodded. "We have to unveil her in front of as many people as possible. And the Fairfest Ball will be the perfect opportunity to do that. Royals and nobles from all the kingdoms will be attending. To expose Garringsford using shadow magic before all of them would guarantee her execution without condemning ourselves."

Luna frowned as she walked. "But how do we get in? If Garringsford thinks you're dead, then you can't go as yourself. We'll need fake invitations—"

Rose glanced over her shoulder at Luna with a grin. "Who needs a fake invitation when you're the Queen of Eradore?"

Orion huffed a laugh. "Convenient."

"And Rose's invitation permits her three escorts," Quinlan said, one hand stroking the nose of his palomino mare. "So Asterin, Orion, and I will accompany her into the ball. We'll need to find disguises, of course, and damned good ones if we don't want to risk getting recognized—"

Luna suddenly dropped her horse's reins and squeezed her eyes shut, slamming her palms into her temples as color exploded behind her lids.

A village, an inn—and a plump, boisterous woman with rosy cheeks who she called Maman. Two other children—Maman's children—brother and sister. Her best friends.

The two children, Luna realized.

"Nathan and Clara," she said aloud.

"Luna?" Asterin said, but Luna could barely hear over the roar in her ears, her world knocked askew by the whirlwind of memories. She snatched up as many as she could, desperate and lost, and tried to piece together the mystery that had become her life.

A wailing girl with hair like silver-blond gossamer chasing after a lanky boy, a bright blue ribbon the same shade as her eyes clutched in his grubby fist. "Poor, pretty little moonflower, her pretty little ribbon stolen," Nathan sang, a devious grin lighting his face.

A second girl sharing Nathan's close-set eyes and freckles lunged out of nowhere. The two tumbled to the ground, brawling in the dust, rolling and growling and snapping at each other like feral dogs. Clara, clothes streaked with dirt, emerged victorious, and handed the ribbon back to its rightful owner, who stopped her wailing for a smile of thanks.

The three of them, scurrying upstairs to a bland attic room with dingy gray walls after a hard day of chores and errands, playing cards and telling stories late into the night. Falling asleep on the floor even when there were three perfectly good beds right beside them, just so they could be close enough to touch, backs pressed to stomachs, clutching one another's hands like lifelines.

The three of them, sitting in a meadow of wildflowers. Nathan and Clara ogling up at the sky while the third child with the gossamer hair—Luna—summoned illusion after illusion, her magic always waiting at her fingertips, creating entire worlds for all of them to dream and play in together.

The memories fast-forwarded as if disturbed by a great gust of wind, and everything went dark. The next thing she saw was Asterin's face, smiling and young.

"Mother said that you're to be my lady-in-waiting, but I think we should be friends first," said the young princess.

Luna remembered nodding shyly, nervous because she had never had a friend before. Or at least, that was what she had believed at the time …

"Luna!"

Luna's eyes flew open at the shout, her chest heaving. She found herself on her knees on the path, the edges of the stones digging through her riding breeches. Asterin's hands clamped Luna's shoulders. The others crowded around them with mirrored expressions of worry.

"I—I saw my childhood," Luna gasped. "But I can't remember how I ended up at the palace. I forgot everything." She stared at her hands. "I forgot about my magic."

"What do you mean?" Asterin asked, helping her onto her feet.

"My magic," Luna repeated. Her appearance, her powers. "Priscilla … she isn't your mother, Asterin, she's mine. And since I'm her daughter, I must have inherited her illusion affinity, even though it was suppressed along with my memories."

"Wait," Rose said, and bent down. She picked up a smooth pebble from the ground, muttering beneath her breath. Slowly, affinity stone in hand, she carved a crude sigil into its surface and held it out. Luna recognized the sigil as Lord Pavon's—God of Illusion. "This won't work as well as a proper affinity stone, but …"

Luna rolled the pebble between her fingers, recalling the hours she had spent in the wildflower meadow with Clara and Nathan. A luminescent drop of light slid from her fingertip like morning dew at her command, filling her with a euphoric feeling she hadn't experienced for many cold, dark years. The drop transformed as Luna spread her fingers, winding outward in gossamer threads. As her friends looked on, just as Clara and Nathan once had, she wove a brilliant, gleaming illusion in the air. A peacock, its tail feathers shining brighter than a thousand dazzling jewels. It moved and bent at her will, bearing down upon them with its hooked beak before soaring upward, feathers fanning out, the fading daylight casting a ripple of iridescence over them. With her cheeks flushed with heat, Luna watched, transfixed, as the peacock stretched its magnificent neck and let out a terrific screech, so real that her friends gasped aloud.

She—*she* had created this thing of beauty. This gift, this power—it was hers.

Tears pricked her eyes, threatening to spill over. *This* is what she had missed, all these years. Her magic, her memories. Robbed.

The illusion dissolved as her fingers curled around the rock. When she opened her fist, only sand remained, the rock crumbling down to nothing. Her magic had overwhelmed its capacities.

"Did you say that you needed disguises?" Luna asked quietly, looking up at her friends, shocked into speechlessness. Only Harry didn't seem surprised, just impressed.

"Yes," Quinlan said, eyes still wide. "That would be very helpful."

"If I may," interjected Harry. "I could use your help too, Luna. But it will be dangerous."

Luna's stomach twisted nervously. *No*, she thought to herself. *You can do this.* She had done too much sitting around, too much waiting.

And she decided that she was done waiting.

So she smiled and asked, "What do you need me to do?"

CHAPTER THIRTY-SIX

"A letter for you, Your Royal Majesty," a servant squeaked, bowing down to the crimson carpet before Queen Priscilla's throne. The pudgy boy carefully offered her the scroll of parchment, his hands quaking.

Priscilla snapped up the scroll in her fist. "Dismissed." The boy struggled to his feet, scampering out as fast as his chubby legs would take him. After he disappeared, Priscilla glanced around the room, noting the four guards stationed by the entrance to Throne Hall. "A moment," she commanded, her voice reverberating up to the cavernous ceiling.

The guards marched out, but only when the heavy doors swung shut did she finally allow herself to look at the letter.

The dark purple wax of the King of Ibreseos's seal melted away at her touch, leaving only the faint indent of the heads of three rearing vipers—for Lady Ilma, Goddess of Air and House of the Viper. Priscilla pulled the scroll open and scanned the harsh, midnight-black strokes of ink, tracing her forefinger along the length of the parchment.

When she finished reading the letter, her eyes lingered on King Jakob's signature and the final line at the end of his message. She sighed, pressing the discolored parchment to the hollow of her throat.

How many years had passed since she had last seen him? Since they had frolicked together in the gardens of the Ibresean stronghold, a duchess and a prince, young and hopeful?

Fifteen years, of course. Two months. Twenty-one days.

A knock sounded at the entrance and a moment later, Carlotta Garringsford nudged the doors open. "My queen, the royal florist awaits you."

Tucking the letter beneath the collar of her dress, Priscilla pushed herself out of her throne and strode out into the hall, the general escorting her back to her quarters. Servants already flitted about the corridors, perching atop ladders and hanging decorations in preparation for the Fairfest Ball. Of course, Priscilla had begun planning this year's ball as soon as the last one had ended. Anticipation bubbled away just beneath her skin as she ascended the grand stairway. This year, she was pulling out all the stops. This year would be more spectacular than ever before.

Because this year, King Jakob had finally accepted her invitation to the ball.

Two men waited outside the door to her quarters with four of her personal guards when Priscilla arrived at the top floor of the palace. One of the men was as spindly as a flower stem and the other a nervous wreck.

"Ah, Your Royal Majesty," the spindly one—the florist—said. Priscilla wondered if a strong enough wind could blow him away. The head gardener stood behind him, sweating and fidgeting. "As always, it is an honor."

The guards opened the doors and Priscilla beckoned the pair into the sitting parlor. Garringsford didn't so much as glance at her for permission before slipping inside as well.

Priscilla extended a hand as she lowered herself onto the gray velvet settee facing the entrance. "Please, have a seat."

The florist and the gardener complied, sitting in stiff-backed chairs opposite the queen. Garringsford took the seat at the other end of the settee.

"These are the arrangements we previously discussed, Your Majesty." The florist laid out a half-dozen arrangements on the low table for her inspection. He smiled thinly. "Are they to your liking?" At her nod, he displayed two more bouquets. "Would you prefer silver spring lilies or coral gardenias at your place setting?"

"The gardenias, thank you." They would complement the lavender lisianthuses decking the ivory columns in the ballroom. Priscilla paused, struck by a sudden idea. “I want flowers hanging from the ceilings in glass baubles. Like little moons.”

The gardener made a noise. “H-how are we to put flowers into blass gaubles? I mean, gas blaubles. I mean—”

The florist shushed him. He peered at Priscilla from overtop the half-rimmed tortoiseshell spectacles perched upon his hawk-like nose. “About how many baubles is Your Majesty thinking?”

The gardener’s lips flapped. “Your Majesty, there are only two days left before the ball—”

Priscilla tapped her fingers on the armrest. Her mouth thinned in a cool smile to match the florist’s. “Thousands,” she decided.

“Thousands?” the gardener squeaked, eyes as round as gold notes. “B-but, Your Majesty, the *cost* of such a thing—”

“I assure you, the Fairfest Ball is more than enough justification for a little added expenditure,” Priscilla cut him off. “Should the head accountant give you any trouble, you may direct her to me.”

The gardener shriveled like a dead blossom under her icy stare, squeaking in compliance and bobbing his chin in a terrified nod.

“After you approved the lavender-lilac color theme a month ago, Your Majesty, the floral arrangements have now been confirmed,” the florist went on, unruffled by Priscilla’s demeanor in the slightest. “In the meantime, have you any other requests?”

She found his nonchalance amusing. “I don’t believe so.”

He tipped his chin, and began bundling the flowers away in bolts of silk with careful, nimble fingers. He rose to his feet. “Then that will be all, Your Majesty. Good day.” With an elegant bow and a dainty sniff, he strode away, the gardener scurrying after him, tail between his legs.

Once the doors shut behind them, Priscilla exhaled through her pursed lips, her thoughts going to the letter pressed against her bosom.

As if reading her mind, Carlotta asked, “Who was that letter from earlier?”

Priscilla scowled. “As if you don’t know.”

The general stretched her arms up to the ceiling, spine popping loudly, and folded them behind her head. "Poor Tristan," was all she said, with a little smirk.

Someone rapped on the door. Priscilla swallowed her annoyance. Between preparations for Fairfest and other matters, she had hardly gotten a moment of peace all week.

"Enter," she called. A guard peeped in. "State your business."

"The first overseas guests have begun to arrive, Your Majesty," said the guard. "As well, a messenger just delivered the news that His Royal Majesty, King Jakob Lucas Evovich the Third, ruler of Ibreseos—"

"I know his name, for hell's sake." Priscilla's stomach curdled with dread. Had he changed his mind about attending the ball after all?

"A-apologies, Your Majesty," the guard stammered. "King Jakob will be arriving one day early. He hopes that the early intrusion upon Your Majesty's hospitality will not be a problem."

And just like that, her dread vanished. *One day early*, she thought, heart skipping a beat. *He wants to see me as much as I want to see him.*

"Thank you very much for bringing this to my attention, soldier," Priscilla said, suddenly dizzy with expectation. "Respond that I shall be honored to receive his presence early. Have the servants begin preparations immediately."

"Yes, Your Majesty."

Once the guard had departed, Carlotta tutted, her gray eyes sharp. "Oh, my queen."

Priscilla resisted the urge to strangle the general. But everything had a price, and Priscilla still needed to pay her dues to this woman. "What?"

Carlotta's mouth tilted into a wicked smile. "Nothing. It's just that if you wish so badly to play in the viper's pit … you'd best prepare yourself for the fangs."

CHAPTER THIRTY-SEVEN

Luna rubbed her palms on her trousers. She had only managed to slip in a few hours of restless slumber in her room at the Singing Sword, a stately lodge in Axaris's trade district, before the first rays of morning light had awoken her.

To say that she was nervous would be a severe understatement. The milky-green jade illusionstone Eadric had bought her was already spotted with her fingerprints, smudged and slippery with sweat no matter how many times she wiped it off.

Fairfest Eve was tonight.

When they had arrived in Aldville on their way back to the capital, Eadric had sent a message ahead for the Elites at the palace. Thankfully, no wyverns attacked them this time. Once they reached the outskirts of Axaris, they found a pair of Elites waiting for them—Alicia and Silas. They left their horses—along with their belongings and most of their weapons—in the care of Alicia's uncle, who owned a small equine veterinary practice nearby. The practice was busy enough that no one would question the sudden appearance of five horses, but small enough that hardly anyone would notice anyway. Afterward, the Elite pair departed with careful instructions from their captain and the promise that the rest of the Elites would be ready at hand in case the plan went awry.

Asterin had flagged hansom cabs to take the rest of them into the city, but they ended up walking the last few blocks because the trade district streets grew too crowded for the cabs to pass. Jostling through throngs of Fairfest celebrators, they finally made it to the Singing Sword. Since there was no chance that anyone would recognize him, Harry had taken Asterin's money and paid for a one-night stay. The rest of them kept their hoods up until they made it safely to the Diamond Suite on the top floor, which consisted of a large common room and several bedrooms and bathrooms. Despite the title it boasted, there wasn't anything particularly luxurious about it, but they at least had the entire floor to themselves.

They had gone to bed early. Luna wondered if anyone else had slept as poorly as she. By late afternoon, they would leave for the palace. But first, she needed to completely disguise and transform the faces of four of her friends. Although both Asterin and Quinlan wielded a little bit of illusionary magic, being omnifinitied, neither were powerful enough in that affinity for their illusions to hold for longer than a few minutes, so the responsibility weighed solely on Luna's shoulders.

Luna had tested her abilities nonstop since they had left the Aswiyre Forest. She'd changed the wallpaper in her room seven times already, and it never faded until she commanded it to.

Now, her friends crowded around her in the common room, cornflowers blooming across the walls at their backs and melting into robins pecking at berries. Everyone except Eadric, who stood guard by the fire-exit door, had draped themselves over various pieces of mismatched furniture or on the floor, just like they used to back at Harry's cottage. The only thing missing was the crackle of the hearth.

"We're ready when you are," said Asterin.

Luna rolled the illusionstone in her fingers, calmed by its smoothness, and gave the princess the firmest nod she could muster. "Who's first?"

Quinlan stood. "I'll go," he volunteered. "I'm not as recognizable as Asterin or Orion. Experiment, make mistakes."

Luna nodded gratefully and beckoned him closer. Taking a deep breath, she squared her shoulders and brought the illusionstone to Quinlan's face, one hand grasping his jaw, leaning in so close that she could count each of his eyelashes.

Focus.

That was what Quinlan always said to Asterin. Not in a thousand years had Luna thought that all those weeks of lurking on the fringes of their training sessions, hanging just out of sight from the garden or by the barn, would ever be of use to her. And even though Luna had believed her magic would always be painfully weak, she had still observed.

She would be eternally thankful for the knowledge she now possessed.

Luna drew a drop of magic from the deep gorge that had cracked open inside of her, letting it slowly well out of her fingertips and onto Quinlan's skin.

The prince exhaled, breath featherlight on her face. "Keep me pretty," he joked.

"No promises," said Luna, and then began to mold.

It reminded her of carving a sculpture. Years of working on busts made this almost easy—and she suddenly wondered if her love of sculpting had, in fact, been a manifestation caused by the suppression of her powers.

First, Luna softened Quinlan's bone structure—lowering the arch of his brow, weakening his chin and smoothing away the sharpness of his jawline. It was slow work. She proceeded with extreme caution, only daring to let tiny drops of magic leak out at a time. She feared loss of control—she had no idea what might happen.

His hair came next. She dug her fingers into his scalp. To her alarm, the strands briefly flashed canary yellow, but no one commented or even stirred. They watched intently as each of Quinlan's locks gradually lightened, dark brown graying to ash. She took a step back and circled him—an artist, inspecting her completed masterpiece. Finally, she deemed her work satisfactory and gave him a nod of approval.

The others stared at Quinlan and Luna clasped her hands behind her back, waiting anxiously for their verdict.

Quinlan's eyes still gleamed indigo, and she hadn't altered his height, but his chest was broader and his shoulders rounder. His face, of course, was unrecognizable.

Asterin's lips parted in amazement. "Garringsford has no idea what she's got coming for her."

Luna flushed at the praise, unable to keep the smile off her face as she took in her friends' expressions of awe. She tossed the illusionstone up and down in her palm casually, her magic bubbling beneath her skin. "So … who's next?"

Orion rubbed his palms together. "Me. Could you give me a tattoo? I've always wanted one."

While she worked on Orion, the others began discussing contingency plans.

Asterin stood from her seat and began pacing. "After we expose Garringsford in front of the royals—"

"Hold on," Orion interrupted, jaw shifting beneath Luna's fingers. "How are we going to do that, exactly? Why would any of them believe us?"

"In order to borrow dark magic from King Eoin," said Harry, "you must pay a price. King Eoin demands two things: one half of your life and whatever you hold dearest. Those who wield dark magic are granted something like temporary immortality. Once that immortality expires, they can continue to pay for dark magic by halving their lives again and again. This creates a sort of inescapable paradox. As the years pass and they absorb more and more shadow magic in place of their dwindling life, their appearance becomes increasingly grotesque and disfigured—more monster than human—but shadow magic can conceal that. So, if we lift the concealment in front of all the guests, there would be no question of her crime. Her fate would be sealed."

Luna shivered. "So we reveal her in front of all the royals at the ball. But how?"

"That," Eadric said, patting a distinct bulge in his chest pocket, "will be up to me."

Three hours later, Luna stood in a room of strangers. Orion sported a new haircut, jet black and cropped close to his skull. He stood even shorter but stockier, a cleft in his chin and a fearsome scowl etched between his brows. At his insistence, Luna inked a tattoo of a serpent onto his neck, a symbol of his allegiance to his temporary new kingdom, its head curled beneath his earlobe, a ruby tongue flicking the cartilage of his ear. The rest of the reptile disappeared beneath the collar of the elegant black getup that

Laurel, the wily Elite who Eadric had described as "the only person in the world capable of stealing the boots off your feet," had delivered just that morning. Both Asterin and Quinlan were clad in identical outfits, and with Orion, the trio matched perfectly.

Rose had been tricky—the ball would be her public debut as Queen of Eradore, so her appearance had to be kept as true as possible, since whatever face the guests saw would be the face they recalled on future occasions. Luckily, because Rose had taken such care to keep her face hidden from the Axarian court, it was unlikely that anyone would recognize her at all, save the Elites. All the same, Luna managed to project a layer of illusion *over* her face, so that her features blurred slightly unless examined at close range. *Just in case*, Luna thought.

She helped Rose into the ball gown that Laurel had snuck right out of Asterin's closet back at the palace. The Queen of Eradore did a slow, admiring twirl, the streaks of gleaming silver beads and jewels on the bodice cascading all the way down the skirts to the floor like fallen stars. "It's gorgeous."

"I know that dress," Asterin said. "It was too big around the bust."

"But it fits Rose perfectly," Luna said. So perfectly—so *queenly*, that it took her breath away.

Rose laughed. "If it makes you feel any better, I'm wearing my combat suit underneath it."

Luna couldn't help but smile as she hung Rose's cloak around her shoulders, transforming the black fabric and crimson underside to a deep plum and trimming it with gold. Lastly came Asterin's tiara. Luna replaced the rubies with sapphires and adorned it with flourishes of white diamond.

Once the preparations for Rose's outfit were finished, Eadric helped Luna fold the dress back into the box. Afterward, he hefted it into his arms and went downstairs to send it off with Laurel, who would deliver it to their next destination—the lavish Grand Hotel. A royal carriage that would take them to the palace was scheduled to collect them at six in the evening.

Finally, there was Asterin. Luna spent nearly two hours altering her best friend. She widened the cut of her jaw and forehead, dipping the bow of her mouth, stretched the crease of her eyelids and the arch of her brows. She bleached the ebony from Asterin's hair and began layering in a faded brown from root to tip. In the likely event of combat, Luna decided that the more Asterin's opponents underestimated her, the better, so she made the princess's frame willowy, delicate. She looked breakable, even though the muscles and strength were still there, hidden beneath the surface of the illusions.

"Do you want to take a break?" asked Quinlan when Luna took a moment to roll the tension from her shoulders. "We've still got more than enough time."

Luna ignored him and asked Asterin, "Any preference for eye color?" Even now, despite the rest of the disguise, those emerald irises belonged unmistakably to the Princess of Axaria.

"Whatever is easiest for you," responded Asterin.

Luna's jaw clenched. "Right." As she began to work, she tried to forget the way her stomach had twisted at Asterin's comment. *Whatever is easiest for me?* She could do better than that. So much was at stake here. Maybe she couldn't call lightning or summon waterfalls, but she could help in her own way. The least she could do was try, do whatever was *best* for everyone—not easiest.

Lips pursed, she pressed the pads of her thumbs into the outer corners of Asterin's eyes. Slowly, the bright green neutralized, stripped to a glassy, clear hue. Luna injected spurts of muddy brown, struggling to control the tiny amounts of magic she allowed to escape, perfecting the little details until the muscles in her shoulders throbbed in pain.

Her fingers trembled as she put on the finishing touches—a spray of freckles across Asterin's cheeks, a handful of scars across her brow, neck, and arms. Another tattoo, reminiscent of Orion's.

When at last she withdrew, the room had fallen silent. Luna had a feeling that even if Queen Priscilla stared at the girl before them for days on end, she would never guess her true identity.

Quinlan appeared at Luna's side, holding out a glass of water. "Drink, Luna," he murmured.

She felt sore just raising it to her lips. When she returned the glass, Quinlan's eyes lingered on her trembling fingers before flicking back up to meet her stubborn gaze.

She tucked her hands behind her back. "I'm fine."

"Sure," he replied.

Luna collapsed into the armchair that Quinlan had vacated, sighing loudly in satisfaction to cover the true extent of her exhaustion. Much to her relief, the first part of the plan had been executed successfully.

A wild grin rose to her face. For once, she felt useful. For once, she had actually made a difference.

Over by the fire exit, Eadric reached inside his jacket, pulling out a little pocket watch. "Two hours to rest," he said, focusing on anywhere and everywhere but Luna.

Her next swallow was like a mouthful of ash. She understood his worry, she really did. But she wasn't a porcelain doll, for the love of the Immortals! Who was he to treat her as if she were made of glass? If Quinlan had shown up, battered and bloody, she doubted Eadric would spare him a second glance. And yet, here she was, with an infinitesimal tremor in her hand, and Eadric couldn't even look her in the eye.

Luna took a deep breath, fighting down the rising resentment. She refused to hold it against him. *I'm just tired, that's all*, she thought. Throat tight, she drew her knees up to her chest and stared blankly through the window by Harry's head.

Bruised purple and gray clouds threatened the sky over the city, but it was the palace atop the mountain shining in the distance that drew her gaze. Clouds smothered the topmost turrets, but the palace only seemed to stand brighter against the soot-stained horizon, a beacon of light resisting the inevitable darkness.

Thunder rumbled off into the distance, promising an oncoming storm.

Let it come, Luna thought. She was ready to taste the rain.

CHAPTER THIRTY-EIGHT

Priscilla folded her arms across her chest and narrowed her eyes at the angry clouds gathering on the horizon, her breath fogging up the great glass windows of her bedchamber. Rubbing the fog away with her palm, she stared at her reflection. With a heavy sigh, she swept her fingertips across the bags beneath her eyes, glaring at herself.

She was beginning to look *old*.

A sharp knock sounded from afar, and a moment later Carlotta poked her head into Priscilla's chambers. "My queen, His Royal Majesty King Jakob has arrived."

Priscilla's heart leaped. She took a final glimpse at herself in the mirror across the room, her figure bathed in a golden halo from the glow of the chandelier. Her tiara threw crystalline shards of light with every movement, sitting perfectly atop platinum curls her maids had spent two painstaking hours plaiting and styling. Just getting her into the gown had taken all afternoon.

If things went as planned, all that work would go to waste. Hopefully, King Jakob would be in a favorable mood—and how could he not be, after fifteen years?

Priscilla hurried through the adjoining antechamber and over to the general, who waited in the sitting parlor, polishing a scuff on her boots.

Carlotta raised an eyebrow. "Your Majesty, are you quite sure you don't want to send for him? It's hardly right for a queen in her own palace to heed the beck and call of anyone else."

"No, Carlotta," said Priscilla, turning her nose up in the air. "It is simply good manners to welcome him in person."

"As you wish it, my queen," the general grumbled.

It wasn't a long walk to the quarters King Jakob occupied—in fact, they were right beside her own. No one had used them since Tristan's death, but Priscilla thought it more than appropriate to allow Jakob to use them. After all, those quarters were meant for a king.

Priscilla gathered herself in front of the double doors, Garringsford still at her side, and shot a quick glance at the pair of soldiers standing guard—one Axarian and one Ibresean. She rubbed her suddenly clammy palms together and smoothed down nonexistent rumples in her newest pearl-white silk gown. In her daze, she watched her hand rise seemingly of its own accord, as if it belonged to someone else. Her fingers splayed against the wood, caressing it. And then she knocked.

Her hand hadn't even fallen back to her side when the door swung open.

Before her stood the King of Ibreseos in all his intimidating magnificence, nearly knocking the breath from her lungs. He had slicked back his sandy blond undercut, and his signature heavy crown glinted atop his head. He had grown a beard in the time they had been apart—fifteen years ago, he'd only ever allowed the faintest golden stubble to grace his chin.

"Queen Priscilla," said King Jakob, his expression unreadable.

Her heart pounded faster at the sound of her name on his tongue. "Welcome to Axaria, King Jakob," she said, pleased with the evenness of her voice.

Jakob stepped aside and beckoned to her. "Where are my manners? Please, come in."

A warm flush of excitement crept up her neck, mind already whirling with flashes of bare skin and cries of pleasure. "Carlotta, you may leave."

Carlotta, to her credit, didn't even bat an eyelash. "Yes, Your Majesty."

Once the general had departed and Priscilla had seated herself beside Jakob near the hearth, she spoke at last. "I daresay you've gained weight, Jakob," she teased with a smile. "Too many sweetcakes?"

When his expression didn't so much as soften, just as unreadable as before, something cold settled in her gut.

"Perhaps," he replied at last, voice gruff.

She couldn't help but frown at his response. Before, he would have teased her back, eyes twinkling, the smirk she had missed for so many years rising to his lips. He would have grinned, seized her hand to kiss the inside of her wrist, gazing up at her through his lashes with those lovely cornflower-blue eyes …

"The beard suits you," she tried.

His hand—oh, those lovely, broad fingers—ran through his beard briefly. "Thank you." A small smile reached his face, finally, and his eyes focused on something far away. The familiar crease between his thick brows faded for a moment, and she wondered what he was thinking about. He hesitated, returning his attention to her, and suddenly she did not want to hear his next words, but by then it was too late. "Adrianna suggested I grow it out."

"Adrianna?" Priscilla echoed in disbelief. "You still speak to her?"

He nodded. "We're getting married."

She stared at him.

And stared.

And then she threw her head back to the ceiling and burst into hysterical laughter. Relief flooded her. *He was just playing*, she thought. *Oh, Adrianna, you poor sad thing.*

Expecting Jakob to join her but hearing only silence, Priscilla paused long enough to glance at him.

He was glowering at the wall, jaw tight and eyes stormy with annoyance.

She felt the blood drain from her face, her stomach clenching as her relief vanished just as quickly as it had come. *What sort of cruel joke is this?* she wondered. Her fingers curled into fists around her skirts. "You can't be serious."

"I am," he replied, the two words a poison. "In fact, the main reason I came to Axaria in the first place was to personally invite you to the wedding."

"Of all people …" Priscilla trailed off, thinking of the girl who had once been the sun to her moon. Her shock quickly dissolved into despair. "But … but what about us?" she demanded.

Jakob's eyes hardened to ice. "What about us?" he asked. "There is no *us*, anymore, Priscilla. There hasn't been, not for years. Not since Elyssa died—"

"Do *not* say that name," she spat. "After everything I did for you? You're just going to throw me away?"

Jakob suddenly took her hands. "Of course not," he said, and his demeanor shifted, softening. The slightest flicker of hope filled her as his touch heated her to the core. She leaned forward. He gave her a kindly smile. "I will always cherish you as a dear friend."

Priscilla felt her heart, her life, her entire *world* shatter at those words. Yanking her hands away as if he had burned her, she stood and stormed over to the door. She rested her fingers on the handle, so cold after the warmth of his touch. "I will never be your friend. That was Elyssa's job." She smiled sweetly. "I'll make you regret this, Jakob."

"For the sake of old times," Jakob implored, "let us be friends. We will have a wonderful time at the ball together, and I truly do hope that you will honor Adrianna and me with your presence at our wedding, Priscilla. You know how much it would mean to her—"

She scoffed. "It would mean nothing to my sweet, *sweet* baby sister."

"Priscilla—"

"Do you know how many letters Adrianna has written to me?" she hissed. When Jakob didn't respond, she went on, voice trembling with fury. "Two. In nearly fifteen years, she has written *two* letters to me. And not once did she mention your … relationship," she sneered, chest heaving. "Nor have you, for that matter. Since when have you ever had any interest in her? The last time I checked, the two of you bore nothing but disgust and hatred for one another."

"We did," Jakob agreed, running a hand down the back of his neck. "But it's been fifteen years, Priscilla. It was time I moved on." He looked up, eyes filled with genuine pity. "It's time *you* move on."

She shook her head. "My dearest sister best watch herself."

In a flash, Jakob was out of his seat. He covered the space between them in five strides and towered over her, expression thunderous. "Taunt me as you please, but do not threaten her in my presence. Touch her, and I promise that no one will ever hear from you again."

Priscilla's jaw dropped. "You *dare* speak to me like that?"

He swallowed, mouth thinning. "I apologize." To her disbelief, he took a step away. The old Jakob would never have backed down like some weak-hearted craven. "That was most tasteless of me."

Her hand tightened on the door handle. "After all the pain and struggle I went through to do what *you* asked of me …" She almost choked on her unshed tears. "You have no right."

Jakob grimaced. "Perhaps not. But look where you are now."

"I would undo everything to have you back," she whispered shamelessly, and the tears fell down her face. "I should have stayed a pathetic, powerless duchess. I should have never left you. Then we would have been together and happy forever."

"But you never made me happy either, not truly, even back then," he told her softly, brushing a hand across her cheek. "It's not your fault."

Priscilla slapped his hand away with a *smack* that echoed like a cannon blast in the silence. "No." She gritted her teeth, seeing red. "You're right. It's all *her* fault."

"This has nothing to do with Adrianna—"

"Not her, you fool. *Elyssa.* She deserved to die sooner, before she birthed her little brat."

Jakob glowered. "You promised me you wouldn't hurt the girl. I heard that she wouldn't be at the ball. Where is she?"

Priscilla's lips curled upward. "You promised that you would love me forever."

"Where did you send her, you blasted woman?" Jakob seethed.

"She's gone. Just like Elyssa." Priscilla wrenched the door open, darting outside before he could grab her. She found Carlotta waiting in the corridor, ever the loyal hound, but she signaled for the general to heel when the woman started forward with a hand on her sword. Her smile widened at Jakob's infuriated growl. There was no chance in hell that he would try and lay a finger on her now. "But don't worry," she went on. "You wouldn't have been able to help her, anyway. And besides …" She lowered her voice to a whisper. "It's time you moved on."

With that, she slammed the door in his face and strode away.

CHAPTER THIRTY-NINE

About an hour before they were due to leave, Quinlan slipped out of the Singing Sword and into the bustling streets to hunt for food. The trade district was a maze of avenues and winding alleys, throngs of people crowding every shop and corner. He passed jewelers, florists, and brewers of ale and brewers of potions galore. He navigated through an entire street strung lamp to lamp with arrays of scarves and shawls of every color and design imaginable. On the next street he briefly peeked into a shop boasting knives with blades as sharp as Ignatian steel. False, of course. His nose guided him onward until the street unfurled like a great flag into an open market, mouthwatering scents and sights spreading before him like a personal feast as he drifted in a trance to the first food stall he saw, his stomach rumbling loudly.

The back of his neck prickled as he paid for a cheese pastry and stuffed the whole thing into his mouth. He glanced backward and caught a shadowy blur darting out of sight behind a cart of fat green melons.

Frowning, he continued on his way until he found a vendor selling beef skewers. He ducked beneath the cheerful, orange-and-white striped awning decorated with lines of faerie lights and flower baubles in the spirit of Fairfest. He handed the vendor some coins, one hand casually perched on the hilt of the dagger at his hip, waiting for some poor fool to slip a hand into his pocket.

Quinlan's pulse quickened when the prickling intensified. He held his breath, nodding blankly as the beef skewer vendor gossiped about the upcoming ball and the expected attendance of the new Queen of Eradore. Then, as he felt the faintest touch at his hip, Quinlan whirled around his stalker and pulled his dagger out in one smooth motion, sliding it beneath their chin from behind with the beef skewer still in his other hand.

The vendor let out a startled squawk and cowered behind his cart.

"Nice try," he murmured into the fabric of his stalker's hood. "How about you give me one good reason not to spill your insides right here in the middle of the street, hm?"

"Whoa. Your voice gets really sexy when you're threatening people."

Quinlan snatched his blade back. "Asterin?"

She turned around, smirking, and he recognized the face Luna had given her. "I'm taller than you now."

He sheathed his dagger. "Yeah, whatever." Hearing her voice from the mouth of a stranger unnerved him more than he cared to admit.

"Oh, Immortals! What is that?" Asterin exclaimed with a theatrical gasp, pointing over his shoulder.

He whipped around. "What?" There was a pinch between his fingers. When he turned back, his mouth fell open in shock. "My beef skewer!"

In response, Asterin took a triumphant chomp of the stolen skewer. With a withering sigh, Quinlan offered a few more coppers to the vendor, who eyed the pair of them warily until they departed.

Shooting Quinlan a sly grin, Asterin linked her arm in his and nudged him onward to the next stall. She leaned close enough that he could smell the woodsmoke clinging to her hair every time she laughed and shook her head. They toured the square, bickering and teasing one another as if nothing was out of the ordinary, as if they weren't wearing strangers' faces, trying to stave off thoughts of what was left to do.

Quinlan polished off a lemon meringue and licked his fingers. "You should've stayed at the inn."

Asterin cocked a brow at him. "What's the big deal? No one can recognize us, anyway." She batted her eyelashes. *Doe eyes*, he thought. "And besides, if anything happens, you'll be right here to save me."

"No, I just meant that you should be resting." Gruffly, he added, "And you don't need anyone to save you. In fact, I'd bet good money that by now you can wield magic without the omnistone."

Her eyes widened. "You really think so?"

"I do. I wasn't expecting us to return so suddenly, so we didn't get a chance to practice, but I do." He exhaled. "Don't count on it, though. Just … if something goes wrong, and—and you don't have one …"

"Quinlan," Asterin began. "If we die—"

His heart leapt into his throat. "Shut up," he said. "Just shut up."

She made an impatient noise. "Quinlan, please. The odds aren't at all in our favor—"

"Don't say that. We'll beat the odds. We have to."

"Quinlan—"

"*No*," he said, the words coming so forcefully that he stopped walking right in the middle of the sidewalk. He closed his eyes, breathing. Just breathing.

Anxious fingers scrabbled for his. "Hey," Asterin said. "I'm sorry."

He didn't respond.

People jostled past them, but he still couldn't bring himself to move.

A moment passed and Asterin spoke.

"My father and I made a bet once," she began, fingers still wrapped around his. "I think I was four. Whoever lost had to eat whatever the winner wanted them to. I lost, and he made me drink an entire pot of beet juice."

The thundering in his head began to quiet as he focused on her words, her voice, her touch.

"When I went to go relieve myself, I thought he'd poisoned me because … well, everything was blood red."

A small grunt of laughter escaped him.

"I locked myself in my room for three days, crying my eyes out, until a healer revealed the cause. As revenge, I spent the next few years sneaking beets into my father's food so he was forced to constantly consult the healer about defecation. The healer was in on it, though, so he would just advise my father to eat only cabbage for an entire week."

Quinlan couldn't keep the smile off his face. "You are unbelievable," he muttered, eyes still closed.

"I know." Her hands cradled his jaw and then guided him to her lips.

The sounds of the streets around them faded, and he lost himself to the kiss, anchored in the darkness by her touch.

When they parted, still blocking the sidewalk, Quinlan opened his eyes, heart heavy and aching in his chest. "Promise me you won't die."

She brushed his nose with hers. "I'll try my very best."

The declaration in no way eased his anxiety, but she took his mouth with hers when he tried to speak again. A growl rose from his throat and he caught her bottom lip between his teeth, hands roving possessively up her waist. She made a noise of surprise and then nipped back tentatively.

Damn, Quinlan thought, tilting her backward by the waist to deepen the kiss.

Some passerby cleared their throat loudly and Asterin broke away, cheeks tinged a most attractive pink. "W-we should head back."

Quinlan tipped his chin in a grudging nod. As they walked, he intertwined their fingers and she grinned at him, bright as sunshine. And even though it wasn't her face, it still took his breath away. Because somehow, beneath the illusion that concealed her appearance, it was still *her*.

"So, what was your favorite part of our little excursion?" she asked. "The lemon tarts? I liked those poached egg buns with the bits of bacon …"

Quinlan's brows creased, the answer so painstakingly obvious that it almost hurt. "You."

She punched his shoulder, hiding a smile, but she couldn't conceal her blush. "You're disgusting."

The others were already waiting for them when they made it back up to the Diamond Suite. The walk to the Grand Hotel from the Singing Sword might have taken about twenty minutes—but with the increasing mobs of Fairfest celebrators cramming into the streets as evening fell, it would take far longer, and navigating as a group of seven would be near impossible. They could have split up into smaller groups, but Eadric was adamant about staying together, and Asterin claimed that she had a better idea, anyway.

Orion held open the door to the fire escape. He looked at Quinlan. "Ladies first."

Quinlan rolled his eyes but complied, stepping onto the rickety metal stairs. The others filed out behind him, ascending the narrow escape to the roof. Tension filled the silence, thick and palpable. Their plan tonight counted on too many variables for Quinlan's liking, but they had been short on both time and resources. Other than the few orders Eadric had sent through Alicia and Silas to the rest of the Elites, they could rely on no one but themselves.

Quinlan climbed onto the landing, Rose at his heels. *You still have a duty to fulfill*, he reminded himself. He couldn't let anything happen to his queen tonight. Nor to Asterin. A grave thought lurked in his head, making his blood run cold. Tonight, if anything happened, Immortals forbid, and he had to make the fatal choice between them …

He stole a furtive glance at Asterin while Orion trudged up the stairs last. She exchanged hushed words with Harry, a few tendrils of brown hair escaping the hood of her cloak.

Once everyone had made it onto the roof, Orion shot them all a grin. "Everyone ready for a bit of roof jumping?"

"Don't fall," Asterin advised, bouncing on the balls of her feet. "Roof jumping is actually quite safe as long as you make it to the other side."

Quinlan snorted, jittery with anticipation. "We'll try to keep that in mind, thanks."

"Knees bent on the landing," she added. "Don't overthink it. And whatever you do, don't look down."

"Exactly *how* many times have you done this?" demanded Eadric. "I still can't believe I've never been informed of this … this sport. What if one of you had fallen?"

Orion raised his eyebrows. "Sorry, mum." He backed up toward the edge of the roof and blew a kiss to the captain. "See you on the other side!"

With that, he barreled forward and launched himself over the vast chasm between the buildings, suspended over his death for a tantalizing second.

Quinlan's breath hitched.

But Orion hit the ground—or rather, the roof—running, and rocketed onto the next without the slightest hesitation.

"Good luck, everyone." Asterin flashed them a toothy grin. She cast Eadric an apologetic glance—not convincing in the least—before sprinting toward the gaping void. She soared over it, and then the next, and the next, never once looking back.

Just watching her made Quinlan's stomach drop. "Immortals."

Rose shot him a delighted grin, tugging at his sleeve like an overeager child. "Come on, then, Quinnie. We mustn't fall behind."

"Your keenness to throw yourself from rooftops is slightly troubling, cousin dearest," he said.

Rose ignored him and sashayed toward the roof edge. Her expression shone with glee as she tore forward. She let out an elated whoop when she landed with scarcely a sound on the other side.

Luna stepped forward.

Quinlan watched Eadric give her a resolute pat on the back. "I'll catch you if you trip," he promised.

She gave him a look. "And why would I trip?" Without waiting for an answer, she barreled forward, leaving Eadric to scramble after her.

The two successfully made it across, which left Quinlan and Harry.

Quinlan cleared his throat. "Well?"

Harry shrugged, eyes dancing with mirth. "Ladies first."

Quinlan chuckled half-heartedly. "Right."

Taking a deep breath, he retraced the steps that the others had taken. He gathered his courage, and then dashed forward in a burst of speed. The edge of the roof rushed toward him and his heart leapt into his throat—

At that moment, when the ground yawned before him, much farther down than he remembered, he almost faltered. But then, in his mind, he saw Asterin take the jump. How effortlessly she had crossed that intimidating gap.

His magic sparked from his palms, a gust of wind shoving him forward.

He shot across and landed squarely on the other side, his heart pounding and adrenaline surging through his veins.

Quinlan trusted his body to do the work for him after that, his magic at hand when he needed a little boost, focusing instead on timing his leaps, growing more and more confident with each stride. A calm settled over him as he flew across the rooftops, sure and swift, soon overtaking Eadric and Luna, then eventually catching up to Rose and darting past her in a blur.

Up ahead, Asterin's silhouette stood stark against the backdrop of coal clouds above the city sprawl. Her hood had fallen back, her hair catching the last of the daylight. He could almost see the wolf in her then—the agility and strength and *purpose* filling each powerful stride.

He joined her, and together they raced across the sky, perfectly in sync, their heavy breathing and the thud of footsteps the only sound in their ears as Axaris bled past them like watercolor on parchment.

His muscles burned. Every breath was fire in his lungs, hot and painful, but the ache only made him push himself harder. His heart beat like a drum, pounding in time with each footfall.

He felt alive.

A single misstep—that was all it would take for one of them to plummet off the roofs, toppling to their death. Quinlan saw it in his mind—a loose stone, maybe. The tumble through empty air, floundering desperately, trying to grab ahold of something, too stunned to do anything except fall. The ringing *crack* and the blinding pain that would follow, before blinking out into eternal blackness.

But he never lost his footing, and the stumble never came.

The storm clouds overhead had only darkened by the time Quinlan caught his first unobstructed glimpse of the mountain. The palace rose from it like a majestic, fiery crystal. Tendrils of fog and mist curled around the topmost turrets like the smoky breaths of a sleeping dragon, sullen rain clouds shrouding the crimson pennants snapping in the wind. Amber light spilled out of the windows and winked from the lanterns lining the mountain road. He could already see the bright carriages snaking up the mountain like a handful of scattered sweets, disappearing beneath the Wall one by one.

Before he knew it, Quinlan spotted Orion waiting for them at their destination up ahead. Together, he and Asterin leapt for the final rooftop and skidded to a halt.

He doubled over, bracing his hands against his knees and gulping in lungfuls of oxygen, wheezing for a solid minute before he began to laugh.

Asterin wiped her forehead, shoulders heaving. "What?"

"That was …" He paused to catch his breath, pulse still galloping. "Ridiculous. Utterly ridiculous."

Orion snickered. "I thought you would have been in better shape, Quinnie."

Asterin squinted. "Speaking of out of shape, where are the others?"

Quinlan zeroed in on a growing speck in the distance. "There's Rose." Luna, Eadric, and Harry were nowhere to be seen.

His cousin's face broke into a weary grin as she crossed the last gap and then collapsed onto the roof in a disheveled heap. "That," Rose panted, "was exhausting. Still better than a carriage, though." She looked up at Quinlan. "Let's do it again when we get home."

"I don't think that's such a good idea, Rosie," he said. "Our roofs are curved. You'd probably twist something."

Rose pouted. "Would not."

"Would too."

Orion shielded a hand over his eyes. "Ah, here come Luna and Eadric."

Asterin let out a little gasp. "No way."

Rose craned her neck. "What? What is it?"

"I think … Immortals, Luna is beating him!"

Captain Covington was, in fact, lagging behind the lovely lady-in-waiting, his face haggard and expression decidedly flustered.

"Yes!" Asterin cackled. Rose scrambled to her feet and started cheering, both Quinlan and Orion joining her. "Go! Run, Luna!"

Luna made it over the final jump and staggered into Asterin's waiting arms, both girls laughing.

"You've been sitting on your ass too long, Cap!" Orion yelled as Eadric made the second-to-last jump.

As he barreled forward, the captain's head snapped up to reveal his scowl. "Oh, shut it—"

And that was when things went awry.

Quinlan watched in horror as the distraction caused Eadric, less than three feet away from the final gap, to trip. Time slowed. Eadric's expression morphed from irked embarrassment to shock, his face slackening. He skittered sideways, flailing wildly, his arms shooting out to try and keep upright—

The toe of his boot caught on the roof ledge and he somersaulted into the void. Luna lunged forward, crying out, her hand outstretched as if to catch him. Quinlan saw the very scene he had dreaded earlier play out before his eyes. The stumble, the desperate floundering, Eadric too stunned to do anything else except fall.

The ringing crack and the blinding pain that would surely follow, before blinking out into eternal blackness.

The rest of them summoned their magic, but Eadric was already falling, arms spread like broken wings, abandoned by the Immortals.

CHAPTER FORTY

A blur of shadow surged out of absolutely nowhere, a pair of jaws opening and latching onto the fabric of Eadric's cloak. Sinewy wings unlocked and sprang free into the air, beating once, twice—powerful strokes, stronger than oars on a stormy sea—pulling out of the dive.

Harry swooped onto the roof in his demon form, buffeting them with gusts of wind as he lowered Eadric safely and deposited him at their feet.

"Eadric," Asterin and Luna breathed as one, running for him. The latter flung her arms around his neck.

Harry transformed back into his human form, fur rippling into that dark, armor-like skin. His neck glistened with sweat.

"How did you just … appear?" Rose asked Harry.

"I heard Luna's shout," he explained. "And then I shadow jumped." His legs quivered and he looked up at Rose, shoulders heaving. "That's how I escaped that trap you caught me in."

"That was close," Eadric mumbled to himself.

"Cap, I'm so sorry," Orion stammered out, flushed red with distress.

In a daze, Eadric waved him off. "It wasn't your fault. I should have paid more attention."

Harry crouched down beside Eadric, eyes filled with concern. "Are you all right?"

The captain jostled himself out of his stupor and rose to his feet, ignoring protests from both Luna and Asterin. Quinlan held his breath as Eadric regarded Harry for a long moment, fists bunched.

Silence fell.

Finally, Eadric said, "You saved my life."

Harry shifted, staring at the roof tiles. "It was nothing, really—"

"I must confess that I never trusted you," the captain went on. "But you easily could have let me fall, and no one would have blamed you. Instead, you saved me, even when you didn't have to." He bowed deeply. "Thank you, Harry."

Harry kept his gaze averted. "I'm sorry," he muttered.

Eadric frowned. "What on earth for?"

"That you feel you can't trust me."

The captain held out his hand. "*Felt*," he admitted grudgingly.

Harry's lips twitched upward. He accepted Eadric's hand and the two shook firmly.

"I hate to interrupt," Rose said, "but the carriage is due to arrive in a few minutes. And the sooner we get back on the ground, the better. We've caused enough commotion already. Hopefully no one saw that, as heroic as it was."

Harry nodded. "Let's go."

Orion looked at Harry with a strange gleam in his eyes. "I could kiss you right now, you know that?"

Harry's eyebrows shot up to his hairline, ears flaming scarlet. "Seriously? I—I mean, if you really want to—"

Rose smacked herself in the forehead. "Immortals. Can't you people take a hint about when *not* to flirt?" Without another word, she stalked off toward the fire escape on the side of the hotel, shaking her head, and descended.

Everyone except Quinlan stared after her in stunned silence.

He sighed. "Sorry about that. She's been like that since Kane."

"Kane …" Luna trailed off. "He's the one that got Rose expelled, right? From the Academia Principalis?"

Quinlan's brow furrowed in surprise. "How did you know that?" Kane was a very sensitive subject that only came up when he made the mistake of even mentioning the name. He couldn't imagine Rose talking about him.

Luna glanced at Eadric. "She didn't tell us his name specifically, but she told us that she helped a classmate on his final examination. Twice. You could see it in her eyes that she loved him." His face must have shown his disbelief, because Luna held her hands up defensively. "I know it sounds sappy, but it's true."

A long moment passed. At last, he admitted, "I think she still loves him, after all this time. I don't know why she hasn't done anything about it, though."

"Kane must have known that Rose would be expelled for helping him," Luna reasoned. "He knew that they would be separated. And instead of trying to pass on his own merit, he put himself before *them*, not once, but twice. If that didn't prove to her how little he valued their relationship, I don't know what would."

Quinlan blinked at her, suddenly ashamed that her conclusion had never so much as occurred to him, even after all this time.

"All of us have someone we're ready to sacrifice anything for," Luna went on. "Someone we're willing to protect, no matter the cost. And most of the time, others don't realize the lengths we're willing to go. Sometimes, we don't even realize it ourselves, until the moment it matters most." Eadric wrapped an arm around her waist, smiling at her.

But Luna wasn't looking at the captain.

Instead, her eyes flicked to Quinlan's. "Don't we?" she asked.

Quinlan stared at her, into the eyes that were so very much her mother's, and yet entirely her own. Understanding sparked in his chest. "Yes," he answered softly, turning from her to look at Asterin. "I suppose we do."

CHAPTER FORTY-ONE

The tightness in her throat had long eased by the time Rose scaled down the building and strolled toward the door marked Deliveries. She found Laurel sitting on a barrel, swinging her legs and whistling a sea shanty. The package with the dress—and shoes, she would later discover—rested in the Elite's lap. Rose had hardly accepted the package by the time the Elite was flitting around the corner and out of sight with nothing more than a quick wink.

With the package in her arms, Rose slipped into the private toilets by the lobby. Once changed, she loitered by the sinks for a few minutes until she heard Quinlan's knock and emerged. Her three escorts surrounded her protectively—Harry and Luna had concealed themselves elsewhere, and Eadric was long gone.

As one, the rest of them made their way to the reception.

The concierge immediately fixed her attention on them, peering over a delicate pair of half-moon spectacles. "Good evening. How may I help you?"

"Her Royal Majesty of Eradore has a carriage scheduled for six o'clock," Quinlan replied gruffly.

The concierge bowed respectfully to Rose. "Certainly. It is our great honor to receive your presence, Your Royal Majesty. Your carriage is already waiting outside, though of course you may leave at your leisure.

Should Your Majesty desire anything else from us at all, please do not hesitate to ask."

There were a lot of things she desired, like a steaming hot bath, but they were running short on time. So instead, Rose thanked the woman and nodded to Quinlan.

Asterin and Orion flanked her sides as Quinlan led the way out of the hotel and to the waiting carriage. Rose couldn't help but ogle at it, the exterior dusted in swirls of silver and green for the House of the Serpent and bedecked with a league's worth of silk ribbons and fresh flowers. And that wasn't even mentioning the six handsome white stallions drawing the carriage, or the coachman and two footmen.

"Isn't this a little excessive?" Rose said as Asterin helped her up into the carriage.

Orion winked. "It *is* your first public appearance. Might as well enjoy it."

Once they were all seated among the plump velvet cushions, a whip cracked and the carriage lurched forward. Hopefully, Luna and Harry had safely hidden themselves in the carriage's luggage compartment when the footmen hadn't been looking. If all went to plan, the two would sneak out of the compartment just before they reached the Wall, where the guards would perform inspection.

The rattling of the wheels reverberated in Rose's bones as they swung onto the west road which divided the trade and entertainment districts, the more upscale shops and boutiques of Axaris lining one side and the Pavilion hugging the other. Three theaters, an opera house, and an enormous concert hall made up Axaris's most popular destination for the arts. The music of street performers drifted into the carriage, and Rose gave into the temptation to draw back the lacy curtains and peek out of the window, catching a glimpse of masked actors in the middle of a sword fight on a makeshift outdoor stage. She felt eyes on the carriage and reluctantly drew the curtains closed. While it certainly wasn't the only vehicle on the road, none could have outdone *six* horses, Immortals help her.

Dinner at the ball was to be served at seven thirty. At eight, Harry and Luna would meet with Garringsford. At eight thirty, after collecting Grey from Alicia's uncle, Eadric would thunder back to the palace. The moment he arrived at the base of the mountain, he would send the signal—a blast of lightning powerful enough to light the ballroom white.

And then the show would begin.

Quinlan's knee bounced to some beat in his head, his eyes closed and head resting on the back of his seat. Orion sat next to him, nibbling at his lower lip and drumming his fingers against the carriage door in time with Quinlan's knee. Beside Rose, Asterin brooded in gray-clouded silence.

Rose's stomach twisted as the carriage eased to a halt. She tugged the corner of the curtain to find the mountain looming high up before them. The guards had heaved open the iron gates at its base to admit the near-constant stream of guests. Here, the guards would check the guest list and detain anyone that appeared suspicious.

A familiar brown-haired guard appeared at the carriage window, saluting. *Carlsby*, Rose realized, the handsome sentry Orion had favored at the beginning of their journey. She glanced at Orion to gauge his reaction, but the disguised Guardian now only spared him a genuinely uninterested glance.

"Queen Orozalia Saville of Eradore," Quinlan said to Carlsby.

Carlsby bowed and smiled brightly before directing their carriage into the right of two lanes. The left lane teemed with carriages crawling up the mountain at a snail's pace, presumably for lesser nobility and other guests. Rose's carriage passed all of them.

The power of the wards swept over Rose in a sudden rush of head-spinning vertigo. They must have been reinforced recently—with good reason, of course. Luckily for them, the wards allowed illusionary magic. According to Asterin, too many royals had too many wrinkles to conceal for it to be banned.

Engrossed in her worrying for Luna and Harry, Rose didn't even realize they had reached the Wall until the carriage came to a halt. Her pulse quickened as the luggage compartment hissed open. One guard checked the carriage's underbelly. The compartment slammed shut a moment later, and to Rose's relief, another guard waved them onward, past an extravagant display of potted red hydrangeas and Axarian poppies arranged in the outline of the Axarian crest.

It wasn't long before the door on Rose's side opened to reveal a crisply dressed butler with a curling, snow-white mustache. A ruby brooch of a wolf head sparkled on his tuxedo lapel, the only splash of color amidst his otherwise pristine ensemble.

"Welcome to Axaris, Your Royal Majesty of Eradore," he said with a deep bow. He extended an arm to her. "May I?"

"Thank you." She took it daintily and he helped her down, her entourage piling out after her. The butler released her, one white-gloved hand clasped behind his back, and then gestured for her to continue up the steps.

"Come, guards," Rose commanded. Quinlan immediately went to her elbow, escorting her past the row of soldiers lining the stairs while Asterin and Orion followed quickly behind.

Rose could hardly believe her eyes as they ascended the steps. The entrance hall was nearly unrecognizable beneath the hundreds of blooming garlands and wreaths and bouquets, perfuming the air with an artful combination of sweet fragrances. Luminous glass orbs filled with purple and fiery orange-red blossoms for which Rose had no name hung from the ceiling like a celestial galaxy, illuminated by the golden flames of a thousand candles.

Guests clustered in the hall, milling about and enjoying glasses of champagne while eyeing the newcomers. Every pair of eyes locked on her, glowing predatorily in the candlelight.

With every word you speak, every step you take, every person you smile at, remember that you will one day be Queen of Eradore, her mother's voice echoed in her mind.

And now she was. She had to act experienced, even though it was her first time attending an event outside of her kingdom without her mother by her side. Gaucherie and lack of social grace were out of the question. Mistakes would be blown to excessive proportions, and she'd learned the hard way that gossip spread like wildfire among royals. But if she played her cards just right …

Rose hid a wicked smile.

She was going to manipulate the ever-loving hell out of these people.

Rose led her entourage through another corridor, following the flowers and the sound of laughter and music. Asterin and Orion flanked her while Quinlan brought up the rear, guarding her from all sides but the front. Eventually, the corridor opened into a massive chamber with a domed glass ceiling.

Four guards saluted them as they approached the large double doors that led to the ballroom, two of them friendly faces—Hayley and Jack, looking splendid in their full dress uniforms.

Jack's eyes widened ever so slightly, a dumbfounded smile inching onto his face. "Good evening."

"May I take your cloak?" Hayley asked, feigning ignorance.

Rose nodded and Asterin and Orion stepped forward to lift her cloak off her shoulders. Carefully, she watched for some sort of reaction, but neither Jack nor Hayley paid the slightest attention to the princess or her Guardian.

"Have a wonderful time," Jack wished Rose with a conspiratorial wink, and the grand doors swung open.

Feeling more than a little bit wobbly in her heels, Rose glided through. She held back a gasp of delight as they emerged onto a balcony of gilded ivory overlooking the ballroom with a staircase leading down to the main floor. Below, the hall brimmed with guests, awash with color and light. More candles hung just beneath the high ceiling, bathing everything in a soft golden glow. From a raised stage on their left drifted the sounds of a cheerful waltz, flitting between bursts of laughter and unintelligible babble like a flock of twittering birds. Jewels and gems glinted from all directions, worn on bodies or stitched onto dresses of every color imaginable, and dancers twirled around the room like flower petals carried by a wayward wind.

Straight ahead, at the opposite end of the ballroom, Queen Priscilla held court atop a makeshift dais. Asterin stiffened but showed not the slightest emotion otherwise.

The herald took one look at Rose and blew loudly into his horn. "Her Royal Majesty, Queen Orozalia Saville of Eradore and the House of the Serpent!" he declared.

Conversation ceased. If Rose hadn't been struggling to ignore the anxiety bearing upon her, she might have snickered at the simultaneous swivel of every head in the room.

There was an awkward cough from the orchestra's conductor. Music sheets shuffled, and then, with a wave of his baton, the orchestra launched into the Eradorian anthem.

Court lessons swirled in Rose's head as she took her first step down the stairs, chin raised. The entire room drew in a collective breath.

Kick, step. Kick, step.

Lady Anthea's etiquette lectures rang in her ears. Lady Anthea, with her perfect lipstick and perfect posture and perfect manners. *Never lift your skirts above the ankles. Look directly ahead. Shoulders back, chest raised—not* that *raised, you fool.*

Immortals, how she had despised Lady Anthea. Actually, she still did.

Her gown trailed down the stairs like a waterfall of diamonds as she continued her descent to the melody of a single trumpet, and she wondered how people would react if she tripped. She thanked the Immortals when she made it to the main floor without mishap. Her eyes flicked to the Queen of Axaria, who watched her approach with avid interest in those teal eyes.

What sort of dark sorcery had Garringsford cast upon her?

Kick, step. Kick, step.

The words became her mantra while Rose promenaded down the seemingly mile-long hall as if she had all the time in the world. Violins swelled over a tide of cellos. The crowd backed away at her approach, clearing a path to the dais. It was tradition for royalty to personally greet their host, so Rose made Priscilla her destination. *Kick, step.*

Hundreds of stares bore down upon her, setting her skin afire, sizing her up—many undoubtedly debating whether it would be worthwhile to take the pains of cultivating an alliance with her, the very new and very young queen of what was nonetheless a very powerful kingdom.

Frankly put, Rose was terrified. Her stomach lurched with every movement and her heart raced, thumping in her throat. She prayed it wasn't audible, because *she* could certainly hear it.

She forced a slow breath into her lungs, skin still tingling. *Come on, Rose.*

As the orchestra crescendoed, she found the pulse of the music, each leisurely step filled with purpose and falling in rhythmic harmony with her country's anthem. The skirts of her dress swayed to the soaring melody, each bead catching the light and reflecting it around the ballroom like a twilight sky brimming with stars and suns and fire.

The Queen of Axaria smiled indulgently, rising from her throne as Rose counted down the number of strides it would take to reach her. She tried not to shrink beneath the woman's scrutiny, her customary hood no longer hiding who she truly was.

The serpent and the peacock—two queens of two very different kingdoms.

Rose met Priscilla's gaze head on.

CHAPTER FORTY-TWO

Harry looked like a piece of grass.

Or, rather, Luna had *made* him look like a piece of grass. Or just grass in general, since when he stared down at himself that was all he saw. He couldn't see any part of his body, not even when he waved his hand directly in front of his face—or, at least, what he *assumed* was his hand. And, of course, that would only be the case if what he *hoped* was his face was actually his face, and if that were so, then—

"Stop thinking about it, Harry," Luna mumbled.

"I wasn't," said Harry, glancing up at the Wall rising ahead. Rose's carriage had passed beneath a few minutes earlier.

"Fine. But in case you *were*," said Luna, "I just wanted to let you know that I can't see you. At all."

Harry was used to blending into the shadows—literally—so it wasn't *that* weird. But this was different. This was grass, apparently.

"Are your knees okay?" he asked. When they had broken out of Rose's luggage compartment, while Harry landed like a cat, Luna had scraped her knees against the road. Luckily, no carriages followed Rose's in the right lane, and no one in the left lane seemed to have noticed the trunk open for two people to tumble out.

"I'll survive."

"Sorry," said Harry. Unlike mortal magic wielders, he didn't have the capability to heal anyone other than himself.

"Stop apologizing. Just remember not to move too abruptly," Luna reminded him. Sudden movements would only make it that much harder for her to maintain their guises.

"You can get us past the Wall, right?" They had a little more than a quarter of the way to go up the mountain before they reached the Wall.

"Yes." A nervous pause. "Probably. All right, slowly now."

Together, they crept along the side of the road, crawling on all fours through the grass. Harry watched the carriages in the left lane, as sluggish as they were, pass one by one.

"We need to move faster," he said.

"Okay," Luna whispered. "Stand up. One step at a time now."

Harry couldn't see the girl, but he could taste her fear as they prowled closer to the Wall—the salty tang of the sweat trickling down her neck. He could hear her heartbeat quickening tenfold, each inhale more raspy than the last. But still—still, Luna persisted.

Finally they made it to the crest of the mountain, the gated entrance to the Wall just fifty paces away. Beyond lay what must have been the palace gardens. Harry narrowed his eyes at the soldiers patrolling the ramparts above, and the dozen soldiers standing guard at the gate itself. Six guards checked the luggage trunks of three carriages at a time, two per carriage.

"We have to get past all those guards first," Harry whispered as the carriages passed inspection and moved onward.

Something brushed his arm. He looked down, but of course, there was nothing. Then a hand latched around his wrist, tugging him behind the third carriage in the line, its wood-paneled exterior painted in rich strokes of fuchsia. With awkward coordination and a lot of elbow bumping, Luna camouflaged them into the background and led Harry around the two inspecting guards as silently as she could. The next carriage alternated navy and gold, which Luna also managed to copy. They had almost reached the final carriage when Harry made a mistake. His shoulder brushed against the hindquarter of the bay stallion harnessed to the carriage. The horse reared, spooked, and Harry, distracted by the hoof swinging at his head, didn't notice the soldier running to calm the animal. The soldier rammed right into Harry's back. The impact didn't harm either of them, but the soldier's reaction to crashing into an invisible person, on the other hand—

"Halt!" the soldier shouted, startling the other guards. He drew his sword, eyes darting to and fro. "Show yourself!"

"Close the gate!" another guard yelled.

Harry cursed under his breath. He grabbed what he prayed was Luna's hand and yanked her forward, nearly tripping over a potted hydrangea. "Hurry!"

"This is *so* not according to plan—"

The soldier closest to them pulled out his affinity stone. "*Astyndos*!"

They ducked beneath his outstretched arm. The hydrangea pot exploded, terracotta fragments shattering against the side of the third carriage in a shower of petals.

"*Ovdekken*!" another guard yelled.

Luna let out a near-silent gasp. Harry's eyes widened as the edges of their shadows began to appear, nothing more than a watery gray outline—but there, nonetheless. He immediately banished them away, but the damage was done.

"I saw something!" the hydrangea-killing guard shouted. "Close it! Close the gate!"

"Ah, to hell," Harry muttered, grasping Luna's hand. "Run!"

Luna didn't argue.

They made a break for it, sprinting as fast as they could through the growing throng of soldiers. They managed to evade the rest of the spells, but if they couldn't make it past the Wall and the wards—

The gate lowered, faster than they could run.

"Come on, Luna!"

Ten strides.

Harry squeezed her hand. "Luna, hold your breath when I say."

Five strides.

"Hold my breath?" Luna squawked. "What in the world for?"

One more stride—

They dropped to the ground and slid beneath the gate just before the bars settled into the ground with a hollow *clank*, sealing them off from the soldiers on the other side of the gate, though more were currently running in their direction from posts on the Wall's interior.

"Now!"

Harry sucked them into oblivion.

The shadow dimension had no air. Sometimes, it felt as though walls enclosed him on all sides, pressing closer and closer until he was certain his body would burst. And other times, it was as easy as slipping into a lukewarm tub of water. Shadow travel was strange that way.

Luckily for Luna, on this occasion, it was the latter. He couldn't see her, and he didn't bother trying. His only anchor to her was the solid grip of her hand in his. Shadow travel reshaped one's physical form into whatever it pleased. Furniture and people whizzed by. As if in a gaseous state, he—and whomever he traveled with—simply passed through.

Harry didn't know anything about the interior of the Axarian palace, so he simply thought *closet* in his mind. When the shadow dimension spat them out, Luna crashed on top of him in what indeed seemed to be a closet, towels and bath soaps raining down upon both of them. In her struggle to stand, she kicked him in the face. Eventually, she managed to squirm into the small gap between Harry and some wooden crates.

"Sorry," she said, both of them visible once more, while Harry rubbed his cheek. "Are you okay?"

His ragged panting filled the silence. "Just give me a minute." The intense scent of lavender hung heavy in the air. He sneezed a few times and cursed quietly, waiting for his breaths to even out. "I wish I was better at shadow jumping," he confessed. "If I was, I could have saved us a lot of time going from the forest to the palace. But I only use it as a last resort, when it could mean the difference between life and death."

"It wasn't your responsibility to get us here, Harry," said Luna. "We're thankful enough that you even came along. And I …" She trailed off and raised her hand, a blue ribbon weaving into existence in her open palm. "I wouldn't have discovered *this* if it hadn't been for you."

He ducked his head, still impressed by her newfound abilities. "And yet … especially after all the trouble I caused, I can't help but feel selfish."

Luna spread her fingers through the air, the ribbon looping and spiraling in an intricate dance. She observed her own hand as if it belonged to someone else. "I've had the experience of living both with power and without," she said. "I don't know my limits yet. Once I do, I *will* push past them—on no one's terms but my own. That's not selfishness. It's survival."

A hero protects the good people, but a hunter does anything he can to survive.

In the end, Harry couldn't figure out a response, so he fiddled with the closet handle instead. "Come on, let's get out of here." He cringed as the door creaked in protest, and then he forced it open a little further to peek out into the hallway. Unable to distinguish anything through the oily murk, he semi-shifted. Though still in his human form, his every sense intensified. He couldn't keep it up for long—a few more minutes, at most, already feeling as though he stood with one foot in a pool of churning water and the other upon shaking ground. He inhaled, the musty air filling his nostrils. From afar came a peculiar trickling sound, perhaps from a spring or fountain deep below them.

"We're in a servants' passage," Luna said as they emerged from the closet. "Hallways and tunnels like this run all throughout the palace. Actually …" She slipped back into the closet, where Harry could hear her digging around. When she reappeared, she waved a little paper package with a flaky golden label at him. "Lavender bath soap. I know for a fact that Queen Priscilla is the only one in the palace that uses it. We must be below her quarters."

Harry sniffed. "Hold on. What's that smell? Not the lavender." Something else, a very particular scent, inexplicably dark. "There's something wrong," he whispered, blood thrumming. "I think—I could be mistaken, but … we have to go and investigate."

Luna stared at him in disbelief. "But what about Garringsford?"

"It'll be quick," Harry promised. "Just follow me and stay close."

"What's wrong?" she demanded. "Are we in danger?"

"It's nothing like that. We'll be fine. I … I just need to make sure of it myself." Harry started forward, only to be jerked back by the wrist. He looked over his shoulder in surprise.

"No," said Luna. She had her feet planted steadfast into the ground, looking for all the world like she might tackle him at any moment.

"No?" Harry echoed.

"We have a task, Harry. A crucial task that we must complete. Eadric's success depends on ours. I won't allow us to be the ones that fail." Luna tightened her iron grip on him. "Asterin comes first."

"But—"

"If we have time afterward, I promise that we can come back."

She's right, he thought. Everyone was depending on them. They needed to meet General Garringsford alone, before Eadric arrived, or all their careful planning, everything that they had worked for, would be worthless. "Okay," he agreed.

"Pardon?" Luna stammered, her stance faltering.

"I said, okay. You're right."

A small huff of wonder escaped her. "You … you're actually listening to me?"

He tilted his head in confusion. "Yes?"

"Oh. Right." Luna smiled. "It's just that no one usually listens to me," she said, staring at the ground, her fingers knotting together. "Ever."

Harry regarded her in astonishment. To think that no one—not even Asterin—took Luna seriously … He imagined what it must have been like for Luna, suffering in the silence of her own mind, destined to be surrounded by some of the most powerful individuals in the world while she could barely summon anything more than a spark of magic.

He tipped his head toward the hallway. "Well, I'm listening now. So lead the way."

CHAPTER FORTY-THREE

Rose curtsied to Queen Priscilla, barely smothering her envy for the other woman's unreal elegance and grace when she returned the gesture.

The queen smiled warmly. "It is my greatest honor to welcome you to my kingdom, Queen Orozalia," she said as the orchestra transitioned from the Eradorian anthem to a lively jig. Most of the guests chattered among themselves, but Rose knew some still eavesdropped on their conversation. Her escorts hung back, quickly lost in the ever-rippling crowd—making her appear all the more independent, though she couldn't help but feel their absence.

Rose dipped her head. "The honor is all mine, Queen Priscilla. Axaris is a magnificent city, and I already look forward to any future visits."

"Axaria will accept you with open arms," Priscilla said. A pause, accompanied by a puzzled frown. "Do excuse me, Your Majesty, but I must say that you look … awfully familiar."

Rose's gut clenched as she thought of Luna's illusion work. She let her lips tilt up, playing it off. "People often jest that I am my mother's duplicate, though I always found her nose to be a little taller than mine."

Priscilla hummed. "I confess that it has been many years since I last saw the late Queen Lillian. She never seemed to be able to attend the

Fairfest Ball, but all the more honor to have you with us. And my sincere condolences for your loss."

"Your Majesty is most kind."

"Well, then," Priscilla said with another curtsy. "Do enjoy the festivities."

Rose mirrored her. "A million thanks."

Before the relief at getting away with Luna's disguise could set in, Rose was immediately swept off the dais by a group of chattering ladies curtsying atop one another and cooing excessively over her dress, their own corsets drawn so tight that Rose wondered how they managed to breathe. Several guests made requests to dance with her later on, all of which she graciously accepted.

For an hour, she played her part as the Queen of Eradore, charming and flirting her way into the good books of every single damned noble and royal present. After all, she had alliances to secure for her country, business partnerships to establish, and most of all … she needed to show that she wouldn't let anyone take advantage of her inexperience in the slightest.

Rose set an empty glass of champagne on a passing tray, keeping an eye out for Garringsford. Asterin leaned against the far wall, Orion kept watch by the balcony, and—

"Rose," a familiar voice breathed behind her.

Her heart leapt into her throat.

Kane.

How in the all-loving name of the Immortals had he managed to sneak in? There was no chance he could have gotten his hands on an invitation, and slinking past all the guards … if only he had put those wily wits to better use at the Academia. She couldn't decide whether to be furious or impressed.

"What are you doing here?" Rose hissed, without turning around.

"I happened to be in the next kingdom over, and I heard you would be coming to Axaris for the ball. I had to see you, of course." The lingering hand brushed against her hip, but the prickle up her spine that followed wasn't from his touch. A slip of paper had found its way into the cup of her palm. She curled her fingers around it. It was still warm. "Just a little thank you. For … everything. From before." She could feel his eyes roving up her body, burning hot, but she refused to spare him even a glance. "Rose, I want to fix things between us—"

Her jaw clenched. *Three times is far too many to fall for this act again.* "Don't." She exhaled through her nose, flashing a coy smile at a random passing lord. She closed her eyes briefly and then snapped them open when she heard a growl.

Quinlan stood before her, glaring over her shoulder at Kane with his teeth bared. "You."

A choked cough from Kane. "Qu-Quinlan?"

Quinlan was unrecognizable beneath Luna's illusion—nevertheless, anyone who knew him as well as Kane once had would recognize that wrath in his voice.

"Yeah. Remember me?" said Quinlan, tone dripping with sarcasm. "Next time I see you talking to my cousin, you eat fire. Now beat it."

Rose opened her mouth, then closed it. Before, she might have said something in Kane's defense … but no, it didn't matter now. He had hurt her in more ways than she cared to admit.

"Rose, wait …"

She shook her head. "Just go, Kane."

A bell rang, not a moment too soon, and the guests cleared out of the way as guards filed into the ballroom, levitating heavy oak tables between them upon currents of air. They arranged them in impeccable lines down the length of the hall. The guests burst into lengthy applause as silverware and decorations even more lavish than those already present materialized from thin air, hidden behind layers of illusion.

By the time the applause had died, Kane was gone.

Quinlan reached for Rose's hand and gave it a squeeze. "We need to talk about that sometime. I … I have apologies to make."

"Okay," Rose whispered. When she was certain he had turned away, she allowed herself a little smile.

Later, after they had been seated as per ornate cursive notecards and Queen Priscilla had made her first grand speech of the night on Axaria's behalf, the servants paraded from the kitchens bearing steaming platters that caused half the hall to drool over their lotus-folded napkins.

Rose picked up her spoon. Quinlan, at her side, had already finished half of his soup. She spared a glance at her other two disguised escorts. Only one personal guard was permitted per guest for dinner, and only for the royals seated at the head table. The others stood vigilant along the walls, eyes sweeping the room. Asterin and Orion blended in perfectly, garnering no more attention than the occasional once-over. After mentally marking their location, Rose took a moment to observe her dinner companions for the night.

King Jakob Evovich of Ibreseos sat stewing silently at Priscilla's right. He'd only spoken with Rose long enough to exchange a cool greeting. On his left was the willowy Queen Belinda of Oprehvar—Priscilla's second cousin—and her towering husband, King Marcus, so gigantic that he was seated in a custom-made chair, low enough so that his knees wouldn't bang against the table every time he moved. King Nori and Queen Kinsa of Cyeji were notably absent.

Across from Rose was a familiar face—Prince Sol of Morova, with his olive skin and pretty gray eyes, chin tipped regally toward his soup. His mother, Queen Calla, was deep in an animated discussion with King Marcus. Prince Sol had often accompanied his father, King Bas, on visits to the Eradorian palace, and the prince had even studied briefly at the Academia Principalis to learn how to control his untamed light affinity. Even before King Bas had disappeared at sea on a voyage to Artica, Sol had taken it upon himself to guide Morova and contribute to its global status. He had negotiated with world leaders to create several new overseas trade routes in order to expand Morova's import-export activities, and under his command, the institutions in Morovis had begun amassing books and papers from all over the kingdom for deeper analysis and to help the kingdom establish a stronger foothold in the advancement of magic.

Next to the prince and his guards were two other frequent visitors to Eradoris—albeit only recently. All night, King Allard of Galanz and his daughter, the scholarly Princess Rowena, had kept to themselves. Rowena's mother, Queen Madeleine, was quite ill, and it evidently weighed upon the pair. Rose herself had arranged the care of the highly esteemed Doctor Ilroy from Ermir, the second largest city in Eradore.

Glancing up, she caught the brazen amber stare of Prince Viyo, the Volterro royal that she had only heard about in passing. He adjusted his bright yellow finery, vivid against his dark umber skin, and raised an eyebrow at her. Beside him sat his older sister, Queen Valeria, in shimmering gold, a thick torque choker of yellow diamonds encircling her slender neck.

Rose stared right back at Viyo until he began fidgeting. He finally turned away, directing his stare instead at the occupants of the next table over, where the Duchess of Ignatia, one of Quinlan's distant cousins, chattered away to Lord Tylas of Ermir. And beside her sat the Duke of Orielle with his bristly mustache, engrossed in a heated debate with the Countess of Ichaqar.

Deciding that she had enough privacy—or as much privacy as one could have in a room full of hawk-eyed snoops with no qualms when it came to juicy gossip—Rose unfurled Kane's message underneath the edge of the table, hidden in the shadows of the satin lilac tablecloth. Quinlan's gaze was seemingly elsewhere, but she knew better.

Rose,

Watch out for the peacock's fangs.

K

Rose frowned. She looked up at King Jakob and Queen Priscilla, but gleaned nothing from either their muted conversation or their body language. Peacocks didn't have fangs—but vipers certainly did. While lifting a spoonful of soup to her lips, she passed the note to Quinlan. There was a quiet hiss as he burnt it to cinders. She waved a hand beneath the table to disperse the thin curl of smoke drifting upward.

With her mind on other things, dinner passed in a blur. Garringsford had yet to make an appearance. Soon after dessert was cleared and the tables spelled away, a chime silenced the room. The guests turned their attention to the throne, where Priscilla stood, glass raised.

"Tonight," the queen began, her voice melodious, "we celebrate the eve of Fairfest." A light smattering of applause. "We have already feasted, and soon we will rejoice at the arrival of summer with a night of dancing and music." More applause. "However, some of you may have puzzled over the absence of a person of great importance to our kingdom." A few nods of agreement. "At this very moment, my beloved daughter, Princess Asterin, courageously defends Axaria. Some of you have perhaps heard of a demon terrorizing our people. This is true—and the princess has taken it upon herself to eradicate this monster in a valiant act of fearlessness." Priscilla's eyes glittered turquoise in the light of the chandeliers. "And so, I should like to propose a toast in her name. To the heroic bravery and successful return of the princess!"

"To Princess Asterin!" the ballroom chorused, glasses raised in salute. Asterin drank alongside everyone else, as if for reassurance.

"And now," Priscilla announced, "let us honor Fairfest!"

CHAPTER FORTY-FOUR

Luna knew the Immortals were on their side when she and Harry made it all the way from the passageway to Throne Hall undetected. The celebrations had worked in their favor—most of the guards were posted by the ballroom, but they found two disgruntled soldiers stationed at the entranceway to Throne Hall. Judging by the guards' menacing glowers, they were not pleased with their exclusion from the festivities.

Luna skirted back around the corner to where Harry crouched behind a pillar. "We need to get through those doors without the guards noticing," she whispered. Shadow jumping wasn't an option—Harry had already done it twice today, and Luna could see it taking its toll on him. She didn't have a watch, but it couldn't be much longer before Garringsford arrived.

Harry stood. "On it."

And then he walked back down the corridor behind her in the opposite direction from the guards.

"Harry," Luna hissed. "Where are you going?"

He only lifted a finger, signaling her to wait as he retreated further and slipped into a door that led into servants' passageway.

Luna fidgeted, toe tapping as she craned her neck to glance back down the hallway at the guards, praying that Harry hadn't decided to just ditch her.

Then, from afar, came a slurred, "Hey, Yagnov."

Luna's eyes narrowed at the pair of guards, but neither were the source of the voice.

The voice went on. "Do you think anyone will take this bottle of wine if I leave it here?"

The two guards perked up, straining to listen, obviously interested in hearing more about the wine.

"I doubt it," came the loud response, a new voice, echoing through the deserted halls. "Besides, there's more than enough to go around."

Luna stifled a giggle. The second voice belonged unmistakably to Harry, and she realized that the first sounded like an impersonation of Quinlan—that is, if he were extremely drunk. The hunter must have used the servants' passageway to pass right beneath the guards' feet.

"Did you hear that?" whispered the first guard.

From afar, Harry let out a lusty sigh. "I guess I'll just leave this here, then. I can hardly carry these two bottles as it is."

"Should we take it?" the second guard asked his companion, and then muttered, "S'not like anyone's around here, anyway. Besides, you heard him. There's enough to go around."

"I'll get it," the first volunteered, licking his lips. He had already disappeared around the corner when the second guard shot up in realization.

"Oi, you bastard, you're just going to keep it all to yourself, aren't you?" he cried, rushing after his fellow soldier.

Luna took that as her cue. Just as she grabbed the door handle, Harry melted from the shadows around the corner the guards had just rounded. She bit down hard on a grin, holding the door open as he swaggered in, hands in his pockets.

"That was amazing!" she exclaimed once the doors had closed.

"Thanks," Harry said, bravado vanishing as they stepped onto the long carpet leading to the throne. They reached the dais and he slumped upon it with an exhausted sigh, eyes drifting shut.

While Harry napped, Luna prepared herself. She shook the tension from her shoulders and took a deep breath. Then, gripping her illusion-stone, she conjured an image of a lidded wooden chest. Imagining it as a slab of clay, she began to sculpt, fashioning elegant ridges and intricate embellishments. Inside the chest, she added a bed of rich green velvet, and then on top of that … based off the anatomical diagrams Rose had sketched for her, she wove what hopefully looked like a human heart.

"Gross," Luna whispered to herself, astonished by her own ability. But now came the difficult part—pushing past the visual limits of the illusion and adding texture, weight, physicality. She mangled the glistening organ with claw marks and scratches, and added the overpowering reek of fermentation.

"Luna." Harry's eyes had snapped open, his pupils dilated. "The Woman. She's coming."

Luna swallowed her anxiety and inspected the chest a final time. Then she passed it to Harry and skittered up the steps to the throne, concealing herself with a layer of illusion as she huddled down behind it.

Outside, the sharp, even *click-click* of heels along the corridor. *Heels?* Luna wondered, her entire body buzzing with adrenaline. Garringsford only ever wore boots, though perhaps for the ball …?

Before Luna could ponder it further, the doors swung open.

"Demon."

Luna's breath stuttered. She knew that voice, and it certainly didn't belong to General Garringsford. No, but it wasn't possible …

She could see Harry, but not the other speaker. His head bowed in submission, the obedient servant. "Milady."

A figure sauntered past Harry, toward the dais. Heart pounding, Luna peeked around the back of the throne to find herself staring straight at Queen Priscilla.

Immortals help me, Luna thought, both hands pressed to her mouth to stifle the sound of her breathing. *All this time …* Priscilla was "the Woman" Harry spoke of.

It had been the queen trying to kill them, all along.

Priscilla turned her back on the throne, her gown swishing like a phantom whisper. "Is it done?"

When Harry looked up, his eyes glittered with a cold, black malice that sent a shudder down Luna's spine. This was not the Harry she had come to know. This was a heartless killer, a warrior without mercy, and she thanked the Immortals that the anygné was on their side.

Instead of answering, he dropped down onto one knee and proffered her the chest. His eyes lingered on Priscilla's crown, and it was obvious he could tell that this wasn't Garringsford.

Priscilla raised a perfectly arched eyebrow. "What is this?"

Harry didn't falter. "Her heart in a velvet case."

Priscilla's mouth dropped open.

And then she began to laugh.

Peals of laughter shook her entire body, tears running down her cheeks. She doubled over, arms clutching her waist. "Oh, you darling," she cried. She took the chest with one hand, so absorbed in her amusement that Luna's illusion passed beneath her notice without a hitch. Priscilla lifted the lid and then recoiled, nose wrinkling. "Immortals. How utterly vile." She shut the box with a snap and thrust it back into Harry's hands. "And what of Luna?"

"I left her alive, as you requested."

Priscilla nodded in satisfaction. "I must return to the ball. People will begin to wonder."

"Milady …"

"What?"

"Are my services still required?"

Priscilla picked an invisible speck of dust from her bodice. "We shall see, demon. Now, get out of my palace." And then she was gone.

After the doors fell shut, Harry turned to Luna. No trace of malice remained in his eyes. "So … that wasn't Garringsford, was it?"

"No," Luna breathed. "It was Queen Priscilla. My … my mother." On one hand, the betrayal had shaken her, but on the other … she wasn't taking it as hard as she might have expected. She relinquished her hold on her recent illusions, allowing both her concealment and the chest in Harry's hands to dissolve. On a whim, she collapsed into the throne, but stood back up a moment later. It was a lot less comfortable than it looked.

"Luna," Harry said softly. "You did well. Really well."

Luna managed a weary smile. "You too. But while I'm sure we'd both like to take a decade-long nap, we have to tell Eadric about Priscilla before it's too late."

As if on cue, a sudden blast of lightning forked outside the tall windows, blazing Throne Hall in white light.

Whatever Harry said next was drowned by an explosion of thunder, but Luna didn't need any further indication. They were out of time.

"Run?" she asked.

And so they ran.

CHAPTER FORTY-FIVE

Asterin tried to calm the bundle of nerves in her stomach, glancing up at the ornate clock hanging above the makeshift dais. It was almost nine. As time dragged on, she grew more and more anxious, waiting for Eadric's arrival and worrying that something had gone wrong.

He'll be fine, she told herself. Garringsford had yet to show up, anyway.

The dancing had begun an hour or so earlier, and Rose hadn't gotten a moment of peace since. Asterin watched from a pillar at the fringes of the main dance floor as the Queen of Eradore whirled from partner to partner with every modulation of key, never faltering, the perfect picture of beauty and majesty.

A handful of other escorts and guards had approached Asterin herself, but her dark scowls had sent all of them running. Her hackles rose as an arm slinked around her waist, her hand seeking the comfort of Amoux's pommel, but then she remembered she had left her sword with Alicia's uncle.

Her glower vanished when she realized that the arm at her waist belonged to Quinlan.

"A dance, my lady?" he asked, bowing and extending a hand.

"I've been rejecting fine young men left and right," she grumbled. "What makes you any different?"

His eyes twinkled at her through his lashes. "I'm the one you've been waiting for."

Asterin allowed herself a small smile. *Perhaps you are*. "Fine," she said. "Just one dance."

She placed her hand in his and let him lead her onto the dance floor into a lilting Galanzy five-step swing. He was a splendid partner, guiding her with smooth, experienced ease and elegance. With her cheeks flushed and aching from the endless ear-to-ear grin she bore, "just one dance" quickly turned into two, and then five. The drumming pitter-patter of the rain only added to the rhythm as they spun and twirled and leapt in unison, and Asterin forgot herself in his arms.

And then came the lightning, so blinding and unexpected that white spots that she mistook for dancers pirouetted across her vision. Cries rang through the ballroom as guests floundered and tripped over one another, releasing their partners and flinging arms over eyes in surprise as another bolt crackled right by the windows. The music stuttered as one of the violinists fumbled his solo.

The thunder that followed shook the very mountain beneath their feet. The quickest of guards with air and wind affinities brandished their stones and whisked up glasses and silverware that toppled to the floor, while others rushed about to restore the objects to their rightful places.

It was their cue. The captain had finally arrived.

Quinlan's hands settled onto Asterin's waist, warm and steady. "You have both of the vials?" he asked. She nodded. "How much longer do we have?"

"A few minutes at most." Nicole and Silas would escort Eadric inside. Sudden fear gripped Asterin. What if their plan didn't work?

Quinlan tightened his hold on her. "Hey. It's going to be okay," he whispered. "We're going to be okay."

She managed another nod, still feeling a little sick. In her peripheral vision, she saw Priscilla—reassuring several guests with witty jokes and sweet laughter, but to Asterin's dismay, General Garringsford was still missing in the sea of faces.

The seconds ticked by. She kept her eyes on the entrance.

Just as Asterin prepared to hunt down Garringsford herself and drag her to the ballroom, the doors opened and the general finally marched in, her expression stormier than the sky outside as she headed straight for Priscilla.

The doors hadn't fully closed when they crashed open again to reveal a disheveled Captain Eadric Covington, drenched from head to toe and panting in the entryway, his uniform covered in mud and rust-colored stains.

Bloodstains.

The room fell deathly silent.

His ragged breaths and the pounding rain were the only sounds as he staggered forward, joined by the rustle of fabric as the crowds hastily backed away, just as they had for Rose—though this time they cleared faster than if he had brought the plague. Behind him were Nicole and Silas, soon joined by Hayley and Jack.

Eadric shoved past Garringsford and onto the steps of the dais, landing in a crumpled heap at Priscilla's feet, brown and crimson-tinged water pooling beneath him.

"Captain," said Queen Priscilla, softer than the caress of a feather, danger edging the inflection of each syllable. No one dared speak, not even Garringsford. "What happened?"

"Your Royal Majesty," he rasped, lifting his face. Tears stained his filthy cheeks. Eadric opened his mouth, only for his voice to crack on an anguished sob, chest rising and falling in rapid heaves. "Th-the … The …"

Priscilla's expression darkened. "What happened?"

"The Princess of Axaria," the captain whispered at last, "is dead."

Miss M first taught him to cry at will, but these came quickly enough.

Eadric bowed his head, shoulders hunched, and whispered, "The Princess of Axaria—" *Pause for climactic tension …* "—is dead."

The ballroom exploded with wails of dismay and exclamations of disbelief. Some people fainted. Eadric couldn't have asked for more—the pandemonium gave him the perfect opportunity to get to his feet. He bumped into a server, who held out a fresh glass of wine to Queen Priscilla. From the corner of his eye, Eadric caught Asterin and Quinlan shouldering closer to the dais.

When the noise reached its climax, the Queen of Axaria gathered herself, face whiter than a corpse. "Silence!" she ordered, the crack of a whip through the din. She reached forward to accept the wine glass from the server, grasping the stem with unsteady fingers. "Silence," the queen repeated even as the commotion ceased, her lips parted and eyes lowering to the ground.

"Not moments ago," Priscilla began, "I anticipated the return of Princess Asterin—the return of … of my daughter." A tremor shook her hand. "And now … I wish to tell you all that Princess Asterin was one of the bravest … and the fiercest of warriors the world has ever seen. As a mother, I begged her not to go. As a future queen, she convinced me to let her leave. She sacrificed herself … she sacrificed everything to defend her kingdom. Her people. And so," Priscilla continued, eyes sparkling with unshed tears, "I ask you all to join me in a toast—not one of sadness or remorse. But of remembrance and joy. Princess Asterin was the light and star of Axaria—"

Eadric saw Asterin valiantly resist an eye roll, but he could tell she was touched by her mother's—or rather, her stepmother's passionate words. So Harry hadn't managed to tell her yet. His heart filled with pity for the princess.

"—and today we have lost her. Today, you have lost one of the most treasured people in all of Axaria. Today, I have lost my daughter. But tomorrow—tomorrow, and every day forth, we shall remember her. On the eve of Fairfest, let us remember Asterin Faelenhart forevermore." Priscilla raised her glass, the tears finally spilling over—crystalline droplets that fell so perfectly from her eyes that they did not even ruin her flawlessly kohl-lined lids and lashes. "To Princess Asterin!"

"To Princess Asterin!" the room bellowed back.

CHAPTER FORTY-SIX

Mere seconds before Eadric had reached the ballroom, Harry had ambushed him and dragged him into the coat room, out of both sight and earshot of the hundreds of royal and noble guests.

"What in hell are you doing?" Eadric hissed. "Garringsford walked into the ballroom. I have to get in there before she tells Queen Priscilla about Asterin and they hold the toast!"

"We were wrong," said Harry. "*Priscilla* is the Woman, not Garringsford."

Eadric could only stare in disbelief. "Have you lost your damn mind?"

"Captain, please. I don't have time to explain, but … please. Just *trust* me."

At that, Eadric almost turned and left, but the earnestness of his tone and the desperate glint in his eyes triggered the memory of the moment the ground had disappeared beneath him, his death looming below. He swallowed and tipped his chin, making his final decision just before bursting into the ballroom.

With Nicole and Silas at his heels and Hayley and Jack falling in behind them, Eadric stumbled up the dais, all too aware of General Garringsford only feet away. He crushed his doubt and fell to his knees before the Queen of Axaria. Tears dripped off his chin—years had passed since

Eadric watched as Garringsford raised her glass to her lips and tipped back its contents. And then his eyes flicked to Priscilla, transfixed on the bob of the pale column of her throat—once, twice.

For a few horrifying seconds, nothing happened.

His heart stammered. Had Harry been wrong?

And then, a screech like a banshee's ripped through the air, broken by the shatter of Priscilla's glass onto the dais.

Asterin rushed forward, eyes wide with shock, but by then Eadric was already running for her, hands locking onto her shoulders and holding her back.

She fought to see Priscilla. "Eadric! What in hell? Let go!"

He shook her, hard. "Asterin, listen to me. Priscilla is not who we thought she was."

The blood drained from her face. "No. *No.* You don't mean—"

His grip on her tightened. "I do."

Asterin's lips moved in silent denial. "But Garringsford's suspicion-dampening spell—"

The realization struck him like a slap in the face. Everything clicked into place. "Asterin, it wasn't Garringsford's spell. It was *Priscilla's.*"

At that moment, Priscilla collapsed to the ground and curled up into a ball, moaning. Guards and guests alike rushed to her aid, but scrambled backward when a black gas began oozing from her contorted body.

The easiest part of Eadric's job had come after his announcement—slipping the cork off the vial filled with contralusio in his pocket. As he had risen from the ground, he bumped into Laurel, who had disguised herself as a server. She now joined the four other Elite Royal Guards forming a protective circle around Asterin. After Eadric stealthily emptied the vial into Priscilla's drink instead of Garringsford's, as they had originally planned, it had simply been a matter of waiting—and praying that he had chosen right in trusting Harry.

A man with sand-gold hair, who Eadric recognized as the King of Ibreseos, strode forward, his expression thunderous as he pushed through the whispering crowd. He made to help a writhing Priscilla when she threw up a hand, halting him in his tracks.

"No, Your Majesty, please," she hissed. "Stay back." She staggered to her feet, covering her face in the crook of her elbow and ducking away from the eyes of hundreds.

And then she bolted from the dais, diving into the crowd and shoving her way past the guests in an effort to flee the ballroom.

"Stop her!" Eadric shouted, lunging after her and leaving Asterin behind.

The Duke of Orielle's eyes bugged out of his head. "How dare you speak of Her Majesty like so!"

Priscilla made it halfway through the dense throng of people when the bare skin on her shoulder blades began to swell. Eadric forgot how to breathe as two spindly protrusions burst forth, tearing through her dress, unfolding into a pair of leathery wings—

Guests screamed, royals and servers alike scrambling away from Priscilla, which only allowed her to flee faster.

"Shadow! She's using shadow magic!" Queen Valeria of Volterra cried out. Gasps of outrage rippled through the hall.

From the entrance to the ballroom, the other five Elites flooded in with Alicia in the lead. Eadric signaled, both to the Elites and the palace guards. "Seize Queen Priscilla!"

Many of the guards froze, conflicted at the order to assail the woman they had sworn to protect. Some shook off their dazes quickly, their deep aversion to dark magic outweighing their qualms.

And some, to Eadric's dismay, turned on their fellow soldiers. Guards in Axarian colors that he didn't recognize, guards General Garringsford had recruited without his approval. *There are so many*, he thought numbly. *I was gone for too long.*

"Witch!" Prince Sol of Morova snarled at Priscilla, palms blazing with white light. His escorts tried to drag him to safety, but he wouldn't budge.

Several guests roared their assent, shaking their fists and adding their own disgusted cries. "Witch!"

"Guards!" Priscilla screamed. She had drawn her affinity stone from her bodice to amplify her voice. "Defend me!" Then she plunged into the churning sea of guests, losing herself in the crowd. Commands drowned in the clamor. No one knew who to trust. The Elites wrestled their way closer to Priscilla, but Garringsford's soldiers—Priscilla's soldiers—met them with swords and spells.

Meanwhile, the guests still present had also joined the melee—royals, nobles, and their escorts alike. As Eadric elbowed his way toward Priscilla, he saw the crackle of energy as his own distant kin—the House of the Falcon—blasted past guards defending the queen. The dancing flames of candles and torches guttered out as the King of Galanz and his daughter, Rowena, as well as other descendants of the House of the Stallion, sent explosive gusts of wind howling through the room, throwing the guards attacking the Elites into the air like rag dolls.

Reinforcements poured through the ballroom entrance. Eadric almost breathed a sigh of relief until he realized that they were reinforcements for *Priscilla.* And they didn't stop coming.

The ground trembled as Queen Valeria, an earth-wielder of the House of the Stag, stepped forward. Cracks splintered down the floor as she stomped, sending a dozen reinforcement soldiers toppling. Young Prince Viyo giggled as he smacked a couple more with a large chunk of floating marble, exclaiming, "Traitor!" every time one went down.

The ballroom plunged into darkness, the light sucked away before folding like paper into flashes of white to reveal Prince Sol of the House of the Lynx, moving as fast as light itself, attacking enemy guards from every direction at once.

Rose herself was a hurricane, stationed in the center of the room. She had shed her beautiful dress to reveal her dark blue combat suit. Half a dozen of Priscilla's guards tried to open a route for Priscilla to escape, but Rose simply raised her arm. Beads of liquid bent and twisted at her will, cramming themselves down the traitors' throats and drowning them right where they stood.

The most powerful individuals on the planet, all packed into a single hall.

And fighting back-to-back with Rose was a single warrior, clad in a hooded gray uniform that gave away no hints of his identity or origin. He used no magic—only his mind-blowing skill with his knives, a dazzling blur of steel and iron, so fast and precise that even Quinlan would have been envious. He and Rose moved around one another in a graceful dance of destruction, as fluid as water itself with the practiced ease Eadric knew could only have come from training together for years on end.

Priscilla staggered forward, thrown off-balance by her *still* growing wings. Eadric had almost caught up to her when he heard the shriek of metal at his left. He drew his own blade just in time to meet the blow, inches from his neck.

General Garringsford quirked a brow at him over their crossed swords. He barely managed to parry her next thrust. "You're out of practice, Captain Covington," the general taunted as he struggled to keep up.

Eadric whirled around to strike. "I've been busy hunting demons." She danced away from his blade. "Why are you doing this, General?"

Her counterattack ripped through his sleeve, steel biting into his skin. He felt almost nothing, numbed by the adrenaline pumping through his veins. "I have no choice," said Garringsford. "I'll kill anyone to bring them back."

Eadric faltered, which nearly cost him his head. "Them? Who's them?"

The general clenched her jaw, breathing hard. "Who else?"

"Your sons are dead, Carlotta," Eadric said.

She lunged forward again. Their swords clashed as they trembled in a deadly duel of strength, neither willing to back down. "Priscilla promised she would bring them back."

He scoffed, sweat rolling down his temple. "You can't bring back the dead."

Garringsford snarled, ramming him back in a surge of strength. "She *promised*."

Eadric tripped and crashed onto his back. He rolled just in time for her sword to cleave a gash in the floor where he had fallen a mere heartbeat before. She struck with such force that a chunk of marble flew up and nearly took his eye out. Like a feral dog, she pounced once more, her usual vicious grace giving way to something desperate, something primal. He threw his sword up to block her, one hand braced against the flat of the blade. Blood ran down his palm as Garringsford pressed harder. He bit down on an agonized groan, arms shaking. Just as his hand began to slip—too much blood—Garringsford's eyes widened and the pressure against his sword relented.

Eadric looked from their locked swords to the bright-scarlet steel point protruding from her chest.

Slowly, Garringsford's gaze followed his. Her grip loosened on her sword, and Eadric finally disarmed her. She sagged to her knees, the light fading from her eyes.

Behind her stood Alicia.

"Captain," the young Elite panted, hands still wrapped around the hilt of her own sword—which she had just plowed into Garringsford's back. Blood pooled around Alicia's boots. "Captain … please tell me that I just did the right thing."

Eadric staggered to his feet. *Priscilla, I need to get to Priscilla.* "You—you did. You saved my life."

The tension in her frame deflated, and she pulled her sword out of the general's back. "Thank the Immortals." Her eyes were still glued to Garringsford's face when a guard attacked from the side. Eadric sprang forward to shove her away, deflecting the blade. Even with his injury, the soldier was no match against him. Eadric slammed the hilt of his sword into the soldier's forehead, knocking him out cold.

"Regroup with the other Elites," Eadric ordered, but Alicia didn't budge, her gaze dragging up and down the blood still dripping down her sword. Her first kill. "Alicia. I know it's hard, but you have to forget about this for now. You have to stay focused. I'm depending on you. *Asterin* is depending on you."

The spark returned to Alicia's eyes. She saluted. "Yes, Captain!" With that, she dashed toward the exit, where Silas and Hayley were evacuating guests.

Eadric ran in the opposite direction—into the chaos.

Priscilla forged her way toward the exit like a valiant knight, hissing and thrashing out at random, but just as Eadric managed to get within an arm's reach of those monstrous wings, two colossal spires of ice erupted out of the marble floor, knocking the woman onto her knees. Jagged shackles of frost surged from the spires and encircled her wrists and ankles, yanking her high off the ground.

The Elites ran forward, affinity stones drawn, and surrounded the dangling woman on all sides.

Priscilla Montcroix-Faelenhart was truly a sight to behold. The midnight-black leathery wings had ripped the back of her silk gown to shreds. No one could stop staring at her, but not for the usual reasons—her stunning features were nothing now. Her skin seemed like an ill-fitting coat, pulling taut in some places and sagging off her frame in others. The hue of her once pale skin had darkened to a mottled yellowish-gray. Her soft, pink mouth had been replaced by lipless fangs and a long tongue covered in ridges. Several people retched.

Asterin stepped out of the crowd, palms crackling with frost. Orion and the two Eradorians jostled their way to her side.

"Priscilla Alessandra Montcroix-Faelenhart," the Princess of Axaria announced. Eadric shivered as the temperature dropped, frost creeping along the floor. Priscilla's bloodshot eyes slitted. "Before hundreds of witnesses, I charge you with treason and the use of the forbidden tenth element, thereby breaking international magic law. Such acts are punishable by death."

"And who might you be?" Priscilla spat, straining against her bonds, her voice diminished to nothing but a dry rasp.

Asterin pulled out the second vial of contralusio and downed it in one go. "The rightful ruler of Axaria," she said as Luna's illusions faded. Unlike Rose, Asterin had never shied from the public, and every guest who had attended the Fairfest Ball in previous years had no issue in identifying her immediately.

The entire hall burst into a cacophony.

Asterin raised a hand. Silence fell. She addressed the crowd. "What all of you have just seen," she began, gesturing to herself and Priscilla, "—is the work of contralusio, a substance that strips the falsities of anything it touches, leaving only the truth. There were three vials. One for Priscilla Montcroix, one for me to prove that I hide nothing from you all. And finally …" She turned to Princess Rowena, the earth-wielder from

Galanz. "One for you, Princess Rowena. Your scholarly papers on magical substances and their properties are most esteemed in my kingdom and its academies. Should anyone doubt what has happened here tonight, I ask and entrust you to verify my claim. Do you accept?"

Rowena's brows rose in surprise. "Honorably, Princess Asterin," her distant cousin answered.

Asterin tossed the third vial to Rowena, the contralusio catching the light like a mysterious jewel. "You have my gratitude."

"And what of this witch?" Queen Valeria demanded, raising her chin toward Priscilla.

"She deserves death!" cried Prince Viyo, which earned him a glare from his older sister.

Asterin leveled Priscilla with a look so cold that it sent chills up Eadric's spine. "Do you have anything to say in your defense?"

A look of absolute murder descended onto Priscilla's face as she looked Asterin dead in the eye and snarled, "I hope you burn."

A deafening *bang* tore through the air.

An explosion of blackness threw Eadric backward—an explosion of shadow. He landed hard on his side, agony tearing up his chest as a ribbon of shadow wrapped itself around his torso and *squeezed.*

"Son of a bitch," he wheezed over the screams ringing through the ballroom, his vision flashing red as something hot and wet dripped down his face. Cursing, he tried to grab at the shadows, but they slipped through his fingers like eels, branching and spreading out until he managed to free his skystone and conjure a jolt of electricity. The shadows solidified for a beat before finally dissipating with a hiss.

Eadric blacked out.

CHAPTER FORTY-SEVEN

If not for her training and the reflexes Quinlan had forced her to hone, Asterin was fairly sure that she would have vaporized on the spot when Priscilla had shattered her ice restraints in an explosion of shadow.

Even then, Asterin just barely managed to hurl up a shield in time to deflect the onslaught of darkness and the barrage of ice chunks. Quinlan, standing beside her, reacted even more swiftly, shielding several of her Elites and the other guests closest to the blast. Dozens of other shields crackled alive like weak torches against the storm of shadow around the ballroom.

Priscilla fled—her hulking, demonic wings flexing as she leapt into the air and spread them wide, launching over the bodies and debris. She nearly slammed headfirst into a wall, but after a few more experimental flaps, she soared out of the ballroom.

From across the room, Rose locked eyes with Asterin behind her own wall of green light, a single word moving on her lips.

Go.

"Silas!" Asterin shouted at the oldest Elite. "Assemble the Elites and evacuate the guests. No one follows—it's too dangerous. Understood?"

At Silas's firm nod, Asterin and Quinlan thundered out of the ballroom after Priscilla.

Unfortunately, flying proved to be much faster than running.

"She's getting away," Quinlan said. He reached for Asterin. "Take my hand."

Asterin only had a moment to acknowledge the strange, euphoric sensation of Quinlan's magic surging through their locked hands like an electrical current before a gust of wind swept her off the ground. Her stomach dipped as he angled them forward, increasing their speed, their toes skimming the floor.

Flying—they were flying.

The corridors whizzed by as they gained on Priscilla. The woman's enormous wingspan cost her precious time—narrow hallways and sharp turns forced her to pull her wings in and extend them again every flap.

As they closed in on her, Priscilla let out an angry screech, sounding more beast than human. She clutched her affinity stone and pelted them with orbs of swirling darkness. Quinlan swerved wildly, doing his best to dodge them. The orbs splattered onto the walls and floor, corroding the marble to sludge. Asterin yelped as one missed her face by a mere inch.

Priscilla swooped up the grand stairway. Quinlan swore and lurched after her, nearly popping Asterin's arm right out of its socket before he managed to wrangle his wind affinity back under control.

With each flight of stairs, they grew closer to Priscilla. Fingers outstretched, Asterin could almost reach out to rip off a wing—

Priscilla veered onto the third floor and smashed a hole through the first door on the left.

With another bitten-back curse, Quinlan steered them through the hole. They landed hard on the marble floor of a large antechamber used for court meetings.

Priscilla skidded across the long oak table on all fours, her talons leaving deep gouges along its surface. She leaped off the end and glanced over her shoulder at Asterin, twirling her affinity stone between spindly fingers. Asterin saw that the once azure illusionstone was now clouded jet black.

A shadowstone.

"Daughter," she said, the word dripping off her tongue like sweet poison.

Asterin balled her fist around her omnistone. "Don't you dare call me that."

Priscilla giggled. "Finally figured it out, did you? Clever girl," she crooned. "Only took you a decade."

Rage swelled through Asterin, drowning out every sound, every thought. Cracks shuddered across the floor. She raised her arms, and two enormous slabs of marble quivered upward.

Then she closed her eyes and hurled the slabs with all her might at the woman she had once called her mother.

Except there came no screech of pain, of death—only a peculiar sensation wriggling at the base of Asterin's skull.

You can't close your eyes in battle, Rose had told her in Aldville.

When Asterin opened her eyes, Priscilla smiled, false pity written across those horrid features. Standing at the far end of the oak table with the marble slabs suspended in stillness above her, the woman brought her shadowstone down in an arc, as if delivering a fatal blow in slow motion. *And perhaps she is*, Asterin realized when her arms lowered against her will, bringing the slabs to a gentle rest at the queen's feet.

Beside her, Quinlan summoned his fire, but his arm lurched downward at the last moment and charred the tables and chairs instead of Priscilla. Waves of heat rippled over them. Beads of sweat rolled down Quinlan's jaw as he struggled to extinguish the flames before they could cause Asterin and him any harm.

Priscilla laughed, cruel and cold. "Naive little fools." With a flick of her wrist, Quinlan's eyes rolled back into his skull.

Asterin cried out, barely catching him as he crumpled. He convulsed against her, and Asterin felt that wriggling again—a little coil of darkness burrowing into her mind, spreading faster than hellfire.

And then her greatest fears and her worst nightmares rushed from the deepest, darkest recesses of her soul and became *real.*

The room around her crumbled to ash, the floor caving inward. She fell with it, crashing down, tumbling in a heap atop the remains of the palace. The charred mess of what had once been the Wall piled around her, and below—oh, almighty Immortals—below, her city was unrecognizable, nothing but a ruin of smoking cinders. She could hear the chanting of spirits, of angry ghosts, a chorus of spine-chilling whispers.

The rubble shifted at her feet.

She stifled a scream as three corpses clawed their way out into the open and crawled toward her.

Her father. Frail and white as the first snow of winter. His milky, clouded eyes fixated on her, as if to say, "This is your fault," even though it never could have been.

Luna. Sweet Luna. Her *before* face, kind and open, the one Asterin had known—but now … her throat, slit.

Asterin kicked the third corpse in the face as hard as she could, her eyes turned up to the scarlet sky so that she wouldn't see its owner, but she still caught a glance of a signature crimson cloak—

A moan drifted to her through the still, arid air like a lone horn, crescendoing as more voices joined in answering. Dozens upon dozens of corpses clawed up the crest of the mountain toward her. They were all faceless, but she knew they were her people, the people of her kingdom. Asterin backed away as they jerked to their feet, closing in from all sides. She sobbed as Amoux materialized at her hip, bile rising in her throat. With no choice, she drew her sword forth, weighing a thousand tons in her hand.

"Please," she begged the dead, falling to her knees. "I can't." But they continued to lumber forward, reaching out to her. Asterin buried her face in her hands. Amoux clanged to the ground as she felt their clammy touch on her arms, on her neck—

And then, just as quickly as it had begun, everything stopped.

Asterin let out a heaving, broken gasp as that horrible, suffocating sensation faded from her head. Her face itched from the salt of her tears, and the taste of blood was sharp in her mouth—she had chewed her cheek raw. In the midst of her hallucinations, she had ended up near the entrance to the antechamber, leaving Quinlan abandoned and unconscious midway between her and Priscilla.

Before Asterin stood Luna, palms braced outward to shield them with her own waves of light from the oncoming tide of darkness about to wash over Quinlan.

"Mother!" Luna shouted, raising her illusionstone high above her head.

Priscilla gaped. The darkness withered away. "Luna?"

A great beast soared over Asterin's head, wings stretching up to the ceiling like sails caught in a ferocious gale. *Harry.* With Priscilla distracted, the demon torpedoed to the floor, wings tucked close to his body. At the same moment that he clamped his teeth around Quinlan's collar, he unfurled his wings. Faster than Priscilla could react, Harry hauled Quinlan into the air and swooped toward Asterin, depositing the Eradorian safely at her side.

Luna gave her mother a frigid smile. "Surprised to see me?"

Harry landed and prowled in front of them protectively while Asterin checked Quinlan's pulse. *Steady.*

Priscilla stammered in disbelief. "Y-you broke the spell."

"Yes," said Luna. "The spell that took everything from me. My powers, my memories—"

Priscilla threw her hands in the air. "I was trying to *protect* you!"

"From *what*?"

"You were a mistake," Priscilla said, her expression softening. At Luna's flinch, the woman hastily added, "The greatest mistake I ever made. But you don't understand—he never wanted a child—he would have killed you if he had found out, so I had to hide you—"

"Who would have killed me?" demanded Luna. "Other than you, by conjuring a demon and then lying about it? The thirty guards, the slaughtered villagers. You sent us to avenge them, but you just wanted us dead!"

"I never sent *you*!" Priscilla shouted. "You were never meant to go!" She pointed at Asterin. "That little bitch was just supposed to take some of her precious Elites. How could I have guessed that she would drag *you* along with her? She ruined everything!"

Asterin barely had time to fling up an energy shield as Priscilla sent a blast of darkness at her, propelling her three feet backward and nearly causing her to trip over Quinlan, still out cold on the floor.

Luna threw herself into the line of fire again, shining brighter than a star as she used her magic to push Priscilla further back. "Don't worry," Luna said to Asterin over her shoulder, sparing her a single glance filled with sincerity and burning resolve. "I won't let her hurt you."

At that moment, all Asterin could think about were the many times she had doubted Luna. But with or without powers, Luna had always possessed a goodness in her heart that Asterin had never quite been able to fathom. Despite everyone's misgivings, Luna had remained brave and loyal.

With a growl, Harry launched into the air and shot toward Priscilla, forcing her to defend against both his and Luna's attacks at the same time. Luna gained another foot, pushing the darkness farther and farther away, conquering Priscilla's magic with her own.

"Luna," Asterin choked out.

"Hush," Luna cut her off, a smile playing on her lips. "I can handle my mother." The smile slipped away when Priscilla's darkness gave Luna a particularly brutal shove.

"Get out of the way, Luna," Priscilla hissed, ducking as Harry's fangs snapped an inch from her neck. "You don't understand—"

"What I understand," said Luna, voice trembling, "is that you want to take away the person who has stood by my side all the years that you did not."

"I made you her lady-in-waiting so you could live a life of comfort and luxury!" Priscilla's face twisted in grotesque frustration. "I gave you anything you could ever desire, and this is how you repay me?" The next time Harry hurtled for Priscilla, she grinned and held up a hand. "Shadow demon! In the power of our blood bond, I order you to kill Asterin Faelenhart."

To Asterin's horror, Harry halted midair and turned his glazed stare upon her. *Didn't he say blood bonds were myths?*

Asterin latched onto Quinlan and began lugging him away from the fight. "Harry," she shouted, "snap out of it—"

And then Harry's barbed tail lashed across Priscilla's face.

Priscilla screamed, holding her cheek. "Shadow demon—"

Harry shifted, human hands wrapping around Priscilla's throat. "For the last time, it's *Harry*."

"Enough." The black veins in Priscilla's neck bulged. Harry swore and recoiled as spikes erupted from her skin, piercing clean through his palms. A blast of shadow sent him careening into a column, and Asterin's ears rang at the ominous *crack* of fractured marble. Harry slid to the floor and Luna gasped, the column teetering above him. Asterin conjured a barrier of ice over his body just as the column gave way with a deafening *crash*.

"Why are you doing this?" Luna screamed at Priscilla, voice breaking. "Why are you trying to hurt my friends?"

But Priscilla's attention had shifted. For the second time, her shadow magic receded, collecting around her body in a shield. Her eyes fixed beyond Asterin and Luna, glinting with something akin to wonder. "Jakob?" she said. "You … you came for me?"

Both Asterin and Luna whirled around to find the King of Ibreseos in the ruined doorway.

A snarl ripped from Luna's lips. She assaulted Priscilla's shield with a fork of blue light. "Answer me!"

Priscilla struggled to keep her footing. "Jakob, help me!"

The king moved a fraction forward.

Luna howled. "Answer me, Mother!"

King Jakob froze. "Mother?" he echoed.

Priscilla's eyes widened. To Luna, she shrieked, "What are you on about, girl?" Her voice raised an octave. "How dare you even suggest such a thing? You disgust me with your nerve!"

Luna turned to face Jakob. It would have taken a blind idiot to miss the resemblance between her and Priscilla, now that the spell had been lifted.

"Priscilla," Jakob rumbled, striding into the room. "Who is the father?"

The former queen released a tiny whimper.

"*Who is the father*?"

Priscilla's shoulders slumped with each punctuated syllable. At last, she surrendered.

"You."

CHAPTER FORTY-EIGHT

King Jakob inhaled sharply, stopping just behind Asterin and Luna.

Luna's face paled. "What?"

"You kept this from me," said the king, expression shuttering.

"You said you never wanted a child!" Priscilla cried.

Luna barked a sarcastic laugh. "What a lovely family reunion." She curtsied to King Jakob. "Father." And then without warning, she rammed a dozen arcs of light into Priscilla's shield.

Stepping away from Quinlan, still unconscious at her feet, Asterin shook off her own surprise and summoned her magic. Together, she and Luna bombarded Priscilla with ice and light, reducing her shield to tatters.

"Jakob, help!" Priscilla shrieked again.

The King of Ibreseos stared at her.

And then he took a step back.

Priscilla let out an anguished wail of betrayal. "How could you?" she shrilled. "I did anything and everything you asked of me! The reason I came to this damned kingdom in the first place, the reason I even began practicing dark magic—"

"I never asked you to do any of those things," Jakob thundered. "*You* were starving for more power. *You* were starving for the throne. You couldn't kill the heiress of your own House, so you stole another one instead. You've pushed yourself past the brink, Priscilla, and I will not fall with you. After you killed Elyssa over a misinterpretation—"

"Elyssa," Asterin whispered, the name lighting some abyss deep inside of her. "Elyssa," she repeated, her magic petering out. "I—I know that name."

Jakob's expression softened. "You look exactly as she did, all those years ago."

Asterin's heart stuttered. "You mean …"

"Yes, child," he said gruffly. "She was your mother."

"And you …" Asterin trailed off. "You knew her?"

Jakob swallowed. "She was once one of my dearest friends."

"And Priscilla killed her."

The king's jaw clenched. He dipped his chin once.

Without another word, Asterin thrust out her hand and launched a volley of ice spears at Priscilla, their razor tips glimmering with jagged rage. Priscilla screeched and conjured shadows to deflect the attack, but one spear made it past her shield and struck her across the shoulder, leaving a ragged slash.

With a gasp of pain, Asterin stumbled backward, one hand gripping her own shoulder. No weapon had struck there, nothing at all, and yet bright red droplets streamed through her fingers, splattering on the floor. *Where did that come from?*

"Asterin!" Luna cried.

"Jakob," Priscilla wailed.

The king shook his head. "Forgive me, but this is not my fight. I have no business here." Then he spun on his heel, vanishing through the exit.

"Luna, do you see how he treats me?" Priscilla panted, staggering toward them. "The person who loves him most? You can say whatever you want about me, but I love you like no one else ever will. I'm your mother. We're family—"

"You may be my mother," Luna whispered in a voice that promised terrifying wrath, "but you will never be my family."

Priscilla gaped at the rejection, poison building behind her expression.

Asterin summoned a second volley of ice, but hands closed around her wrists and she turned to find Quinlan behind her. She hadn't even noticed him awaken. "Don't," he said. His next words came in a messy, inarticulate cascade. "You can't injure her. Reflective spell. Like the ropes from Harry's traps. She's cast it on herself. If you attack her, it will rebound." His fingers hovered over her shoulder. "You're bleeding pretty badly. Haelein."

"What are we going to do?" Asterin breathed as her wound closed up.

"Why can't we just cast reflective spells on ourselves?" asked Luna.

Asterin shook her head. No one had tutored Luna before, so she wouldn't know. "It's only possible to cast such a spell on inanimate objects. That is, unless you use shadow magic."

"Luna," said Quinlan, distracting Priscilla with a swarm of fire arrows, hot enough to redden his skin from her reflective spell, but not burn. "Can you buy us some time with your illusions? We might be able to do Priscilla some damage and heal ourselves at the same time. Even then, there's no way to get a kill shot unless one of us …"

"I have an idea," Luna said. "If it doesn't work …" She shook her head. "Either way, I'll handle it."

Something in her voice told Asterin exactly what she meant by *handle*.

She grasped Luna firmly by the shoulders. "I've lost enough already to Priscilla," Asterin growled, forcing her friend to meet her gaze. "And I sure as hell won't lose you to her, too."

"Always, Asterin," Luna whispered. "I'll always stay by your side. *You* are my family. I will always choose you."

Asterin swallowed the thick knot in her throat. "So what's your idea?"

Before she could answer, however, Quinlan let out a curse and Asterin looked up just in time to watch a shower of dark arrows rain down upon them. Quinlan shielded them from the worst of it, but one arrow slipped past his defenses, slicing him all the way from his wrist to his elbow.

Priscilla cackled and conjured a second barrage. Quinlan grimaced, the deep gouge leaking black sludge down his arm.

Without thinking, Asterin's fingers brushed over the wound. "Haelein." She watched his skin mend. Yet to her utter disbelief, it reopened not moments later. "*Haelein*," she said again. And again, and again, but to no avail. "Quinlan, I can't heal it."

"What do you mean?" he said, still focused on blocking Priscilla's arrows.

Fear surged through her veins at the breathy rasp of his voice, the bluish-gray pallor of his skin. "Quinlan, you have to stop!"

"I'm fine," he panted, every inhale growing more laborious.

Priscilla grinned at them from the other side of Quinlan's shield, its strength waning with every blow. The woman's tongue darted over her teeth, as if she could already taste victory.

Quinlan fell to his knees. Asterin lunged for him. She had no plan, no idea how to help. Perhaps ... perhaps, if she could somehow let him borrow her power, let their magic fuse into one ...

Exhaling, she laced her fingers with his, imagining her magic flowing through their connection and into him. Slowly, a current like the one she had felt when they had chased Priscilla hummed through her and fueled the weakening inferno beside her. She willed the shield to become more powerful.

And to her wondrous awe, it did.

Only, the arrows kept coming. Asterin felt each blow to the shield like a punch to the gut. How Quinlan had managed on his own for this long was beyond her comprehension.

The shield wavered, and Asterin looked up just in time to watch an arrow sail through and strike Quinlan, tearing into his abdomen and halfway out his back.

"No!" Asterin shouted.

The grip on her hand fell slack and his body sagged to the ground, his eyes slipping shut again.

The shield flickered out.

Asterin swore, releasing Quinlan's fingers and pushing her palms outward with all her might to defend against the unrelenting arrows. Priscilla pummeled her shield without mercy, and Asterin could only manage to throw up small shells of magic to deflect the worst of the storm.

Her only remaining hope was Luna, crouched at Asterin's side with her eyes squeezed shut in concentration.

"Luna," Asterin gasped. "If you've got anything planned—"

"Give me a moment."

Asterin missed an arrow. It landed dangerously close to Quinlan's unmoving form. Then she missed a second, a third. Her arms might as well have been made of lead. Every muscle burned.

Her legs gave out and she crashed to the ground. With a grunt, she deflected three arrows aimed for her chest, but a fourth skimmed her face.

Pain exploded from her cheek, an acidic burn eating through her flesh. Her vision blotted. *How did Quinlan endure this agony for so long?*

Another arrow glanced off the surface of Asterin's shield and ricocheted upward. With a last, feeble crackle, the shield faded.

Asterin had nothing left to give. She closed her eyes, wondering if her death would be swift, but realized Priscilla would never let her go that easily. She understood what Quinlan had meant back in the forest—that it was never a mercy to be at another's mercy. *It only means you will suffer longer.*

But death did not come.

Instead, Asterin heard a sob. When she opened her eyes, tears cascaded down Priscilla's face, her lips moving in a silent, futile plea.

Asterin turned, trembling from exhaustion.

Behind her, King Jakob's body lay splayed out across the floor. One hand gripped the shaft sticking out of his chest, blood seeping between his fingers.

His heart—pierced by a single black arrow.

Beside Asterin, Luna smiled.

CHAPTER FORTY-NINE

"No," Priscilla whispered. "Jakob."

The crying grew unbearably shrill. Broken, anguished sobs wracked her body and grated against Luna's ears, making it hard to focus. She could only pray that the real King Jakob was far away as she poured every drop of energy she had into her illusion of the king's body, an imaginary shadow arrow protruding out of his chest.

If it had been anyone else, Luna would have felt terrible. But not *her*—not now. Luna felt powerful, more than she had ever been in her entire, helpless life. Something warm settled in her stomach. Satisfaction.

Everything has a price, Mother.

Priscilla had held Luna's life in her hands for so many years. But no longer.

Luna would make her pay.

She hoped that the image of Jakob's dead body would be forever seared into Priscilla's mind. She hoped it would haunt her every time she closed her eyes. She hoped it would cause her as much pain as she had caused Asterin. She hoped it would drive her over the edge.

Luna pressed a hand to her mouth and staggered away from her masterpiece, rounding on Priscilla. "What have you done?" she cried. "He came back for you, and you killed him!"

To Luna's everlasting delight, her mother flinched. "I—I didn't do anything!" Priscilla cowered beneath Luna's disgusted stare. "I have no idea how … It was an accident. Jakob, forgive me!" she wailed. "Oh, my love, forgive me—"

"It's no use now, you witch," Luna spat. "He's dead!"

Priscilla howled, burying her face in her hands.

"Luna," Asterin said, voice hoarse. Her hands clutched desperately at Quinlan's wounds, the cut on her own face still dribbling gray sludge. "The dark magic … his pulse is getting weaker and weaker. He's dying, Luna, and I can't heal him."

"You can," Luna whispered ferociously. "I know you can. You must."

At the sound of their voices, Priscilla's neck swiveled toward them. She pointed a gnarled claw at Asterin, her eyes rimmed with crimson. "This is all your fault," Priscilla rasped, every word laced with fury. "I will end you."

Luna screamed as Priscilla fired a shadow arrow, aimed straight for Asterin's heart.

It stopped not an inch short of its destination.

"Or better yet," Priscilla said, eyes glittering as they flicked from Quinlan to Luna, something truly ugly overtaking her expression. "I will *break* you."

And before Luna could comprehend her meaning, two black masses slithered from Priscilla's palms toward them. One leapt at her, and the other at Quinlan, slipping beneath their chins and yanking them upward.

The coil of shadow only tightened around her neck as Luna struggled, Quinlan hanging limp beside her.

Fight, Luna. You're better now. She kicked and screamed, fighting the darkness creeping upon her.

For Asterin, she fought.

Asterin's words echoed in her head. *I sure as hell won't lose you to her.*

For Asterin, Luna refused to break.

CHAPTER FIFTY

When Eadric finally came to amidst the wreckage, he could hardly recognize the ballroom. With a groan, he tried to push himself up only for his arm to collapse beneath him, pain shooting through his wrist. His uninjured hand came away red when he brushed it across his temple.

Ears ringing, he heaved himself to a sitting position, the dull thud of his own heartbeat intermingling with the low moans and faraway shouts. Breathing deeper revealed the stab of a fractured rib or two. Holding his injured wrist close to his chest, he flexed his other hand, gripping his affinity stone, and summoned his magic to help him onto his feet. He attempted to heal himself as best he could, which, frankly, wasn't very good at all, but he had survived worse. At least the gashes from Garringsford's sword had clotted.

Surveying the damage, Eadric realized that Priscilla must have escaped. Several people—guests and guards alike—lay on the ground, unmoving. Dust floated thick in the air. A pillar had collapsed, and past it he saw a hole that had been blasted through the far wall, wisps of black, putrid smoke still curling from the rubble.

Where was Asterin?

She had been right in front of Priscilla when the woman had released that demonic explosion. Eadric prayed to every Immortal he could think of that she had managed to shield herself in time.

Eyes stinging from the smoke hanging in the air like a thick veil, he scanned the faces around him, trying to find any of them—Asterin, Rose, Orion, Quinlan.

"Eadric!"

He spun around. A man with a prominent serpent tattoo winding around his neck clambered over the fallen pillar, his dark hair lengthening and lightening back to gold even as he approached.

"What are you doing?" Orion exclaimed. "Don't just stand there!"

"Where's Asterin?" demanded Eadric.

"Went after Priscilla already, come on." Orion slung an arm around Eadric's waist and swiftly guided him over the pillar. "You sure look beat up."

Eadric only grunted in response. The other side of the ballroom had fared better than he'd expected, though that wasn't saying much. He spotted Rose flitting about, sending up swirls of debris as she brandished her affinity stone, healing people left and right. That mysterious figure in gray from the earlier battle trailed behind her, his knives sheathed at his sides. He had taken off his hood—Eadric caught a brief glimpse of his flat, stormy expression and a shock of unruly white hair.

"Any internal injuries?" asked Orion, glancing at the blood dribbling down Eadric's temple.

"Rib and wrist, but I healed them. Sort of."

Orion raised a skeptical eyebrow. "I see." He waved his arm. "Rose!"

The Queen of Eradore rushed over to them. She placed a hand on Eadric's chest, as if she could sense his pain, and muttered under her breath. He winced at the tugging ache of the bones mending at her touch. Two deft fingers prodded at his wrist, then pushed back his matted hair to heal the gash on his forehead, her gold eyes meeting his. He found comfort in their steadiness.

At last, Rose exhaled. "Better?"

"Better." He stepped away. "Thank you."

"Are you coming?" Orion asked Rose.

"A lot of people here are injured. I need to help them first," the Eradorian said. "But I'll be there as soon as I'm finished with the worst of it."

"Captain!" Eadric heard someone call.

He turned to find Gino jogging over the rubble toward him. "Gino," he said with a sigh of relief. "Are all the other Elites all right?"

Gino bobbed his head, gelled hair sticking up in every direction. "We're still evacuating guests. Asterin told us to stay here, sir, but we wanted to tell you that we found a trail probably leading to her location."

"If we aren't back in a quarter hour, come after us. Bring reinforcements, and do *not* underestimate Priscilla."

Gino saluted. "Understood."

Orion tugged at Eadric's sleeve. "Let's go."

They left Rose and the ballroom behind, dodging the stream of evacuees, and tore through the corridors, their path unmistakable thanks to the black sludge leading down the hall and up the grand stairway. They followed it up three flights and dashed left, where they found the end of the trail leading through a pair of double doors—or rather, the gaping hole that remained. Eadric could hear the screaming and yelling of a duel beyond.

Orion sprinted for the hole, only to be launched sideways back into the corridor by an unseen force. He sailed into the air and crashed through a window in a shower of glass.

"Orion!" Eadric rushed to the window, expecting to find a broken form on the ground far below. To his relief, the Guardian clung to the stone ledge of the shattered window, bloodied and peppered with cuts but otherwise unharmed. Eadric grasped him by the forearms and heaved him back to safety.

They approached the destroyed doorway. Eadric aimed a kick at the hole, but it was blocked by some sort of invisible air barrier.

Orion's eyes widened with terror, staring beyond the hole. "Almighty Immortals."

Eadric followed the Guardian's gaze. Inside, Harry lay crumpled beneath a melting shell of ice that protected him from being crushed by the remains of a fallen column. Eadric shoved Orion aside for a better view and saw a grinning Priscilla, pupils blown to bottomless pits of hatred. And closer, just a few paces from the door, Princess Asterin on her knees.

But nothing could have prepared Eadric for the sight of Quinlan and Luna—*his* Luna—being yanked up by nooses of pure shadow, their bodies dangling five feet off the ground. Quinlan appeared to be unconscious, but Luna thrashed and clawed at her noose like a lion, face steadily purpling.

Eadric could have sworn his heart stopped beating. "What are Luna and Harry doing in there? They were supposed to—"

"Never mind that," Orion exclaimed. "We need to get inside."

Together, they blasted magic at the air barrier, dodging whatever ricocheted back at them.

"It's no use," Eadric panted, overwhelmed by the sudden urge to throw his affinity stone out of the window Orion had broken. He saw Asterin raise her palms, struggling to conjure two pitiful shields. "It's too powerful."

Orion let out an animalistic snarl and pitched himself at the hole again. Eadric lunged forward, preparing to seize the Guardian when he went flying, but to his astonishment, Orion fell right through and landed in a heap on the other side.

A burly man with sandy-gold hair appeared beside Eadric, the crown on his head tipped askew. "You'd better hurry if you want to save my daughter."

Daughter?

But instead of dwelling on the thought, Eadric just thanked the Immortals above and plunged through the hole.

CHAPTER FIFTY-ONE

Shackles bore down on Asterin's every muscle, each limb driven so far beyond exhaustion that she could scarcely move an inch. So when Priscilla wrapped those nooses of shadow around Luna's and Quinlan's necks, she could do nothing but watch.

She had never felt so worthless in her life.

"Aren't I wonderful?" Priscilla sang. "I'm giving you a choice. Isn't that what everyone always wishes for nowadays? I hope you have it in you to save one of your friends, Princess Asterin. If you don't … well, you'll just have an extra funeral to attend."

Two arrows appeared, one on each side of Priscilla.

And suddenly, Asterin understood what she meant by a *choice.*

Priscilla was making her choose between Luna and Quinlan.

The world ground to a jarring halt.

"And I'll tell you what, dearest Asterin—I'll even count down from ten," Priscilla went on with a cheery smile. "Ready?"

Asterin heard a crash behind her, but she couldn't bring herself to look.

"Ten … Nine …"

Asterin's eyes widened. She attempted to conjure two shields of energy, but they both glowed so weakly that she could barely see them.

"Eight …"

Asterin gritted her teeth, her heart hammering in her throat, and summoned every last drop of energy in her body to squeeze into her shields. Immortals help her—Harry—but no, he was still unconscious.

"Seven …"

The shields solidified, but still … still they couldn't have been thicker than a pane of glass. Neither could deflect Priscilla's arrows alone, which of course Priscilla knew. The only way would be to combine the power of the two shields into one … to choose. But … who would she choose? How *could* she choose?

Or better yet, I will break you.

Asterin cursed quietly, begging herself to try harder.

"Six—oh, this is taking forever." Priscilla giggled, the sound like the scrape of knives. "Three …"

The oxygen in Asterin's lungs vanished in one *whoosh*.

"Two …"

Her body quaked. Oh, gods, *oh Immortals*, the shields wouldn't be strong enough.

Luna or Quinlan?

"One."

The arrows flew.

CHAPTER FIFTY-TWO

As the arrow whistled toward Luna, her imminent death was nothing compared to the ugly emotion that rushed through her when Asterin collapsed the two shields together and threw it … not before her, but before Quinlan.

Asterin had chosen Quinlan over her.

Asterin had chosen *Quinlan* over *her.*

After all these years, after so much together … death was nothing in the face of this betrayal.

Luna released a choked sob and forced her eyes wider. She would not close them. She was not afraid of her death, not after *this*—and she vowed to greet her end without fear.

But all she could see, replaying over and over in her mind, was Asterin collapsing the two shields to form one and hurling it to protect a person she had only met months before.

Making her choice.

A sudden burst of lightning blinded her. *This must be death*, she thought as she prepared to embrace the darkness. But she didn't expect the stench of sulfur or the overwhelming metallic taste filling her mouth, much less the sight of the shadow arrow dissipating before her, the debris just nicking the tip of her nose while Asterin's shield deflected Priscilla's other arrow from Quinlan. Luna hardly noticed when the constriction around her neck released, nor the coolness of the marble tiles against her heated skin when steadfast arms caught her and gently lowered to the ground.

She wished she could have fallen—fallen and broken every bone in her body. It would have been better than this hateful, aching emptiness within her.

Appearing out of nowhere, Eadric reached forward to brush Luna's cheek, but she turned away. He tensed, little bolts of electricity jumping up and down his hands, but eventually retreated. In the end, he had stopped the arrow meant for her. He had been her savior.

"Luna!" her best friend cried, rushing over to her. Luna did not move. She felt Asterin's trembling arms wrap around her, holding her close. The scent of home enveloped her.

Because for Luna, Asterin *was* home.

Asterin was everything to her.

And like a fool, she had never, not even for a second, doubted that Asterin felt the same way.

She had been so blind.

"You chose Quinlan," Luna whispered.

Her eyes trailed down from where Orion hovered over Quinlan, still unconscious. The Guardian applied pressure to the dribbling gash in Quinlan's stomach. Even now, with the prince soaked in a puddle of black sludge and his own blood, his face as pale as snow, a stray curl of dark hair sticking to his damp forehead … she wanted to hate him. She really did. But how could she?

Asterin faltered. "I—I know. I could only choose one of you … and …"

"You chose him over me. Your best friend."

"I know, and I'm sorry, but—"

"I can't believe you, Asterin," Luna breathed, ignoring the swell of tears rising past her bruised throat.

"But I *love* him!" Asterin burst, throwing her arms toward Quinlan. "I love him, and I love you, but I listened to my heart and that was the hardest decision I have ever made in my life and I hope to the Immortals that no one, and I mean *no one* will ever be forced into that kind of situation." Asterin panted, her grip tightening. "Luna …"

Asterin's fingers suddenly felt like claws.

Something in Luna shut off. It corked her every emotion before it had the chance to bubble to the surface, stopped her from *feeling*.

"Asterin, I don't know how long I can keep this up," Eadric said through gritted teeth. The electricity jolting from his arms fed into a sphere of white lightning imprisoning Priscilla in the center of the room. Every time the woman tried to get close to the surface, Eadric upped the voltage and zapped her. She snarled at him, but she had gone slightly cross-eyed.

Asterin swallowed. "Luna—"

"No," Luna breathed. "It's fine." She pried off Asterin's hands, banishing the tendrils of bitterness from her stomach and tilting her lips up in what might have been a smile. "Forget it. We have more important things to deal with. Like my mother."

Eadric glanced sideways at Luna, his attention still mainly on the sphere. "Are you okay?"

"I'm alive," she said. "Thank you for—" Her voice hitched slightly. "For being there."

"You don't ever have to thank me for that," Eadric told her. Then, to Asterin he said, "The Elites should be arriving with backup any minute now, so we just need to keep Priscilla imprisoned until then."

"Asterin," Orion called, standing up over Quinlan. "Staunch this wound. I need to get Harry."

Asterin seemed torn between staying by Luna's side and going to Quinlan, but Luna swallowed and jerked her chin. "Just go."

Without another word, she complied, shedding her cloak and using a discarded arrow on the floor to shear off strips of fabric to bind Quinlan's stomach.

While Eadric continued to struggle with containing Priscilla in the sphere, Orion ducked beneath Asterin's ice shell to retrieve Harry, who seemed to just be awakening. Both of his legs and one arm were twisted in strange directions, so Orion picked him up and carried him out from under the shell to where Asterin hovered over Quinlan. Even as the demon blinked himself awake, his limbs began righting themselves, bones popping and cracking back into place.

Not moments later, boots squealed in the hallway and Rose skidded through the hole. She took one look at Quinlan and sprinted for him, dropping to her knees and sliding the last few feet, her hands engulfed in green light. "What—" Her voice cracked. "What happened?"

"I—I tried to heal him," Asterin stammered. "I used the spell, but the wounds won't close ..."

Rose exhaled in a shaky rush. "We need to stop the bleeding." She stood, head whipping around. "Fire—I need fire!" she hollered.

Orion dashed out of the door and returned with a torch from the corridor, iron bracket and all. He thrust it at Rose. "Hurry."

Rose swiftly unstrapped the knife from Quinlan's hip, holding the blade over the flame until the silver glowed red. Luna could barely stand to watch as Rose snapped off the arrowhead sticking out of his back with one steady hand and slid the shaft out of his body, immediately applying pressure to the exit wound. Once the blade cooled back to silver, she lined the flat of the knife along the entry wound, face grim, and pressed down.

Luna's stomach lurched at the hiss of burning flesh, toes curling inside her boots. Despite her best efforts, she couldn't help but turn away, staring at Quinlan's legs instead.

Asterin cursed softly as Rose levitated Quinlan onto his stomach and repeated the process on his back and arm.

They waited. Luna hardly dared to breathe, her heart racing in her chest.

An eternity later, Rose let the knife slip from her white-knuckled grip and clatter to the floor. "Well, that was a close one," she said with a faint, airy chuckle. "Lucky bastard."

They all released a collective sigh of relief.

And then, just when Luna began to think that the worst was finally over, Eadric groaned, the veins in his arms and neck bulging from strain as he gripped his affinity stone. They whirled around to find Priscilla thrashing wildly in the sphere, darkness flooding from her skin and shrouding her entire being.

"I don't know how much longer I can hold her for!" Eadric shouted. "My magic—"

But before he could finish his sentence, the sphere exploded and Priscilla broke free.

CHAPTER FIFTY-THREE

A horrific screech ripped through the room as Priscilla took to the air, wings beating a flurry of wind that forced Asterin to grapple for Quinlan to keep him from sliding backward.

Eadric's hands glistened scarlet, shards of his affinity stone imbedded in his palms and littering the ground.

Priscilla trembled with rage, raising her shadowstone above her head. "You dare lock me up like an animal—"

A blast of ice knocked the stone right out of her hand, sending it skittering across the floor. "Shut up, you bitch!" Orion hollered. He flicked his wrist and the black stone came whizzing to his feet. He brought his heel down upon it with a satisfying *crunch.*

"No!" Priscilla screamed.

Orion grinned, razor-sharp. "Oh, yes." His next surge of ice struck Priscilla between the shoulder blades, shooting upward and encasing her wings. She plummeted to the ground, shrieking.

"Orion!" Asterin exclaimed, staring at the thick slab of ice coating his entire backside, mirroring what he had just done to Priscilla. "She's cast a reflective spell upon herself, you can't—"

Orion ignored her and raised his palms to fire another blast, binding Priscilla's legs together as she tried in vain to shake off the ice on her wings. More ice raced down her shoulders to her fingertips, but even immobilized, she still attacked, hurling shadow arrow after shadow arrow at Orion. All of them missed by leagues.

In turn, Orion was buried to his chest in ice.

Eadric growled, raising his sword and smashing the hilt on the ice over and over until it splintered and Orion could wriggle free.

Then a sleek blur tore over their shoulders and struck Priscilla. The ice surrounding her disintegrated in a shower of black frost. Another blur hurtled by from behind them, and Priscilla staggered backward, a thin blade hewn from darkness piercing clean through her shoulder.

Behind them stood Harry, snarling in pain while silvery fluid leaked from his own shoulder.

"Harry!" Orion cried. "Stop! Rose, heal him—"

"Get away from me!" Harry shouted. Dozens more blades materialized around him, all aimed for Priscilla.

His intention dawned upon them. The blades were not just meant to stop her … but to kill.

"Harry, the reflective spell!" Rose exclaimed.

"I know," he answered simply. "The time Priscilla borrowed from Eoin isn't quite up yet, but I'm taking her to a place that she'll never come back from. Where no one will find her. Where she won't be able to touch any of you ever again."

"And you?" Asterin demanded.

The demon didn't respond. Instead, he raised his hand, clenching it into a fist as he conjured more shadow blades—until an army of terrifying darkness had assembled above his head. He began to shift uncontrollably from his human form to his demon form, his ears popping out from his skull and his fingers extending into claws before retracting again. A black silhouette rose from his shoulders—wings, looming over Priscilla, his own promise of eternal damnation.

Priscilla blanched at the sight and shrieked, "If you kill me, you'll kill yourself!"

"See, the problem with killing an immortal," Harry growled, his hellish wings continuing to grow, "is that you *can't*."

He snapped his wings to their full span and the blades flew, ripping into her body, her tortured screams shattering the air.

"Harry!" Orion yelled as the demon doubled over, silver blood gushing onto the floor. Orion scrambled forward, only to be knocked off his feet by a jerk of Harry's chin.

"I said, stay back!" Harry bellowed, face twisted in agony. His eyes blazed pure white, brighter than the sun. A dark spiral formed behind Priscilla, who lay spread eagle on the floor, twitching in a growing pool of her own blood. The spiral swirled and widened, caving inward and beyond itself, leading to nowhere and everywhere all at once.

"Harry," Orion snarled.

"I'll be back," Harry swore. "But this I owe to all of you."

And with that, he surged into the air. He clutched one last dagger in his fist.

As the portal of darkness yawned open, Harry swooped down and grabbed Priscilla by the neck. She flailed pathetically, a final attempt to escape, gurgling and foaming at the mouth.

And just before the shadow portal swallowed them whole, Harry plunged the dagger into Priscilla's heart.

In her shock, Asterin hardly heard Orion shout. When he bolted forward, her hand shot out by pure reflex, latching onto his wrist to yank him backward, but he wrenched himself free and lunged for the rapidly shrinking portal.

"Orion!" she screamed, racing after him, fingertips brushing the fabric of his sleeve, so, *so* close—

He dove into the darkness headfirst. The shadows enveloped him, sucking him away, and in less than a blink the portal ceased to exist.

Vanished. Right into thin air, taking Orion and Harry and Priscilla with it.

As the dust settled, no one spoke.

The seconds ticked by, filled with tension as they waited. Waited—for something.

Anything.

And then, just as Asterin lost hope, a pinprick of black appeared midair, spreading outward like a bleeding blot of ink.

She exhaled in a choked rush, stumbling toward the swell of darkness.

Vaguely, almost as if from another universe, she heard the sound of boots thundering up the stairs. Guards—her Elites were coming.

The portal opened and out lurched a bleeding, bedraggled, but very much alive Harry.

"Stand down!" Eadric ordered as the Elites burst through the door, weapons drawn.

Asterin ran to the anygné, supporting him as his strength left him, his legs wobbling and chin slumping to his chest. Meanwhile, her eyes darted to the portal, wondering anxiously how long Orion would take to come back through.

Panic stabbed through her when the portal began to swirl closed and Orion had yet to reappear.

"Harry!" Asterin exclaimed, shaking him. "Where's Orion?"

Harry's head snapped up, eyes suddenly alert. Confused. "What?"

"*Where is Orion*?"

Rose came up beside them, face pale. "He followed you through the portal."

Harry froze, his lips parting as he stared into the portal, looking … afraid.

Asterin's blood turned to ice in her veins.

"Why didn't you stop him?" Harry breathed.

"She tried to, Harry," Rose said, when Asterin found herself unable to utter a single word. "She really did."

Asterin's tongue finally began functioning. "Can't you … can't you just go in and get him back?"

Harry swallowed. "No. He wasn't in physical contact with me when I went through. Where I took Priscilla … he … he could have ended up anywhere."

"Oh, Immortals," Asterin whispered.

"Where did you open that portal to, Harry?" Eadric demanded.

Harry stared at them, stricken. His mouth began moving, but no sound came out. When he finally managed to speak, it was no more than a devastated rasp. "The Immortal Realm."

CHAPTER FIFTY-FOUR

Days passed, but Quinlan did not wake. Both doctors and healers from all over Aspea convened in the Axarian palace, but none were able to coax him out of his coma. Eventually, a man named Doctor Ilroy arrived from Ermir at Rose's request. Although he couldn't rouse Quinlan, the doctor stabilized his worsening condition and erratic heartbeat. The color returned to his face soon after, and Ilroy deemed his condition stable enough for transport back to Eradoris, where he could continue treatment.

Until then, Asterin spent every moment she could at Quinlan's bedside, her fingers entwined with his, listening to his every breath. Ilroy had also succeeded in healing the cut on Asterin's face. The only remnant was a thin, silver scar tracing down her cheek—reminding her every time she saw her reflection of what she could have lost. *Had* almost lost.

She was, however, forced to abandon Quinlan's side now and then to deal with her royal duties. With Priscilla … not so much dead, but gone, Asterin ruled as Queen of Axaria, though the title wouldn't be official until her coronation. Eadric bombarded her with paperwork—this needed her approval, that needed her signature or her seal. She had citizens lining the halls waiting to speak with her at all hours. No matter how little sleep she had gotten, she listened carefully to each one, doing her best to address their concerns while trying to imagine what her father might have said or done in her place.

Asterin wondered how long it would take Harry to find Orion. According to the anygné, one could compare the Mortal Realm to the Immortal Realm like an apple to the Earth. She wanted nothing more than to search for Orion herself, but Eadric sternly reminded her of her obligations as queen, and Harry refused to bring any mortals into the Immortal Realm until he found a concrete lead on Orion's location.

Thoughts of Orion and Quinlan plagued her waking hours, but sleep was worse—hounded by grisly nightmares filled with the most vile of beasts and monsters. She awoke drenched in cold sweat, her heart pounding, the moment when Orion had disappeared into the portal replaying over and over in her head—her fingers just catching his sleeve, so close. So *damned* close. But she always missed, and then he was gone.

Some days later, while Asterin leafed through tedious documents, there was a knock at her door. She opened it to find Harry waiting outside—the anygné had gratefully accepted her offer to stay at the palace until he had recovered from his injuries and his exhaustion from opening the portal. Wordlessly, she invited him into the sitting parlor.

Bruises circled his bloodshot eyes. He looked ravaged, worn right down to the bone. But even then, Harry being Harry, he wasted no words on pleasantries. "I thought about trying to contact some of my immortal kin for leads on Orion's location, but … I would really rather not risk King Eoin finding out about this." He sounded as weary as he looked. "The sooner I get to the Immortal Realm, the better."

"Take me with you," said Asterin.

Harry's shoulders sagged. "I'm sorry, Your Highness. The Immortal Realm is simply no place for mortals, the Shadow Kingdom even less so. And you have your duties here, as soon-to-be Queen of Axaria." It was true—the arrangements for her ceremony were already being made. Still …

"Orion is down there," she said, refusing to yield. "I can't just stand by and wait for his return. It was my fault that he got away in the first place."

"No," Harry growled. "It wasn't. It was his decision to follow me. He didn't know about the consequences, and that was *my* fault. He must have thought that ..." He hung his head. "That I wouldn't come back." After a moment, he shook himself and inhaled sharply. "Rose asked if I might be able to help transport Quinlan to Eradore since he's in a delicate state right now, so I'll depart for the Shadow Kingdom directly from Eradoris. If I can find a lead, I will see what I can do to ensure safe passage for a mortal queen, but I cannot make any promises."

Asterin nodded. It wasn't good enough, but it would have to do for now. "Thank you." She bit her lip. "Will everything be all right between you and King Eoin? I mean, you did annihilate one of his clients."

Harry sighed and got to his feet. "Don't worry about that. It was my choice, and I'll deal with the consequences. I've got a good track record, and believe it or not, Priscilla was fairly insignificant to him, anyway." He shot her a sly grin. "Besides, he's easily bribed. And I'm his favorite shadowling." At her confused frown, he explained, "My immortal kin. There are three of us in total, although the oldest retired recently, just a few decades ago."

"Recent indeed," Asterin muttered.

"Killian came second in our little family," he went on, making his way to the door. "She was only a child when Eoin claimed her, and they've never really gotten along. I was third, the youngest sibling of sorts even though I was nearly twenty when I signed my contract." He ran a hand through his hair and scrunched his nose. "It's dreadfully complicated."

Asterin huffed at that, thinking of her own family. Though she tried not to show it, Priscilla's treachery had affected her more deeply than she could have imagined possible, and she was still reeling. "I guess all families can be a little messy, can't they?"

"I suppose so." Harry let himself out the door, tipping his chin in parting. "Have fun finishing your paperwork."

The following afternoon, two days before Harry and the Eradorians' scheduled departure, Asterin was studying a list that Eadric had compiled of potential candidates to replace Garringsford as General of Axaria. She thumbed through the candidate profiles he had also helpfully provided, her legs propped up on the table in the sitting parlor. A long-stale tray of tea and sandwiches lay untouched by her feet.

There came a knock at the door, but before she could so much as set the papers down, Luna let herself in.

And for the first time in her life, Asterin could not read her best friend's expression, now transformed into a cold mask.

Her resemblance to Priscilla nearly knocked the breath from Asterin's lungs.

Since the battle on Fairfest Eve, Luna had thrown herself into her sculpting, making herself so scarce that the only time Asterin saw her was when she had deliberately loitered outside of the girl's workshop. After two hours of waiting, Luna finally slipped out, stiffening as she caught sight of Asterin. Gaze averted, Luna had asked if "Her Royal Highness" required any assistance. Something leaden settled into Asterin's gut and she had shaken her head, too stung to speak.

"Luna," Asterin said, the list sliding from her grasp and onto the floor. She stood, pushing her legs off the table so forcefully that it scraped against the mahogany floor with an awful screech.

"Your Highness," Luna said once Asterin had re-collected her wits. "There's something I need to tell you."

"Yes, of course, anything," Asterin said, fumbling with the tea tray. "Please have a seat. I'll ring for fresh tea."

"Don't bother. I won't be long."

"Oh." Asterin cleared her throat, her hands twisting behind her back. "Right." *Where to begin?* she wondered. *Apologize?* What came out instead was a shaky, "What can I do for you?" She cleared her throat, trying to dislodge the sudden tightness. "How … how have you been?" *I miss you.* "I've been worried about you, and—"

"I'm leaving."

Asterin froze.

Luna pushed on. "The King of Ibreseos—my father. He's invited me to stay at the Ibresean palace. He wrote to me yesterday. Apparently he wants to get to know me better, as well as open a gallery of my work. I just wanted to let you know where I was going."

The room tipped sideways. Asterin's mind whirled as she tried to steady herself, gripping the edges of the tea tray as Luna's words sank in. "You … you can't leave, Luna."

"Can't I?" Luna challenged. "You would deny me the opportunity to meet my father?"

"No, no, of course not, but—"

"I could have just left when the letter came, but—I respect our … friendship too much. And if you respect it as well, I hope that you'll let me leave with your blessing," Luna continued, grimacing even as she tried to conceal it by turning her face away.

"Luna, please, I know that I've done something terrible—to us—but let me *fix* it," Asterin pleaded.

"It's not something you can fix like a broken toy, Asterin. I just need some time away," Luna said in a gentle voice, as if consoling a child.

The teacups on the tray began to clatter quietly. "Luna … I don't expect you to forgive me, ever, but please know that I am so, so sorry."

Luna remained silent.

"Do you have *any* idea how difficult making that decision was for me?" Asterin exclaimed, overwhelmed by the tumult of emotions. "To hold the lives of the people that I love most of all in this damn world in my hands and be forced to *choose between them*?"

"No, I don't, but—"

"Well, what do you want me to tell you, Luna?" Asterin erupted. The tray tilted and the cups slid off, shattering on the floor, spilling tea onto her boots and soaking the rug. "What would you like me to say? That I regret protecting him? Because I don't! I will never regret saving him." She clenched her eyes shut. She wouldn't allow herself to dwell on that feeling of absolute helplessness.

That was a dark, bottomless hole, and she refused to fall in.

Asterin took a breath, forcing herself to meet Luna's eyes. "I will always regret not being powerful enough to protect both of you—"

"Orion," Luna interrupted. His name sent another wave of fresh grief rolling over Asterin. "I have to—I have to know, Asterin. Tell me—if it had been between me and Orion, who would you have chosen?"

Asterin stopped short, stunned.

The silence that followed was the most agonizing she had ever experienced, because they both knew that she was stalling.

"I—" She swallowed, averting her gaze. "Luna …"

And that was answer enough.

Luna's mask cracked for the briefest second, revealing the despair beneath. Asterin felt as though her heart had been cleaved in half.

"I understand," Luna said.

"How can you do this to me?" Asterin demanded, hurt. "You know I love you!" She scrabbled for words, voice rising in desperation. "If—if it had been between me and Eadric, who would you have chosen?"

"Always you, Asterin," Luna responded without the slightest of hesitations. Her voice broke on her next words, a lone tear rolling down her cheek. "I will *always* choose you."

"She took my family," Asterin whispered hoarsely. "She killed my parents."

"And she took me from my family, too," Luna said. "Somehow. I don't even remember how, but I'm going to find them, wherever they are."

Asterin stared at her. "What?"

"I had a brother and a sister and a mother that I couldn't call mine, but they still called me their own."

"You mentioned names during the battle," said Asterin, racking her brain. "Maman and Nathan … and …"

Luna looked away. "Clara."

"Do you miss them? Since—since you remembered?"

"Every second," she murmured.

"Please, Luna," said Asterin. *What am I going to do without you?* "Stay. Please stay. I'll have a hundred galleries display your beautiful sculptures—"

"Asterin," Luna hissed, her demeanor changing so suddenly that Asterin flinched. "It's not about the damned gallery. I am going to Ibresis, whether you allow it or not. But I hoped that my departure wouldn't ruin what is left of … us. Obviously, I was wrong." Luna shook her head. "Wrong about so many things. I need some time away from … here. From Axaria."

"You need some time away from me," Asterin translated.

"Yes, Immortals help me. Yes, I do. I have my things packed already." Luna turned and walked to the door, hand resting on the knob. "You made your choice, and now I'm making mine."

"You're leaving … forever?" Asterin croaked.

There was a lengthy pause. "No," Luna sighed at last. "I don't think so."

"Write to me," Asterin begged. "Write to me when you're ready to come home."

"Home," her best friend whispered, opening the door. "I don't even know what that means anymore." She snapped the door shut, rattling the ink bottles on Asterin's desk.

And as Asterin slid to the floor, alone in the silence, her family falling to pieces right before eyes, everything in her life on the verge of collapse like a glass tower she had not known was quite so fragile, she wished—not for the first time—that Priscilla's shadow arrow had been aimed for her heart instead.

Just days after Luna departed, Asterin found herself standing with Rose and Harry on the outskirts of the Wall.

"Thank you for everything, Asterin," Rose said, the late evening breeze ruffling the locks of auburn that managed to escape the hood of her cloak.

Jack and Laurel emerged from the gardens beyond the gate, levitating Quinlan—bundled to a flat wooden plank—between them.

Rose turned to Harry. "Again, I cannot express in words how grateful I am that Quinlan no longer needs to risk a long trip across the ocean. Without you … the journey would have taken ages."

Harry tipped his head. "It is my honor."

"The first thing I will do when he awakens," Rose told Asterin, "is yell at him. The second will be to write a letter to you." The Eradorian shot her a wry smile. "The yelling may take a while."

The thundering of hooves announced Eadric's arrival. He pulled up beside the gate and swung out of the saddle, leaving Grey to paw and huff at the road.

Captain Covington had seen better days. Exhaustion lined his features, and it looked as if he hadn't run a comb through his hair—or even slept, for that matter—since Luna had left. He had volunteered to carry out Garringsford's responsibilities and obligations as temporary General of Axaria until a worthy replacement was found, and on top of that, he had demanded to personally oversee background rechecks for every guard in the palace, *plus* recruit new guards to replace the ones they had lost in the battle.

"Leaving so soon?" asked Eadric.

"Yes, but I'm glad you caught us, Captain," said Rose.

He bowed his head. "As am I, Your Majesty."

Rose raised an eyebrow. "Why, Captain, I thought we were well past those sorts of formalities."

That drew a chuckle out of him. "You're the one calling me captain."

"Well, I'm the Queen of Eradore," she shot back, though there was no fire behind her words. "I can do whatever I please."

Eadric sighed, but his mouth twitched into a tired smile. "Undoubtedly, Your Majesty." He coughed. "I mean … Rose." At her smile, he seemed to summon up the courage to ask, "That fellow with the knives who fought beside you during the ball … was that Kane?"

Rose's mouth thinned, but she nodded. "He disappeared as soon as I left the ballroom to find all of you. Only the Immortals know what he's up to now. He mentioned something about a neighboring kingdom, though, so you probably don't have to worry about him."

Grey whinnied and Eadric shifted. "Well, I'm afraid that I must be off." To Rose, he said, "I pray for your safe journey and Quinlan's restoration to full health." He gave them all a final brisk nod before striding toward Grey, posture as stiff and rigid as a wind-up toy.

"Eadric," Rose called at the last moment, just as he mounted Grey and wheeled him around.

He glanced over his shoulder. "Yes?"

"Visit us soon."

He looked taken aback. "Should you wish it—"

"I do."

Eadric's hands tightened on the reins, his gaze glinting onyx in the moonlight. "I will, Rose."

They watched him round a corner and disappear behind the hedges.

When all was silent once more, Rose spoke. "He's not so good with goodbyes, is he?"

Asterin held her arms open, and Rose fell gracelessly into her embrace. "Well, this isn't goodbye," she murmured into Rose's hair.

Rose chuckled softly. "From one queen to another, a million thanks."

"A million thanks," Asterin echoed, and they parted. To Harry, she anxiously asked, "Will you be okay going back and forth so many times?" He could only transport one extra person per shadow jump.

"I devoured enough food to feed the entire royal court," reassured Harry. "And thanks to your fancy palace pillows, I'm more rested than I've been in weeks."

Asterin sighed. "Safe travels, then."

The anygné held out a hand for Rose to take, the air charged with the sheer weight of his power. "Ready?"

"Ready," said Rose and placed her hand in his.

They vanished.

When Harry returned for Quinlan a few minutes later, he gave Asterin an awkward pat on the shoulder. "Asterin, I'm going to—" He squeaked in alarm as Asterin threw her arms around his neck. They stayed like that until Harry exhaled, rubbing her back. "I'll find him. I promise."

"I'm counting on you, Harry," Asterin whispered fiercely. "I need him back."

"So do I," he said with such emotion that she drew back in surprise. Harry blinked, and then blushed bright pink. "I mean—"

"Oh," Asterin said. "*Oh.*" How could she be so stupid? *All those times* … She hadn't even noticed. "So … you …"

"Well, yes." Harry reddened further. "You don't mind, do you?"

It took her a moment for his meaning to sink in. "What? Of course not."

His smile lit up his entire face. "Thank you, Asterin."

She bit her lip, turning to where Quinlan lay on the plank. She swept back a few strands of dark hair from his forehead and pressed a kiss to his brow, blinking away the sudden prickle of tears, and stepped back. "I've lost half of my family," she whispered. She took a breath, letting it cool the heat in her veins. Beyond the gate in the Wall, she could just glimpse the districts of Axaris glittering and twinkling away below, as they always did. When the stars emerged from behind a stubborn mist, it seemed as though the night sky itself reflected the city.

"You can't think like that," Harry said. "Or you're just letting Priscilla win. The things I've done for King Eoin … I can't let him win, either."

"If all goes well, maybe I'll get to meet him."

A crooked little grin played on Harry's face. "Pray that you don't ever find yourself within ten leagues of the Ruler of Darkness, Your Majesty."

"If it means that Orion has been found, I will dream of nothing else."

Harry hefted Quinlan higher onto his back. "Very well. I shall see you soon."

Asterin forced herself to look away from Quinlan's face. "May the Immortals protect you, Harry … wherever you must go."

The anygné smiled. "Have spirit, Asterin Faelenhart, and till 'morrow."

Asterin stood alone beneath the Wall long after Harry and Quinlan had faded into evanescence. The voices of Jack and Laurel floated to her, the two Elites sprawled in the grass by the guardhouse and pointing at the stars. She stared out into the night, the magic of the wards beyond the Wall humming like a lullaby in her bones, and the light of Axaris burning like a promise in her heart.

"Till 'morrow," she whispered.

EPILOGUE

A cool night breeze kissed Asterin's bare skin, causing her to shiver and roll onto her side. Drawing the covers to her chin, she dozed for a moment longer before her breath caught and her eyes flew open.

She always locked her windows shut when she slept.

Slowly, cautiously, she craned her neck to survey the dim, moonlit room, eyes trailing up the hulking shadow over her bed to meet a luminescent green stare. The covers slid from her grasp as she sat up, her heartbeat thumping loudly in her ears. "Lord Conrye."

The wolf's ears twitched as he continued staring, front paws perched on the foot of her mattress.

"Aren't you forbidden from being here?" she asked, unable to keep the bitterness from her voice. "Why now, instead of during the battle?"

The Council of Immortals would not allow me to … interfere with trivial mortal matters.

Asterin's eyes widened. The god's voice swept through her head like soft thunder, but she could still hear the disdain dripping from his words.

Asterin bristled. "Trivial? The meddling of dark magic by the leader of a kingdom and the near deaths of not one, but *four* heirs is considered trivial?"

There words, not mine, Conrye rumbled, lips curling back in a snarl. *I was overruled.*

"Well, you're too late," said Asterin. "My Guardian is gone. The battle is over. So why are you here now?"

Because you have already made your choices. I cannot influence the path you now walk.

Her fists clenched. Perhaps it wasn't the wisest choice to direct her anger at an ancient god, but she couldn't help it. He could have *helped* her. Helped all of them. He could have stopped Orion from going into the portal. Killed Priscilla himself, like he had the wyvern, so Harry wouldn't have had to open that portal in the first place.

Conrye regarded her, appearing unsurprised at her hostility. *There is something you must do, Asterin. This is the only thing I may offer you. After Priscilla seized control of the throne, she imprisoned dozens of people she believed posed a threat to her—liabilities. People who she could not sway, could not fool with her illusions.*

"Yes, thank you for the reminder that I was one of those fools," muttered Asterin, collapsing back against her pillows.

That was not my point. She kept one of those people in the holding cells below the palace.

Asterin sat back up, stunned. "Cells? You mean—you mean we have a dungeon?" There were jailhouses, of course, in Axaria, but below the palace itself …

Indeed. They are spelled to provide enough necessities to keep their inmates alive for as long as necessary. You must go down there.

Her pulse quickened. "What's in there?"

Not so much what, but who, Conrye corrected. *Take the servants' passage in the west wing, and locate a storage room marked with an X on the door. Find a brick, smoother than the rest, and pull it to the left. Twist the knob of the door without a knocker twice and enter. Follow the stairs as far down as you can.*

Asterin wasn't sure she wanted to know what—or rather *who* was down there, but she took careful note of Conrye's instructions nonetheless.

Come forward, Princess Asterin.

She hesitated only a moment before scooting toward him, the hairs on her arms prickling from the sudden chill.

He bowed his head. *Around my neck.*

She threaded her fingers into the tufts of his silky fur and paused. Beneath her palms thrummed his pulse, fluttering—almost like the wings of a bird, almost like the omnistone, yet heavier—much heavier. The immortal heartbeat of a god. Swallowing, she found a leather cord around his neck and pulled it over his head. From it dangled a heavy, tarnished key, ancient runes etched into its surface.

"What's this for?"

You will know when the time comes.

Asterin raised it over her own head, feeling its warm weight settle between the hollow of her breasts. She shut her eyes and felt the sharp bite of winter wind ruffle her hair.

When her eyes opened, the window had closed and the wolf was gone.

Asterin found the stairwell easily enough. Navigating in the dark had long since become second nature to her after spending so many hours with Orion exploring the hidden passageways of the palace as children.

Eadric followed at her heels, peering into every corner. After telling him everything—from Conrye's visit to his claim of a dungeon deep beneath the palace—he had demanded to accompany her, and she'd been secretly relieved. She had no idea what to expect down there, and she was thankful for the solid presence beside her.

Asterin lit their way down the stairs with a glowing orb of magic, taking care to test each rickety step, a faint, unnameable stench reaching them from below.

At last, after what seemed like hours, they reached the bottom.

Asterin levitated her orb higher, its glow shuddering along the length of the walls around them as she came to a standstill, arm trembling.

Behind her, Eadric swore softly.

A long corridor of prison cells stretched out before them, plunging deep into an endless gloom so thick that her light could scarcely penetrate it.

They crept along the aisle, peering into each murky cell.

"They're empty," Asterin said. She let out a frustrated grunt. "There's nothing here." She nearly jumped out of her skin when a hand fell on her shoulder, but it was only Eadric.

He gestured further on. "I just saw something move."

As they approached the final cell, there was a rustle of fabric.

Asterin stumbled backward, colliding into a startled Eadric. Her light had fallen across a pale, gaunt face, spindly fingers gripping the metal bars.

It was a woman, with a tangled nest of long, black hair. She stared at Asterin with rich emerald eyes, brighter than the stars themselves.

Asterin stared back, feeling as though she had been slapped, her mind stuttering as it tried to comprehend the sight.

Emerald eyes, whose shine had not yet dulled, even in such isolation. Whose resolute expression had never crumbled to one of hopelessness. Who had never surrendered herself to the darkness.

Asterin *knew* that face—she had seen it in her dreams. In her flashbacks after the contralusio.

In the mirror.

"Almighty Immortals," Asterin breathed, her hand clapping to her mouth as she staggered closer to the bars.

"Asterin, get back," Eadric said, brandishing his affinity stone—but she just shook her head.

"Asterin?" the woman asked, her voice like gravel after years of disuse. She cleared her throat. "My … my Asterin?"

"Who are you?" Eadric demanded.

Asterin's knees wobbled as she raised her hands to the woman, tears flowing down her face. Both of their faces. The woman she had not seen for over a decade let out a strangled sob of joy and disbelief.

Asterin turned to Eadric. "Eadric, this …" It all came back to her in a rush of golden light. She swallowed. "This is Elyssa Calistavyn-Faelenhart, the *true* Queen of Axaria."

The woman smiled, her bony wrists sliding through the bars to cup Asterin's cheek. She leaned into the touch, her throat catching on a tear-choked laugh.

So warm, so gentle, so loving.

So familiar.

"My mother," Asterin whispered.

ACKNOWLEDGMENTS

Sometimes I can't believe I wrote a book. Like, an entire book! Of words! That I wrote! Myself! When and where and how did this happen?! Then I take a moment to think about all the people that made *Shadow Frost* possible and it makes a lot more sense.

First, I want to thank my editor, Scott Allie. I was so nervous at the prospect of working with someone whose job was to basically roast my writing, but you only did that like, twice. Your hard work and devotion to *Shadow Frost* truly made it into what it is today, and I will never forget that.

A humongous thank-you to my agent, Richard Curtis, who has gone far above and beyond to support/tolerate me from the very first moment (and for letting me get two milkshakes that one time I clearly only needed one). Thank you to Marco, and David and Matthew for all your help as well! Shout out to my From the Top fam for all of your support. And of course, I definitely couldn't have done this without my team at Blackstone—Rick, Josh, Josie, Lauren, Mandy, Jeff, Bryan, and many others. You are all absolute angels and I am so grateful for your dedication to *Shadow Frost*. Also, a very special shout-out to Kathryn G. English. You promised me that I would get the cover of my dreams, and you came through 110 percent with the most gorgeous creation I have ever laid eyes upon. On the note of the most gorgeous creations, colossal thank-you to my freakin' dad, who hand-drew that freakin' amazing map of the Mortal Realm at the beginning of the book. Yeah, that's right. My dad drew that!!! Go look at it again, right now! No offense to you, but my dad definitely wins Best Dad.

Now, where would I be without my mentors? Ms. Clark, you ignited my passion for English. Mr. Wade, *Shadow Frost* literally would not have begun if not for your class. Ms. Lomp, I think you unintentionally let me write about 50 percent of *Shadow Frost* during your class instead of practicing the saxophone, so thank you for that. Ms. Greenspoon, I adore you. Veda "Feyda Lachinsky" Kaplinsky, you are my icon in every imaginable way. And a big thank-you to Arsha for all your love. Shout out to Jim for always cheerleading my writing from the very start. Juna, I probably would have burnt out mentally and physically a long time ago without your wisdom and guidance. Thank you to Ms. Lee, the sunshine and candy-provider on all my stormy days, to Mr. Ajerman, for always being there for me with a cup of tea and a hug, and to *Christopher*, for being a star and introducing me to attack badgers and *la jeu de poule* and always making me laugh when I needed it most or not at all (by the way, call your mother). And thank you to Professor Berry and Professor Piñango for keeping me sane during my first year at Yale. AH! There are so, so many more. I know who you are, and if you're reading this, then you know who you are, too. From the bottom of my heart, thank you. Jeez, I've had so many awesome teachers. Stay in school, kids.

Right then, moving on. Three years ago, I forced two of my friends to beta the first draft of *Shadow Frost*. You have my utmost gratitude, Angela "Moomoo" and Adam "Dadam." Angela, you were so savage most of the time, but *Shadow Frost* probably would have ended with Asterin becoming a cake chef or something without your sensible suggestions. Massive thanks to Umi for being the best godmother ever to my characters, and Ysa for blazing through the whole draft in like, two days! Love you all.

Trillions of hugs to Thomas and Dorothy, the best kiddos ever, and Yi-heng and Max, the best adults ever. Lowkey, please adopt me.

Time for some more shout-outs to my squad. Amy, my homaka. Emma, a heckin' fren. Jona, you beautiful, perfect-eyebrowed human.

Catherine, who *always*, always wanted to read what I wrote no matter how crap it was. Tyson, the bestest buddy to ever exist and my human definition of A Canadian™. Hiroko-chan, you precious, artistic gem. Tomas, for everything. Margret, for so, so much chocolate. Elli, you deranged psychopath with more talent in one eyelash than most people have in their whole bodies. Yuja, an untouchable goddess, and Kiki and LX, who have never failed to inspire me in every possible way (except shoe choice). And Miron, who my adoration for cannot be intelligibly expressed in words. *I love you guys.*

My Yale fam. Mona, the most fierce team of athletes and beautiful friends anyone could ever ask for. Pianists 2018–2019. Wei-Yi and Chris and many others for definitely caring about me more than I care for myself. And to Qiancheng and Jérémie for being the best neighbours/babysitters (of me) in the history of existence.

Also, shout out to Colin Firth and Taron Egerton, who aren't *yet* part of my squad, but are kings among men (did you see what I did there?!). Frankly, my writing career began with the two of you. Don't ask. You are my true heroes.

My most sincere gratitude to Mrs. Hewitt. Your love and support helped me get to where I am today.

V. E. Schwab, Leigh Bardugo, Holly Black, Marie Lu, Sarah J. Maas, Tamsyn Muir, Kelly Sue DeConnick, Rainbow Rowell, Victoria Aveyard, Jennifer L. Armentrout, Marissa Meyer, Alexandra Bracken, Natasha Ngan, Mackenzi Lee, Rin Chupeco, Michelle Kwan, Adam Rippon … all of you have had an immense influence on me and are the unconquerable queens of my life.

AND IF YOU, YES YOU, ARE READING THIS AT ALL, thank you, thank you, thank you! Especially if you're from Twitter, Instagram, or Goodreads. Or if we met at BookExpo America or BookCon and you loved the *Shadow Frost* ARC enough that you bought a copy. MANY HUGS FOR YOU.

All my thanks again to the incomparable Emanuel Ax. I could not think of a more wonderful and deserving human being to dedicate my very first book to, and I know that anyone and everyone who knows you at all would agree with me on that without hesitation. Also, you read *Shadow Frost* when it was just a thirty-page jumble of absolute nonsense … yet loved it (or at least pretended to, haha). The ferocity of your enthusiasm and encouragement for my writing truly motivated me to fight through every struggle until I typed out *THE END*. I still owe you dim-sum.

And finally … Mum and Dad, thank you for putting up with me for eighteen consecutive years, an honestly Herculean feat. Neither I nor *Shadow Frost* would exist without you. Literally.

EXCERPT FROM

GOD STORM

THE SECOND BOOK IN

THE SHADOW FROST

TRILOGY

PROLOGUE

down and down and down …

He couldn't remember the light. Here, the deepest of shadows gave way to a murk that seemed only a little less menacing, a little less sinister. The sky never lightened beyond a bruised purple before it darkened to an impenetrable, inky gloom.

To think that he had *reached* for that gaping blackness instead of fleeing far, far away and never looking back.

… and down and down and down and down …

How many days had passed? How many hours had dragged by since that fateful moment when his heart had told his body to move, to *move, you idiot,* to hurl himself without hesitation into that swirling, infinite void—

… and down and down and down and down and down …

The portal had devoured him, and he had begun to fall. Ribbons of shadow entangled him, strangled him, laughing and singing and whispering to him in tongues he couldn't understand.

Now, he wouldn't stop falling. *Couldn't* stop falling. The shadows laughed and stole the screams right from his throat. He tried to keep track of the seconds, but he never made it past one thousand before losing count. He wondered when this would end, how it would end, if it would ever end at all—

The world flared white for the briefest second, and when he came to, the ground was moist against his bare face, filling his nostrils with the scent of rain and something he did not recognize.

Orion Galashiels pressed a kiss to the land and thanked the Immortals.

Then he rolled onto his back, closing his eyes as he sank into the wet ground, and breathed.

When he opened his eyes, he looked up into the dark heavens and thought them more beautiful than anything he had ever seen before.

With a smile, he lifted a hand toward the unfamiliar constellations scattered above as if to capture them.

The ground rumbled, low thunder in his ears. Orion had no chance to react when clods of dirt erupted skyward, slamming into his shoulder and arm, enclosing him in a death grip of mud and rocks before wrenching him down. He struggled to free himself as the ground began to *swallow* him. To bury him alive, one limb at a time.

Heart hammering, Orion let out a desperate cry. His fingers plunged through the roiling dirt, searching for his pocket and closing around his affinity stone. He held it aloft in triumph, but the moment he uncurled his fist, it crumbled to dust right before his eyes.

"No," he choked out. Dirt filled his mouth and nostrils, suffocating him. *No, no, no, no—*

In a burst of blinding light, his magic exploded from every pore of his body. The ground shied away from his radiance, relinquishing its hold upon him at last.

Blood roared in Orion's ears as he scrambled up the sides of the crater that had formed around him, clawing at straggly roots to haul himself out. Once clear of the crater, he ran for all hell's worth, his skin still pulsating with magic, certain that the ground would seize him once more if he so much as faltered for a second too long. Only when he couldn't bear the burning of his lungs did he finally slow—and thankfully, the ground didn't try to gobble him up again.

Resisting the urge to vomit, Orion took in his surroundings. Trees of silver towered over him on all sides, glimmering with iridescent bark, their filigree leaves tinkling prettily in the breeze. Still panting for breath, he braced his hand against a trunk, but recoiled immediately. His palm came away slick, coated in an oily sap that reeked like hot tar. Upon closer inspection, he realized with horror that the sap was *moving*, churning and writhing in agitation along his skin, lapping up his fingers like tiny maggots.

Once more, his magic surged forth, this time with a scorching heat that sizzled the sap right off his skin and sent it skittering back up the tree trunk.

Orion stared up at the sliver of sky just visible overhead through the dense tangle of branches. Ragged exhales tore at his lungs as he tried to calm the fear coursing through his veins.

Everything was alive here. The rocks, the dirt … even his magic. It felt almost foreign in his body, as if he had suddenly sprouted a new organ. Here, his magic need not bend to his beck and call. It refused to be summoned, controlled. Gone was his loyal hound, his most reliable tool—replaced with something primal and wild.

Something powerful had always dwelled deep inside him, his skin, his blood, his soul. But now, it was *free*. Orion could run from the forests and the monsters within, but he couldn't run from himself.

And that was the most terrifying thought of all.

He still tried, though. He ran until his legs gave out, until he collapsed in an exhausted heap and hit his head on something sharp. White starbursts exploded across his vision. His groping fingers came away scarlet, and wherever the droplets fell, small red blossoms sprang forth.

As the world blurred beneath his half-closed lids, the shadows began to sing anew, their voices pouring over him in honeyed waves. There was no laughter this time, only a soothing, haunting melody filling his ears as the shadows wrapped him into their satiny midnight folds.

The ground shifted beneath him, and as his consciousness faded, he heard the *fwip fwip* of a thousand fluttering wings.

His eyes slipped shut.

He dreamt of flying, of being carried far away by a great darkness high above a city of daggers and blood.

GUIDE TO SHADOW FROST

SPELLS

Avslorah aveau — to summon water

Avslorah fiere — to summon fire

Haelein — to heal

Helt Avsloradovion — (non-self) to all summon

Skjyolde — to shield

Náxos — to strike

Reyunir — to unify

Lumi — to flare

Ovrire — to open

Explosa — to erupt

Astyndos — to blast

Ovdekken — to expose

THE COUNCIL OF IMMORTALS	BLOODLINE
Lady Siore (See-**ore**-ay), Goddess of Earth	House of the Stag
Lord Tidus (**Tie**-duhs), God of Water	House of the Serpent
Lady Fena (**Fee**-nuh), Goddess of Fire	House of the Fox
Lord Conrye (**Con**-rye), God of Ice	House of the Wolf
Lady Reyva (**Ray**-vuh), Goddess of Wind	House of the Stallion
Lady Audra (**Ow**-druh), Goddess of Sky	House of the Falcon
Lady Ilma (**Ill**-muh), Goddess of Air	House of the Viper
Lord Ulrik (**Ool**-rick), God of Light	House of the Lynx
Lord Pavon (**Pah**-von), God of Illusion	House of the Peacock
King Eoin (**Ay**-oh-in), God of Shadow	None

THE ROYAL ELITE GUARD

Captain Eadric Covington (26)

Hayley Zalis (27)

Nicole Dwyer (26)

Laurel Kuru (24)

Rose Fletcher (19)

Alicia Lormont (15)

Silas Atherton (30)

Jack Lintz (25)

Gino Satoré (23)

Casper Castille (23)

Quinlan Holloway (19)